W9-AJL-981

FOOD NETWORK
best of **The Best Of**

FOOD NETWORK
best of The Best Of

Jill Cordes and
Marc Silverstein

HPBooks

HPBooks
Published by The Berkley Publishing Group
A division of Penguin Group (USA) Inc.
375 Hudson Street
New York, New York 10014

First HPBooks trade-paperback edition: October 2004

Visit our website at
www.penguin.com

Library of Congress Cataloging-in-Publication Data
Cordes, Jill.
  Food Network best of the Best Of / Jill Cordes and Marc Silverstein.
     p cm.
  ISBN 1-55788-436-6
  1. Restaurants—United States—Guidebooks. 2. Best Of (Television
program) I. Title: Best of the Best Of. II. Silverstein, Marc. III. Food
Network (Firm) IV. Best Of (Television program) V. Title.

TX907.2.C665 2004
791.45'72—dc22

                                                                                2004053997

Printed in the United States of America
10 9 8 7 6 5 4 3 2 1

To my wonderful husband, Phil.
Despite the many times I've left you at home with an
empty refrigerator, you are always there at the end of my
journey, with a hot meal, a clean house, and a big heart
that is full of encouragement, support, and love.

—Jill

To my son and best buddy, Spencer, whose welcome home
hugs made each trip bearable, to my gorgeous baby daughter, Lexy, who sat with me typing late each night, and most
of all, to my sweet and beautiful wife, Kathy, whose love
and support make all our dreams possible.

—Marc

Acknowledgments

The logistics are staggering. Think about it: Two hosts and their respective crews traveling around North America to hundreds of restaurants. Incredibly, it doesn't take an army, just *The Best Of* professionals—people we're fortunate enough to also call our friends.

Our thanks and appreciation go to Segue Productions and the incredible leadership of Dan Sitarski, Eileen Matthews, and Nick Satiritz, who make the dream a reality every day. To Kathleen Quaid-Weisz and Karen Fox, who routinely pull off the impossible.

To Food Network for this incredible opportunity. In particular, thanks to Judy Girard and Kathleen Finch. And to Eric Ober and Jim Zarchin, who invited us to be part of their creation.

For the professionals at Scripps in Knoxville—who made sure the shows aired without a glitch. Terry Richani, Matt Mullins, and Todd Blackburn: Your attention to detail is greatly appreciated.

FROM MARC TO HIS CREW: Photographer/buddy Larry Deal, who had my back from the moment we met. To producer/friend Jill Littman, the true heart and soul of the team. To Bud McHugh and Steve Sullivan, who added just the right touch to our road family. And to Patti Power with thanks for keeping my voice in your head. A special thanks to Malachi "Arty" McGlone.

FROM JILL TO HER CREW: To my incredibly gifted photographers: Dave Dennison, Dan Dwyer, and Chris Peterson, who have a remarkable eye for capturing the heart and soul of a place and doing it with style and grace. To my producers: Jodi Langer, without whom I'd be lost—except for the many times you got us lost!; Amy Shea, who puts on a smile even in the stickiest situations; and Tanya Jones, who came aboard later, yet hit the ground running. To my sound guys: Tom Forliti and Paul Dahlseid, who hear the good, bad, and ugly but only remember the good! And Tom: Next time, let's pass on dessert.

To our agent, Peter Goldberg of N.S. Bienstock, for his guidance and, more important, for the gig.

To our book agent, Ian Kleinert of The Literary Group International, for making this project a reality.

To our publisher and editor, John Duff at HPBooks/Penguin, for his brilliant leadership. And to recipe editor Jeanette Egan, for keeping all the measures and instructions straight.

Our heartfelt thanks go to the chefs, restaurant owners, and employees who *allowed* us into their lives and shared their stories and recipes.

Most importantly, we thank the viewers who invite us into their homes. We're humbled by the honor.

FROM JILL: A heartfelt thanks to my mother-in-law, Beverly Johnston, who spent many a night proofreading and recipe-testing this book. To my Mom and Dad, who always encouraged me to follow my dreams, no matter how steep the climb. My sister and brothers, who keep life interesting—Kelly: Your free spirit is contagious. And a special thanks to my entire extended family, without whom life would be dull.

FROM MARC: To my parents, Marlene and Sheldon Silverstein, whose laughter and love are my inspiration. To my brother, David, for his life-long support. To my sister, Sheryl, for setting the bar high. To my buddy, Ron Suskind, for the laughs. To Rosita Brewster, for her incredible help. And most of all—to my wife, Kathy, son, Spencer, and daughter, Lexy, who fill every moment with love.

Contents

Introduction   xi

New England   1
Maine, Vermont, New Hampshire, Massachusetts,
Rhode Island, Connecticut

The Mid-Atlantic   23
New York, New Jersey, Pennsylvania, Delaware,
Maryland, District of Columbia

The South   69
Virginia, West Virginia, Kentucky, Tennessee,
North Carolina, South Carolina, Georgia, Florida,
Alabama, Mississippi, Louisiana, Arkansas

The Midwest   127
Ohio, Indiana, Illinois, Michigan, Iowa, Missouri,
Wisconsin, Minnesota

The Mountains and The Great Plains   177
Kansas, Montana, Idaho, North Dakota, South Dakota,
Wyoming, Nebraska, Utah, Colorado

The Southwest   207
Arizona, Nevada, New Mexico, Texas

The Pacific   229
California, Oregon, Washington, Alaska, Hawaii

Index   279

Introduction

IF WE GET you hungry, then we're doing our jobs. On Food Network's *The Best Of,* we visit the nation's top restaurants to find out what makes them great. We don't care if they are expensive five-star establishments or Mom-and-Pop eateries. We search for those fascinating culinary discoveries that make a night out perfect, a vacation fun, or a detour on a road trip memorable.

We do more than just review food. Let the professional food critics tell you why a dish is "whimsical" or how the taste of some dessert "made their knees wobbly." We don't talk like that. Instead, we're storytellers. To us, a restaurant stands out because of the people, the neighborhood, the history, or some other intriguing bit of lore. Yes, food is often the reason for a restaurant's success—and we certainly don't ignore it, but sometimes it's only part of the story. We've collected recipes—some of which have never been in print before—from some of the nation's top chefs to help you deal with that hunger we've induced.

We've arranged the book by region and by state, but our picks are in no particular order. You'll find fancy dining emporiums next to casual diners, French haute cuisine cheek-by-jowl with home cooking. Occasionally, we even included a restaurant that didn't ring our bells but got raves from the critics. We figure you should know their opinion as well as ours.

Oh, the Places We've Been . . . and Gone

Running a restaurant is hard work. But many of them, even the good ones, do go out of business. There are countless reasons why: long hours, hot kitchens, bad management, or busted relationships (business and otherwise). Food trends change, chefs leave, the economy heads south, and the public heads elsewhere . . .

At *The Best Of,* we're very careful about the restaurants we profile. Our researchers do lots of legwork before we commit to a place. Almost all the restaurants that have appeared on the show are still thriving. Many tell us of a significant increase in business after their stories air. But every once in a while we get caught by events that no one can control.

For instance, there was the place in Boston that was struck by lightning right around the time our story hit the air. It has yet to reopen.

A historic restaurant in Las Vegas was in business for 70 years but closed suddenly just before its debut on the show. Jill had to rework the piece into a memorial tribute, even though none of their video or interviews had been shot with that in mind. It was a challenge, to say the least.

A fondue joint in the South was severely damaged by—what else?—fire, although not from burning cheese, but from a space heater.

Sadly, a few cooks have passed away. A few patrons have, too.

A professional football player we invited to be part of shoot because of his expertise in food and wine was cut from his team before the piece was broadcast. One couple called us from the road to thank us for our report . . . on their *former* restaurant. Turns out they had just sold it.

Britney Spears's restaurant in New York was a mess even before it opened. Fortunately, we had front row seats to that train wreck and told the story on the air exactly as it happened.

In most cases, we update the pieces the best we can and then move on.

Same for this book. Each restaurant has been checked and double-checked. But if something happened after we went to press, blame it on the nature of the business. Or the economy. Or lightning or Britney Spears. Just don't blame us. We had nothing to do with it. Honestly!

Use the book as a traveling companion, or just enjoy the stories and have a few laughs as you get a look behind the scenes. But one note about the recipes: Although chefs are the most passionate, hardworking professionals you'll ever meet, they often are not as inspired when it comes to writing down their recipes. They're artists, after all. So we've done our best to translate a "handful" of this and a "dash" of that to actual measurements. (Let us know if you have any secrets or tips of your own at our website, www.bestofbook.com. And send us your other comments as well.) You can e-mail us both through the website. We would love to hear from you.

Our Top Picks

Q.: "What's your favorite restaurant?"
A.: "All of them. We eat anything."

In an attempt to answer this most-asked and ever-so-difficult question, we've compiled a top ten list (in no particular order) of places we've enjoyed the most—whether it's for the story, the adventure, the uniqueness of the place, or the food. We hope it will give you a glimpse into what we believe *The Best Of* is all about.

Double Musky Inn
Girdwood, AK
(Page 268)

Tribute
Detroit, MI
(Page 146)

Gino
New York, NY
(Page 30)

Pink's Hot Dogs
Los Angeles, CA
(Page 247)

Mirror
Nashville, TN
(Page 81)

Smokey's on the Gorge
Lansing, WV
(Page 75)

The Herbfarm
Seattle, WA
(Page 264)

Shack Up Inn
Clarksdale, MS
(Page 109)

Charlie Trotter's
Chicago, IL
(Page 133)

Pat's King of Steaks
Philadelphia, PA
(Page 49)

New England

Maine, Vermont, New Hampshire, Massachusetts, Rhode Island, Connecticut

IN MAINE, THE welcome sign should read, "Welcome to our state. How do you like your lobster roll?" In Rhode Island, it should say, "Quahogs and Clam Cakes rule."

In this section, we'll explain these all-American seafood creations and tell you where to find the best. After all, many of our country's favorite dishes were founded here, along with life, liberty, and the pursuit of happiness. Boston boasts of having our country's oldest restaurant and one of our oldest neighborhoods. It's where a walking tour will work up your appetite for all things Italian.

With its historic ports dotted along the coast, you'll find scrumptious seafood and a seafaring spirit that makes New Englanders a hearty lot—

and a bit superstitious. Thus, our trip to Salem, home of the witch trials and a frighteningly good restaurant where the food is so tasty there's one ghost who doesn't want to leave. Dare to sleep in Lizzie Borden's house? Think you know where Grilled Pizza was created?

It's all here in New England.

Maine

Red's Eats

41 Water Street
Water and Main Street
Wiscasset, ME 04578
(207) 882-6128

Red's is the main attraction in Maine, at least foodwise. Haute cuisine on a hot dog roll.

Take a pound, or more, of succulent cooked lobster meat, and slap it into a toasted bun. A lobster sandwich? Actually, around here it's called a Lobster Roll. What could be more American?

A mandatory stopping place in Wiscasset since 1938, Red's is a small shack that's hard to miss along busy Route 1. Open from late March through October, it offers a large, 70-item, fast food-style menu that also features Crab and Clam Rolls, plus mouthwatering Onion Rings.

Keep in mind, the best-selling Lobster Roll isn't cheap at $14 apiece. But Red's does all the dirty work by cleaning out the shells and giving you every piece of chunky lobster meat, including the claws. Red's goes through about 10,000 pounds of lobster a season, which means, even at that price, Red's can be wicked crowded, as they like to say in Maine.

The vote is in. Red's Eats wins in a landslide.

photo courtesy of Jill Littman

The Results Are In . . .

Red's Eats appeared in a "Viewers' Choice" episode of *The Best Of*, where fans write in to tout their favorite restaurants. We chose to cover Red's because of the incredible number of letters recommending the place. It wasn't until we started doing interviews that the truth slipped out. It seems Red's was behind a successful write-in campaign to get on the show, offering customers photocopied letters to sign. Good for them! As they say in Maine, "As Red's goes, so goes the nation." Or something like that.

The Lobster Shack

225 Two Lights Road
Cape Elizabeth, ME 04107
(207) 799-1677
www.lobstershack-twolights.com

Quick, describe Maine. On second thought, save yourself the effort and just say "The Lobster Shack."

This Portland-area restaurant offers a picture-postcard setting. Visualize a pair of historic lighthouses, logically called Twin Lights, sitting on a bluff. Just below is the eatery itself, overlooking the Atlantic Ocean. A fixture in these parts for decades, it's perched atop a rugged beach, made entirely of rock, called Maine Shale. As the waters pound the shore, diners fill the picnic tables around the large outdoor patio. Throw in the freshest seafood around and a few seagulls circling overhead, and you've got the scene at The Lobster Shack.

The locale is so perfect it was used in an old postage stamp commemorating Maine's statehood. See what we mean?

The Lobster Shack is another Maine restaurant that specializes in Lobster Rolls, hot-dog rolls filled to overflowing with lobster meat. Open from April to October, the restaurant also offers hearty Lobster Dinners, Maine Shrimp,

Maine

photo courtesy of Jill Littman

Welcome to Maine. How do you like your lobster?

Maine

and a whole assortment of other seafood delicacies. Plus, there's nothing like a creamy bowl of "chowda." You tend to talk that way when you're in a place that just says, "Maine."

Lobster Roll

ADAPTED FROM THE LOBSTER SHACK,
CAPE ELIZABETH, MAINE

MAKES 4 TO 6 SERVINGS

2 (1-pound) lobsters
4 to 6 hot dog rolls
4 to 6 lettuce leaves
Mayonnaise

Boil lobsters in water in a large stockpot for 10 to 12 minutes, or until the tail section reaches 175°F. Drain and cool. Pick the meat from claws, knuckles, and tails. Cut meat into medium-size chunks. Toast rolls on both cut sides. Fill with lettuce and lobster meat. Top with a dollop of mayonnaise.

Merriland Farm Café and Golf

545 Coles Hill Road
Wells, ME 04090
(207) 646-5040

Besides offering a fantastic breakfast and lunch, Merriland Farm perfectly blends two popular pastimes, golf and berry picking. On second thought, it may seem an unusual pairing. But somehow, these two outdoor activities mesh to make for an interesting afternoon.

In 1980, Julie and James Morrison bought a rundown 62-acre farm near Kennebunkport with vague plans to create a business. It evolved into a success story. On one end, they built a challenging nine-hole golf course. A round costs a very reasonable $11. It's just $5 more if you want to play again. Bring your clubs, or rent them onsite.

Then, they planted about 10 acres of blueberry and raspberry plants. Ripe for the picking, you're invited to take what you want and pay on the honor system—$1.25 a pound. Leave your money right there by the scale.

With all those berries around, Julie started making jams, jellies, and pies. At first, she sold them at a roadside stand, but business was so good they opened up a café. The Morrisons' son Jon, who's taken over the whole operation, does most of the cooking. The 75-seat, indoor/outdoor restaurant is busy for breakfast and lunch. The homemade Belgium Waffle, loaded with berries, naturally, is a big hit to start the day. The Grilled Portobello and Sundried Tomato Pesto on Homemade Focaccia is popular at lunch. Plus, many people make it a point to load up their trunks with pies and jams. That is, if they still have room with all the berries and golf clubs in there.

———

Vermont

NECI Commons

25 Church Street
Burlington, VT 05401
(802) 862-6324
www.necidining.com

The chefs who make your meal at NECI Commons are also trying to make the grade. They're students at the New England Culinary Institute (NECI), an esteemed cooking academy based nearby.

This is real on-the-job training. NECI Commons is one of seven local restaurants owned by the school. Virtually from day one, students learn what it's like to work in the real world. Some days they make salads; a few days later it's pasta. They continue throughout the restaurant until they learn the business from front to back. Seventy-five percent of their two-year education is spent in this kind of hands-on environment.

Sometimes, their inexperience shows. In fact, guests are encouraged to fill out comment cards—sort of pop quizzes on a daily basis. But the food is always perfect. Often, it's due to the students' developing skills and continued training. Other times it's because veteran chef-instructors carefully supervise the students' every move.

Located on Burlington's Church Street pedestrian mall, the bustling two-story NECI Commons building is more like several dining spots in one. There's the large restaurant with its open kitchen, a carryout, a bakery, and a bar.

The reasonably priced menu features cosmopolitan American fare, from simpler items like Rotisserie Chicken or fresh Pizza, to more of a complex dish like Sautéed Fillet of Salmon. One hundred percent of the students who graduate from New England Culinary Institute get work. Who knows? The next world-renowned chef might be cooking your meal.

———

Waybury Inn

457 East Main Street
East Middlebury, VT 05740
(800) 348-1810 or (802) 388-4015
www.wayburyinn.com

You'll probably recognize the Waybury from the old *Newhart* TV show. The historic Waybury Inn has been a fixture in central Vermont for nearly 200 years, but it's best known to television viewers as the Stratford Inn, the place owned by Dick Loudon (Bob Newhart). Picked for the show because of its quaint look, the building's green front was repainted white for its TV close-up, and fake snow was brought in for the lawn. The Waybury Inn first appeared on *Newhart* in 1982, and its alter ego lives on forever in repeats. But there's a lot more going on here than just Larry, Darryl, and his other brother Darryl.

In the 1950s, the great American poet Robert Frost was a regular diner, apparently deciding the road to the Waybury was indeed the one to take. He often held court in the Inn's pub. There's a guest room named in his honor.

And in room number 9, there's another poetic tradition: In the late 1980s, a honeymooning bride left a note hidden in the room's antique desk, inviting future guests to write about their visits. Hundreds of letters have been left over the years. The topic usually concerns love, whether it's about a couple who have just met, or another celebrating their 25th anniversary. Sometimes, the notes are from people emerging from bad relationships, or just about a weekend getaway with friends. Men write more often than women.

Since the inn opened in 1810, it has been a favorite local gathering spot. Early on, it was a stop for stagecoach travelers crossing Vermont, which is why the restaurant's named The Coach Room. You don't have to be a guest to eat here; in fact, most diners aren't. It's known for its American cuisine with a New England touch, like the Vermont Cheese and Ale Soup. The menu also features plenty of steak and seafood from the region. The intimate pub is crowded most nights, filled with as many locals as tourists.

With its fame, history, and traditions, the Waybury Inn has hosted thousands of guests, even the actors who played Larry, Darryl, and his other brother Darryl. But there's still no word from its famous TV "owner." To this day, Bob Newhart has yet to make a reservation.

Waybury Inn Vermont Cheese and Ale Soup

ADAPTED FROM THE WAYBURY INN, EAST MIDDLEBURY, VERMONT

MAKES 8 SERVINGS

1/4 cup butter
1/4 cup all-purpose flour
1 medium onion, minced
2 cups chicken stock, preferably homemade
1 cup Otter Creek Copper Ale or other fine ale
2 cups half-and-half
2 cups grated cheddar cheese
Salt, black pepper, and cayenne to taste
Croutons or popcorn to serve

Melt butter in a soup pot over medium heat. Stir in flour, and cook, stirring frequently, for 10 minutes. Be careful not to let it burn. Add onion and cook, stirring frequently, until transparent.

Add stock and ale, and cook, stirring frequently, for 15 minutes. Reduce the heat to a simmer. Add half-and-half and cheese, stirring so cheese does not settle on the bottom of the pot and burn. Season with salt, black pepper, and cayenne.

Ladle into bowls. Serve with croutons.

New Hampshire

Lindy's Diner

19 Gilbo Avenue
Keene, NH 03431
(603) 352-4273

Lindy's Diner isn't just an all-American favorite; it's an all-American *presidential* favorite. The town of Keene is the epitome of small town USA—until the presidential primaries heat up. That's when all the wannabees flood this quaint, picturesque place to stop and have a cup of joe with your average Joe.

So why come here? Well for starters, when Arietta and George Rigopoulos first opened in 1961, they invited presidential hopefuls to stop by and, thus, a tradition was born. Plus, this is New Hampshire, and folks here expect to meet their candidates face to face. When Jill asked Arietta which candidate over the years she liked best, she said, "All of them." Answered like a true politician.

The second reason they come? The food. Politicians are a hungry lot, and there's no better place to kill two birds with one stone than a restaurant. They can meet, greet, and eat all at the same time. Lindy's is renowned for its New England clam chowder, homemade macaroni and cheese, and Salisbury steaks—all the grub a candidate needs before grubbing for votes.

After the hoopola is over and the citizens of the state cast their ballots, Lindy's goes back to being a regular blue-plate diner, but one that still gets our vote.

Ya Mamma's

75 Daniel Webster Highway
Merrimack, NH 03054
(603) 578-9201
www.yamammas.com

As a young boy, Michael Ferrazzani says a day didn't go by without his friends asking, "What's your mamma making for dinner tonight?"

Inspired by the Italian dishes cooked by his mamma, young Michael grew up to be a chef and eventually owner of his own restaurant, named for whom else? His mamma.

Coming here means never leaving hungry. In true Italian style, they don't skimp on portions, and it's all made from scratch. In fact, they've been voted southern New Hampshire's best Italian restaurant eleven years running.

But to give Michael's mom all the credit wouldn't be fair to the Ferrazzani family tree. The recipe for Michael's red sauce is from his grandfather Luigi and dates back more than 100 years. There's also a lot of history in his house specialty, the Veal à la Michael.

It's a dish he created for a wedding—his own. He and his wife, Michele, didn't have a lot of money at the time so they made all the food themselves for their big day. Talk about being married to your work!

On many nights you'll find Michele and Michael's mom, Joan, greeting customers and welcoming them into their home. The restaurant has a real family feel. You may even find his son, 14-year-old Michael Anthony, in the kitchen helping his dad plate the lasagna or put his finishing touch on the tiramisu. After all, he's hoping to follow in his dad's footsteps. If he does, you can guess what his restaurant will be called: Ya Papa's.

Veal à la Michael

ADAPTED FROM YA MAMMA'S, MERRIMACK, NEW HAMPSHIRE

MAKES 2 SERVINGS

6 green olives, pitted
3 pepperoncini
1 tablespoon chopped garlic
1 tablespoon grated Romano cheese
¼ cup oil-packed sun-dried tomatoes, drained
1 stick (½ cup) butter
2 (6-ounce) veal medallions, pounded until thin
2 slices provolone cheese
2 slices prosciutto
1 red bell pepper, roasted, halved, and seeds and
    stem removed

1 egg
½ cup all-purpose flour
1 cup seasoned bread crumbs
Olive oil

In a food processor, process olives, pepperoncini, garlic, and Romano cheese until the mixture resembles a paste. Set aside. Clean the food processor, and process sun-dried tomatoes until puréed. Add butter, and pulse until smooth. Set aside.

Lay veal medallions flat on a work surface. Spread olive paste evenly over each medallion. Layer provolone cheese, prosciutto, and roasted pepper on top of veal. Fold veal in half, and place in the freezer for 30 minutes to firm up.

Preheat the oven to 350°F.

Beat egg in a shallow bowl. Dredge veal in flour, place in beaten egg, and roll in breadcrumbs. Heat olive oil in an ovenproof skillet. Add veal, and sauté until golden brown, turning once. Transfer to the oven, and cook for 20 minutes.

Spoon a dollop of tomato butter over the top. (Extra tomato butter can be refrigerated for several days.)

New Hampshire

Massachusetts

Harbor Sweets

Palmer Cove
85 Leavitt Street
Salem, MA 01970
(800) 234-4860
(800) 243-2115 for 24-hour phone orders
www.harborsweets.com

It began with a simple question that candy man Ben Strohecker posed to people in the early 1970s. He asked friends and family if they could eat only one piece of candy before they died what would it be? The most frequent answer? A chocolate-covered almond butter crunch.

So Ben set out on a sweet pursuit to make the best butter crunch in the world, regardless of cost. In 1973, while working out of his basement, he founded Harbor Sweets with his signature butter crunch confection: The Sweet Sloop. Formed in the shape of a sail and dipped in white and dark chocolate, this nautical nugget instantly received rave reviews and was the beginning of a whole fleet of sweets.

More than three decades later, Ben's business is out of the basement and into a quaint factory store in downtown Salem. When you visit this candy corner, think Willy Wonka meets Santa's elves. You can gaze upon the factory floor and watch—and smell—the butter crunch cooking in copper kettles. You'll see vats of chocolate flowing like waterfalls, and at the sound of the bell, all hands are on deck to be sure things like warm caramel dots are topped with nuts before they cool. There is very little automation aboard this tight and tasty ship. Everything from cutting, to dipping, to molding, even packaging, is done by hand.

Another added bonus: Employees are allowed to eat their mistakes. In fact, Harbor Sweets is known as a place that treats their workers pretty sweet. There is only one rule in this factory: If you're not having fun, you're fired! No wonder most of the employees have been around for a decade or more. Take Phyllis Leblanc, who started here in 1977 as a part-time candy dipper. Two

college degrees and several promotions later, she now owns the company! She bought it from Ben when he retired in 1998.

The business is primarily mail order, although they also sell their chocolates in specialty stores like Dean & DeLuca and have been commissioned to make custom chocolates for organizations like the Smithsonian, the Guggenheim, and Harvard. There are about seven types of chocolates to choose from, and even if you aren't planning on dying anytime soon, the signature Sweet Sloop is certainly a safe bet.

As Ben told us when shooting for our *Best Of Sweet Sensations* show, "An entrepreneur's greatest tool is serendipity." If that's true, then this is sweet serendipity at its best.

———

Ye Olde Pepper Companie

122 Derby Street
Salem, MA 01970
(866) 393-6533 or (978) 745-2744

59 Main Street
North Andover, MA 01845
(978) 689-3636
www.yeoldepeppercandy.com

Before Hershey's or Mars, there was Ye Olde Pepper Companie, America's oldest candy company.

Its history dates to 1806 and a rock-hard confection called the Gibraltar. The story has an English woman named Spencer surviving a shipwreck with little more than a family recipe for the candy. Opening shop in Salem, she made a good living selling the treat to seafaring crews who liked its durability. The sugar rush helped, too.

The company got its name from its next owner, John Walter Pepper, who built it into a real moneymaker. He sold it to the Burkinshaw family, and it's been in their hands for more than a century. The fourth generation's now in charge.

The diamond-shaped Gibraltar comes in lemon and peppermint and is so hard it's guaranteed to make you think twice about your fillings.

Massachusetts

The company is also the birthplace of the molasses-flavored Blackjack, believed to be the oldest stick candy in the country.

In the Salem store, there's a large jar on display filled with aging Gibraltars. One is believed to be 170 years old, yet the company says it probably tastes brand new. We'll take their word for it.

—

Lyceum Bar and Grill

43 Church Street
Salem, MA 01970
(978) 745-7665
www.lyceumsalem.com

The seaside city of Salem, Massachusetts, has, over the years, risen to supernatural status. After all, the 1692 witch trials continue to haunt this quaint New England town. One walk through the cemetery, and you'll sense restless spirits like Giles Corey, who is reportedly a regular apparition here. He was one of 20 people put to death in 1692, only instead of being hanged, he was crushed. His cruel, violent death (big rocks were put on him to weigh him down and it took several days of severe suffering for him to finally meet his maker) was one of the reasons the witchcraft court was ultimately shut down.

But if you're not into hanging out among the dead, then head to the Lyceum, where you can hang among the living—well, sort of. We guess we should say it's also a place to hang out with those who aren't ready to leave this world.

The Lyceum was built on the site of what was once the apple orchard of Bridget Bishop—the first person put to death for witchcraft in 1692. Owner George Harrington and many others believe Bridget is still hanging around. For example, there's the former waitress who quit because every time she came to work, her watch stopped. There's also a certain time of year that some of the staff claim to smell apple blossoms upstairs—which is far away from the kitchen. There are even reports of photographers who have taken pictures inside only to find they came out blurry, despite the fact their film worked fine outside.

Not only is the building haunted, it's also historic. The definition of a lyceum is a lecture hall, and that's exactly what this place was. People like Emerson, Thoreau, and Fredrick Douglas all gave speeches here. But perhaps the biggest event happened in 1877, when Alexander Graham Bell made the first long-distance phone call. He called his friend Watson at the *Boston Globe*, forever changing the course of history.

While you're waiting for Bridget to rattle her chains, you can settle your rumbling stomach with fine dining New England style. Chef James Havey hails from California and describes the cuisine as contemporary American and quintessential New England. Clam chowder is always on the menu, along with fresh fish and juicy steaks. After eating some of his food, Jill figured out why Bridget sticks around. If she's a hungry ghost, she's in the right place.

—

Richardson's Ice Cream

156 South Main Street (Route 114)
Middleton, MA 01949
(978) 774-5450
www.richardsonsicecream.com

If you think kids scream for ice cream, wait until you see what happens at Richardson's.

Located in the Boston suburb of Middleton, Richardson's claims to be the largest ice-cream stand on the East Coast. Even that description doesn't do it justice. It's really more of a complex dedicated to the entire ice-cream food chain, from cow to cone and beyond.

The centerpiece is the Dairy Barn, where you can pick from more than 90 flavors—or try to pick, anyway.

But the activities are just getting started. Around back, there's a large dairy farm—with more than 350 cows—where the public is invited to walk around and get a close-up look. The Richardson family has been farming in these parts since the 1600s. It wasn't until 1917 that they started bottling milk. The ice-cream stand was opened in 1952. These days, the company supplies restaurants and stores all over New England.

Massachusetts

On a typical day, it produces 4,000 gallons of ice cream.

So much for the cow to the cone. Here's the beyond part. On the other side of the Dairy Barn, there are two—count them—two 18-hole miniature golf courses, along with a driving range and batting cages. Any or all of the sports go perfectly with eating ice cream.

It seems incredible with all the excitement, but somehow vanilla remains the most popular flavor here. Sure it tastes good, but it's also the last word you would use to describe Richardson's.

———

North End Market Tours

Six Charter Street
Boston, MA 02113
(617) 523-6032
www.micheletopor.com

In Paul Revere's backyard, tour guide extraordinaire, Michele Topor, revolutionizes the way you look at one of Boston's most historic neighborhoods. Only it has nothing to do with the Redcoats. Red sauce? Now that's another story.

Boston's North End is one of the country's oldest, most authentic Italian neighborhoods. It's filled with Old World–style bakeries, greengrocers, butchers, and, of course, restaurants like Mamma Maria (see below). Several times a week, Topor leads visitors on a three-and-a-half-hour tour, during which she shares her expertise on why such a small area—less than $\frac{1}{3}$ of a square mile—is so vibrant.

The Puritans were actually the first "immigrants" to live in the North End. Paul Revere became a resident in 1770. Over time, the neighborhood became a haven for a succession of different ethnic groups, first Irish, then Russian Jews, Portuguese, and finally Italians. Topor says it was 90 percent Italian in the 1920s. Although the numbers have declined, the heritage remains on display. Topor is proud to show it off and wants others to grow comfortable with the ways and customs.

Her tour offers a long list of stops, and plenty of samples along the way. At Maria's Pastry Shop, *sfogliatelle* may be hard to pronounce, but one bite makes it clear it's a breakfast pastry. At Alba Produce, Topor explains how dandelions are a familiar ingredient in spring salads. Salumeria Italiana brings a passionate discourse on the difference between authentic balsamic vinegar and weak imitations. And at Y. Cirace and Son, one of the top Italian wine shops in the United States, there's a toast over Limoncello, a lemon liqueur.

One thing you won't find is a large supermarket. Topor says the custom here—as in Italy—is to go from store to store on a daily basis, socializing at every stop. Topor speaks the language as if she were from Italy. She's visited there more times than she can count. So it's somewhat fascinating to discover she's 100 percent Polish. But her soul is Italian, she says, and that's what counts. Her connection to the culture started when she moved to the neighborhood 30 years ago. She's been sharing it ever since, serving up a tasty course in history.

———

Mamma Maria

3 North Square
Boston, MA 02113
(617) 523-0077
www.mammamaria.com

How did a guy named John *McGee*, an Irishman through and through, come to own an upscale Italian restaurant in Boston's North End? If you ask him, he'll give you two good reasons. First and foremost: The Irish were here first. Second: He worked as a waiter at this restaurant for years when it was a simple spaghetti house—one that had red and white checked tablecloths with empty Chianti bottles as candleholders—so he's as regular here as anyone.

You'll find the restaurant in the historic North Square. It has been everything from a doctor's office to a funeral home and, since the 1960s, a restaurant. In 1989, when it went up for sale, John bought it. He kept the name but transformed the menu, focusing on regional Italian dishes like Osso Buco and Grilled Yellow-Fin Tuna, puttanesca-style over homemade squid-ink

Massachusetts

linguini. Depending on what's in season, nearly all the dishes are made with local ingredients, often cooked "slow and low."

In other words, if you're just looking for spaghetti and meatballs, you've come to the wrong place. But if upscale Italian cuisine in a historic setting is your choice, Mamma Maria's is our choice. Not bad for an Irishman, aye?

———

Union Oyster House

41 Union Street
Boston, MA 02108
(617) 227-2750
www.unionoysterhouse.com

The main draw on the menu at the Union Oyster House is . . . well, oysters, of course. But you can also expect a serious helping of history on the half shell, if you will. Opened in 1826, the Oyster House is the oldest restaurant in Boston and the oldest continuously operating restaurant in the United States. The building itself is more than 250 years old, and it feels it. With every creak, a bit of its storied past is revealed.

The legendary statesman Daniel Webster was a regular at the Oyster Bar. To this day, you can sit where he sat, eat what he ate, and drink what he drank. But be careful not to drink as much as he drank! Old Daniel was known to toss back a rather hefty tumbler of brandy and water with each helping of oysters.

A century later, John F. Kennedy was another Oyster House regular. Many Sundays, JFK would plant himself in booth number 18, where he'd read six or seven Sunday newspapers. He'd frequently stay from noon until 5, not leaving until he'd read them all.

Today, the Union Oyster House is as popular as ever, albeit extremely touristy. But in this case, tourists have good reason for making this a destination. The oysters are truly irresistible. On a busy day, they'll shuck more than 3,000 of them. The lobster, steamer clams, and New England clam chowder are also excellent.

So plan on visiting the Union Oyster House with a hunger for seafood and a hearty appetite for American history. You're likely to leave sated on both counts.

———

Finale Park Plaza

One Columbus Avenue
Boston, MA 02116
(617) 423-3184

Finale Harvard Square

30 Dunster Street
Cambridge, MA 02138
(617) 441-9797
www.finaledesserts.com

Curtain up, light the lights, this is Boston's century-old theatre district. In fact, at the Shubert Theater, Marlon Brando made his debut in *A Streetcar Named Desire*. Naturally, dinner and a show make for a perfect night out, but when the check is paid and the curtain comes down, where do you go for the finale? How 'bout Finale?

This is a dessert lover's dream and the success story of two Harvard grads, Kim Moore and Paul Conforti. They cooked up the idea of a dessert café for a class project, calling it Room for Dessert. After they received their academic credit, they started thinking, *Maybe we should actually try and execute this idea.*

While most Harvard grads were fielding multiple offers and deciding on six-figure salaries, these two went to work in local restaurants, perhaps holding the record as the lowest-paid Harvard grads out there. But they were smart; they knew they needed to learn the business from the ground up. After a year of trying to convince investors to give them some credit, in 1998 they made the grade and were able to raise enough capital to open Finale.

Now, six years later, they have a second location in Harvard Square—just in case their professors want to check up on them. By the way, we give all their desserts an A, but the crème brûlée and chocolate molten cake each get an A+. However, don't trust us, trust their Harvard professors who also gave them an A on the project. Sweet success.

Massachusetts

Finale Cheesecake

ADAPTED FROM FINALE, BOSTON, MASSACHUSETTS

YIELD: 1 (9-INCH) CHEESECAKE OF 12 SERVINGS

*2 cups graham cracker crumbs (or cookie
    crumbs)*
1 cup plus 1 tablespoon sugar
1 stick butter
3 (8-ounce) packages cream cheese, softened
3 eggs
1 teaspoon vanilla extract
1 tablespoon lemon juice
1 cup heavy cream

Preheat oven to 350°F. Mix together crumbs and 3 tablespoons sugar. Melt butter, and stir into crumb mixture. Press into the bottom of a greased 9-inch round springform cake pan. Set aside. Using an electric beater, blend together cream cheese and remaining sugar until creamy, wiping down the sides of the bowl and the beaters with a spatula to incorporate all the cheese. Add eggs 1 at a time, beating after each addition. Add vanilla and lemon juice to cream, then slowly stir into cheese mixture.

Put the prepared round cake pan into a slightly larger rectangular pan. Pour cheese mixture into the prepared pan. Set both pans in the oven, and fill the rectangular pan with water, halfway up the sides of the round pan. Bake until firm and golden brown, approximately 45 to 50 minutes. Cool completely before removing from the pan.

No. 9 Park

9 Park Street
Boston, MA 02108
(617) 742-9991
www.no9park.com

As a young girl, Barbara Lynch never dreamed of eating in a restaurant like No. 9 Park, much less owning it. The restaurant, which sits in the historic wealthy neighborhood of Beacon Hill, is a far cry from where Barbara grew up in the South Boston housing projects. Her single mom worked four jobs to put food on the table for Barbara and her seven siblings.

It wasn't until she was in high school that her life took an unpredictable turn. Barbara discovered she had a knack for cooking while taking a home economics class. Likewise, her teacher saw in her pupil plenty of passion and encouraged Barbara to cultivate her culinary skills. After high school, Barbara took that teacher's advice and moved to Martha's Vineyard to cook, which is where her passion really heated up. Eventually she returned to Boston, working in several high-end Italian restaurants before opening No. 9 Park in 1998. Almost immediately, the accolades came pouring in.

Named one of the top 25 restaurants in America by *Bon Appétit* and one of the top 50 by *Travel & Leisure,* Barbara won the coveted James Beard Award for Best Chef in the Northeast in 2003. She's now opened two other places: B & G Oysters Ltd. (550 Tremont Street, 617-423-0550) is an oyster bar in the south end and right next door, a gourmet butcher shop and wine bar simply called The Butcher Shop (617-423-4800).

Despite her success, she's never forgotten her roots and remains humble. When asked by Jill what advice she has for others in a similar situation, Barbara said, "Do what you love, and the money will follow," adding, "It wasn't easy, but it was worth it." No doubt Bostonians would agree.

Bomboa

35 Stanhope Street
Boston, MA 02116
(617) 236-6363
www.bomboa.com

A Boston food writer once wrote, "Bomboa is a 7-dollar vacation." That's the cost of their signature drink—the Mojito—a rum concoction mixed with mint, loads of limes, and sugar. One sip and you're transported to the tropics—pretty refreshing in a city where the cold hangs in for about eight months of the year.

Massachusetts

This tropical hot spot, located in the shadow of Boston's John Hancock Tower, serves up odd and unusual foods and drinks that have a distinctly Brazilian flair. If you're in an adventurous mood, try the Feijoada—the national dish of Brazil—made with braised pork ribs, sausages, and beans. It'll definitely stick to your ribs on a cold winter night.

The bar offers fruity and amusing libations—appropriate considering *Bomboa* is a slang word for "fun." There's the Kool-Ade, a mixture of raspberry vodka, ginger ale, and Chambord, and the Stumbling Islander, an all-rum drink that could cause you to stumble out. But the number-one favorite is the refreshing Caipirinha. They sell 500 of these Brazilian babies a week. It's made with fresh limes, crushed ice, lime juice, simple syrup, and Brazilian liquor. You might not be able to travel to the tropics, but you can get a taste of them here. Brazilian in Beantown. Who knew?

—

Radius

8 High Street
Boston, MA 02110
(617) 426-1234
www.radiusrestaurant.com

Radius is so ultra-hip, it would work in New York City. There are pros and cons to that observation, because athough this stylish financial-district hot spot certainly compares to the big boys, you also get the feeling that you've seen it all before.

There's the slightly self-important staff, the fashionable dining room, a happening bar scene, and a communal dining table—*de rigueur* in all places cutting edge. Quite frankly, we had an overwhelming sense of déjà vu, having experienced the same setup in every other big city. But critics can't stop raving about Radius, starting from when both *Food and Wine* and *Esquire* picked it as the best new restaurant right after it opened in 1999.

Still, the seasonally changing nouvelle cuisine is excellent, even if the portions are small. Standout specialties include the Crispy Softshell Crab, Halibut, or the Roasted Quail. The creative desserts also shouldn't be missed. The high-powered clientele isn't bothered by the high-powered prices, yet another trait stylish restaurants seem to share, whether they're in Boston, New York, or Any Town, USA.

—

Lumière

1293 Washington Street
West Newton, MA 02465
(617) 244-9199
www.lumiererestaurant.com

If you think owning a restaurant is glamorous, just head to West Newton, Massachusetts, and spend an hour with Lumière owners Jill and Michael Leviton before opening time. There you'll find Jill washing dishes and picking cigarette butts off the sidewalk. You'll find Michael running around getting last-minute ingredients and putting his kitchen and staff in order. Sounds pretty alluring, huh? But if that's what it takes to make a small French bistro work, then this dynamic duo is out to make it happen.

The restaurant is small and intimate, the décor contemporary and chic, the food exquisite—classified as modern French. The menu only has about six items in each appetizer, entrée, and dessert category, but what they lack in choice they make up for in flavor. Their signature dish is Seared Sea Scallops with Exotic Mushrooms, but really everything here is mouthwatering.

Once the doors open, the earlier frenetic feel bows to a quiet elegance. Beautiful people are seated. The servers are impeccably dressed. The food is perfectly presented. The name, Lumière, which means "light" in French, stems from the Lumière brothers who invented cinema in the late 1800s. And just like a good movie, the picture here is flawlessly orchestrated, leaving the viewer—er, diner—unaware of the frenzied pace that takes place behind the scenes.

Massachusetts

Molten Chocolate Cakes with Rum Caramel and Vanilla Ice Cream

ADAPTED FROM LUMIÈRE, WEST NEWTON, MASSACHUSETTS

MAKES 4 SERVINGS

Cakes:

8 ounces (2 sticks) butter
9½ ounces bittersweet chocolate, coarsely chopped, preferably Valrhona Manjari chocolate
2 eggs
6 egg yolks
¼ cup sugar
Pinch salt

Rum Caramel Sauce:

½ cup sugar
5 tablespoons butter
¼ teaspoon salt
3 tablespoons water
¼ cup dark rum
Vanilla ice cream (homemade or your favorite brand)

Preheat a convection oven to 300°F and low fan. Grease 4 ramekins or soufflé cups.

To make cakes: Melt butter and chocolate separately over simmering water in two double boilers. Remove both from heat when their temperatures reach 110°F. Meanwhile, gently whisk together eggs and egg yolks. Add sugar and salt, stirring to combine. Slowly drizzle chocolate into egg mixture, stirring as you pour. Slowly add butter, continuing to stir gently. Do not overmix (no air bubbles allowed).

Pour the batter into prepared ramekins. Bake for 10 minutes. Remove from the oven, let cool slightly, and turn out onto serving plates.

To make sauce: Cook sugar, salt, and water in a small heavy saucepan over medium to an amber caramel color. Stir in butter. Remove from the heat, and slowly add rum.

Drizzle cakes with sauce, and top with ice cream.

Mr. Bartley's Burger Cottage

1246 Massachusetts Avenue
Cambridge, MA 02138
(617) 354-6559
www.mrbartleys.com

Any restaurant can have a hamburger special, but at Mr. Bartley's Burger Cottage they like to say, "We have really special hamburgers."

Located in Cambridge, Massachusetts, Mr. Bartley's is a Harvard Square landmark, famous for their 7-ounce burgers, onion rings, and sweet potato fries. And although "Mr. B," as Bill Bartley is affectionately known, retired from his post behind the grill in 1978, he's still almost as famous in these parts as his burgers. You'll find him on many a Saturday keeping the crowd in check and greeting customers at the door.

His son Bill Jr. keeps things cooking. College students looking to satisfy their carnivorous cravings can choose from 20 different burgers, each one with a special title and saying on the menu. To name a few, there's The Bill Gates where *money can't buy a better burger;* The Viagra Burger that'll *rise to the occasion;* The Dick Cheney—*a heartbeat away;* The Tiger Woods—*get up to par;* and The Ted Kennedy— *a plump, liberal amount of burger.*

As Jill helped Bill Jr. grill up the Mr. & Mrs. B Burger—commemorating his parents' 52 years of marriage and still speaking to each other—he told her the most important rule in the kitchen is to not tamper with the cook's buns. Fair enough.

Whatever burger you choose, wash it down with a Lime Rickey, made with lime juice, soda water, and sugar; or one of their fabulous frappés, which is the New England term for thick milkshakes. Seems like it's everything an undergrad needs to earn that freshman 15. And, as an added bonus, some say their burgers are brain food to boot!

Salts

798 Main Street
Cambridge, MA 02139
(617) 876-8444

It looked like a potential disaster. Not long after Marc and his crew started taping at Salts in Cambridge, a car went out of control and struck a nearby power pole. No one was hurt, but the electricity was knocked out for the night.

So what do you do when you're faced with a tight schedule and can't come back? You keep taping, that's what, even in the dark. It couldn't have worked out better. The reason? Salts was scheduled to appear in an episode of *The Best Of* about hidden treasures. The pitch darkness seemed to emphasize the restaurant's "hidden" quality. The fact that none of the customers left made it even more of a "treasure."

Opened in 1997, Salts is a small and intimate place owned by husband and wife team Steve Rosen and Lisa Mandy-Rosen. He cooks while she manages. The cuisine is based on their Eastern European backgrounds. She's Italian-Polish, while he's Russian-Romanian. Steve's cooking adds a gourmet touch to Old World favorites like Chive Pierogi with Mushrooms, Skewered Lamb, or Maine Crab Kugel, a noodle dish.

Even with the outage, Steve was able to keep the kitchen going, and customers got their food. Bathed in candlelight, the dining room was even more romantic than usual. The restaurant was back running at full strength the next day. But even in the dark, Salts deserves the spotlight.

Rosemary Skewered Lamb with Black Olive Crust

ADAPTED FROM SALTS, CAMBRIDGE, MASSACHUSETTS

MAKES 8 SERVINGS

Olive Crust
1 cup olive paste
¾ cup pitted kalamata olives
1 teaspoon capers
1 teaspoon chopped garlic
1 teaspoon pine nuts
1 teaspoon chopped fresh parsley
1 tablespoon olive oil
Juice of 1 lemon
Salt and freshly ground black pepper, to taste

2 pounds boneless lamb leg, cut into 1-inch cubes
2 red bell peppers, cut into 1-inch squares
2 green bell peppers, cut into 1-inch squares
8 rosemary skewers

To make olive crust: In a food processor, process olive paste, olives, capers, garlic, pine nuts, parsley, olive oil, lemon juice, salt, and pepper until puréed.

Toss olive mixture with lamb to coat. Skewer lamb and bell peppers, alternating pepper colors, on rosemary skewers. Preheat the grill. Place the skewers on the grill rack, and grill for 6 to 8 minutes or to desired doneness.

Lizzie Borden Bed and Breakfast-Museum

92 Second Street
Fall River, MA 02721
(508) 675-7333
www.lizzie-borden.com

Prepare for a bloody great getaway. The Lizzie Borden Bed and Breakfast-Museum invites you to check in to the actual Borden family home, the scene of the crime of the nineteenth century. Then, enjoy a breakfast to die for similar to the victims' last meal. It's so hauntingly good, it will make your head spin.

Even if you don't know the details, you've probably heard the children's ditty about Lizzie Borden. It's where she took an axe and gave her mother 40 whacks, only to follow that performance with 41 for dad. The poem's easy to remember, but it's not exactly what happened on August 4, 1892.

Lizzie discovered her father Andrew's body first. The wealthy banker was found on a sitting room couch, the victim of 10 blows—not 41— from an unidentified object. Moments later, the

Massachusetts

photo courtesy of Steve Sullivan

CSI: The Best Of. Recreating the crime at the Lizzie Borden Bed and Breakfast.

Massachusetts

family maid and a neighbor looked upstairs to find the body of Lizzie's stepmother, Abby. She had suffered 19 blows from the same weapon.

Lizzie was arrested but got off after a sensational trial. She might have had a shaky alibi and stood to gain a large inheritance, but there was little evidence, no murder weapon, and plenty of speculation about other potential suspects.

More than a century later, the house is open for tours and overnight stays. You can sleep in Lizzie's room, but the most requested suite is where stepmom Abby bought it.

The authentic "last-meal" breakfast includes eggs, bacon, bananas, and Johnnycakes, an old-style New England pancake. There's also an axe-shape sugar cookie, its edge lined with a blood-red frosting.

The Museum portion is light on artifacts. There are a couple gory crime scene pictures, a dress worn by Elizabeth Montgomery in a TV movie about Lizzie Borden, and the family crest. Ironically, it's an animal holding an axe. Lizzie's favorite books are on hand, including one on gardening called *With Edged Tools*. It's a stay that will make you think you died and went to heaven.

Rhode Island

Al Forno

577 South Main Street
Providence, RI 02903
(401) 273-9760
www.alforno.com

The next time someone asks where Grilled Pizza was invented, raise your hand and proudly answer "Al Forno." Granted, the subject doesn't come up that much. On the other hand, this respected Providence restaurant is frequently discussed.

Al Forno is generally considered the best place to eat in New England. Opened in 1980, chef/owner/couple George Germon and Johanne Killen are the recipients of almost every major culinary award and are often lauded in the media. Plus, they invented Grilled Pizza.

Of course, the next logical question is, what's Grilled Pizza? It's wafer-thin dough gently sprinkled with extra virgin olive oil, then topped with a minimal amount of ingredients, like tomatoes, cheese, and herbs. George is very particular about not overdoing it. The pizza goes into the oven until the crust gets crispy, and grill marks add just the right amount of flavor.

There's much more to the Al Forno's Northern Italian cuisine than just the pizza.

Critics often tout the Baked Pasta or the Vegetable Entrée that's grilled to perfection. The key to Al Forno's success has been the owners' insistence on keeping the dishes "painfully simple."

The only thing that isn't simple is being forced to decide your dessert at the same time you order your meal. The reason is because every dessert—including ice cream—is made to order while you dine. The early decision-making challenge is something most people can handle, though.

Flo's Clam Shack

324 Park Avenue
Portsmouth, RI 02871
(no phone)

4 Aquidneck Avenue
Middletown, RI 02842
(401) 847-8141

Flo's Clam Shack is an institution here, not only for the fried clams, chowda and clam cakes, but also for its resiliency. More than a handful of hurricanes have battered Flo's over the years, and the place is still standing.

In 1936, Flo Vares and her husband took a chicken coop from their family farm and set it up on this location in Portsmouth, Rhode Island—about 10 miles from Newport. She started selling her seafood specialties, and business was booming until 1938, when a hurricane demolished the place. They rebuilt. Business went on until 1955, when another hurricane hit—and again in 1963. By 1978, Flo was fed up with the wacky weather and constant rebuilding, so she sold the business.

Sold it, you ask? Who in their right mind would buy it? Komes Rozes, that's who. You probably think he is pretty crazy right? Well, actually, not really. He's just a fun-loving guy who likes to "go with the flo." He's always been in the restaurant business, and when Flo's went up for sale, he wanted to keep her tradition going. That he does . . . hurricanes notwithstanding. In fact, he expanded her tradition and built a second Flo's in Middletown, Rhode Island, with indoor dining and an upstairs bar. Across the street, you'll find Overflo's—a good place to go for drinks.

Clam cakes are by far their most famous specialty. Komes says they've served more than 40 million of 'em (how they keep track we're not sure). They're also known for their quahogs, which are gigantic clams baked with stuffing inside.

Both locations are just a "reach from the beach," as Komes is fond of saying. The Shack is classic. You just walk up to the window, order, and then either eat on the beach or on the benches nearby.

Although it's a wonderful spot, come hurricane season they're never quite out of the path of those whipping winds and high waters. After Hurricane Bob hit in 1991, the Shack was once again wiped out. Komes took matters into his own hands and was able to salvage the original siding and weathered shingles on the outside, but rebuilt the inside with steel columns and a floodgate. Now he says, this Shack ain't going anywhere. So when you come to Rhode Island, take Komes's advice: Relax, and realize life's a beach. No matter which way you go, when you go with the flo, you'll be happy as, well, a clam.

Flo's Clams Casino

ADAPTED FROM FLO'S CLAM SHACK, MIDDLETOWN, RHODE ISLAND

MAKES 4 SERVINGS

16 littleneck clams
¼ cup butter
Juice of 1 lemon
¼ cup chopped fresh parsley, plus additional for garnish
Hot pepper sauce
¼ cup diced green bell pepper
¼ cup diced red bell pepper
¼ cup diced onion
½ cup crushed butter crackers
4 strips bacon, partially cooked and quartered
Lemon wedges, for garnish

Preheat the oven to 350°F.

Shuck and drain clams. Leave clams in bottom shells; set aside on a baking sheet. Melt butter in a sauté pan over medium heat. Add lemon juice, parsley, and several dashes of hot pepper sauce. Add green and red bell peppers and onion, and sauté until softened. Remove from the heat, and stir in crackers.

Spoon a small amount of cracker mixture on top of each clam, and top with a piece of bacon. Bake for about 10 minutes or until bacon is crispy. Garnish with parsley and lemon wedge.

Rhode Island

Castle Hill Inn and Resort

590 Ocean Drive
Newport, RI 02840
(401) 848-0918
www.castlehillinn.com

Don't call it happy hour. There is no such thing in Newport, Rhode Island. It's actually illegal. The way places get around it is to call the evening imbibing "social hour." There is perhaps no better place for "social hour" than here, at this beautiful Victorian mansion overlooking Narragansett Bay.

Castle Hill was built in 1874 as a summer residence of famed Harvard marine biologist Alexander Agassiz so he could study marine life. Nowadays it is a 40-acre retreat, complete with 25 guest rooms, 8 private beachfront cottages, and of course that water view that'll knock your socks off.

The food is as impressive as the view. With four dining rooms, Chef Casey Riley keeps busy heating up the kitchen. Everything he touches seems to turn to gold. From his Rack of Colorado Lamb with Sheep's Cheese and Rosemary Crust to his Georges Bank Cod Loin, complete with a Toasted Hazelnut Crust and an Apple Pear-Beurre Blanc.

On warm summer nights, when the sun starts to set, you'll find every Adirondack chair on the lawn taken. People sit back with their cocktail or wine and toast to the good life. It's the perfect place to gather and be happy—even if, technically speaking, you're just being "social."

The Chanler at Cliff Walk

117 Memorial Boulevard
Newport, RI 02840
(401) 847-1300
www.thechanler.com

They called them summer cottages—"they" being families like the Astors and the Vanderbilts. These "cottages" are now the number-one attraction in this seaside city. Just strolling along Mansion Row is enough to blow you away. The Vanderbilt place, for example, is a mere 138,000 square feet. The family only stayed here for 6 to 8 weeks each summer.

Today many of these mansions are open to the public, and no matter what your social status, you're invited to tour these magnificent properties. In a few instances, you can dine, drink, and even spend the night.

The Chanler was originally built as a summer cottage for Congressman John Winthrop Chanler and his wife, who was a member of the Astor family. Over the years it's been a home to a Greek ambassador to the United States, a boarding house, and a school for girls. In 1999, the Chanler was shut down and completely renovated. During the summer of 2003, the $10 million renovation was unveiled, and this 20-room boutique hotel opened for business.

The rooms are works of art, each decorated in unique themes. The Louis XVI Room, complete with handmade tapestries and inlaid wood furniture, will make you feel like royalty. By contrast, the Nantucket Suite has a nautical feel along with its own private entrance, courtyard, sauna, and hot tub.

It is clear just by stepping into any of these that no expense was spared. (Jill still raves about the beds, saying it was the best night's sleep she's ever had.)

Their signature restaurant, the Spiced Pear, is where Executive Chef Richard Hamilton works his magic in his open exhibition kitchen. The dining room overlooks the ocean, so whether you look at it or at Chef Hamilton cooking, you'll be entertained.

His food is first rate. Each night he offers a four-course prix fix menu. Starters include items like Hudson Valley Foie Gras and Lobster Mac and Cheese. Entrées range from prime beef to spiced squab. The menu is constantly evolving and changing with the seasons.

Right outside the dining room is the beginning of Newport's famed Cliff Walk—three and half miles of trails that go along the ocean, following Mansion Row. So after lunch or dinner, you can work off your meal and at the same time soak up some of that spectacular scenery. An experience here will leave you feeling, if only for a moment, like a member of the upper crust.

The French Dip with Peach Mustard

ADAPTED FROM SPICED PEAR, NEWPORT, RHODE ISLAND

YIELD: 1 SANDWICH

1 piece beef tri tip
Salt and pepper for seasoning
2 (½-inch-thick) pieces foie gras
1 small baguette
Peach mustard
Baby arugula leaves
Summer truffle, shaved
Truffle oil

Season tri tip with salt and pepper. Cook meat until medium rare on rotisserie (or grill) about 20 minutes, depending on temperature of cooking medium. Heat pan for foie gras.

Season foie gras with salt and pepper, then sear in hot pan.

Slice and toast small baguette, and spread bottom piece with peach mustard. Slice tri tip, and place on bottom half of baguette with peach mustard. Place foie gras on top of tri tip, and add a dollop of peach mustard on foie gras. In a separate bowl, mix baby arugula leaves, shaved truffle, truffle oil, salt and pepper. Place greens-and-truffle mixture on top of sandwich, spread peach mustard on top half of baguette, slice, and serve.

The Black Pearl and Hot Dog Annex

Bannister's Wharf
Newport, RI 02840
(401) 846-5264
www.blackpearlnewport.com

You wouldn't think you'd find a fine dining restaurant that also boasts of a hot dog annex, but then again, The Black Pearl isn't like most places. For starters, there's the "clam chowda." They go through about 100 gallons a day and ship it all over the world. (The recipe is top secret so, unfortunately, it won't appear in these pages.)

Then there's the chef. Daniel Knerr, a New Jersey native, wasn't sure what he wanted to be when he grew up. He started out pre-med in college, then tried drama, then joined a rock band. Cooking never crossed his mind simply because he says there were no role models in the 1950s for kids who wanted to be chefs.

Eventually he got a job in a deli dicing celery and onions, and it hit him: He liked to cook. Thinking back, he says he remembers helping his grandmother and mom cook their home-made meals, but he never thought it would be a profession he would aspire to. Once he found his calling, he worked at some of the finest restaurants in New York and Philadelphia before landing at The Black Pearl in the mid-1980s.

The owner of the restaurant told him he could change anything on the menu except the chowder. Daniel serves up gourmet foods with a New England twist like the Lobster and Scallop Enchiladas and cockles cooked in a Thai sweet chili sauce.

As for that hot dog annex, it opened in the 1970s when Newport starting hosting a lot of festivals, including America's Cup. They had to find a way to feed a lot of people really fast. What better way than a walk-up hot dog window where you can also get some chowder to sate your hunger while you wait for a table in the restaurant? Just don't fill up too much because you might not make it inside—and believe us, this is a meal you don't want to miss.

Jill and Chef Daniel Knerr of The Black Pearl with purveyor Paul Pritchard.

photo courtesy of Debra Girard

Rhode Island

Cheeky Monkey

14 Perry Mill Wharf
Newport, RI 02840
(401) 845-9494
www.cheekymonkeycafe.com

This is a business all about monkey business. Everywhere you look at the Cheeky Monkey, you'll find portraits and paintings of the simian family. No wonder, considering these mischievous monkeys are the inspiration behind owner Hank Kates's restaurant.

When Hank was building Cheeky Monkey, he was going ape. He couldn't think of a name. First, he came up with the Funky Monkey, until a British friend playfully grabbed his cheek and said in her highly civilized accent, "No Hank, you want to call it *Cheeky* Monkey." (In Great Britain, this a compliment to someone who is a little devilish.) Hank took her advice and even took it a step further, making a menu he describes as "devilish."

If you're not someone who likes to share your food, then you might want to cross this one off your list. Executive Chef Jeff Cruff serves much of his menu on tasting tiers. And because the British Empire once had tremendous influence around the globe, they have a worldly menu with food infused from all over.

You'll find towering tiers of entrées like Wasabi-Crusted Scallops on one level, Grilled Moroccan BBQ Salmon Filet on another, and a Panko-Crusted Tuna Nori Roll on top.

They even do tasting tiers for dessert. To keep those monkeys happy, Bananas Foster is usually on the top tier.

So if you're in the mood to monkey around, check it out. We're pretty sure this is one monkey you *won't* want off your back.

Connecticut

Olde Tymes Restaurant

360 West Main Street
Norwich, CT 06360
(860) 887-6865
www.oldetymes.com

Rodney Green sure can hambone. A big guy with a Tennessee twang, the owner of Olde Tymes Restaurant in Norwich is well known for performing his country-meets-rap lyrics on radio commercials.

"Breakfast lunch or dinnertime, Old Tymes is really fine,
Our home cooking makes you say, home is just a taste away."

The act comes complete with the mandatory hand and knee slaps that give hambone its rhythm. It's the perfect image for this down-home country-style restaurant that serves big portions of comfort food.

"This is Rodney talking now. Telling all of you just how.
We try so hard to make you feel, at home with food you know is real."

But old times weren't great times for Rodney and his wife, Lucille. After a long career in the food service industry, they thought they were doing very well with their restaurant in Illinois. But almost overnight, their landlord went bankrupt, which left them virtually locked out of their own business. While in Connecticut visiting relatives for the holidays a few months later, they saw a "For Rent" sign on an empty building and knew they should start over. Rodney met with the building's owner at a McDonald's on Christmas Eve and signed a deal written on a napkin. Olde Tymes opened in 1984, and Rodney has been happily hamboning ever since.

———

B.F. Clyde's Cider Mill

129 North Stonington Road
Mystic, CT 06355
(860) 536-3354

B.F. Clyde's is as American as apple pie. Located on a winding road in rural Mystic, Connecticut, this family-run mill makes the best apple cider this side of the Big Apple. It also produces some pretty impressive hooch, too.

Hooch? Actually, it's called hard cider. Like grapes, apples can be aged into a pleasantly intoxicating drink. Clyde's has been making hard cider longer than any mill in the country. Benjamin Franklin Clyde first started pressing the juice out of apples in 1881. Back then, it wasn't really thought of as booze. It was just fruit juice that had a heck of a kick. His success continued, even during Prohibition. He could still sell nonalcoholic cider and apple vinegar. It was Mother Nature's fault if it fermented into moonshine after you took it home. One time his wife, Abbie, was nearly arrested for bootlegging, but legend has her meeting the lawmen at the front door with a shotgun. Somehow, all charges were dropped.

After Prohibition, hard cider's popularity waned as other libations became more fashionable. These days, Clyde's continues to make and legally sell plenty of it—to those 21 and over—but most of its business comes from producing regular cider, without the alcohol. It's sweet and much more robust than regular apple juice, because it hasn't been processed.

Clyde's is only open in the fall when the leaves change to remarkable shades of red and gold. Along with cider, people flock to this 3-acre wonderland to buy homemade apple pies, jams, jellies

and other goodies. Several times a day, you can watch the apple pressing process on the same historic steam-powered mill B.F. Clyde used. It's really a heart-warming experience, especially after a couple stiff shots of hard cider.

Splash

The Inn at Longshore
260 Compo Road South
Westport, CT 06870
(203) 454-7798
www.decarorestaurantgroup.com

Splash is all about the scenery. We're not just talking about the picturesque Long Island Sound nearby, surrounded by multimillion-dollar vacation homes. We also mean the attractive see-and-make-a-scene regulars with their multi-million-dollar trust funds.

An affluent community within commuting distance of New York City, Westport is known as Hollywood East because of the celebrities who live here. Paul Newman, Robert Redford, and Michael Bolton are often mentioned. In the 1960s, Frank Sinatra proposed to Mia Farrow on a yacht anchored off the waters of Westport. And long before that, F. Scott and Zelda Fitzgerald summered in the very building where Splash is located. The setting is believed to have inspired his work, but if he were writing now, *The Great Gatsby* might have ended up as a blog of the couples' good times at the restaurant.

With its waterfront location, Splash is a mandatory place to go in warm-weather months and especially on weekends. The restaurant itself is eye-catching, with vibrant blue tiles that accentuate the crowd noise. There's a top-quality raw bar to start and large servings of Pacific Rim–inspired dishes. The perfectly steamed Chilean Sea Bass, wrapped in a banana leaf, and the Maine Crab Cakes are popular entrées.

Outside, the crowd gathers either on the large veranda or at the popular Patio Bar. And everyone checks out the scenery. Occasionally, that doesn't even mean the people.

Connecticut

Thomas Henkelmann—Homestead Inn

420 Field Point Road
Greenwich, CT 06830
(203) 869-7500
www.homesteadinn.com

There's a reason the word *green* is in "Greenwich." It's home to some of the wealthiest and most powerful people in the country. When you play host to this elite set, you better know what you're doing. Thomas Henkelmann—Homestead Inn does.

Forty minutes from New York City, this remarkably updated 200-year-old Victorian inn and French restaurant evokes words like *exquisite, artful,* and *graceful*—even if those adjectives aren't normally part of your vocabulary. In co-owner Theresa Henkelmann's own words—often sprinkled with French phrases—the inn is much like a French auberge, a destination where one stops for an extraordinary meal and then spends the night.

The 3-acre farmhouse wasn't much of anything when she bought it with her chef-husband, Thomas, in 1997. After renovations, Theresa decorated the eighteen guest rooms herself; filling them with *"objets d'art,"* as she says, and creating a look she calls "sophisticated and very eclectic, with a thread of whimsy everywhere." Those who aren't as concerned with design will still be impressed with the heated tile floors in every bathroom.

Thomas (pronounced *TOE-mahs*) went about creating his showcase restaurant. His cooking, which Theresa says is his *"raison d'être,"* is rooted in traditional French technique but updated with a light contemporary touch. He won't do fusion. Theresa explains that when people go to "a French restaurant, they don't want the best Japanese meal of their life." Thomas is certainly passionate about his food. While demonstrating his signature Mousseline de Fruit de Mer recipe for Marc and his crew, he dove into the finished product virtually before the camera started rolling. Declaring his love for the dish, he said "I really should sit down as a customer at my own restaurant. It's so good." That's ardor.

But again, it's Theresa who best explains the Inn's certain *je ne sais quoi.* When asked who else visits besides big-buck tourists and powerful company executives, she responded that there are plenty of local guests. According to her, they need someplace nice to stay when they're redecorating their mansions.

Check, Please

We often eat for free. There, I said it. It's out there for the world to see. It's a magnificent perk of the job, but certainly not something we require of restaurants. Our crews have limited expense accounts, and we're more than happy to use them. But when there's an invite, hey, we're human. And we'd hate to be considered rude.

But some places just "get it" more than others. They know that exposure on *The Best Of* is helpful, and their promotional budgets can cover a free meal or two. Besides, there's no better way to get a feel for a restaurant than to sit down and dine. Sure, that's a giant rationalization, but it's also the truth.

The only time it gets awkward is when a host insists we eat, and then hits us with a large bill. It's happened, several times. The one situation that really stands out occurred when a restaurant owner and her spouse joined us for dinner, and encouraged us to keep ordering, especially dessert. When the unexpected (and expense account busting) bill came, it totaled several hundred dollars. Fortunately, it didn't include their portion.

The single most unanticipated bill came at a small place we were profiling in Chicago. We didn't eat there, but imagine our surprise when we were handed a bill, for the food we took pictures of for our story—on them.

The Mid-Atlantic

New York, New Jersey, Pennsylvania, Delaware, Maryland, District of Columbia

WHAT MAKES THIS region great is its brash attitude. New Yorkers are blunt; Philadelphians have their own unique swagger; while power-hungry Washingtonians exhibit the best of Northern hospitality and Southern efficiency. When it comes to discussing restaurants in the Mid-Atlantic states, the only way to keep everyone happy is to keep them arguing. Fortunately, there's plenty to debate in this chapter.

You'll discover how wings took flight in Buffalo and why a one-time government attorney left the bar to became a baker. You'll also be introduced to a Marine who served our nation with pride and now serves the public great food. We'll explain how french fries ended

up on sandwiches in Pittsburgh and why a Big Apple chef raises bees on his rooftop.

But will New York food snobs be impressed by our top picks? Will Philadelphians agree on the best cannoli? Or will Washingtonians caucus at the restaurant known as the real party headquarters? Yo, who wants to know?

New York

Jean-Georges

1 Central Park West
New York, NY 10023
(212) 299-3900
www.jean-georges.com

For some reason, the man thought by many to be the world's greatest chef is bending over backward to help out Marc and his crew. Jean-Georges Vongerichten is on the patio of his flagship New York City restaurant, obeying our requests to pose in various uncomfortable positions so we can get just the right shot. Our plan is to frame him in the camera so it looks like he's holding the giant globe sculpture that sits outside the restaurant on Columbus Circle.

The point we're trying to make visually is that Jean-Georges owns the culinary world. But as the shoot drags on, we learn something else. Jean-Georges really cares about service, no matter how ridiculous the request.

He doesn't need the publicity. He's enjoyed every accolade. Perhaps his most notable accomplishment is twice earning the elusive *New York Times* top rating of Four-Stars, the first time at age 29 and the second, just months after he opened Jean-Georges in the Trump International Tower.

He now owns about a dozen highly rated restaurants worldwide. He obviously knows something about serving the public.

To look behind the scenes at Jean-Georges is a rare privilege. In his open kitchen, Vongerichten's passion for aromatic spices is clearly evident in every dish, but his unusual combinations—fusions—are only the beginning.

When it comes to real service, the waitstaff at Jean-Georges is unparalleled. But this doesn't come without effort. Each day, just before opening, the dining room becomes the stage for a *Paper Chase*–style grilling of the staff about every minute detail of the night's offerings. The questions put to them are excruciatingly exact, down to the seasonings in the soup or whether an entrée includes turnips or radishes. No one's

criticized for getting a wrong answer, but everyone makes sure they get it right.

Dinner at Jean-Georges is expensive, with a seven-course tasting menu costing north of $100. But it's an event worth the expense: The food arrives, and several waiters remove the globe lids simultaneously from the plates around your table with a flourish. And many dishes are brought to perfection at the table with a last touch of sauce or cream.

If you're going to do it, why not be the best? Not that Jean-Georges really needs us to say it, but we will anyway. This man owns the world.

Katz's Delicatessen

205 East Houston Street
New York, NY 10002
(212) 254-2246
www.katzdeli.com

If Jean-Georges represents New York at its most glamorous, then Katz's is New York at its, well, most authentic. It's one of the oldest delicatessens around—and a bit overpriced in our opinion, but hey, this is New York—it's also the first—and only—place that Jill ate tongue. But we're not going to talk about that. If you're curious, try for yourself.

At Katz's, pastrami is king, and boy, does it reign supreme. Arguably, they make some of the best in the world. The brisket of beef is cured in a brine solution, then rubbed with coriander and black peppercorns before being smoked. Eating it is truly an out-of-this-world experience. If you can't make it here, they will come to you. They ship their specialties all over the world.

Katz's opened in 1888 in the area known as the Lower East Side. A gritty, textured part of town with a hugely historical past. Four-fifths of the Jewish population in this country came to the Lower East Side after landing on Ellis Island. In fact, just around the corner on 90 Orchard Street is the Lower East Side Tenement Museum (www.tenement.org), which is one of Jill's favorite museums in all of Manhattan. Seeing what those early immigrants

"Larry Fat"

Viewers frequently ask us about the volume of food we consume in the course of our work. The questions usually go something like this: "You and Jill eat at so many great restaurants. How does *Jill* stay so thin?" They may mince garlic, but apparently, Food Network viewers don't mince words. To answer that question: Jill exercises. I just eat everything—but then nobody was asking about *me!*

Long ago I decided not to skimp on these tasting opportunities. I rationalized my decision because I have some of the greatest chefs in the country preparing food just for me. I'd be crazy to miss out.

But sometimes it does take its toll on Jill, me, and our entire crew. At one point, photographer Larry Deal was trying to drop a few pounds. After weeks of hard work, Larry was feeling pretty good about how he *thought* he looked. That is until he saw a picture of himself on the beach during a taping in Mexico. That's when Larry came up with a term everyone can relate to: "Larry Fat." It's when you think you've lost a lot of weight but haven't dropped a pound. Sample usage: "After switching to diet soda and low-fat cookies, I thought my pants would actually fit. But it turns out, I'm just Larry Fat."

The picture that inspired the term "Larry Fat."

photo courtesy of Jill Littman

went through when they first arrived will make places like Katz's seem like the Taj Mahal of restaurants—even if the guys behind the counter make a fuss when you don't know the drill.

The drill: When you walk in, you have to take a ticket, which under no circumstances should you lose! Stand in line, then step up and order. If you ask for mayonnaise or something special on your sandwich, you might be given the death stare by some of the counter guys. They don't deal with demanding customers very well, so if you're one of *those,* you might want to skip this place. You order your drinks at a separate spot down the line. Don't ask those meat-slicing men for your diet soda . . . they might turn the meat slicer on you.

Get your sandwich and soda, then look for a table. Most days this can be a challenge considering how hugely popular this place is. Good luck.

Important tip: Hold on to your ticket. After they scribble on it, that's your bill. You don't get out of the deli without it.

The desserts always look good, but it's hard to save room. Plus, after eating that huge meaty

sandwich, you might be better off having some antacid tablets instead.

———

Tavern on the Green
Central Park at West 67th Street
New York, NY 10023
(212) 873-3200
www.tavernonthegreen.com

Tavern on the Green is like New York City itself—bold and gaudy, while also beautiful and mesmerizing. Its world-class location in Central Park makes it a major draw for tourists. Usually, that's more than enough to keep away often-cynical Manhattanites, but they remain faithful, too, lured by the romantic atmosphere and enormous portions.

Today, the Tavern is one of the country's most financially successful restaurants. But in 1870, it was a barn for 200 sheep that grazed in a neighboring field. That field is now a popular hangout for sunbathers but is still known as the

Sheep Meadow in the heart of Central Park.

It wasn't until 1934 that city officials realized they could do more with the building and converted it into a restaurant. The first incarnation of Tavern on the Green was an instant success and remained a social center for New Yorkers for 40 years.

But like the city, the restaurant fell on hard times in the 1970s. Closed in 1974, it was bought by Warner LeRoy, a restaurateur known for his "over-the-top" way of doing business. LeRoy poured $10 million into renovations and created the Tavern's jaw-dropping Crystal Room, a glass-enclosed chandelier-filled masterpiece. There are five other dining rooms, each one different and just as fascinating.

The Tavern sprang back to life in 1976 and has remained one of New York's see-and-be-seen destinations. The perfect spot for movie premiere parties and celebrity outings, it's also ideal for romantic couples and surprise engagements. Each year, more than half a million people dine here—out-of-towners as well as those often-cynical Manhattanites who seem to have a soft spot for Tavern on the Green.

photo courtesy of Bud McHugh

Jill keeps a safe distance from Carl Redding as he harvests honey on the rooftop of his restaurant, Amy Ruth's.

Amy Ruth's Restaurant

113 West 116th Street (between Lennox and 7th Avenue)
Harlem, NY 10026
(212) 280-8779
www.amyruthsrestaurant.com

Jill's husband calls Amy Ruth's most popular dish the equivalent of eating a chicken donut. That may not sound too appetizing, but trust him on this one. It's the best chicken either of them has ever had. The dish we're talking about is Councilman Bill Perkins Southern Honey-Dipped Fried Chicken. Owner Carl Redding harvests his own honey on the roof of his Harlem restaurant, fries up his chicken, then drizzles that fresh honey all over along with crushed red pepper and cinnamon.

Carl named his restaurant after his grandmother, Amy Ruth, with whom he spent summers in

Alabama learning how to make her soul food specialties. By the age of six, he had learned many of Grandmother Ruth's secrets. By the time she passed away in 1989, Carl had mastered her recipes and knew his calling was in the kitchen.

However, before he could answer that call, he needed to satisfy another passion: politics. For nine years, he worked as Reverend Al Sharpton's chief of staff and personal assistant. During that time, he met a lot of prominent African Americans, many of whose names appear on his menu—like that chicken donut dish.

On Mother's Day 1999, he opened Amy Ruth's in the heart of Harlem in honor of Miss Ruth—his mentor, his cook, and his teacher.

Carl has seen his share of prominent politicians come in (one day when Jill and her husband were eating up here, Governor Pataki made a stop, although all he ordered was lemonade), but there is still one he is waiting for—former President Bill Clinton, whose office is just a

New York

few blocks away. Carl says that when he does make his way to Amy Ruth's, he knows just what he wants to serve him—honey-dipped chicken.

But you shouldn't wait for President Clinton to drop by before tasting some other must-try dishes such as Reverend Timothy Wright's Fried or Baked Catfish and Attorney Johnnie Cochran's Fried or Smothered Pork Chops. If you can possibly save room for dessert, try Jill's favorite, Janette Rucker's Red Velvet Cake.

Mama Mexico

2672 Broadway (between 101st and 102nd Streets)
New York, NY 10025
(212) 864-2323

214 East 49th Street (between 2nd and 3rd Avenues)
New York, NY 10017
(212) 935-1316
www.mamamexico.com

If there were ever a poster child for the modern American Dream, it would be Juan Rojas Campos. In 1982, he left his tiny Mexican village in search of a better life. Five times he attempted to cross the border. Five times he failed. On the sixth try, he made it and found himself in New York City with only the shirt on his back and a couple pennies in his pocket. He knew no English.

He took a job in a factory making $135 a week. It wasn't long until he got his start in the restaurant business, first as a dishwasher, then a busboy, and finally a waiter. He learned—and perfected—his English along the way. He worked tirelessly, he saved every cent, and one by one, brought his seven brothers across the border to join him.

In 1997, the Campos Clan opened Mama Mexico in honor of their mom—the family's matriarch and culinary mistress. This band of brothers proudly calls themselves "mama's boys."

Forget the typical enchiladas and burritos here. Instead, be adventurous and trust Juan's mom. From lobster fajitas to veal chops smothered in mushroom tequila sauce, these mama's boys have learned well.

We're not sure who taught them how to make the drinks, but they have more margaritas on the menu than you can imagine. Not to mention on many nights, a mariachi band that really lights the place up.

At Mama Mex, not only will you go from Manhattan to Mexico in a single meal, margarita, or mariachi, you'll also be toasting to a place that made the most far-fetched dream come true.

Metrazur

East Balcony
Grand Central Terminal
New York, NY 10017
(212) 687-4600
www.charliepalmer.com

Perched on the East Balcony of the magnificently restored Grand Central Terminal, Metrazur is the ultimate place to sit and watch the world go by. Below, half a million people—a crowd that roughly numbers the population of the city of Cleveland—rush by every day, heading to or from a vast network of commuter trains.

Opened in 1913, Grand Central came to symbolize New York—hectic and loud, but with a purpose, and always Grand. Much like the city, it fell into disrepair for many years, but came back strong, helped by $200 million in recent renovations.

Metrazur, part of Grand Central's rebirth, is the work of Charlie Palmer, one of the country's most respected chefs. The cuisine, best described as contemporary American, features favorites like Seared Salmon and Tempura-Coated Soft Shell Crabs.

Seared Salmon with Braised and Raw Endive and Beet Reduction

ADAPTED FROM METRAZUR, NEW YORK, NEW YORK

YIELD: 10 PORTIONS

For Salmon:
10 (7-ounce) portions of salmon (skin on)
Salt and pepper to taste
½ cup olive oil

Season salmon with salt and pepper. Sear both sides in olive oil in a hot pan.

Remove salmon from the pan, and reserve.

For Horseradish Crust:
1 cup panko breadcrumbs
2 tablespoons fine herbs, chopped
1 cup fresh grated horseradish
2 tablespoons wasabi paste
Salt and pepper to taste
¼ cup olive oil

Mix panko, herbs, horseradish, and wasabi in a bowl. Season with salt and pepper. Drizzle in olive oil while mixing to incorporate.

For Braised Endive:
5 heads endive
1 tablespoon sugar
Salt and pepper to taste
1 tablespoon unsalted butter
¼ cup olive oil
¼ cup chicken stock

Cut endive in half, and trim the core (reserve any extra leaves for garnish). Lightly sear in olive oil, cut face down, in a sauté pan. Sprinkle with sugar, salt, pepper, and butter, and cover and place in a 350°F degree oven.

When just tender, place on stove top and deglaze with chicken stock. Reduce liquid to a syrup, and season with salt and pepper to taste.

For Beet Reduction:
3 sprigs thyme

1 cup mirepoix (a mix of diced carrots, onions, and celery sautéed in butter)
2 tablespoons olive oil
½ cup ruby port wine
1 cup red wine
1 cup red beet juice (strained)
1 pound unsalted butter
Salt and pepper to taste

Caramelize thyme and mirepoix in olive oil in a sauté pan. Add port wine and red wine, and reduce to a syrup. Add beet juice, and reduce to syrup. Whisk in softened butter. Season with salt and pepper. Strain, and reserve warm.

For Garnish:
30 endive leaves
10 sprigs mache

Place fish on a baking sheet, top with horseradish crust, and bake at 350°F degrees until desired temperature (5 to 7 minutes). Warm endive, and place on a warm plate. Remove salmon from the oven, and arrange on the plate overlapping endive. Drizzle beet sauce around. Season raw endive leaves and mache with olive oil, salt, and pepper. Place endive leaves in braised endive, and top with a sprig of mache.

Grand Central Oyster Bar and Restaurant

Grand Central Terminal (lower level)
89 East 42nd Street
New York, NY 10017
(212) 490-6650 or (800) 622-7775
www.oysterbarny.com

The pearl of all oyster bars is much like the mollusk it's famous for. Burrowed downstairs in the historic train terminal, its vaulted ceilings give the restaurant a shell-like feel. There's even an acknowledgment of an occasional imperfection.

"We're winging it, that's pretty much how we operate," admits general manager Michael Garvey, adding, "We don't know until 11:30, when

New York

we open, exactly how the menu is going to turn out. Believe it or not."

Flexibility is best when you're dealing with a restaurant this size. Each day, it offers up to 30 different types of oysters from around the world. If it's fresh, it'll be here. The place sells more than 5 million oysters a year. That's in addition to the nearly 2 million pounds of fresh fish and seafood.

Here's a mind-boggling tidbit: The menu is completely handwritten and printed every day, so it can be changed on the fly as the newest deliveries arrive. That's some incredible juggling when you're dealing with more than 70 different offerings. Like Garvey said, nothing's finalized until the place opens.

One must-have dish that's always available: the Oyster Pan Roast. It's a creamy soup steam-heated so the oysters plump up like pillows.

About a half a million people a year eat here. Amazingly, a majority of diners aren't even commuters, which makes the Grand Central Oyster Bar a destination of its own. Or as they prefer to say, it's a landmark in a landmark.

―

Gino

780 Lexington Avenue (between 60th and 61st Streets)
New York, NY 10021
(212) 758-4466

Every conversation about this classic Italian restaurant always seems to include a few words about its unique wallpaper. Occasionally, the comments are even nice.

It's an unusual design to say the least, row after row of leaping zebras avoiding arrows. The look covers almost the entire place.

Gino Circiello, who founded the restaurant in 1945, gets the credit—or blame. It's said he snapped up the wallpaper because it reminded him of his favorite sport—hunting—and because it was on sale.

In 1972, regulars feared renovations would doom the zebras. But television star and Gino faithful Ed Sullivan insisted the look be restored. It was. (Sullivan also complained when

Leaping zebras on the wallpaper at Gino
photo courtesy of Marc Silverstein

a long-time phone booth was removed. It, too, was returned and remains there today, without the phone.)

Gino is known for much more than its wallpaper, but the enduring design shows how little the restaurant changes. It still doesn't take credit cards, and the recipes are much the same as when Frank Sinatra and his Rat Pack were regulars. (Sinatra also used to bring his family here on Mother's Day.)

The Osso Buco alla Gino has always been a favorite but it's only served on Mondays and Tuesdays. The place is also famous for its Segreto (secret) Pasta Sauce, made with a formula employees are forbidden to discuss.

Osso Buco alla Gino
ADAPTED FROM GINO, NEW YORK, NEW YORK

YIELD: 4 SERVINGS

1 onion, finely chopped
½ cup butter
4 veal shanks (approximately 2½ inches thick)
Flour, for dusting
¾ cup fresh sliced mushrooms
3 to 4 dry porcini mushrooms
1 carrot, thinly sliced
1 celery stalk, thinly sliced
Salt and pepper
¼ cup fresh sage, chopped
1 cup dry white wine
3 cups tomatoes, peeled
2 to 3 cups veal stock

Sauté onion in ¼ cup butter in a wide shallow skillet until soft and golden. Dust veal shanks with flour, then fry them in the same skillet, turning several times until they are golden on all sides. Stand them on their side to prevent the marrow in the bones from slipping out during cooking. Add fresh mushrooms, porcini mushrooms, carrot, and celery, and season with salt and pepper. Add sage, and simmer for 4 minutes. Add wine, and let evaporate. Add tomatoes and veal stock, and simmer gently for about 1 hour or until cooked and tender. Add more wine or stock to sauce if needed.

Ruby et Violette

457 West 50th Street (between 9th and 10th Avenues)
New York, NY 10019
(212) 582-6720 or (877) 353-9099
www.rubyetviolette.com

You'll find a slice of heaven here in the heart of Hell's Kitchen along with a woman who is one tough cookie.

Wendy Gaynor always wanted to have her own baking business and refused to let the fact that she was a single mom—without a college degree—get in the way. In 1989, she combined her two loves: her daughters—Ruby and Violet—and baking, and started up her cookie shop.

Business was going well, and success was at her fingertips. In 1995, her chocolate-chunk confections were being shipped to more than 200 stores. Then tragedy struck.

Her 18-year-old daughter Ruby was in a terrible car accident and suffered a traumatic brain injury. She was in a coma for weeks.

Ruby's injuries were so severe, her rehabilitation turned into months, then years. She had to learn how to walk, talk, and feed herself again. Needless to say, the cookie business was put on hold.

But as Wendy will tell you, miracles do happen, and slowly Ruby began to recover.

So after a 6-year hiatus, and at the encouragement of both daughters and her new husband, Michael, Wendy returned to baking. In May 2001, she reopened, this time in a tiny storefront in the heart of Hell's Kitchen. It didn't take long for people in the Big Apple to take

Wendy Gaynor of Ruby et Violette.

notice. Rave reviews poured in from the *New York Times* to *Bon Appétit* and *Gourmet*.

She has more than 52 variations on the chocolate-chip cookie: Champagne, rose, lemon, espresso, toffee, banana—you name it, she probably has it. She bakes more than 1,000 of them a day and ships them all over the country. And although the flavors and prices may change, one thing stays the same: 5 percent of all her profits go to Mount Sinai Hospital's Traumatic Brain Injury Unit. As she told Jill, "They took Ruby from a wheelchair unable to speak and care for herself and turned her back into my daughter . . . It was payback time."

Today Ruby is a graduate of Columbia University with a degree in Childhood Education and is getting her Masters. Her goal is to work with disabled kids. Wendy's other daughter Violet works at *Shape* magazine as the associate fashion editor. And even though they're all grown up and doing well, they still love Mom's cookies. We're pretty sure you will, too.

New York

New York

"Kitchen Sink" Chocolate Chunk Cookies

ADAPTED FROM RUBY ET VIOLETTE, NEW YORK, NEW YORK

YIELD: 36 COOKIES

2 sticks unsalted butter, at room temperature
1 cup dark brown sugar, packed
½ cup granulated sugar
2 large eggs
1 teaspoon natural vanilla extract
2¼ cups all-purpose flour
1 teaspoon salt
¾ teaspoon baking soda
½ cup peanut butter chips
½ cup toffee chips
½ cup mini-marshmallows
2 cups imported semisweet chocolate chunks

Cream butter in an upright mixer until fluffy. Add dark brown sugar and white sugar, and mix until thoroughly blended with butter, scraping sides and bottom of bowl from time to time.

Add eggs, one at a time, and mix until thoroughly blended, scraping sides and bottom of bowl from time to time.

Add vanilla extract, and mix on low speed (to avoid splashing) to combine well. In a separate bowl, mix flour, salt, and baking soda. Add flour mixture to butter-sugar mixture, and mix on low speed until thoroughly blended, scraping sides and bottom of bowl from time to time. Mix briefly on medium speed until completely combined.

Add peanut butter chips, and mix on low speed until thoroughly combined. Add toffee chips, and mix on low speed until thoroughly combined. Add mini-marshmallows, and mix on low speed until thoroughly combined. Add chocolate chunks, and mix on low speed until thoroughly combined. Refrigerate batter for a few hours or overnight until cold.

Preheat oven to 350°F (300°F if using convection oven). Line baking sheet with parchment paper, and drop heaping teaspoonfuls of batter 2 inches apart. Bake for approximately 12 to 18 minutes (depending on type of oven), turning tray once during baking. Cookies are done when they are golden brown around edges and soft (not bubbly) on top. Let cool on wire rack.

Serving suggestions: Fill two cookies with your favorite ice cream or gelato, and freeze for the "perfect" ice-cream sandwich. Or fill with chocolate butter for an utterly divine sandwich cookie. Serve with a cold glass of milk.

Cafeteria

119 Seventh Avenue (at 17th Street and 7th Avenue)
New York, NY 10011
(212) 414-1717

One bite is all it takes to discover this ain't your high school lunchroom. While the name implies vinyl seats, plastic trays, and gum-snapping waitresses, you'll find none of that here.

At this "cafeteria," diners enjoy sitting on leather seats and eating tuna tartar, crab cakes, and filet mignon served up by a waitstaff decked out in designer duds.

Granted, you can still find familiar comfort food favorites at this modern mess hall. Dishes like meatloaf, mac and cheese, and chicken and waffles are on the menu—they are just elevated to appeal to a slightly more sophisticated palate.

The clientele isn't your run-of-the-mill cafeteria crowd, either. They have their fair share of celebrities stop in—from Mariah Carey and Julia Roberts to Jennifer Lopez and Harrison Ford. Mind you, not together, or in that order, lest we start a rumor we didn't intend.

If sleep isn't on *your* menu and you have a hankering for a hip *and hearty* meal, this 24/7 joint also boasts a full bar and a lounge downstairs. But the best part about Cafeteria: the prices. They're not "cafeteria-cheap," but they're not bad. Pretty much all the entrées are well under $20.

Zen Palate

34 East Union Square (at 16th Street)
New York, NY 10003
(212) 614-9345

663 Ninth Avenue (at 46th Street)
New York, NY 10036
(212) 582-1669

2170 Broadway (between 76th and 77th Streets)
New York, NY 10024
(212) 501-7768
www.zenpalate.com

Zen, of course, is an ancient philosophy that requires serious thought. On the other hand, deciding if Zen Palate is the right place to eat is a no-brainer.

This is one vegetarian restaurant where confirmed meat-eaters can feel comfortable. The meals are tasty and filling. There are plenty of pasta dishes and meat substitutes (Vegi-Ham, Vegi-Burgers) for those committed more to good taste than to eating vegetarian. But for those following a more serious approach to healthy eating, Zen Palate should be filled with the sound of one hand clapping.

——

Rosa Mexicano

1063 First Avenue (at 58th Street)
New York, NY 10022
(212) 753-7407

61 Columbus Avenue
New York, NY 10023
(212) 977-7700
www.rosamexicano.com

(Other locations in Washington, DC and Atlanta, GA.)

Rosa Mexicano was one of the first restaurants to introduce New Yorkers, and the rest of the United States, to upscale Mexican food.

You don't come here for enchiladas and burritos. (There's even a note on the menu not to expect "some of the more popular Americanized dishes often associated with Mexican food.") Here you'll find lamb shank wrapped in parchment paper or crepes filled with shrimp.

The Guacamole en Molcajete appetizer is virtually mandatory. It is mixed fresh at your table, and the chunky consistency makes it more like a salad than a dip.

And when they say "authentic Mexican" around here, it does include margaritas—rather strong ones, actually. But the house specialty is made with pomegranate juice. Remember, it's upscale.

——

The Cowgirl Hall of Fame

519 Hudson Street
New York, NY 10014
(212) 633-1133

Half bar, half restaurant, this friendly honky tonk celebrates in pictures and attitude the true heroes of the prairie—the cowgirls. After all, what would Roy Rogers be without Dale Evans? The cowgirls not only cooked up the steaks, they rounded up the cattle and branded them, too.

Depends on what y'all are hankerin' for, but the Cowgirl can rustle up some serious victuals (excuse me, vittles). A real slop-and-serve favorite is the Frito Pie. It's chili ladled into a bag of corn chips, and just like down home in Texas, it comes complete with the bag. 'Course there's also Chicken Fried Steak and Corn Dogs for the youngins'. Don't forgit the baked potato for dessert. A baked potato, you ask? This one's made with ice cream and dressed up real purty with cocoa to make it look like it's out of the ground. Annie Oakley never had it so good.

So round up the posse, and ride off into the sunset to "The Cowgirl." And don't forget, y'all come back now, y' hear?

——

Grimaldi's Pizzeria

19 Old Fulton Street
Brooklyn, NY 11201
(718) 858-4300
www.grimaldis.com

In a city that takes its pizza pretty seriously, it's not easy to be called the best. But this inconspicuous little place under the Brooklyn Bridge has achieved superstar status.

Grimaldi's has won Zagat's vote for the best pizza in New York City 5 years running. What does that do to a small pizza place? Well for one, it turns it into controlled chaos, which is why you need to know the rules.

No slices, no credit cards, no reservations, no deliveries, and no fancy toppings. Just the tried and true: pepperoni, peppers, mushrooms, sausage—you get the idea.

What makes it the best? Well for one, their dough. It's a top-secret recipe baked fresh to order. Second, their cheese consists of fresh mozzarella squares placed atop the pie. The sauce is simple—just fresh crushed tomatoes and spices. And as an added touch, each pizza is garnished with a few fresh basil leaves before it goes into the oven to bake.

And that's where the real secret lies. While no longer legal in New York, their coal-fired brick oven was grandfathered in when these types of ovens were outlawed several decades ago. The temperature inside this baby reaches 900 degrees, which means these pies are into the mouths of you mouthwatering customers pronto!

Expect long lines. After all, that's just one of the prices customers have to pay when they go for the best.

———

The River Café

1 Water Street
Brooklyn, NY 11201
(718) 522-5200
www.rivercafe.com

Known as "the restaurant that launched a thousand chefs," one of The River Café's claims to fame is that it has been the training ground for more great chefs—from Charlie Palmer to David Burke—than any other restaurant in America. But the skill of the chefs who have passed through this kitchen is not the only thing that blows this place out of the water. Situated on the Brooklyn waterfront in the shadow of the Brooklyn Bridge, the restaurant offers a breathtakingly beautiful view of the Manhattan skyline. So when dining here, the challenge is in deciding what is better, the food or the view. In our opinion: Both are out of this world.

When owner Michael "Buzzy" O'Keefe set out to construct the restaurant, he didn't realize the bureaucracy he'd have to fight. Beginning in the 1960s, it took him 12 years just to get permission to build. He wrestled his way through reams of bureaucratic red tape and New York City politics. He was called crazy by more than one person—and even had his life threatened. But nothing could stop him. In 1977, the restaurant opened its doors and is still going strong more than 25 years later.

The River Café has been called one of the most romantic restaurants in the city, and with justification. O'Keefe claims that there are more marriage proposals made here than at any other restaurant in the United States. In fact, the staff often jokes that on any given night they have

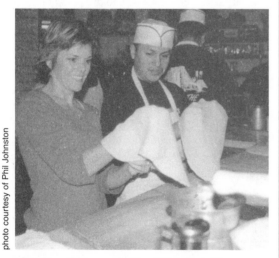

photo courtesy of Phil Johnston

Jill with a pizza pro at Grimaldi's in Brooklyn.

more rings flashing about in the restaurant than the diamond case at Tiffany's.

Although the ambience and the menu always get high ratings, it's their most famous dessert that's particularly noteworthy because it literally allows you to taste the view. Called the Chocolate Marquise Brooklyn Bridge, this is an edible rendition of the famous landmark. The base is made of devil's food cake. Piped chocolate creates the sweet side rails. And a river of chocolate mousse floats under the whole structure. They serve 400 to 500 a week.

No matter what you order or where you sit, this fine dining destination is guaranteed to leave a lasting impression. And you can bet the Brooklyn Bridge on that.

———

Dizzy's

511 Ninth Street (at 8th Avenue)
Brooklyn, NY 11215
(718) 499-1966

It was a brisk fall morning in 1998 when Cherry Valentine showed up at Dizzy's in Park Slope, Brooklyn. She was dressed only in a housecoat and, according to owners Ben Hoen and Matheo Pisciotta, looked quite confused. They sat her down and gave her some food and a hot drink. She handed them a piece of paper and told them she didn't know what it meant. Turns out it was an eviction notice. Upon further investigation, Ben and Matheo learned that at the age of 83, this one-time Cotton Club dancer not only had a serious case of dementia, but she was also a victim of elder abuse.

Apparently the people who were supposed to be taking care of Cherry, weren't. They were taking her money and leaving her to fend for herself. Ben and Matheo decided to take charge of the situation as best they could and contacted the city's Adult Protective Services, spoke to her landlord, and helped Cherry get her life back under control.

For 5 years, Dizzy's effectively became her surrogate family/parent. Every day she came in and was fed, talked to, and nurtured. If she didn't show up—even for a day—someone from Dizzy's

would go to her apartment to make sure everything was okay.

In the fall of 2003, Cherry passed away. Dizzy's was praised at her memorial service for coming to her rescue. A picture of Cherry hangs proudly on their wall.

That's Dizzy's in a nutshell—a neighborhood restaurant where you'll leave with much more than a full stomach. It's a place where everyone knows your name and one that truly serves the community of Park Slope.

When Ben and Matheo opened it in April 1998, they wanted to create "a finer diner" that would feel like home. The food is certainly finer than most diners. Incredible breakfasts served all day long, homemade mac-n-cheese topped with Rice Krispies, wonderful salads and sandwiches, and delicious dinner entrées. In fact, on most weekends, there's a wait to get in for brunch. Many in the neighborhood claim their coffee is the best around. Ditto that for their Brooklyn Egg Creams.

On the menu are pictures of the prominent people in Park Slope. There's Joey Ups, the UPS guy; Tommy Bones, the local chiropractor, and Ronny the mailman, to name a few. You'll regularly see Father Bob Lawsine, who calls himself the "Chaplain of Dizzy's," enjoying coffee and talking to the local rabbi about issues in the neighborhood. You'll even see some of the regulars helping themselves to coffee as if it were their own home. And for many people, it is a home away from home. It certainly was for Cherry Valentine, just one of many who found a hot meal served up with a lot of heart and soul.

L & B Spumoni Gardens

2725 86th Street
Brooklyn, NY 11223
(718) 449-6921-restaurant
(718) 449-1230-pizzeria
www.spumonigardens.com

"Everything in life is a situation," according to Brooklynite Camille Barbati, whose family owns the legendary Spumoni Gardens in the Gravesend section of Brooklyn.

Talking to Camille and her alleged husband and executive chef Lenny Kern is a story in itself. As Jill and her crew sat around a table full of fresh pasta, chowing down on Italian favorites like Eggplant Romano Nero and Broccoli Rabe with Italian Sausage, we heard about the man who fell over in the restaurant's bathroom, grabbed the sink, and ended up taking the whole thing with him onto the floor (or "wid," as Camille said). And how she and Lenny aren't really married, but sometimes they claim to be and sort of are (we never quite figured that one out and they went back and forth on it so many times, we gave up trying). Oh, and we can't forget Camille's story about how her grandmother used to spy on her brothers from an upstairs window adjoining the restaurant. If they weren't working hard enough, she'd shout down obscenities from the window.

We had arrived on a brisk March night to do a story on Italian dishes. We got Italian all right—and stomachs that ached from laughing so hard. Ludovico Barbati came over from Italy and started selling spumoni out of his horse-drawn wagon on the streets of Brooklyn in 1939. For those of you not familiar with it, spumoni is chocolate, vanilla, and pistachio milk sherbet. If you want all three, order a rainbow.

His Italian neighbors loved his icy treats so much that in the late 1940s, he set up a permanent location here on 86th Street. The spumoni stand launched a pizza joint, the pizza joint launched a restaurant, and eventually Ludovico owned the entire block. He named it L & B, after his initials.

Camille's brother Louis "Lulu" Barbati runs the pizza joint, serving up square-sliced Sicilian-style pizza, while Camille and Lenny run the restaurant. They officially took it over in the early 1990s and elevated the cuisine to a finer Italian fare, while still keeping the atmosphere laid-back and intact with the rest of the block.

Lenny started in the restaurant when he was just 13 as a prep cook. (Forget child labor laws. He loved it.) Whatever the status is with him and Camille, he is definitely considered family around here, and that means he can cook. Seeing him in action, you'd swear he was Italian—remember, his last name is Kern. Besides the traditional pasta plates like Fettuccini Alfredo and spaghetti and meatballs, you'll also find other examples of his creative genius at work. The night we were there he pan-seared some salmon, drizzled it with olive oil and Romano cheese, added some Dijon mustard and fresh cherries, and let it bake. Superb.

The neighborhood surrounding L & B is a bit rough, but no one seems to mess with the place. As "Lulu" says in his perfect Brooklyn accent, "Yeah, they know betta."

They should, especially if they want to get served some of the best Italian food around.

Classic Italian served up in a classic Brooklyn neighborhood. If you get a chance to hang with any of the Barbatis (that includes Lenny), one word of warning: Your stomach will hurt by the time they're through with you. And we don't mean from the food.

M & I International

249 Brighton Beach Avenue
Brooklyn, NY 11235
(718) 615-1011

It may just be a subway ride from Manhattan, but when you hop off the Q-train at Brighton Beach in Brooklyn, you'll feel like you're a world away. There's a reason this area is nicknamed Little Odessa, but instead of the Black Sea, you have the Atlantic Ocean. Despite that *minor* difference, what you'll find is one of the largest Russian communities outside Moscow.

One of the oldest, biggest, and best places to

start your tour is M & I International. Sophia Vinokurov and her family came here in the 1970s from the former Soviet Union and opened this grocery store/restaurant. From caviar and crustaceans to soups and sweets, nearly everything here has Russian roots. For just a couple bucks, you can get a sampling of pierogi—potato, meat, or sour cherry—washed down with Russian beer. On a nice day, sit outside on the upstairs patio, and you'll find yourself whisked away to the Old World.

———

Gina's Cappuccino Café

409 Brighton Beach Avenue
Brooklyn, NY 11235
(718) 646-6297

For scrumptious salads and piping hot coffee, head to Gina's Cappuccino Café. Gina Sharon, who hails from Ukraine, features specialties of her homeland. The Gina's Salad—lettuce mixed with her special sauce, topped with salmon and red caviar—is delicious. To finish off, try her apple blintzes. The apples are baked in amaretto and rum and topped with sugar.

———

Café Glechik

3159 Coney Island Avenue
Brooklyn, NY 11235
(718) 616-0494

A glechik is a clay pot, and many of the dishes served up by Oleg Bortnikov and his daughter Diana are baked in them. Here you can have a taste of true borsht and dishes like Beef Odessa, a pastry-topped stew made with beef, potatoes, and prunes. Sounds strange, but it's tasty. As Diana says, "It's dishes that your Ukrainian grandmother would make for you."

Trust us—a trip to Brighton Beach is worth it. After all, you can go to Russia and back, all for the price of a subway ride. Now *that's* a Big Apple bargain.

Beef Odessa

ADAPTED FROM CAFÉ GLECHIK, BROOKLYN, NEW YORK

YIELD: 6 SERVINGS

1 (3-pound) beef eye round
2 to 3 tablespoons vegetable oil
4 to 5 Spanish onions, chopped
2 cups beef broth
4 bay leaves
6 to 8 large potatoes
1½ pounds puff pastry
20 prunes
3 large cloves garlic, crushed
Chopped dill, to taste
Salt and pepper

Trim beef from bones, and cut into 3- to 4-inch pieces. To a pot of boiling water, add beef and boil until no longer pink. Drain.

Heat oil in a Dutch oven or stock pot over medium heat until hot, add chopped onions, and brown evenly. Add beef, broth, and bay leaves; cover tightly; and simmer 2 hours.

Preheat the oven to 375°F.

Peel potatoes, cut into 4-inch pieces, and fry until golden brown and tender in oil that has been heated to 350°F. Drain on paper towels. Cut puff pastry into pieces that will fit over 6 ovenproof bowls. Remove bay leaves from the meat mixture. To the bowls, add beef cubes, sauce, prunes, potatoes, garlic, dill, salt, and pepper, and cover with dough. Bake for 20 minutes or until pastry is golden brown.

Elias Corner

24-02 31st Street
Astoria, Queens
New York, NY 11102
(718) 932-1510

Elias Corner doesn't have menus, which can make first-timers to this Greek seafood tavern feel a little like fish out of water. Don't worry; it's easy to catch on.

Located in Astoria, the largest Greek neighborhood outside of Greece, Elias Corner is as

New York

authentic as it gets. Early every morning, owner Elias Sidiroglou goes to the fish market to buy the freshest catch of the day. Back at the restaurant, he puts his selections on display in a refrigerated case from which customers can make their pick. The fish is covered in olive oil and oregano, grilled, then doused with more oil. Some dishes, like octopus, get vinegar, too. That's it. Not real complicated.

The process saves on menus. Why commit to print when the choices always change?

Whole red snapper and shrimp are a couple constants. So is the large Greek Salad. If you're daring, go for the fried white bait as an appetizer. Whatever your pick, be prepared to pay cash. Credit cards, like menus, don't have a place around here.

—

Anchor Bar

1047 Main Street
Buffalo, NY 14209
(716) 886-8920
www.anchorbar.com

The legend of the Buffalo wing first took flight in 1964 and has been flying high ever since. As is the case with so many legends, there are a couple different versions. But pretty much everyone agrees, the idea of the Buffalo chicken wing was hatched at the Anchor Bar in Buffalo, New York (hence, it is not called the Des Moines wing) by a woman named Teressa Bellissimo.

In one version, the bar mistakenly received a shipment of chicken wings (at the time, they were used mainly as stock for soup). Not wanting to waste the wings, Teressa allegedly deep-fried them, concocted a homemade hot sauce, grabbed some celery and the restaurant's house dressing (bleu cheese, of course), and voilà!

The story that the owners of the Anchor Bar favor also involves Teressa and her son Dominic, who worked as a bartender. It was late one Friday night, and some of Dominic's friends were famished (supposedly because, true to Catholic tradition, they hadn't eaten meat all day). So Dominic and the boys begged Teressa to cook them some meat after midnight. The rest, as they say, is history.

Whether Teressa was simply (pardon the horrid pun) *winging* it, we may never really know. But you can't deny the force that the Buffalo chicken wing has become. It is a bar food staple and one of America's most popular appetizers.

As for the Anchor Bar: It's still going strong in its location on the edge of downtown Buffalo. Sure, it's a little touristy, but make no mistake, this is a legitimate restaurant. It was given the James Beard Award for Classic Northeast Restaurant in 2003. Not too shabby for a place built on a wing and a prayer.

—

Twist O' the Mist/The Misty Dog Grill

18 Niagara Street
Niagara Falls, NY 14303
(716) 285-0702

Top of the Falls

Goat Island at Terrapin Point
Niagara Falls State Park
Niagara Falls, NY 14303
(716) 278-0348
www.niagarafallsstatepark.com

Everyone should visit Niagara Falls, even if the road trip conjures up images of a National Lampoon–style vacation.

Shared by two countries, this Wonder of the World offers a better interactive experience than any amusement park. But what most newcomers don't know is that there's more to do than just pose for pictures in front of the Falls. You can get remarkably close to the rushing waters, either aboard a sightseeing boat or on foot. In one place, you can actually stick your head into the torrent. It's incredible given the look-but-don't-touch mentality at other destinations.

Maid of the Mist (www.maidofthemist.com; 716-284-8897)

Step aboard one of North America's oldest tourist attractions, operating since 1846. Passengers are given blue plastic ponchos, because they're going to get drenched. The ride

New York

Clockwise from top left: videographer Larry Deal, audio technician Bud McHugh, Marc, and producer Jill Littman at Niagara Falls.

sails past the American and Bridal Veil Falls and then head-on to the base of the more powerful Horseshoe—or Canadian Falls. With a thunderous 75,000 gallons of water falling per second, it's the perfect storm.

Cave of the Winds (www.niagarafallsstatepark.com; 716-278-1730)

There's no better place to soak up the Niagara Falls experience. This walking tour starts in Niagara Falls State Park, where you don another raincoat as well as a pair of "where-have-these-been?" slippers. Then, you ride an elevator down 175 feet, where you're guided along a boardwalk to the aptly named "Hurricane Deck" at the base of the Bridal Veil Falls. Go ahead; immerse yourself in the roaring waters. Look for rainbows everywhere, even at night.

A family-style trip like this requires proper family dining. You certainly can't miss the cleverly named Twist O' the Mist. No, really. You can't miss it, because it's 27-feet high and shaped like an ice-cream cone. With its unique look, and more than 50 different flavors of ice cream, the Twist claims to be the second-biggest attraction in Niagara Falls.

Next door, the Misty Dog serves standard fast-food fare, along with more exotic choices, like Ostrich Burgers or Duck Sausage.

There's no downside to the Top of the Falls restaurant. With its perfect location on the grounds of Niagara Falls State Park, the tiered dining room provides everyone with an awe-inspiring view of the Horseshoe Falls. The menu features California-influenced, all-American cuisine, like Chipotle BBQ Pork Tenderloin and Sesame Seared Tuna. (Save the jokes; the fish doesn't come from the Falls.)

Keep in mind, even with a new casino spurring development, the city of Niagara Falls, New York, leaves much to be desired. There's more to do on the Canadian side. But even there, with its established casino and scores of arcades and tourists shops, the town still looks like Atlantic City—without the Boardwalk or the beach.

If you want a popular side trip across the border, head to the quaint town of Niagara-on-the-Lake and the Inniskillin Winery:

Inniskillin Wines

Service Road 66 off the Niagara Parkway
Niagara-on-the-Lake, Ontario, Canada L0S 1J0
(888) 466-4754, x311
www.inniskillin.com

Inniskillin is famous for its ice wine. As the name suggests, it's made from nearly frozen grapes that are picked in winter. The juice that's produced is highly concentrated, but surprisingly leads to a tropical-tasting dessert wine.

———

New York

New Jersey

Le Petite Chateau

121 Claremont Road
Bernardsville, NJ 07924
(908) 766-4544

Scott Cutaneo, chef and owner of this fine dining establishment, has a simple dream . . . to
have the best restaurant in the world. Okay, so
maybe it's not so simple, but he's off to a good
start.

Critics and customers alike love his small
French restaurant in the quaint town of
Bernardsville, and he loves them. From the fine
French cuisine to the fine Reidel crystal on the
table, Cutaneo wants every aspect of his cus-
tomers' dining experience to be the very best.

Each night on his prix fixe menu he creates
memorable meals, many of which stem from his
childhood. Take for instance, the foie gras appetizer. He told Jill it was a takeoff on the cream
cheese and jelly sandwich he used to eat as a kid.
He just elevated it to an adult palate. Sound like
a stretch? Here, it's not.

In his kitchen, cream cheese is replaced
with slowly heated frommage blanc. The "jelly"
is actually diced strawberries, fermented in a
strawberry liqueur, lemon juice, and sugar to
bring out the flavor. White bread is replaced
with a healthy slice of brioche. Yet like the childhood classic, the crust is cut off and the brioche
is toasted.

He cooks the foie gras to medium rare and
assembles the appetizer—first the brioche, then
the cheese, the strawberries, that foie gras, and
a handful of micro greens.

If his goal is to be the best, this dish certainly
gets him one big leap forward.

———

The Ryland Inn

Route 22 West
Whitehouse, NJ 08888
(908) 534-4011
www.therylandinn.com

Chef Craig Shelton told Jill to close her eyes and
listen. He had just put perhaps the best beef
she'd ever seen—*cote de boeuf*—in a hot pan.
The steak made a crackling-sizzling noise as it
cooked. He told her to tell him when the sound
stopped.

"Okay," she said. "It stopped."

"Great," he said. "Now open your eyes. It's
time to flip."

Time to Teach Wine

We had shot at The Ryland Inn for two days and were beat. We finally sat down to eat when
Chef Shelton approached the table with a flip chart and marker in hand. I knew what all of
us were thinking: *Oh no, now we have to pay attention to a lesson, and we're exhausted.*

Much to our surprise, Chef Shelton put on an impromptu wine tasting, bringing out sugar and
lemons and a variety of wine to demonstrate how the physiology of any given food can dramatically
change the taste of the wines—for better or for worse. For example, he had us take a taste of sugar, then
sip on a nicely aged white wine. Instead of tasting wonderful like it should have, it seemed highly acidic.
He repeated the experiment with a lemon but this time sipping on a young, highly acidic wine.
Surprisingly, having the lemon first made it taste quite good.

Of course it is no surprise that Shelton is a great advocate of pairing food and wine so carefully, and this
smal demonstration gave us a glimpse into why that is so important. Suffice it to say, you're always treated
special here, even if you don't know it. Would you expect anything less from a mad-but-brilliant chef?

Welcome to Cooking 101 with Craig Shelton—a man who uses all his senses to make his magic.

A Yale graduate with a degree in molecular biophysics and biochemistry, the chef/owner of this Relais & Chateaux, AAA Four Diamond property turns into a mad scientist when he gets in a kitchen. So much so he's made a second career out of it.

Shelton's enthusiasm to enlighten is obvious, from his masterful pairing of food and wine to his messianic approach to cooking slow and low. Then there's the 3-acre organic garden with more than 400 varieties of herbs, flowers, fruits, and vegetables growing.

His mad scientist side comes out here, too, as he dashes into the garden, points to a plant, and exclaims, "They said it couldn't be done! Artichokes in New Jersey! Really, they said it couldn't be done . . . but you see them!"

And when you taste his cooking, you'll feel the same way. From the garden to the table, there's a reason every meal here is magical and memorable.

Daniel's on Broadway

416 South Broadway
Cape May, NJ 08204
(609) 898-8770
www.danielscapemay.com

It might not be in New York's famed theater district, but this restaurant on Broadway still puts on quite a show. Set in one of the 600-plus beautiful old Victorian mansions for which Cape May is famous, Daniel's is one of the finest restaurants in this beachside community.

Try the Horseradish and Herb-Encrusted Red Snapper served on a bed of lobster mashed potatoes, or the Crabmeat Napoleon. If you want to try it with beer or wine, bring your own. At this BYOB, they're happy to pour it; they just can't sell it.

End your evening with a horse-drawn carriage ride on the quiet, historic streets. Watch the moonlight glisten over the ocean. Listen to the waves. It's a long way from the Great White Way, for which, in this case, you'll probably be grateful.

The Lobster House

906 Schellenger Landing Road
Fisherman's Wharf
Cape May, NJ 08204
(609) 884-8296
www.thelobsterhouse.com

There's something fishy going on in Cape May, New Jersey—something that's been reeling in customers by the thousands. The Lobster House is a seafood lover's dream come true. There's a reason they serve 2,000 meals a day—nothing fancy, just downright good food!

Like most good fish tales, this one started small and grew . . . and grew. Owner Keith Lauderman's grandfather was a commercial fisherman in the 1920s. In 1954, his son (Keith's dad), opened up a *small* restaurant on the pier. Over the years, he gained a *big* following. So big, the restaurant expanded several times, and now the family nearly owns the whole dock.

There's a takeout shop for dining along the wharf, a raw bar, a coffee shop, a huge indoor restaurant, and the *Schooner American*—an 1830s fishing vessel—moored dockside, where you can eat outside and watch the sun set.

Be prepared to wait for your table. After all, this is one fish tale that's been told for more than 50 years, and the lines have grown about as long as the wharf itself.

Hennessy Tavern

191 Paris Avenue
Northvale, NJ 07647
(201) 768-7707
www.hennessytavern.com

Marc didn't know what to expect on the drive toward Hennessy Tavern in North Jersey, but he was definitely a little nervous. After all, there were suggestions the big TV star for whom the restaurant is named would only be available for a short time. Marc and the crew walked in prepared to find a diva barking orders at an assistant, a cell phone glued to her ear, and makeup artists toiling anxiously.

New Jersey

At Hennessy's, owner Paolo Mastropeitro, Jill Hennessy, and Marc.

Imagine their surprise when they discovered actress Jill Hennessy is—in a word—*normal.*

The star of NBC's *Crossing Jordan,* and before that, *Law and Order,* doesn't have an entourage, never once spoke into a cell phone, and actually borrowed makeup from Marc because she forgot her own. (Yes, he carries makeup. You have to on TV. And no, he doesn't have a makeup artist, either.) She also talked with customers, posed for pictures, and stayed as long as we needed.

Opened in 1999 in this town an hour outside New York, Hennessy Tavern is the work of Jill's husband, Paolo Mastropietro. He personally restored an old family-owned building and then named it for her even though they were just dating at the time. Smooth move!

Jill's then-co-star from *Law and Order,* Benjamin Bratt, helped with the renovations. The man named one of *People's* Sexiest Men Alive was dating superstar Julia Roberts at the time, and the star-sightings caused plenty of talk in town. But the real tongue-wagging dealt with the best times to catch Bratt working outside, shirtless.

The restaurant was also known as a hangout for the cast and crew from the NBC show, *Ed.* Its famed "Stuckey Bowl" set was just a few doors down.

Hennessy Tavern doesn't boast about its celebrity ties, but it doesn't run from them, either. There are a few articles posted on the walls, but for the most part, the place is best known for its comfort food. There are tavern staples like fish-n-chips, shepherd's pie, and beef stew. There's also a long list of pasta dishes. Paolo's mother, Angie, makes the flourless chocolate cake for dessert.

Jill's favorite dish is, not surprisingly, the Hennessy Chopped Salad.

In short, the restaurant is easygoing and likeable, just like its very normal namesake.

Shepherd's Pie

ADAPTED FROM THE HENNESSEY TAVERN, NORTHVALE, NEW JERSEY

MAKES 1 PIE

Filling:
⅔ *cup vegetable oil*
2 large yellow onions, diced
5 pounds ground beef
1 (16-ounce) package frozen peas and carrots
Salt and black pepper to taste

3 tablespoons olive oil
½ cup regular or quick-mixing all-purpose flour
3 cups beef broth

Topping:
8 russet potatoes
¼ cup butter
¾ cup heavy cream
Salt and black pepper to taste

To make filling: Heat vegetable oil in a large Dutch oven or saucepan over medium heat. Add onions, and cook until translucent. Add beef and cook, stirring to break up the meat, until brown. Drain beef and onions in a strainer to remove fat. Return meat mixture to the Dutch oven. Add peas and carrots, and season with salt and pepper; set aside.

Add olive oil to a medium saucepan over medium heat. Stir in flour, and cook, stirring constantly, until bubbly. Stir in broth, and cook, stirring constantly, until thickened. Season with salt and pepper.

Pour sauce over meat mixture, and simmer for 45 minutes, stirring occasionally.

Meanwhile, to make topping: Scrub, peel, and quarter potatoes. (Drop them into cold water until ready to use. This will prevent them from discoloring.) Cook potatoes in slightly salted, boiling water until tender when pierced with a fork, 15 to 20 minutes. Drain. Return to the pot, and add butter and cream. Mash, leaving some small lumps for this hearty dish. Season with salt and pepper.

Preheat the oven to 375°F.

To finish pie: Place filling in a large casserole, and top with potatoes. Bake for about 30 minutes or until the top is browned and filling is heated through.

CHEF'S NOTES: You may sprinkle paprika on top of the potatoes before baking. You may also serve in individual casseroles.

Grounds for Sculpture

18 Fairgrounds Road
Hamilton, NJ 08619
(609) 586-0616
www.groundsforsculpture.org

Rat's

(located on Grounds for Sculpture)
(609) 584-7800
www.ratsrestaurant.org

J. Seward Johnson Jr. wanted to do away with the loftiness often associated with art. So he built a giant playground of sorts on what used to be the New Jersey Fairgrounds, installed some very large sculptures, and invited everyone to come in and have fun.

You can do that kind of thing when you're an heir to the Johnson & Johnson fortune.

But Johnson isn't some dilettante. An acclaimed sculptor, one of his works is on display in Rockefeller Center in New York and another, called *The Awakening*, is a popular attraction in Washington, DC

Johnson's own works are some of the most approachable of the 200 pieces from dozens of artists spread over 35 acres. He takes the characters in classic paintings, like Renoir's *Luncheon of the Boating Party*, and turns them into life-size figures that invite participation. For instance, his sculpture shows a woman playing footsy under the table, something you don't see in the original Renoir masterpiece. One of the unidentifiable characters in the painting is, in fact, a self-portrait of Johnson.

In keeping with the theme, Johnson installed a rather elegant French restaurant on the Grounds and then called it Rat's. A rather odd name for a fine-dining establishment, but not for Johnson, who claims it's named for a character in a favorite children's book, *The Wind in the Willows*. Or could it be because Rat's spelled backward is "star"?

Who knows? J. Seward Johnson does, but rather than tell you, he'd rather you think about it, laugh, and enjoy, which is precisely the idea at Grounds for Sculpture.

New Jersey

New Jersey

Temple Bar and Grill

Caesar's Atlantic City
2100 Pacific Avenue
Atlantic City, NJ 08401
(609) 441-2345
www.templebarandgrill.com

In a gambling mecca often maligned for its bus-loads of aging slot-machine players, the Temple Bar and Grill is dedicated to one thing: excess.

Located inside Caesar's, this independently owned restaurant is geared toward Atlantic City's high rollers. It's certainly opulent, with towering columns, soaring palm trees, and a PG-13-rated masterpiece on the ceiling. The restaurant's centerpiece is a 22-foot high glass-enclosed wine tower, with the more expensive bottles at the top. That way, other diners know your price range when the sommelier climbs to retrieve your order.

The Temple is one of the few places in Atlantic City to feature real Kobe steak, at $130 a plate—at last check. Kobe comes from Japanese steer that are massaged with gin. The process makes the meat so tender you can literally cut it with a fork. You'd be that way, too, if someone rubbed you with booze all day.

There's also South African Lobster Tail, Alaskan Crab Cakes, caviar, and other dishes for big spenders. Don't worry if you're not in their league, because you can also order sushi, pizza, or burgers.

Subtle is not a word that comes to mind when we talk about this place. *Spectacle?* That's the word! But no matter how you describe it, Temple Bar and Grill is a much better bet than all those slot machines.

Pennsylvania

Reading Terminal Market

12th and Arch Streets
Philadelphia, PA 19107
(215) 922-2317
www.readingterminalmarket.com

Philadelphia's top three destinations are, in this order: the Liberty Bell, Independence Hall, and the Reading Terminal Market.

The first two might be more famous, but Reading Market has much better food. It may well be the world's greatest farmers' market with more than 80 vendors peddling Philadelphia's finest meats, poultry, cheese, seafood, flowers, spices, and produce plus local specialties like steak sandwiches, soft pretzels, and Scrapple.

The Market dates to 1892, when the Reading Railroad built a world-class train station upstairs, while below, the area's produce and pushcart vendors were given a place to sell their goods. It flourished for most of a century. At one point, suburban families would order food from the Market and have it delivered aboard trains for pickup at their local stations. But the Market faced an uncertain future when the Reading Railroad went broke in the 1970s. At one point, city officials talked about its closure, until merchants showed up at a City Council meeting with a petition bearing 70,000 signatures of support.

A new Convention Center has been built nearby, and the Market has been revitalized, welcoming 80,000 visitors a week and promoting the pursuit of happiness that the guys at those other Philadelphia tourist attractions intended way back when.

Susanna Foo

1512 Walnut Street
Philadelphia, PA 19102
(215) 545-2666
www.susannafoo.com

Susanna Foo never aspired to be a chef, let alone one of the country's best. Born and raised in China, she moved with husband, E-Hsin, to the United States in 1967. In 1979, after earning a Master's degree in library science at the University of Pittsburgh, they moved to Philadelphia to help run his family's restaurant. Susanna's job was to greet customers and run the business side of things. She did very little cooking.

That changed when she met Jacob Rosenthal, founder of the Culinary Institute of America. Rosenthal was impressed by Foo's modest efforts in the kitchen and encouraged her to cultivate her culinary skills. She followed his advice and took some courses at the CIA. In 1987, she and E-Hsin opened Susanna Foo. It was an instant hit.

When Jill asked her how she felt about her success, she said, "the higher the mountain you climb, the harder you have to work."

All that hard work has put her restaurant and Chinese cooking on the country's fancy food map. You won't find typical American-Chinese dishes like sweet and sour chicken here. Nor will you find tapestries hanging on the walls or Chinese lanterns on the table. Rather, her Asian equation is high style and spice embodied in her signature dishes like Crispy Duck with Sweet Potato Purée and Nectarine Chutney, Grilled Baby Rack of Lamb with Coconut Sweet Rice Compote, or Lobster Dumplings with Emulsified Coconut Lobster Sauce.

It's no wonder she's called Philadelphia's—and America's—Queen of Chinese Cuisine. One taste and you'll know why her meals reign supreme.

———

Joseph Poon Asian Fusion Restaurant

1002 Arch Street
Philadelphia, PA 19107
(215) 928-9333
www.josephpoon.com

Joseph Poon is the unofficial Mayor of Philadelphia's Chinatown.

Loaded with energy and filled with exuberance, Poon regularly leads what he calls his "Wok and Walk" tours around the 8-block area, introducing newcomers to Asian culture and cuisines. Stops include a Chinese Herb Store, where Joe explains Kumchoi, a plant believed to remove toxins from your system. The crowd is usually more attentive when Joe talks about

The Audition

The shoot at Susanna Foo's was my first crack at the job hosting *The Best Of.* I was flown to Philadelphia to meet the executive producers of our show, Dan Sitarski and Eileen Matthews, who wanted to get to know me over—what else—food. They had me shoot a few pieces with them to "test the waters," so to speak. This way they could see how I did on camera and how I interacted with people.

Needless to say, I was a bit nervous upon meeting them, but they put me right at ease. At dinner that first night, I realized they weren't "foodies" either—rather just regular people who wanted to tell stories on television. The way I held my fork didn't matter to them.

Five years and nearly 1,000 restaurants later, I'm grateful to have passed muster and landed this dream job. I owe part of my success to Susanna. Working alongside her, I felt entirely at ease. She has a subtle way of just making people feel comfortable. It was the perfect place to "try out" for my new career.

an herb referred to as Chinese Viagra. Later at a fruit stand, Poon holds up a Durian, a fruit known as much for its unpleasant odor as for its flavor. Finally, the tour ends at a fortune cookie factory, but by then, the crowd knows they don't need a cookie to determine their fate. Because when Joe Poon's around, there's always good fortune.

Poon came to the United States from Hong Kong at age 25 with $8 in his pocket. In college, he worked seven jobs to pay off his student loans. Nothing gets this guy down. One time, a chef refused to teach him how to carve fruit and vegetables into intricate centerpieces, so Joe bought hundreds of potatoes and taught himself. He's now a recognized expert.

Over the years, he made and lost a lot of money in the restaurant business, but Joseph Poon Asian Fusion Restaurant has brought him nothing but good fortune.

Poon takes classic Chinese dishes and combines them with cooking techniques from around the world. Nowhere else will you find a dish like Peking Duck Tacos or General Joe's Chicken.

You might expect Joe to credit those Chinese herbs for his success. Instead, he explains it this way, "I want to be healthy. Number one. Healthy. Happy, number two. Money, number three. I love money, too." Sounds like something you hope to find in a fortune cookie.

General Joe's Chicken

ADAPTED FROM JOSEPH POON ASIAN FUSION
RESTAURANT, PHILADELPHIA, PENNSYLVANIA

YIELD: 2 SERVINGS

6 to 8 ounces chicken breast (2 large breasts),
   sliced
½ cup cornstarch

Deep-fry sliced chicken breast dusted with 2 to 3 inches dry cornstarch until brown.

Sauce:
1 tablespoon white vinegar
2 tablespoons soy sauce
3 tablespoons chardonnay
4 tablespoons sugar
5 tablespoons chicken broth
1 teaspoon garlic
1 teaspoon ginger
1 teaspoon hot sauce
2 to 3 tablespoons slurry

Mix vinegar, soy sauce, chardonnay, sugar, broth, garlic, ginger, hot sauce, and slurry. Place chicken on a plate. Heat up sauce. Pour sauce on the top to create General Joe's Chicken.

Victor Café

1303 Dickinson Street
Philadelphia, PA 19147
(215) 468-3040
www.victorcafe.com

At this music-lover's rendezvous, you'll find pasta literally served up with a side dish of Puccini. At Victor Café, music makes the menu sing.

Rick DiStefano's grandfather came to Philadelphia from Italy, saved his pennies, and opened up a gramophone and record shop here in 1918. He was a lover of all things opera. With the repeal of prohibition in the 1930s and hard times setting in, he thought he could turn a better profit by making the place an Italian restaurant. When he opened up Victor Café, the "Music Lovers' Rendezvous," you can guess what kind of music was played.

Over the years, the restaurant evolved to the point where patrons took to belting out opera tunes. Then, in 1979, a new tradition was born when a local opera student working here starting singing for his customers. That's when the tables turned and opera students were hired as servers. Every 20 minutes or so, a bell rings to announce a performance. The tunes these aspiring tenors and sopranos sing will bring you to tears.

But the hardest part for servers might be carrying orders from the downstairs kitchen to the dining room. Between belting out arias, they're huffing and puffing up and down the stairs, so remember that when it comes to tipping time.

When it comes to ordering, it wouldn't hurt to bring an opera cheat sheet along. The DiStefanos wrote history into their menu in the form of classic Italian dishes with classical opera overtures. For example, there's the Fettuccine Giuseppe Verdi, made with green fettuccine noodles tossed with fresh spinach and wild mushrooms. Verdi apparently loved to eat and would probably have broken into song when trying this dish.

The Cannelloni Don Carlos is about as dramatic in taste as the opera for which it is named. It consists of two pasta tubes filled with pork, veal, beef, spinach, and ricotta cheese. The Lucia di Lammermoor is named for the famous sextet for that opera and made with six types of seafood tossed in pasta.

Even if you don't know opera lingo, ordering is easy (everything on the menu is explained in English), and just listening to the students sing is an experience. This is one bel canto crowd you don't want to miss.

———

Ralph's Italian Restaurant

760 South 9th Street
Philadelphia, PA 19147
(215) 627-6011
www.ralphsrestaurant.com

Ralph's is a regular kind of place. By that, we mean it's packed with regulars. Most nights you'll find people who eat here more than they eat at home.

Founded in 1900, Ralph's claims to be the oldest family-owned Italian restaurant in the country. Immigrants Francesco and Catherine Dispigno, who named the place after their son, started by feeding neighborhood workers. Ralph eventually took over and saved the business during the Depression by standing out on the street, selling bowls of spaghetti for a nickel. In the 1950s, Ralph's became a popular hangout for entertainers appearing at a nightclub down the

street. One biography of Frank Sinatra says Ralph's was Frank's favorite place in Philly.

You're going to find the classics here, like pasta, seafood, and veal. Many Old World dishes (chicken livers and mushrooms, sweetbreads) have been on the menu since the beginning. The prices may have changed since then, but not by much.

At Ralph's, the servings are large. They pile it on as if they want to keep you full until your next visit. Which, judging by the regulars, won't be all that long.

———

Termini Brothers

1523 South 8th Street
Philadelphia, PA 19147
(215) 334-1816 or (800) 882-7650
www.termini.com

No place makes cannoli like Termini Brothers. In Philadelphia, the two are always mentioned in the same breath, almost as if it's one word: *TerminiCannoli.*

A fixture in South Philly since 1921, this Italian bakery was created by brothers Giuseppi and Gaetano Termini, who spent long hours at work and raised their families in separate apartments above the store. The bakery was the center of their lives.

These days, the traditions live on with the grandsons of Giuseppi, Vinnie and Joseph, who run the business just like their grandfather taught them, working alongside their parents, Vincent and Barbara.

Termini's most popular cannoli—those crunchy Italian pastry shells curled around a sweet creamy filling—is loaded with ricotta cheese and chocolate morsels.

Learning to fill cannoli with the Termini brothers, Joseph and Vincent.

photo courtesy of Kathy Silverstein

Pennsylvania

The Termini difference comes in the preparation of the cannoli shells. To create their cone-like shape, the still-soft pastry is wrapped around maple wood dowels and then lowered into a fryer. Other bakeries use metal rods, but Termini's says the wood infuses flavor.

Another difference comes in the filling: Termini's adds citron—chopped up sugar-cured melon rinds—to the ricotta. When mixed with the chocolate morsels, it instantly becomes TerminiCannoli.

———

Le Bec-Fin

1523 Walnut Street
Philadelphia, PA 19102
(215) 567-1000
www.lebecfin.com

Before Le Bec-Fin opened in 1970, Philadelphia was considered a gastronomic wasteland, known only for steak sandwiches and locally baked TastyKake cupcakes. Georges Perrier from Lyon, France, changed that, putting his adopted city on the culinary map.

For nearly two decades, Perrier's classic French restaurant was awarded the elite Mobile Five-Star rating. Reservations were nearly impossible to get. In addition, his presence helped invigorate the dining scene in Center City Philadelphia, where an impressive list of restaurants has since emerged.

But Le Bec-Fin has taken its hits. In 2000, Mobile knocked its rating down to Four-Stars, still impressive, but a major blow to Perrier. A man well known for his vocal outbursts (usually to underlings), Perrier proudly admits he's a perfectionist. "I am never satisfied," he is often quoted as saying.

So what does a perfectionist do when things aren't perfect? In Perrier's case, he closed his restaurant for a month in 2002 and spent more than $1 million to renovate. He also hired a top executive to oversee his growing Philadelphia restaurant empire (he owns two other local eateries) and returned to the kitchen at Le Bec-Fin. Perrier now oversees almost every meal. He

also redoubled his efforts in the dining room. Service was outstanding before, but he insisted it could be improved. It's the least that customers who are paying upward of $115 for the Traditional Six-Course Prix Fixe Dinner should expect. With all the improvements, and the continuing appeal of its signature dishes such as the house smoked salmon, crab cake and rack of lamb, Le Bec-Fin recaptured its Five Star Rating in 2001 and is currently the only restaurant in Philadelphia with this prestigious designation. After leading the way for more than 30 years, Le Bec-Fin is still making history.

———

¡Pasion!

211 South 15th Street
Philadelphia, PA 19102
(215) 875-9895
www.pasionrestaurant.com

Some places feature a sushi bar. ¡Pasion! features something unique—a ceviche bar.

Executive Chef Guillermo Pernot has taken the idea of "cooking" fish and seafood in citrus juice and turned it into an art form. The results have blown away the critics.

¡Pasion! burst onto Philadelphia's downtown restaurant scene in 1998. Within no time, *Esquire* magazine named Pernot Chef of the Year for 1999 and ¡Pasion! among the Best New Restaurants. *Gourmet* magazine named ¡Pasion! one of America's top 50 restaurants for 2001. The list goes on.

The raves are not just about the ceviche (although that does get much of the ink), but also for Pernot's Nuevo Latino cuisine. The Argentina-born chef, who says he grew up cooking but never took a formal lesson, draws on influences from throughout Latin America. Main courses include Pescado, a crispy whole fish with a black bean sauce; and the Parrillada Argentina, a mixed grill of meats, served on a hibachi to keep it warm.

———

Pennsylvania

Pat's King of Steaks

1237 East Passyunk Avenue
Philadelphia, PA 19147
(215) 468-1546
www.patskingofsteaks.com

photo courtesy of Kathy Silverstein

Marc, doing the "Philly Stoop" with Pat's King of Steak owner, Frank Olivieri.

The late Pat Olivieri didn't care what people said about him, just as long as they talked. The man who created the Philly Steak Sandwich in 1930 was dealing with rumors his legendary product was made with horsemeat. So he issued a challenge, offering $10,000 to anyone who had proof. Business boomed as people came from far and wide to investigate. But no one claimed the money. The reason: The steak was pure rib eye. As for the rumor: Pat started it.

That's how they do things in South Philly.

Superstars and average Joes stand in line together at this outdoor landmark. And the food still has people talking. But around here, you need to know the proper language to order your food.

For instance, you have to specify if you want your steak "wit" or "wit-out." The initiated know we're talking about "with" or "without" onions. And it's not "steak and cheese"; that's for wimps. Around here it's "Cheese Steak."

The current owner Frank Olivieri, Pat's nephew, drives home both points every day. His license plate reads: CHEZWIT.

By the way, "inside out" means they rip out the interior of the bread. Why? Because.

Yougoddaproblemwitdat?

Then there's the stance. It's best to assume what they call the "Philly Stoop" to properly enjoy a Pat's Cheese Steak. Bend your knees—and stand as if you're about to hit a golf ball. That way, when you bite into the sandwich, the grease and cheese drip on the sidewalk, not on your shirt or shoes.

Very important: The cheese? It's Cheez Whiz®. That should keep you talking.

Again, that's how they do things in South Philly, and it's certainly what makes Pat's, King of Steaks.

The Original Pat's King of Steaks® Philadelphia Cheese Steak

ADAPTED FROM PAT'S KING OF STEAKS, PHILADELPHIA, PENNSYLVANIA

YIELD: 4 SANDWICHES

6 tablespoons of Soya bean oil
1 large Spanish onion
24 ounces thin sliced rib eye or eye roll steak
Cheese (Cheez Whiz® is recommended, but American or Provolone work fine.)
4 crusty Italian rolls
Sweet green and red peppers sautéed in oil (optional)
Mushrooms sautéed in oil (optional)
Ketchup (optional)

Heat an iron skillet or a nonstick pan over medium heat.

Add 3 tablespoons oil to the pan, and sauté onions to desired doneness, then remove onions. Add remaining oil, and sauté slices of meat quickly on both sides. Melt Cheez Whiz® in a double boiler or in the microwave, and place 6 ounces of meat into rolls. Add onions, pour Cheez Whiz® over top, and garnish with hot or fried sweet peppers, mushrooms, and ketchup.

Put on the theme song to the first *Rocky* movie, and enjoy!

Pennsylvania

Pennsylvania

Buddakan

325 Chestnut Street
Philadelphia, PA 19106
(215) 574-9440
www.buddakan.com

Buddakan is a Steven Starr production.

Starr, a one-time local concert promoter, realized that restaurants are just another form of entertainment. He now owns some of the most severely chic places in Philadelphia. Buddakan is one of his earliest and most enduring works.

It's a show as much as it is a restaurant. Large and wide open, with 20-foot-high ceilings, its centerpiece is a giant, gold-leafed Buddha. At the foot of the statue, there's a long (22-seat), onyx-topped community table where strangers mingle and share food. The menu is Asian-ish, with large, family-style platters, perfect for passing around. The tables around the rest of the restaurant fill up early, along with the lounge upstairs.

There's a mesmerizing waterfall near the front, not far from the hostess stand that changes colors. The sound system reportedly cost $30,000.

Once the night gets going, this restaurant is loud.

Buddakan rocks. It's appearing nightly, in Philadelphia.

———

White Dog Cafe

3420 Sansom Street
Philadelphia, PA 19104
(215) 386-9224
www.whitedog.com

This City of Brotherly Love needs a lot of love, and Judy Wicks might just be the person to bring it on. The motto of her restaurant: "Eating well while doing good." This place is as much about social activism as it is about food.

Judy and her chef Michael O'Halloran start at the grassroots level, buying their produce from local farms and markets in the area; they make sure all the meat and poultry they buy is humanely raised and that their seafood comes from sustainable fisheries.

The Cafe has helped lead campaigns to ban the sale of endangered fish and the use of Genetically Modified Organisms. Ten to twenty percent of their pre-tax profits go toward organizations like Action Aids and Amnesty International. To top it off: 100 percent of their electricity is generated by wind power, although like most great chefs, O'Halloran uses gas to cook in his kitchen.

If you think you're going to walk into an incense-and-macramé-filled restaurant, think again. The place is classy and cozy; the food is delicious. The menu changes constantly, depending on what the farmers are bringing in, but to give you an idea, you'll find entrées like Pan Roasted Free-Range Amish-Farmed Chicken with Rosemary-Sage Sauce; Balsamic Roasted Organic Portobello Mushroom with Garden Vegetable Ratatouille; and Flame Roasted London Broil with Wild Mushroom-Worcestershire Glaze.

To further the legacy, Judy has opened up a store adjoining the restaurant called The Black Cat. Here you can find social activism in cans, jars, and bottles, like Hood Salad Dressing, bottled by high school students in Los Angeles as a way to fund their college educations.

Judy is a restaurateur who is trying—and succeeding—at making a difference both locally and globally. She even leads tours with her staff and customers to places like Nicaragua, Vietnam, Mexico, and Cuba—a country with which she says the United States has a "misunderstanding." She's developed relationships with restaurants around the world and teaches her tour groups about how U.S. foreign policy in those countries affects those peoples' lives.

Bottom line, when you *open* the door to this revolutionary restaurant, enter with an *open* mind. You might just find yourself wishing you had something like this in your neighborhood. Then again, if you're a revolutionary, maybe you can follow Judy's lead.

Black Bean and Florida Citrus Salsa

ADAPTED FROM WHITE DOG CAFE, PHILADELPHIA, PENNSYLVANIA

YIELD: ABOUT 5 CUPS

2 cups cooked black beans, rinsed
3 Florida navel oranges, peeled and chopped into
    bite-size pieces
1 red bell pepper, seeded, deveined, and diced
    into ¼-inch pieces
1 green bell pepper, seeded, deveined, and diced
    into ¼-inch pieces
½ medium red onion, diced
1 cup fresh or canned pineapple, diced
1 tablespoon diced canned chipotle chiles en
    adobo
1 tablespoon chopped fresh cilantro
Juice of 1 Florida lime
Salt

In a bowl, toss together beans, oranges, red and green bell peppers, onion, pineapple, chiles, cilantro, and lime juice. Salt to taste. Serve at room temperature or chilled. This salsa can be made one day in advance if kept covered and refrigerated.

Scoop it up with crispy tortilla chips, or serve it atop grilled meats and seafood, or as a side for your favorite sandwich.

Tacconelli's Pizza

2604 East Somerset Street
Philadelphia, PA 19134
(215) 425-4983

They take reservations, but not the kind you're thinking of. When you call up this pizza parlor in the Port Richmond section of Philadelphia, what you're reserving is your *dough*.

It all goes back to the oven. When Giovani Tacconelli first came to America from Italy in 1918, he got into the bread-baking business. He built a 20-by-20 brick oven in his row home in this working-class neighborhood. After World War II, the family branched out and started making pizza. In fact, Vincent and Barbara Tacconelli still live above the pizza shop.

Okay, here's the scoop on the dough issue: You have to *plan ahead!* Each morning at 10 A.M., the oil-fired oven is turned on. The oil burns for about 5 hours, and the heat left over from that is what makes the pizza cook. Come 9 o'clock at night, that oven is cooling down, and once that happens, pizza production stops. The dough rests for the night along with Vincent and Barbara.

A One *Man* Show

Tacconelli's is a one man, one oven operation. I don't use the word *man* lightly. It's always been the man's job to pull the pizza out of the oven with their 18-foot paddle. So the ruckus we caused when shooting there came to me by surprise.

My executive producer, Eileen Matthews, and I thought it would be fun if I pulled one of the pizzas out of the oven on camera. No one told us we would be breaking a long-standing tradition. Vincent Tacconelli Jr. and his wife, Doris, were running the shop at the time, and as I pulled the paddle out with a piping-hot pizza on it, Doris gasped. She then exclaimed, "No woman has *ever* held the paddle before, much less pulled out a pizza." She was clearly stunned.

Major protocol had been violated.

I thought I might have just shattered a marriage and broken four generations of pizza tradition. We quickly finished up the shoot, and bid them farewell.

I'm happy to report that at last check the marriage is still intact. In fact, they've even gone off and opened their own Tacconelli's in New Jersey. This one has a smaller oven heated by gas with a much smaller paddle. Even so, Doris says it's still a man's job in the kitchen.

You can find their South Jersey location at:

450 South Lenola Road
Maple Shade, NJ 08052
(856) 638-0338

Pennsylvania

To be fair, there are some nights when you might get lucky and stop in to order a pizza on the spot, but if you want to play it safe . . .

Their other rules include cash only, no delivery, and no booze sold. You have to bring your own.

———

Valley Green Inn

Fairmount Park
Valley Green Road at Wissahickon Creek
Philadelphia, PA 19128
(215) 247-1730
www.valleygreeninn.com

Valley Green Inn is so secluded in Philadelphia's Fairmont Park that it doesn't even have a numbered street address. Its official location, Valley Green at Wissahickon, pinpoints a spot where a park road meets a creek. The restaurant says even MapQuest has problems giving directions here.

Despite its location, or perhaps because of it, Valley Green Inn is a popular spot for romantic meals and weekend brunches. The building, which dates to 1850, looks like something right out of a Norman Rockwell painting—charming and serene.

Both the Inn and Fairmont Park are popular destinations for joggers, families with strollers, and anyone looking for a respite from city life. Amazingly, it's only 10 minutes from hectic Center City Philadelphia. The Inn is open 365 days a year, so don't worry if you get lost. They'll still be there when you arrive.

The menu offers specialties like Roast Duckling, Pretzel Crusted Pork Chops, and Napoleon Meatloaf—a tower of ground beef, veal, and pork layered with potatoes, then wrapped in bacon. It's so big, it might actually show up on MapQuest. And the Challah French Toast stuffed with Brie could be the best brunch meal you'll ever find—that is, provided you first find the Valley Green Inn.

Brie Stuffed French Toast

ADAPTED FROM THE VALLEY GREEN INN,
PHILADELPHIA, PENNSYLVANIA

YIELD: 4 SERVINGS

1 stick sweet, unsalted butter
½ cup walnuts, chopped
2 bananas, sliced
¼ cup banana liqueur (optional)
1 pint real Vermont maple syrup
2 cups half-and-half
2 tablespoons ground cinnamon
2 tablespoons pure vanilla extract
4 whole eggs (not beaten)
½ cup sugar
Pinch salt
8 pieces challah bread
¼ wheel double cream Brie cheese, cut into 8 thin pieces

In a medium-hot pan, melt 4 tablespoons of butter. After butter melts, but before starting to brown, add walnuts. Reduce heat to medium, and lightly cook walnuts until you begin to smell aroma of toasted nuts. Add bananas to walnuts. Cook approximately 3 to 5 minutes or until bananas begin to caramelize. Remove pan from heat (very important, do not add liqueur to pan while still on burner), add banana liqueur, (if using) and return to heat. If pan is hot enough, let most of the liquid evaporate until removing from heat. Add maple syrup, and set aside in serving container. Combine half-and-half, cinnamon, vanilla, eggs, sugar, and salt in a shallow bowl. Stir vigorously to combine cinnamon with mixture. Dip challah bread into egg mixture, turning to be sure bread soaks up liquid.

Heat pan to medium. Melt 1 tablespoon butter. After butter has melted and before it begins to brown, add 2 slices of bread to the pan. Gently lay bread into butter. After approximately 30 to 45 seconds, turn over 1 slice, and place Brie on cooked side of challah. Place other piece of challah bread on top of Brie (uncooked side still facing up). Add more butter if necessary. Cook another minute, turn over, and cook 1 more minute. Continue with remaining bread and cheese in the same manner.

Place on a plate, spoon your syrup mixture on top, and enjoy.

The Mayfair Diner

7353 Frankford Avenue
Philadelphia, PA 19136
(215) 624-4455 or (215) 624-8886

If the saying is true that everything old is new again, then The Mayfair Diner just might be the hippest spot in Philadelphia. Okay, not exactly, but when you're talking about longevity, this dining car—or should we say *cars* because three of them take up an entire city block—continues to stand the test of time.

This slice of neon nostalgia has been around since 1932, and some of the waitresses have been here almost as long, greeting you with a smile and making sure your coffee cup is always full.

You'll find a few things here indicative of authentic diners. For starters, there's the shiny metal siding and long counter with stools. There's the hours: They're open 24 hours a day, 364 days a year. Closed only on Christmas. And there's the owners: The Mulholland family who has owned it since its inception.

As for the food, what can we say? It's a diner—a greasy spoon, serving up homemade meatloaf and mashed potatoes, stuffed chicken, old-fashioned beef pie, lasagna, you name it.

But a diner is much more than a place to eat—it's about community and neighbors knowing neighbors. The Mulhollands have embraced this philosophy over the years by sticking to their traditions and not attempting to modernize too much. Some of their regulars come here simply because the diner *is* their family—their spouse

has passed away or their kids have left home, and this place is the social centerpiece of their life. They are welcomed every day with open arms.

If you're looking for a slice of Americana, then check out The Mayfair. It's a place that will not only fill your stomach, but your heart as well.

—

Ye Olde College Diner

126 West College Avenue
State College, PA 16801
(814) 238-5590
www.thediner.statecollege.com

At Penn State, football rules, and the grilled stickies from Ye Olde College Diner make 'em drool. The diner dates back to 1929 and is as much a tradition as the Nittany Lion. Come game weekend, the diner dishes out about 25,000 of these gooey, goopy goodies. You think that's incredible, consider this: When Beaver Stadium fills up, it becomes the third largest city in Pennsylvania. That's a lot of hungry mouths to feed.

Stickies are basically sweet rolls taken to another level when they're put on the grill—and are a staple in every Nittany Lion's diet. They're delicious anytime, but—as all the students can attest, myself included—they taste best after the bars close at 2 A.M. Not that I would know . . .

True sticky connoisseurs order the "Mt. Nittany," also known as Sticky à la Mode, which has two scoops of vanilla ice cream on top. However, if these sweet treats don't float your

Pennsylvania

When the topic *The Best Of Campus Hot Spots* was suggested for *The Best Of,* I jumped at the chance to showcase some of my old haunts. As a proud Penn State graduate, I think there's a long list of "best" places to visit. But if you just have time to check out a few, I've included some of my favorites here.

Jill with her alma mater's mascot, Penn State's Nittany Lion.

photo courtesy of Bud McHugh

boat (*gasp!*), the diner has all kinds of other foods that you'd expect to find at, well, a diner.

———

The Corner Room

100 West College Avenue
State College, PA 16801
(814) 237-3051
www.hotelstatecollege.com

If anyone says to you, "Meet me at the corner," this is where you go. On the corner of College and Allen Streets, you'll find a restaurant housed inside The Hotel State College, which itself has been around as long as Penn State—since 1855. The Corner Room restaurant came later—in 1926—and has become a landmark in this town, with big helpings of hearty food served up by a loyal and hospitable staff. Owner Michael Desmond got his start working here as a dishwasher when he was in the ninth grade, and many of the staff have been here just as long. This "Corner" caters to every generation and every taste, from Zeno's, their classic basement bar to the casual-yet-fun Corner Room on street level to their fine dining Allen Street Grill upstairs.

———

Café 210 West

210 West College Avenue
State College, PA 16801
(814) 237-3449

There are loads of bars I could talk about here: The Rathskeller, Zeno's, The Phyrst, but for one that does drinks and food in a great outdoor setting, Café 210 West is the place to go.

Café 210 West is famous for its live music, sizzling fajitas, and Long Island Iced Teas. I know they have a host of other, newer tea flavors, but for my trip down memory lane, I can only vouch for the original. On hot summer nights, expect long lines. Once you nab a table, enjoy it. When you settle into your surroundings, you'll know why Penn State students give this place high marks.

The University Creamery

12 Borland Lab
University Park, PA 16802
(814) 865-7535

All it takes is four days to get from the cow to the cone. That's how fresh the ice cream is at The Creamery. This landmark, which has been around since the late 1800s, is a sweet staple for any Penn Stater. On football Saturdays, they'll dip up to 12,000 cones. On a regular day, they do a mere 3,000 or so.

Around the year 2006, I'm told The Creamery will move to a new location closer to Beaver Stadium. I've been assured the taste won't change, but most everyone says they'll miss the old building that has held so many sweet memories.

Nevertheless, bon appétit, and oh yeah, "We are . . . PENN STATE!"

———

Church Brew Works

3525 Liberty Avenue
Lawrenceville, PA 15201
(412) 688-8200
www.churchbrewworks.com

Holy cow! A brewpub that was once a church!

It's a divine sight and the answer to beer lovers' prayers. There's a giant stainless-steel and copper brew house up on what used to be an altar. Pews have been cut in half and used as table benches, and the rest of the wood has been converted (get it?) into a bar. An old confessional

photo courtesy of Church Brew Works

Holy Cow! The brewpub that used to be a church.

booth now sells souvenirs, and stained-glass windows provide a better glow than any drink.

It's all been done with the church's blessing, or at least its approval.

For most of the twentieth century, St. John the Baptist Church was the spiritual home for Catholics in Lawrenceville, a once-thriving blue-collar neighborhood. The church survived a fire, the Depression, and a flood, but Pittsburgh's declining steel industry signaled the end when congregants moved away.

The Pittsburgh Diocese closed St. John's in 1993; the building was de-sanctified, and three years later it became the Church Brew Works.

Owner Sean Casey makes the point that the operation is respectful of the building's history, while successfully restoring it as a vital part of the neighborhood.

The faithful flock here, but now it's for what the restaurant calls its Heavenly Cuisine, which features pierogies, wood-fired (not hell-fired?) pizza, and its other much-better-than-pub-grub dishes. Of course, there's all that awe-inspiring beer.

The Church Brew Works intends to make a believer out of you.

———

Primanti Brothers

(Strip District)
46 18th Street
Pittsburgh, PA 15222
(412) 263-2142
(Various other locations around Pittsburgh and Ft. Lauderdale, Florida.)
www.primantibrothers.com

For a place that sells overstuffed sandwiches, Primanti Brothers is the master of understatement. It bills itself as "Almost Famous," even though its food is required eating in Pittsburgh.

The Cheese Steak (actually a burger) is listed as the "#2 Best Seller," yet #1 is never revealed.

Primanti Brothers knows how to get your attention, especially with its one-of-a-kind recipe. Around here, no one asks if you want fries with your order, because they're included *inside*

your sandwich. Let's make that point again. Along with a heap of grilled meat, coleslaw, and tomatoes, you get a large handful of french fries squished between two slices of Italian bread. The creation easily stands 5 inches tall.

How did it get started? As the story goes, the original Primanti Brothers forgot to buy plates, forks, and knives when they opened their depression-era hole-in-the-wall in Pittsburgh's produce shipping area called the Strip District. So they piled everything onto one sandwich, making it easier for locals to work and eat at the same time. Could be.

In the 'Burgh, Primanti Brothers is as much a part of the local landscape as the Three Rivers. The original Strip District location is open 24/7 and is party headquarters on weekends as well as before and after local sporting events.

We would say the sandwiches are filling, but that would be an understatement.

———

Tessaro's

4601 Liberty Avenue
Pittsburgh, PA 15224
(412) 682-6809

Dominic Piccola is a lifesaver, in more ways than one. On most days, Dominic serves his community as a member of the Pittsburgh Fire Department. But in his spare time, he comes to the rescue of Tessaro's, a popular bar and grill famous for its 8-ounce hamburger, located in Pittsburgh's Bloomfield neighborhood.

Dominic is the restaurant's in-house butcher. Rarely do you find a local joint so committed to hamburgers that it hires a specialist, but at Tessaro's, it was a requirement. For years, the restaurant bought its trademark ground beef from a butcher across the street. But when the shop closed in 1998, customers noticed the difference.

Tessaro's owner Kelly Harrington tried 15 different suppliers, but no place gave him the same quality beef. Then he found Dominic, who had worked at the old butcher shop and knew the proper mix of chuck roast, strip, fillet, and fat.

Now Dominic moonlights at Tessaro's. He comes in early or often late at night, grinding about 900 pounds of beef a week. The fireman is actually on-call at Tessaro's in case of an emergency, like a sudden ground beef shortage. He's also in charge of producing the steaks and pork chops that are nearly as popular.

At Tessaro's, it's truly a case of out of the fire, into the frying pan, or at least onto the grill.

—

Delaware

The Green Room

Hotel du Pont
11th and Market Streets
Wilmington, DE 19801
(302) 594-3100 or (800) 441-9019
www.hoteldupont.com

The tiny state of Delaware is home to more than just your credit card bills, tax-free shopping, and lax incorporation laws. It's also the headquarters of DuPont, the world's largest chemical company. That's a big deal around here. When consumer activist Ralph Nader made national headlines in the 1970s by declaring that DuPont owned Delaware, locals actually celebrated. "Look," they cheered, "we're on the news!"

The company, known for gunpowder, Nylon, Teflon, and Jeff Gordon's NASCAR jumpsuits, opened its namesake hotel in 1913 to offer visiting dignitaries and business leaders a first-class place to stay in Wilmington. Or maybe they just needed *any* place to stay in Wilmington.

The Hotel du Pont has remained one of the most celebrated hotels in the region. Just walking around marveling at the ornate lobby and 700 original paintings—including those from three generations of Wyeths—is time well spent. The breathtaking Gold Ballroom is the hub of Wilmington's social scene. The Green Room restaurant, with its sophisticated French cuisine, has long been known as *the* place for special events, as well as formal everyday dining. Its

enormous Sunday brunch is proof owning a state has its benefits.

Plus, there's no tax on your bill. Take that, Ralph Nader.

—

Maryland

Bertha's

734 South Broadway
Baltimore, MD 21231
(410) 327-5795
www.berthas.com

You know you've seen it somewhere. You'll be driving down the road, anywhere in the country, when a car passes with a green and white bumper sticker bearing the vague message, "Eat Bertha's Mussels."

What's that about? you ask yourself as the car disappears over the horizon.

Bertha's is a funky haunt in Baltimore's Fells Point neighborhood, known for its cobblestone streets and popular nighttime hotspots.

In 1972, Tony and Laura Norris bought what was then a small bar so they could have a place to play their beloved classical music. But the couple soon discovered zoning laws required music joints to serve food, so they started selling mussels. The Norrises claim they had no idea how to run a restaurant, but somehow they managed.

The name of the restaurant comes from a stained-glass window the Norrises found at a flea market that bore the words "Bertha E. Bartholomew." And the bumper sticker was also a spur-of-the-moment inspiration. Tony says he was having beers with friends one night when they came up with the idea. He says he deliberately kept the message brief, with no address or phone number, to make it memorable. The idea clicked, and the bumper sticker is so ubiquitous, there's even one on the South Pole.

People who eat Bertha's mussels remember them even without the souvenir. The plate comes overflowing with nine dipping sauces to choose

photo courtesy of Kathy Silverstein

The message is everywhere. Eat Bertha's Mussels.

from—including a hometown favorite, the capers and garlic sauce. The restaurant sells a ton of mussels a week, but there's a long list of other seafood dishes from which to choose. Afternoon tea has also become a tradition.

A popular pastime at the bar is to cut up the bumper sticker and use the letters to create a new—usually off-color—message. Most that are posted on a wall can't be recorded here, but once again, it makes you think about those three words: "Eat Bertha's Mussels."

Jimmy's Restaurant

801 South Broadway
Baltimore, MD 21231
(410) 327-3273

Jimmy's refuses to put garnish on its meals.

"Nobody eats them," says owner Nick Filipidis. "I'd have a trash can full of garnishes."

He also wouldn't have any room, because the dishes he serves are already loaded with food.

Jimmy's serves up no-frills cheap-eats, Baltimore-style. Located in the heart of eclectic Fells Point, it's a place you'll find the governor, dockworkers, office humps, and doctors from Johns Hopkins. If you want to know what's going on in the city, you go to Jimmy's, especially at breakfast time.

When the old TV series *Homicide* was taping around the corner, its cast would hang out here. Often, they would turn around and shoot a scene inside the restaurant. Jimmy's was a semi-regular on the show.

Fame isn't what makes Jimmy's popular. It's the giant portions of diner-like food, from omelets to burgers and daily specials, too. There's usually a wait for a table, but if you're a regular, your order will be there when you sit down.

Just don't expect any garnish.

Nacho Mama's

2907 O'Donnell Street
Baltimore, MD 21224
(410) 675-0898

Take the hominess of Barry Levinson's *Diner,* put it in the middle of John Waters *Hairspray,* and you start to get the true Baltimore feel for Nacho Mama's. Way past quirky, this is—as the name says—not your mother's Mexican restaurant.

Early flea market is one way to describe the look; another is college dorm room, on a budget. When asked if it's a little cluttered, owner Patrick McCusker says no, "It's a *lot* cluttered."

There's a six-foot Elvis statue outside the front door—sometimes painted in Baltimore Ravens colors. Inside, Christmas decorations are up year 'round. The walls are littered with posters commemorating the Colts, Orioles, and "Natty Boh," a one-time locally brewed beer better known as National Bohemian (longneck bottles sell for just $1.25). The King also makes appearances inside, on artwork as well as in spirit.

Nacho Mama's opened on January 8, 1994. As we all know, it's Elvis's birthday. What's with all the Elvis? Who knows? He just seems to fit. Nacho Mama's is so obsessed with the King, it holds an annual golf outing in his honor. Players dress as the singer, with one person in each foursome coming as Priscilla, Lisa Marie, or any prominent actress in his films. They're allowed to hit off the women's tees.

Certainly, Elvis would enjoy the portion size. Nachos and margaritas are both served in large hubcaps. We said that right—large hubcaps.

Maryland

Owner Patrick "Scunny" McCusker and Marc sampling Nacho Mama's chips and margaritas, served in hubcaps.

photo courtesy of Kathy Silverstein

Maryland

As easygoing as everything is, the place is serious when it comes to food. The most popular dish is the Santa Fe Chicken—chicken breast stuffed with lobster meat, topped with sherry cream sauce. The Ultimate Fajita Thing, as it's billed on the menu, comes stuffed with tenderloin, jumbo shrimp, and portobello mushrooms. Now that's taking care of business in a flash, as Elvis would say.

The cheap eats draw large crowds, and with just eleven tables, the wait can be long. If you're lucky, you'll be able to pull up a chair at one of the small cocktail tables made from upside-down washtubs, order a "Natty Boh," and ponder the scene. As they say around here—in an accent heavy with hard "Os"—this is Bal'mer, hon.

Santa Fe Chicken

Adapted from Nacho Mama's, Baltimore, Maryland

MAKES 4 SERVINGS

4 (10-ounce) boneless chicken breasts, pounded until thin
1 pound ground chorizo sausage
2 cups all-purpose flour
1 cup shortening
2 cups heavy cream
¼ cup sun-dried tomatoes, rehydrated and puréed
2 canned chipotle chiles in adobo sauce (smoked jalapeños), puréed
2 tablespoons chopped garlic
¼ cup grated Parmesan cheese

Preheat the oven to 450°F. Grease a baking pan.

On a floured cutting board, lay out chicken breasts. Place one-fourth of sausage on one side of each breast. Tightly roll breast lengthwise around sausage. Dredge rolled chicken breasts in flour. Heat shortening in a cast-iron skillet or deep sauté pan to 350°F. Brown chicken rolls on all sides (they will only be about half cooked), and cool slightly.

Slice chicken rolls crosswise into about ¼-inch pieces. Place on the prepared pan. Bake for about 15 minutes, or until chicken and sausage are firm to the touch.

For sauce, combine cream, sun-dried tomatoes, chiles, and garlic in a sauté pan. Bring to a boil, and add Parmesan cheese. Simmer sauce, stirring occasionally, until it is reduced by half. Divide sauce onto 4 plates, and arrange chicken over sauce.

CHEF'S NOTE: Dried chipotle chiles can be used. Soak in water for 30 minutes before puréeing.

Sabatino's Italian Restaurant

901 Fawn Street
Baltimore, MD 21202
(410) 727-9414
www.sabatinos.com

Aldo's Ristorante Italiano

306 South High Street
Baltimore, MD 21202
(410) 727-0700
www.aldositaly.com

There are nearly 20 restaurants in Baltimore's 12-block Little Italy, and you won't go wrong at any of them. We spotlight these two because they represent different ends of the dining spectrum.

Sabatino's is classic old-style Italian, famous for its garlicky Bookmaker Salad, homemade pasta, and late hours—it's open until 3 A.M. A large, casual restaurant that begs for red-and-white checkered tablecloths, it's a festive place where you'll find classic Italian dishes done right, and an interesting crowd as the hour grows late.

Just across the street, Aldo's is more upscale and gourmet. It's the perfect place for a special occasion. You'll be impressed by its beautiful Italian villa-like look, which was actually constructed by chef/owner Aldo Vitale himself. Reservations are suggested.

Either way, manga and enjoy. Prego.

Cantler's Riverside Inn

458 Forest Beach Road
Annapolis, MD 21401
(410) 757-1311
www.cantlers.com

In Maryland, people start eating crabs right about the time they're weaned from mother's milk.

You don't grow up around here without knowing how to use a wooden mallet to crack open a freshly steamed, heavily seasoned blue crab right out of the Chesapeake, then pick it apart by hand. You can usually tell a local by the scars on their fingers from the creatures' jagged edges.

The only thing Marylanders like as much as crabs is arguing about which place serves the best. The answer, of course, is Cantler's.

Located on a winding road outside the state capital of Annapolis, Cantler's sits on a tributary of the Chesapeake. The location is not only scenic; it makes it easy for watermen to sail up and sell their catch right out of the Bay. So the stuff is fresh.

Founder Jimmy Cantler was a longtime Bay waterman himself, just like his father and grandfather before him. In fact, many of his 17 siblings are still in the business, so the restaurant has a real "in" when it comes to quality.

When Cantler's opened in 1974, it was little more than a watering hole known for its tough crowd. But it's grown into a family-friendly local institution where people are known to wait hours for a seat. Following longtime state tradition, its picnic tables are covered with brown paper, and the crabs are tossed in the middle. There's a large basin around back where you can wash off afterward.

So grab a mallet and get crackin'.

Maryland

photo courtesy of Jill Littman

Marc, Larry, and Bud crabbing in the Chesapeake for Cantler's.

Chick and Ruth's Delly

165 Main Street
Annapolis, MD 21401
(410) 269-6737
www.chickandruths.com

With his trademark green cap, bowtie, and penchant for magic tricks, you might think Chick and Ruth's owner Ted Levitt is quite a character. But if you spend time with him, you'll discover he's really a *man of character*.

Each weekday morning at 8:30—9:30 on weekends—he asks customers to stand as he leads them in the Pledge of Allegiance. "I guarantee it will get your day off to the right start," he says.

He gladly performs his magic tricks for children—adults, too—usually without being asked. Give him a tip, and he donates the money to cancer research. Same thing with the coins poured into the gum machines in the back of the restaurant. The disease killed his mother. So far, he's contributed hundreds of thousands of dollars.

Chick Levitt and his wife, Ruth, started their delicatessen in 1965 and made it into a landmark in the state capital—known especially for its power lunches. There's a Governor's table in the front, always reserved for the state's highest elected official, past or present. About 40 overstuffed specialty sandwiches on the menu are named for the state and national lawmakers who often eat here. The Middy Burger—with two patties, cheese, and coleslaw—is a favorite among the midshipmen from the nearby Naval Academy. Breakfast is served all day long, and the sundaes are notoriously large.

When Chick passed away in 1995, it was front-page news. Ted, who'd been working here since he was a child, took over and continued the traditions. He still wears a bowtie like his father, because it maintains that mom-and-pop feel. With Annapolis's growth into a tourist and boating destination, Chick and Ruth's is more popular than ever.

It takes more than magic to do that. It takes a man of character.

Ristorante Antipasti

3303 Coastal Highway
Ocean City, MD 21842
(410) 289-4588

Ristorante Fausto's Antipasti

11604 Coastal Highway
Ocean City, MD 21842
(410) 723-3675
www.ristoranteantipasti.com

Tanned and fit, with a hearty Italian accent, owner Fausto DiCarlo makes it a point to greet every guest—especially women. In true European style, he bestows them with a friendly kiss (men receive a firm handshake). He's become famous for it. Women remind him if he forgets. Given the large crowds at his restaurant, this guy could make Richard Dawson blush.

Talented enough to have once been a cooking sensation in Philadelphia, DiCarlo relocated to this vacation playground in 1993. He figured he could work hard in the summer and enjoy golf in the off-season.

He might have a six handicap, but he's busy year 'round. Ristorante Antipasti is a first-class Italian restaurant, but the fact that it's in a resort town best known for chains and all-you-can-eat buffets makes it a true standout.

Fausto's signature dish, Timballo Di Mamma, is made of thin layers of homemade pasta filled with ground veal, tomatoes, and a béchamel sauce. DiCarlo used to call it a "Sunday dish" and offer it as an occasional special, because it required so much work. But it became so popular, he had to add it to the menu. Another mouthwatering specialty is the Garlic Steak, a center-cut fillet covered in Italian herbs and then grilled black. You won't find this anywhere else.

After a decade of success, DiCarlo opened a second Ocean City location in 2003. With his typical style, he scurried between the two restaurants aboard his Italian-made Vespa scooter.

Golf would have to wait. There are guests to be greeted and many kisses to be bestowed.

The Weight-Loss Contest

A few years into the taping of *The Best Of* and we realized there was more of us than before. Eating at all these nice restaurants was having an effect. It wasn't just me; the entire crew was suddenly shopping for Sans-a-Belt pants at the Big and Tall Store. So we decided to hold a weight-loss contest. To make it interesting, we wagered a few bucks.

It was all pretty informal. Our initial weigh-in took place at a Sears store in Portland, Maine. Why there? Because it's the city where we came up with the idea, and no one had a scale. Where better to "test-drive" one than the store where America shops?

Several months and many pounds later, we held our decisive weigh-in on the Boardwalk in Ocean City, Maryland. Why? Because it was the only place we could take off our shirts without getting laughed at—too much. Plus, we couldn't find the local Sears. This time, I brought a scale from home. We're all in television, so we called someone who actually understands math to figure out our weight-loss percentages.

In the end, photographer Larry Deal won, losing about 25 pounds. I was right behind him with about 23 pounds. Audio technician Bud McHugh was out of the running, and producer Jill Littman actually gained weight. It turns out she was pregnant. But we still took her money. Hey, a bet's a bet.

Timballo

ADAPTED FROM THE RISTORANTE ANTIPASTI, OCEAN CITY, MARYLAND

MAKES 12 SERVINGS

Tomato Sauce:
$\frac{1}{4}$ cup finely diced onion
3 tablespoons olive oil
1 (14-ounce) can whole peeled tomatoes
Salt and freshly ground black pepper to taste
6 to 8 leaves fresh basil
1 pound fresh pasta sheets

Bechamel Sauce:
6 cups milk
2 tablespoons butter
2 tablespoons all-purpose flour
$\frac{1}{8}$ teaspoon ground nutmeg
Salt and freshly ground black pepper to taste

2 tablespoons butter
$1\frac{1}{2}$ pounds ground veal
Salt and freshly ground black pepper to taste
$\frac{1}{4}$ teaspoon ground nutmeg
$\frac{1}{2}$ cup (1 stick) butter, melted
2 cups $\frac{1}{4}$-inch diced mozzarella cheese
1 cup grated Parmigiano-Reggiano cheese

To make tomato sauce: Sauté onion in olive oil until brown. Add tomatoes, and bring to a simmer. Crush tomatoes with a fork as they soften. Season with salt and pepper, and add basil. Simmer for about 1 hour.

Cook pasta in boiling, salted water until al dente. Drain, add pasta to a bowl of cold water, and drain again. Lay out pasta on a clean kitchen towel, and dry.

To make béchamel sauce: Bring milk to a simmer in a saucepan over medium heat. Melt butter in a sauté pan over medium heat. Stir flour into butter, and cook, stirring, until bubbly. Whisk in milk, salt, pepper, and nutmeg and simmer, whisking, until slightly thickened, about 2 minutes. Remove from the heat and set aside.

Melt 2 tablespoons butter in a sauté pan over medium heat. Add veal, and cook, stirring to break up meat, until brown and cooked through. Season with salt, pepper, and nutmeg. Drain off excess liquid, and set aside.

Preheat the oven to 375°F.

To assemble: Coat the bottom of a 13x9-inch pan with half of the melted butter. Cover the bottom of the pan with a layer of pasta. Ladle a thin layer of tomato sauce over pasta, and sprinkle with one-fourth of mozzarella cheese. Add another layer of pasta over cheese. Ladle a thin layer of béchamel sauce over pasta. Sprinkle one-fourth of ground veal and one-fourth of the Parmigiano-Reggiano cheese evenly over béchamel sauce. Repeat layering, making 6 pasta layers. Cover the top layer of pasta with remaining mozzarella cheese, veal, Parmigiano-Reggiano cheese, and tomato sauce. Finally, ladle remaining $\frac{1}{4}$ cup melted butter over the top, and cover the pan with aluminum foil.

Bake for about 30 minutes or until bubbly. Let stand for about 10 minutes before serving.

Maryland

District of Columbia

Kinkead's

2000 Pennsylvania Avenue, NW
Washington, DC 20006
(202) 296-7700
www.kinkead.com

In a city known for spin, owner Bob Kinkead is a straight talker. Ask him about the overwhelming success of his best-selling dish, the Pepita Crusted Salmon, and he shares his true feelings.

"And what did this dish build?" he asks, "It built my home in Great Falls, Virginia. And it's a big house. Five thousand square feet, and all paid for with this dish right here."

That's pretty frank. So is his response to people who can't wait to inform him his restaurant is often mentioned in James Patterson's best-selling novels.

"I think I know," Kinkead says, "You're the 400,000th person who's told me today."

Bob Kinkead is crusty but loveable. A beefy guy with a walrus-like mustache, he's often the first person you see as you walk up the stairs to the second-floor main dining room. He's the guy barking orders into a headset, commanding his restaurant's out-in-the-open kitchen.

photo courtesy of Jill Littman

Mr. Silverstein goes to Washington. Taping from atop the Hay Adams Hotel, across from the White House.

Kinkead, who grew up in New England, has been working in restaurants since he was 15. For a while, he tried other careers, including a stint as an insurance salesman. "I hated it," he says with typical candor, "I loathed every minute I was doing it."

Kinkead's gruff charm has made him one of DC's favorite chefs. His stylish restaurant, just four blocks from the White House, is usually filled with the power elite. Reservations are essential, at least a week or two in advance.

The acclaimed menu features seafood. Other than that popular salmon dish, classic entrées include the Black Pepper Crusted Rare Tuna and the Roasted Cod with Crab Imperial.

As for the dish that built his house, Kinkead's recommendation is, as always, blunt. "I've done this at least 250,000 times," he says. "You'll love this dish. I love this dish. I'm sick to death of doing it, but I love it."

———

Café Milano

3251 Prospect Street, NW
Washington, DC 20007
(202) 333-6183
www.cafemilanodc.com

It quietly irks restaurant owners when people suggest their job is simply hosting nightly cocktail parties. And then there's Café Milano owner Franco Nuschese—who really does host a nightly cocktail party—probably the best DC has to offer.

The power hungry, as well as the just-plain hungry, flock to this chic Georgetown hotspot. It's one place where normally buttoned-up Washingtonians cut loose. People-watching here is a contact sport.

Bill Clinton dines at Café Milano, usually in the company of Democratic Party Boss Terry McAuliffe—who claims to pick up the tab. George Clooney makes it a favorite stop. So does Placido Domingo. Looking to see visiting movie stars or network anchors? This is the place. The late King Hussein of Jordan was such a regular, he gifted the restaurant an impressive set of prayer beads. Queen Noor still frequents.

The bulk of the action takes place in the "please, please sit me here" main dining room. By design, it shares space with a large bar. During lunch and dinner, there's nothing to indicate this is anything more than a popular restaurant. But the transformation to cocktail party–central begins as night falls. The crowd grows, the booze flows, and the music gets louder. Soon, everybody is table-hopping, schmoozing, and flirting. On warm nights, it spills out onto the open-air patio. It's all very sexy and European.

Amazingly, Chef Domenico Cornacchia's first-class Italian cuisine isn't overshadowed. Many people come just to eat. Some diners even choose to sit in an upstairs dining room, just this side of Siberia. Lobster and Shrimp Linguine, Veal Milanese, and Portuguese Scorpion Fish in an English Pea Sauce are three favorites.

A key element is owner Nuschese himself, who keeps the glamorous crowd mingling. Not long ago, *GQ* magazine picked him as the "fourth most powerful person in DC you've never heard of." He's the guy movers and shakers want to get in with.

Café Milano is very democratic, so everyone's invited. Even other restaurant owners, who, despite what most people think, don't get out to these kinds of parties much.

———

The Tombs

1226 36th Street, NW
Washington, DC 20007
(202) 337-6668
www.clydes.com

With a name like The Tombs, it makes sense this popular Georgetown pub has strong ties to the movie classic *The Exorcist.*

For one thing, it's right across the street from the infamous "Exorcist Steps," on which a climatic, devil-of-a-fight scene was shot. Thirty years after the film, the location is still a tourist attraction, even though, with 75 steps, it's known as much for exercise as it is for exorcism.

The Tombs founder Richard McCooey was

On the "Exorcist" steps in Georgetown, possessed by the food at the Tombs

also a good friend of William Peter Blatty, the author of both *The Exorcist* book and screenplay. A religious man, McCooey thought the story was too graphic and turned down Blatty's pleas to use The Tombs in the movie. For some reason though, he OK'd its use in the sequel, which nobody saw. Maybe the devil made him do it.

For the most part, The Tombs is a favorite hangout for Georgetown University students and faculty—exactly what McCooey intended when he opened it in 1962. Downstairs from its more formal sister restaurant called 1789, The Tombs offers a relaxed "devil may care" atmosphere, perfect for scarfing down gumbo, fish and chips, or the sinfully good lamb sandwich. *Exorcist* fans should note there is no pea soup on the menu.

The restaurant is so much a part of campus life that it accepts Georgetown's meal program, called Munch Money. Food only—students can't buy booze with it.

The Tombs is sometimes associated with the Brat Pack flick, *St. Elmo's Fire.* It wasn't technically based on the restaurant, but the movie centers on the action at a popular Georgetown student bar. So who's going to argue, other than a devil's advocate?

District of Columbia

The Tombs Gumbo

ADAPTED FROM THE TOMBS, WASHINGTON, DC

MAKES 8 SERVINGS

1 cup vegetable oil
1 cup all-purpose flour
8 celery stalks, chopped
4 onions, chopped
2 green bell peppers, chopped
2 red bell peppers, chopped
4 cloves garlic, minced
2 (15-ounce) cans chicken broth
2 (15-ounce) cans beef broth
2 (28-ounce) cans chopped tomatoes
1 pound fresh or frozen okra, sliced
2 tablespoons hot pepper sauce
5 bay leaves
2 teaspoons ground black pepper
2 teaspoons ground white pepper
2 teaspoons cayenne
2 pounds chicken thigh meat, diced and sautéed
    until brown
1 pound andouille sausage, diced
1 pound (21 to 25 count) shrimp, peeled and
    deveined
4 cups cooked rice

In a large skillet, combine oil and flour. Cook over medium heat, stirring constantly, until dark brown, about 30 minutes. Do not burn (if the roux burns, you will need to start over).

Add celery, onions, red and green bell peppers, and garlic, and cook, stirring constantly, for 10 minutes. Transfer to a large heavy pot, and add chicken broth, beef broth, tomatoes, okra, hot pepper sauce, bay leaves, black pepper, white pepper, cayenne, chicken, and sausage. Simmer for 15 minutes. Add shrimp, and cook for 5 minutes. Remove bay leaves, and serve over rice.

Cakelove

1506 U Street, NW
Washington, DC 20009
(202) 588-7100
www.cakelove.com

Warren Brown had an objection—to his job as a government lawyer. So he called for a recess, taking time off at home to perfect his cake-baking skills. Some time later, he made a motion—to a new career.

Brown's move from torts to tortes culminated with the opening of Cakelove in 2002, his small but successful bakery in DC's up-and-coming U Street corridor. A year later, he opened a coffee house across the street called Lovecafé. His fascinating personal journey was first chronicled in the *Washington Post*, which led to an appearance on *Oprah* and his selection a few years ago as one of *People* magazine's 50 most eligible bachelors—officially making him a stud muffin. Talk about flour power!

All his cakes are made from scratch. Every week he experiments with a new recipe, just to keep things really fresh. Customers fawn over his creations, and—thanks to the publicity—often travel from far away to sample his works. The descriptions of some of his best-sellers are enough to make your mouth water. Susie's A Pink Lady features fresh raspberries between three layers of vanilla butter cake, covered with raspberry purée and butter cream topping. For chocolate lovers, there's the aptly named My Downfall—two layers of vanilla butter cream between three layers of chocolate butter cake glazed with a rich ganache.

The attention hasn't gone to Brown's dreadlock-adorned head. He modestly says he was following his heart and recommends others do the same.

Case closed, in favor of Cakelove.

Sarah's Secret Flat Chocolate Torte

ADAPTED FROM CAKELOVE, WASHINGTON, DC

Ingredients—Melted
10 ounces semisweet chocolate chips
⅓ cup half-and-half
2 tablespoons brandy

Melt above in a double boiler, stir to combine, set aside.

Ingredients—Meringue
7 egg whites
½ cup sugar
¼ cup water

Bring sugar and water to 240°F in heavy bottom pot. With wire whip, whip whites to stiff peak in mixer. Pour syrup over meringue with mixer running. Whip until cool, set aside.

Ingredients—Wet
4 egg yolks
1 vanilla bean
⅓ cup sugar

Ingredients—Dry
1-teaspoon potato starch
1 tablespoon cocoa powder (extra brut preferred, 22% fat)
2 tablespoons flour (all purpose, unbleached)

Whip wet ingredients until you have body; add melted ingredients, add dry ingredients, add one-third meringue, and fold in remaining meringue. Pan into a 10" x 2" bottom-release pan lined with parchment; bake at 325 to 350°F for about 40 minutes. Top will crust, cake will not jiggle, and cake will stick to toothpick skewer when done. Remove and cool completely.

Ingredients—Caramel Crust:
1-cup sliced, almonds (blanched, sliced, and pulsed in processor to large crumbles)
6 tablespoons sugar (melted in copper pot)
3 tablespoons heavy cream in double boiler

Melt sugar in copper pot; slowly drizzle in cream stirring with wooden spoon. Mixture will bubble rapidly—keep stirring. When cream and sugar are combined, pour into processor with blade running. Stop processor when mixture forms a ball.

Using hands, well-dusted with confectioners' sugar, roll into a ball and place between two sheets of dusted parchment paper. Using a gentle motion, roll from the center in a direction away from you until you have a disk about 10 inches in diameter. Be gentle.

Remove one layer of the parchment, invert cake, remove other layer of parchment, place onto cake board, flip over cake, and remove parchment from top of cake. Dust sides with sugar.

The Honor of His Honor

DC Mayor Anthony Williams made an impromptu visit to Cakelove while we were taping. We knew something was up when beefy men wearing sunglasses and dark suits showed up, talking into their sleeves. The mayor, a big fan of Brown's, followed them in to buy cakes for a staff meeting that afternoon.

Being the shy-types we are, we immediately leaked word of the visit to the *Washington Post*. It ran an item the next day in its gossip column, noting that the mayor—well known as a micromanager—actually picked out every treat himself.

Mayor Williams, well aware of Brown's unusual career path, delivered a solid punch line when he said, "I'm very proud that he stopped being an attorney and started doing something useful with his life."

District of Columbia

Old Ebbitt Grill

675 15th Street, NW
Washington, DC 20005
(202) 347-4800
www.clydes.com

The Old Ebbitt Grill is one-stop shopping for all your dining needs.

Looking for a place that's casual and fun? Head to Old Ebbitt. In the mood for something a little more formal? Check out Old Ebbitt. A tourist stops you to ask where to eat? You see where this is going, don't you?

DC's oldest saloon is also its most dependable. A block from the White House, the Old Ebbitt is smack dab in the middle of mover-and-shaker territory. Most nights, the bar is packed with heavy-hitters and the journalists who cover them. The restaurant is so linked to official Washington that it closes for the Presidential Inauguration every four years, mainly because it's on the parade route.

But its convenient location means it's also a perfect refueling stop for tourists, locals showing them around, and just about anyone else who's hungry. The official dress code is "anything goes." It's interesting to watch unsure newcomers peek inside the restaurant, realize they're welcome after scouting the crowd, and break out into a relaxing smile. The Victorian décor is formal enough for dating couples, but just as comfortable for families with children.

The American menu is much the same way. It ranges from its famous chili and hamburgers, to the more expensive—but still reasonable—Jumbo Lump Crab Cakes. The acclaimed raw bar is the best in the region.

The Old Ebbitt has a tradition of hospitality. It started out as a boarding house in 1856, hosting presidents and other famous statesmen. The restaurant has moved several times, settling in its current location in 1983, on the front porch of history, with a welcome mat out to all.

Jumbo Lump Crab Cakes
ADAPTED FROM THE OLD EBBITT GRILL, WASHINGTON, DC

MAKES 4 HUGE CRAB CAKES

1 pound jumbo lump crabmeat
1/3 cup mayonnaise
2 teaspoons Old Bay seasoning
1 tablespoon chopped fresh parsley
1 tablespoon Dijon mustard
1 tablespoon water
4 saltine crackers
Vegetable oil for pan-frying

Pick over crabmeat to remove any shells and cartilage. Mix mayonnaise, Old Bay seasoning, parsley, mustard, and water in a small bowl until smooth. Add mayonnaise mixture to crabmeat, and mix, being careful not to break up the lumps. With your hands, break up the saltines into crumbs, and mix them into crab mixture. Form into patties.

Heat about 1 inch oil in a large skillet over medium heat. Add crab cakes, and pan-fry until golden brown, turning once. Crab cakes can also be broiled.

Zola

800 F Street, NW
Washington, DC 20004
(202) 654-0999
www.zoladc.com

Zola has a secret identity. Known to most in DC for its hip and powerful crowd, it's also believed to have ties to the International Spy Museum next door—a first-of-its-kind attraction dedicated to the history of espionage. It features exhibits on everything from the Trojan Horse to FBI traitor Robert Hanson.

There's no crime in being a museum restaurant—especially for the hordes of customers it provides—but Zola does quite well on its own. Since opening in 2002, it's become one of the hottest restaurants in the sizzling downtown area known as Penn Quarter. Intelligence indicates the restaurant's "straightforward American cuisine" has garnered rave reviews. Locals tend to come more for lunch and dinner than cloak and dagger.

But Zola acknowledges a bond—a subtle bond—to the Spy Museum. The restaurant's name honors a noble figure in the infamous French spy scandal, the Dreyfus Affair. In addition, there are small windows at several tables that let you spy on the kitchen staff. Another portal on the floor allows for reconnaissance into the museum's gift shop. There's a drink called a Spytini and another called the Goldfinger. Don't ask if they're shaken, not stirred. Even without a few stiff ones, many visitors have a hard time maneuvering a revolving *Get Smart*–like wall that doubles as the door to the restrooms.

Is Zola successful because of its see-and-be-seen clientele, or due to its undercover links to the museum? We know, but if we told you we'd have to kill you.

———

Willard InterContinental Hotel

1401 Pennsylvania Avenue, NW
Washington, DC 20004
(202) 628-9100
www.washington.interconti.com

The Willard Hotel is known as the residence of presidents. About the only place you can find more history in Washington, DC is at the Smithsonian.

Located just two blocks from the White House, the Willard has hosted every Commander-in-Chief since 1850. Before his inauguration, President-elect Abraham Lincoln had to be smuggled into the hotel because of assassination threats. Lincoln was so broke he had to wait for his first presidential paycheck to cover the $773 bill.

The Willard was the site of the Peace Convention in 1861, a last-ditch effort to avoid the Civil War. And the same year, Julia Ward Howe wrote "The Battle Hymn of the Republic" while staying at the hotel, inspired by passing troops.

The hotel was considered neutral territory during the war. Northern sympathizers entered through the front doors; Southerners came in the back.

After the war, President Ulysses S. Grant—urged by his wife to enjoy his cigars and brandy outside the White House—would relax in the Willard's lobby. When word got out, and powerful leaders started joining him to press their causes, Grant developed a new term, "lobbyists."

In 1963, Martin Luther King wrote his immortal "I Have a Dream" speech at the Willard. Unfortunately, it's also where J. Edgar Hoover bugged the civil rights leader's room.

Amazingly, the hotel continued its presidential ties even after it closed in 1968, when it housed Richard Nixon's election headquarters.

The building deteriorated for nearly 20 years, and only a court order kept it from being torn down. But new owners and a multimillion-dollar renovation restored its former glory, and the hotel reopened in 1986.

Present-day history makers can often be found in the Round Robin Bar, where it's said the gentle art of conversation is alive and well.

Down the hall, the stately Willard Room restaurant serves regional American and European cuisine. Its formal setting is often referred to as "timeless," an appropriate word in a hotel where history resides.

photo courtesy of Kathy Silverstein

The Willard Hotel, Washington DC

District of Columbia

District of Columbia

Miniature Pumpkins Filled with Maine Lobster Ragout

ADAPTED FROM THE WILLARD ROOM, WILLARD INTERCONTINENTAL HOTEL, WASHINGTON, DC

MAKES 4 SERVINGS

4 miniature pumpkins
Salt and freshly ground black pepper to taste
1 medium butternut squash, peeled
1 quart whole milk
4 ounces green peas
Meat of 2 (2-pound) lobsters or 12 ounces lobster
*   meat*
1 bay leaf, if needed
Pinch juniper berries, if needed
4 tablespoons butter
1 tablespoon chopped shallot
4 teaspoons brandy
1 tablespoon chopped fresh parsley

Cook whole pumpkins in boiling water for about 6 minutes. Drain and cool. Cut off pumpkins tops, about 2 inches below the stems, in a straight line. Remove the seeds, and reserve the tops. Season with salt and pepper.

Cut squash into chunks. Place in a large saucepan with milk. Simmer until very tender, about 20 minutes. Season with salt and pepper. Add squash mixture to a blender, in batches, and blend until smooth. Strain through a fine sieve to make a smooth sauce.

Cook peas in boiling salted water for 3 minutes. Cool peas in ice water to stop cooking.

If using live lobsters: Cook lobsters in boiling water with a pinch of salt, 1 bay leaf, and pinch juniper berries for 8 minutes for a 2-pound lobster. Drain and cool in ice water. Remove meat from the shells.

Melt butter in a sauté pan. Add shallot, and sauté until softened. Add lobster meat and peas, and cook for 1 minute. Stir in brandy, and scrape up any browned bits. Cook for 1 minute. Reserve ½ cup squash sauce. Mix remaining sauce into lobster mixture. Stir in almost all of the parsley.

To serve: Warm pumpkins for 2 minutes in a 350°F oven. Set pumpkins on individual plates, lids off. Fill each pumpkin with some lobster ragout. Drizzle reserved sauce around the base of each pumpkin. Sprinkle remaining parsley on top of ragout. Replace pumpkin tops.

The South

Virginia, West Virginia, Kentucky, Tennessee, North Carolina, South Carolina, Georgia, Florida, Alabama, Mississippi, Louisiana, Arkansas

WHEN WE VISIT cities in the South, locals often ask uncomfortably, "How many meat and threes are you going to do?" They're always relieved to learn we don't limit our profiles to those beloved old-style restaurants that serve an entrée and three vegetables. Make no mistake, we love Mom-and-Pop places, but these days the term can refer just as easily to Mirror, a fantastic cutting-edge restaurant in Nashville owned by a young husband-and-wife team.

Still, you're going to find the classics in this chapter, legendary places like Uglesich's in New Orleans, Lynn's Paradise Café in Louisville, and O'Steen's in St. Augustine. And the South certainly has its share of mouth-watering barbeque joints, including Daddy D'z in Atlanta and a bodacious place called Bubbalou's in the Orlando area. But you're also going to meet world-class chefs, such as Atlanta's Guenter Seeger and Frank Stitt at Bottega in Birmingham. Just for fun, you don't want to miss the antics at the best airport restaurant in the country, the Conch Flyer in Key West. In short, it's meat and threes, and a whole lot more below the Mason-Dixon line.

Virginia

The Inn at Little Washington

Middle and Main Streets
Washington, VA 22747
(540) 675-3800

Critics consistently name The Inn at Little Washington one of the best restaurants in the country. An hour and change outside Washington DC, it's in a small town with no traffic lights, at the foot of the Blue Ridge Mountains. And possibly the only reason most people come here is for this renowned country inn.

But be sure you bring a credit card . . . or two.

A seven-course prix fixe dinner costs more than $150 on weekends, about $30 less during the week. That's without tax, tip, and drinks. Most of the wine in the 40-page wine list tops $100. If you booked a room because of the lengthy drive back, expect to spend hundreds more. Add a $300 surcharge if you're lucky enough to sit at the chef's table in the kitchen.

But for all you get, there is something here you won't find anyplace else. This is the only establishment in the country to receive the Mobil Five-Star award for both its restaurant and its inn—not just once, but for more than a decade and a half. It also received the AAA Five-Diamond Award.

The success story dates to 1978, when chef and co-owner Patrick O'Connell and his partner Reinhardt Lynch opened a small restaurant in an old auto repair shop. A glowing newspaper review weeks later prompted the muckety-mucks from the Big Washington to rush down the road. They soon demanded a place to stay.

These days, reservations are difficult to get, and for major holidays, they are only available if you call during certain times of the day. It's easier to win the lottery—and requires less wear and tear on your phone's redial button.

From humble beginnings to a world-class establishment, success hasn't changed O'Connell. He still frets over every customer. At these prices, he better.

The Globe and Laurel

18418 Jefferson Davis Highway (Route 1)
Triangle, VA 22172
(703) 221-5763

When they talk about service at The Globe and Laurel, it isn't always about the waiter's job performance. Likewise, when they talk about orders, it's not just about the food you select from the menu.

The Globe and Laurel is geared toward Marines. Located barely a klick from the gates of Marine Corps Base Quantico, it's a place to fill up on both patriotism and provisions—make that food if you're a civilian, and you're more than welcome here, too. Families also. That's an order, son.

Major Rick Spooner, USMC (Ret.), served his country for 30 years, in World War II, Korea, and Vietnam, and was awarded four Purple Hearts. He continued serving the Corps—food and drink—by opening the restaurant with his wife, Gloria, in 1968.

Inside, the small pub is like a Marine museum—call it Planet USMC. The walls and ceilings are covered with military memorabilia and artifacts, including a small display about a soldier who—while barely clinging to life during combat in World War II—was saved by the enemy. It takes others to tell you the man was Spooner himself.

In an amazing demonstration of respect and tradition, there are also police patches from departments worldwide. The custom started years ago when officers training at the FBI Academy on Quantico asked if they could post their decals. There are now too many to count. In a sense, it's a symbol of those in uniform sharing an unspoken bond.

Given the clientele, the menu is primarily steak, steak, steak, and prime rib. What do you expect Marines and lawmen to eat?

Spooner, who greets diners with a hearty "Welcome aboard," says the restaurant is a place where Marines can come, swap sea stories, and feel at home with the family. "And believe me," he says, "The Marines Corps is a family."

As for those not in the Corps, he says, "We hope they learn something about us by coming here. We like to share in our values, deep love of Corps, and country."

Semper Fi.

———

The Trellis

403 Duke of Gloucester Street
Williamsburg, VA 23185
(757) 229-8610
www.thetrellis.com

Marcel Desaulniers tells a fascinating tidbit about the public's appetite for all things chocolate. A fan once admitted to him that although she doesn't bake, she bought his *Desserts to Die For* and *Death by Chocolate* cookbooks—because she enjoys reading the recipes before going to bed. Apparently, they're just dreamy.

Desaulniers's over-the-top concoctions are just as decadent as anything you'll find in a Jackie Collins novel—with a lot more calories. His towering multi-layer cakes are loaded with ingredients 3 out of 4 dentists prefer when they're eyeing a new Mercedes. As an author, a television show host, and the owner of The Trellis, Desaulniers has been stimulating chocoholics' passions since 1980.

Incredibly in-shape, the former Marine jokes that his all-chocolate diet keeps him thin. Actually, he's a long-time runner who recently switched to walking. He also gets a workout overseeing all the baking, pastry preparation, and ice-cream making at his restaurant.

While famous for its desserts, The Trellis is about a lot more. In fact, it's a bit of a find in an historic town filled with tourists and people dressed in period costumes. Refined but relaxed, it features top-notch regional fare changed on a seasonal basis.

Desaulniers usually waits until you're savoring the last bite of dessert before he shares another important tidbit. It seems each slice of cake weighs a pound and contains more than 1,300 calories, which means you just enjoyed quite an indulgence.

Suddenly, reading his cookbooks seems to make a whole lot of sense.

———

Steinhilber's Thalia Acres Inn

653 Thalia Road
Virginia Beach, VA 23452
(757) 340-1156

Tell someone in Virginia Beach that you're going to Steinhilber's, and they'll remind you to have the shrimp.

Generations have been raised on it, and it's not unusual for diners to order the shrimp both for their appetizer and their meal.

Technically, the dish, called Original Steiny's Fantail Fried Shrimp, has been on the menu since the restaurant opened in 1939. Remarkably large and plump, the shrimp are lightly breaded and served with a Thousand Island–like sauce.

Steinhilber's is Virginia's oldest family-owned restaurant, built on a vast piece of land that was once home to a country club. Founder Robert "Steiny" Steinhilber was known as a tireless worker who did things his own way. He sometimes closed during the busy summer vacation season. But he wasn't catering to tourists anyway. The restaurant is 10 miles from the beach, in a remote neighborhood just this side of the middle of nowhere.

Steiny's children, Jeanne and Steve, now own the restaurant, live on the property, and make sure traditions are followed. Waiters wear white jackets, and customers are treated to large doses of Southern hospitality. Jeanne sometimes surprises regulars with salads made with vegetables from her garden next door to the restaurant. Otherwise, the menu is loaded with the kind of decadently prepared seafood dishes that were popular in the days before this kind of food became known as "fattening."

And of course, there's the shrimp. You really should have some.

———

Virginia

The Jewish Mother

3108 Pacific Avenue
Virginia Beach, VA 23451
(757) 422-5430

With a name that virtually shouts, "Eat! It's good for you. You're too skinny," you don't have to be Freud to understand why the "JewMo" has been the mother of all hangouts in this friendly resort town since 1975. Its menu is enormous, with a combination of guilty pleasures mixed with just plain guilt. It's kind of Jewish-ish. Naturally, there are overstuffed sandwiches and other traditional deli items; but there are also less conventional dishes, with fun names like Pita and the Wolf, a hot-spiced beef sandwich on a pita with Swiss and ranch dressing. Oy!

This place knows how to carry out a theme. One whole wall is dedicated to paintings of mothers of all backgrounds. So the message to "Sit up straight! Clean your plate!" applies to everyone.

When Mom's not looking, the deli converts into a music bar at night. Some of the most famous bands in the country—and others only a mother could love—have played the stage here.

And never once did anyone yell, "Turn down that music. You can burst an eardrum!" But "Go ahead, have some more. What could it hurt?" That's another story. *Nu?*

Duck-In

Shore Drive at the Lynnhaven Inlet Bridge
3324 Shore Drive
Virginia Beach, VA 23451
(757) 481-0201
www.duck-in.com

With the warm breezes off the Chesapeake and cool drinks on the gazebo, the Duck-In is the perfect beach hangout. About 300,000 people a year stop by, or as they prefer to say around here, Duck-In.

In fact, that's exactly what the name means. Originally an around-the-clock bait stand that became a restaurant in 1952, the place was so small people had to bend over to enter. Or duck to get in.

Since then, there have been seven expansions. It's enormous. No one has to duck anymore. With its size, the restaurant is able to successfully maintain dual identities as both a family-friendly dining establishment offering boatloads of fresh seafood, as well as beach party central. The happenings start every Friday afternoon in season and just seem to keep going.

Pocahontas Pancake and Waffle Shoppe

3420 Atlantic Avenue
Virginia Beach, VA 23451
(757) 428-6352
www.pocahontaspancakes.com

The real Pocahontas twice saved a struggling Virginia colony, married a tobacco tycoon, and inspired a beloved Disney character. By comparison, this place has it easy. All it has to do is churn out a bunch of pancakes and waffles to the vacationing masses and their kids.

On second thought . . .

Let's face it, how much do you really expect from a breakfast-only joint in a family-friendly beach town? Whatever it is, Pocahontas somehow makes it happen. You can find the place just by looking for the extra long lines outside. That's an impressive accomplishment in a town loaded with places to grab an inexpensive bite.

The large buttermilk pancakes are extra fluffy, and the Belgian Waffles have just the right crunch. Smear on the margarine, drench it in syrup, and top everything with whipped cream, and you're talking about a seriously good way to start your vacation day.

This Pocahontas won't be saving any towns from extinction, but it does a pretty good job of conquering tourists' hunger.

Virginia

West Virginia

The Greenbrier

300 West Main Street
White Sulphur Springs, WV 24986
(304) 536-1110 or (800) 624-6070
www.greenbrier.com

It's been described as "The White House on steroids," and when you pull up to The Greenbrier, past the guarded gate, you'll see why. It's that awesome.

Since the early nineteenth century, visitors have flocked to this magnificent place in White Sulphur Springs to be pampered, to relax, to unwind—and in the case of Jill and her crew, get lost. It's massive. With 650,000 square feet inside and 6,500 acres of breathtaking beauty outside, it's easy to get turned around. It's also easy to see why this has long been a place for the country's elite to socialize.

Don't expect a contemporary or modern interior. Much of it is downright old-fashioned with its signature rhododendron wallpaper adorning the walls in the guest corridors. Likewise, the main lobby hasn't changed much since the 1940s. That feel of yesteryear is part of the charm here.

Originally, the upper crust was drawn to the area for the sulphur water, thought to have healing capabilities. Even though research has proved no such powers exist, people still come to The Greenbrier to soak it up.

The spa is pretty incredible. Jill had The Greenbrier Signature Treatment. Although she's a spa addict, this was a new one. First, you soak in your own private sulphur bath. Keep in mind it has a distinct, shall we say, odor. Next, Nurse Ratchet hoses you down with a device that feels like a water cannon. (Modesty must go out the window.) You feel like you're the rubber ducky that people try and shoot to win a prize at the carnival. They call this part of the treatment a Scotch spray, and it's said to break up toxins and cellular blockage in the body. It certainly breaks up something. It's hard, but it does feel good. The treatment ends with a mini-massage that will put you in a state of euphoria.

Fast Facts About The Greenbrier

The Greenbrier is such an extraordinary place that it deserves a "trivia" box all its own.

- James Monroe was the first U.S. president to visit the resort. So far, 26 U.S. presidents have been guests here.
- For the first 2 years of the Civil War, the resort served as both military headquarters and a hospital for the Confederate troops.
- From 1867 to 1869, it was the summer home of General Robert E. Lee.
- In September 1942, The Greenbrier was purchased by the U.S. Army and converted into a 2,000-bed hospital for 4 years.
- After World War II, it was completely refurbished and redecorated. The designer, Dorothy Draper, used more than 30 miles of carpeting, 4,500 yards of fabric, 40,000 gallons of paint, and 15,000 rolls of wallpaper to complete the project.

When you check into The Greenbrier, your breakfast and dinner are included in the rate. But just so you don't get tired of going to the same restaurant time and again, they have a handful from which to choose—plus room service. Just about any food you crave is on one of the menus, and the man who makes it is a master. Executive Chef Peter Timmins is one of the few certified Master Chefs in the country, so you're in good hands.

But there is much more to The Greenbrier than meets the eye. Beneath the massive structure is a 112,000-square-foot bunker, built for Congress when the Cold War was getting hot. It was made to be a safe haven for them, where they could convene and run the country in case of a nuclear attack. Amazingly, it remained top secret for 30 years until 1992 when the *Washington Post* broke the story. Because it was no longer secret, its purpose was defeated.

Now it's open for tours, and believe us when we say it's absolutely mind-boggling. They had several hundred phone lines in the bunker, and the walls were strong enough to withstand a nuclear blast 20 to 30 miles away. They were capable of providing water, food, and power for up to 1,000 people for a 45- to 60-day period.

Ironically, The Greenbrier was built to celebrate the height of civilized living, yet here was a facility built in preparation for the end of it.

Enough to give you the chills, huh?

———

Smokey's on the Gorge/Class VI River Runners

Ames Heights Road
Lansing, WV 25862
(304) 574-0704 or (800) 252-7784
www.800classvi.com

There are certain questions you expect to hear in a restaurant, such as "What's tonight's special?" or "May I have another cocktail?" Then there's Smokey's on the Gorge in Lansing, West Virginia, where a common pre-dinner query is, "Is there any chance I'll die before my meal?"

Okay, some context: Smokey's is the restaurant affiliated with Class VI River Runners. Class VI refers to the most challenging classification of white-water river rapids. Most people who attempt to go rafting on rapids like these are either thrill-seekers or lunatics. Or as in Jill's case, both.

Here's how it works: The rafting trips begin at the same spot as the restaurant. Call it base camp. You meet here at the crack of dawn and get on a bus. They take you to the mouth of the river, give you instructions on how *not* to kill yourself, and off you go with a boat full of people and a colorful character as your guide.

The rapids here are some of the best in the world. Think of it like coming face to face with a tidal wave. You scream, you laugh, you're terrified, and you're elated—all at once. After finishing an extremely tough rapid, everyone high-fives. You'll feel like you're bonded to these people for life.

Six hours later, after nonstop, hair-raising, thrill-seeking excitement, you end up back at the restaurant, tuckered and famished (you do stop for lunch on the river, but with all the energy you expend trying to stay afloat, your calories are eaten right up).

Base camp has showers, dressing rooms, etc. for you to clean up. Dinner is an incredible buffet of fresh salads, fish, meats, and desserts—a first-rate operation with an incredible view. Anyone can eat here; you don't have to raft first. But for those who do, as you sip your wine and look down 1,000 feet to the river where you were struggling just hours ago, you'll smile knowing you survived—and thrived—in the mouth of the monster.

Think of it as an extreme case of surf and turf.

Arctic Char

ADAPTED FROM SMOKEY'S ON THE GORGE, LANSING, WEST VIRGINIA

MAKES 4 SERVINGS

4 (6- to 8-ounce) fillets Arctic char or salmon
¼ teaspoon salt
¼ teaspoon celery salt
½ teaspoon ground thyme
Freshly ground black pepper to taste

Sauce:
1 cup pinot noir
3 sprigs fresh thyme
1 tablespoon honey
Salt and freshly ground pepper to taste

Preheat a grill or broiler. Season fish with salt, celery salt, thyme, and pepper. Grill for 3 to 5 minutes, or until fish begins to flake.

To make sauce: Boil wine until reduced by half. Add thyme and honey, and boil, stirring, for 1 minute. Season with salt and pepper, and stir to dissolve the honey. Remove thyme sprigs, and serve sauce with fish.

———

West Virginia

The General Lewis Inn

301 East Washington Street
Lewisburg, WV 24901
(304) 645-2600 or (800) 628-4454
www.generallewisinn.com

This is an inn full of egos. What do you expect when you have two celebrities roaming the property? The first star has been featured in numerous national publications and now on *The Best Of*. She even has her own e-mail address and business card. The second star came onboard a bit later and got her 15 seconds of fame also on *The Best Of*.

Come to The General Lewis Inn, and you can meet them both, but there's no guarantee they'll sign an autograph. Butterscotch the cat (known as General Butterscotch) and Harley the dog don't have time for that. They're too busy claiming their territory and resting up for the day—or night—ahead.

The inn is a blend of the old and new. The two stars are the newest addition to this property that dates back to 1834. Even with nine lives, General Butterscotch can't possibly compete with that.

Originally a family home, the property was purchased by Randolph Hock and Mary Noel, who opened it up to guests in 1929. It has been continuously family-run ever since.

The 25 guest rooms are cozy and rustic, much like the rest of the home. Parts of it seem more like a museum, with many antiques and relics, some dating back to the 1700s, when the pioneers came to the Allegheny Mountains looking to settle down.

Their food is first rate. Breakfast is delicious—consisting of hearty fried potatoes, country ham, and omelets. For lunch and dinner you'll find Southern specialties like fried chicken, mountain trout, duck, and steak.

If you have any leftovers, you probably know who—or what—would be willing to eat them.

———

The Moxie

Routes 3 and 219 (corner of North and Main Street)
Union, WV 24983
(304) 772-3068

It was the late summer of 1992 in the Adirondacks when Reed and Amy Van Den Berghe's tomatoes froze solid. In frustration, Reed said, he threw them at the barn. They were so hard they bounced off. That's when the couple made a goal: to move somewhere warm enough where they could grow a peach.

Amy grew up in Morgantown, so they decided to give the state of West Virginia a try. Reed, a Culinary Institute of America–trained chef, got a job at the world-class Greenbrier Resort. Life was good—good enough that they grew peaches. There was one problem, though. The couple bought a house in Union—because the price was right—but the commute for Reed was 45 minutes each way on winding country roads.

When the local clothing store went out of business, leaving a beautiful, historic building vacant, Reed decided it was time for a change.

Keep in mind this area doesn't even have a fast-food restaurant. There's no stoplight or interstate in the entire county. Opening a fine dining restaurant in a town of about 500 people seemed like a bit of a stretch. But he thought if he built it, they would come.

Come they did. Since The Moxie opened in 1997, this town hasn't been the same. Seems that Reed's food is so good, people don't mind driving an hour or more to eat here. On some weekends you'll even find the place packed. Granted, they run the restaurant on a skeleton staff and barely manage to eke out a profit, but at least they're managing.

He named the restaurant after the famed soda that dates back to 1884. It became largely popular during World War II when Ted Williams endorsed it, proclaiming, "What this country needs now is a little moxie." *Moxie* means "courage and perseverance."

That's exactly what it took for Reed and Amy to take this risk. Here's toasting them (with Moxie) that it continues to pay off.

Kentucky

Lynn's Paradise Café

984 Barret Avenue
Louisville, KY 40204
(502) 583-3447
www.lynnsparadisecafe.com

You can think of it a few different ways—an art project gone awry, Peewee's Little Playhouse, an adult romper room or *Alice in Wonderland* on steroids. Any way you slice and dice it, this place is a hoot, as is the owner, Lynn Winter. She has way too much energy for one person, but all who know her can't imagine her any other way.

We think she's a creative genius of sorts. Looking at all the kitsch in her place, you'll know why. On one wall you'll find a huge mural she made out of corncobs; on another, a diorama of the restaurant made out of plastic animals; and hanging from the ceiling, you'll see a big pair of pants she made out of tea bags (that she actually wore when posing for *Bon Appétit* magazine). Out front you'll see a zoo of colorful concrete animals, large enough to sit on, as well as a larger-than-life eight-foot coffee pot with cups. In a nutshell, this is Lynn's version of paradise—crazy, creative, and definitely over the top.

You never know who or what you'll find here on any given day. Lamps from her Ugly Lamp Contest; a group of nuns sitting next to a group of punk teenagers; people milling about in pajamas on her New Year's Day Pajama Party Brunch. Then there's her World of Swirl shop next door. Here you'll find purses made out of recycled juice containers, magic pants that magically fit any shape or size (Lynn's own design),

photo courtesy of Lynn Winter

Jill chows down on breakfast at Lynn's Paradise Café.

and quirky, creative store clerks just waiting for you to play dress up.

One thing you can always be certain of: Great food. Breakfast is the specialty and is served all day. Her Kentucky Corncakes, loaded with country ham, then smothered with sorghum butter, will send your taste buds spinning, as will the Cinnamon Swirl Sourdough French Toast topped with Bourbon Vanilla Custard. It might not be the white sandy beaches of the Mediterranean, but for many in this town, including Lynn, it's their own version of paradise found.

Hot Brown Frittata

ADAPTED FROM LYNN'S PARADISE CAFÉ, LOUISVILLE, KENTUCKY

MAKES 8 SERVINGS

12 large eggs
3 cups heavy cream
1 teaspoon salt
½ teaspoon ground black pepper
4 ounces bacon, cooked crisp and chopped, 1 tablespoon bacon fat reserved
1½ cups (about 6 ounces) diced yellow onions
1 (14½-ounce) can diced tomatoes, drained
1 pound diced roasted turkey
1 pound mixed cheddar and Monterey Jack cheese, shredded

Three-Cheese Mornay Sauce:

3½ cups half-and-half
2 tablespoons butter
¼ cup diced onion
2 tablespoons all-purpose flour
⅓ cup grated Parmesan cheese
⅓ cup shredded Monterey Jack cheese
⅓ cup shredded Swiss cheese
2 teaspoons Worcestershire sauce
¼ teaspoon salt
¼ teaspoon hot pepper sauce

Preheat the oven to 350°F. Spray a 13x9-inch pan with nonstick spray.

In a large bowl, whisk together eggs, cream, salt, and pepper. Set aside. In a small sauté pan, heat reserved bacon fat over medium heat. Add onions, and sauté until softened. Stir in tomatoes and bacon, and set aside.

Layer turkey in the bottom of the prepared pan, and sprinkle with bacon and onion mixture. Sprinkle with 1 pound cheddar and Monterey Jack cheeses. Pour egg mixture over all, and press lightly to be sure all ingredients are coated with the mixture.

Bake for 45 to 55 minutes or until puffed and set. After about 30 minutes, rotate and cover with aluminum foil if the top looks brown.

Meanwhile, make sauce: Heat half-and-half in a small saucepan to 160°F; set aside. Melt butter in a medium, heavy saucepan over medium heat. Add onion, and sauté until translucent. Add flour, and whisk to combine. Cook, whisking, for about 1 minute. Pour half-and-half into flour mixture, whisking constantly. Reduce the heat, and bring to a simmer. Cook, whisking, until the mixture begins to thicken. Add Parmesan cheese, Monterey Jack cheese, Swiss cheese, Worcestershire sauce, salt, and hot pepper sauce, and stir well. Taste and adjust seasonings.

Cut frittata into 8 large pieces, and cover with sauce.

Vincenzo's

150 South Fifth Street
Louisville, KY 40202
(502) 580-1350
www.vincenzosdining.biz

Many restaurants in Kentucky are known for carrying on the hospitality and traditions of the Old South, but in this case, the hospitality and traditions came all the way from southern Italy. Brothers Vincenzo and Agostino Gabriele began their culinary journey in the Sicilian city of Palermo, where they grew up listening to their merchant marine father tell tales of faraway places. They said that whenever their dad would talk about America and cities like Boston, Philadelphia, and New York, his eyes would shine.

The brothers were lured to this land of opportunity in 1969. They landed in St. Louis,

A Close Encounter?

When we sat down to eat some of the southern specialties like fried chicken and country ham at Old Talbott Tavern, there was an odd occurrence. With our camera rolling, our ghost hunter, Patti Starr, and I talked about the food and the history of the place. Our photographer Dan didn't notice until months later when he was dubbing the tape, but when he looked closely, he could see a small flying object that passed through the wall behind us. We made it part of the piece and even tried to enlarge it in the editing process, but never did confirm what it was. You can guess what Patti said. She was positive it was a piece of the paranormal, perhaps a hungry ghost, propelling itself from the next dimension into our dinner. I, on the other hand, am not sure, but one thing is certain: I wasn't sharing my supper with the supernatural.

Missouri, and once here, they each went in different directions. Agostino honed his culinary skills at his uncle's restaurant while Vincenzo rose through the ranks managing fine Italian restaurants, first in St. Louis, then in Louisville. In 1986, he decided to go out on his own and open a restaurant. All he needed was a great chef. He knew the perfect person to call . . .

The brothers work together in perfect harmony. While Agostino cooks up wonderful Italian delights from all regions of Italy, Vincenzo runs the front of the house and makes each guest feel at home. After all, when their father would recount his travels on the Seven Seas, he was fond of saying, "The most important thing about hospitality is sincerity." You can bet he'd be proud of his sons now.

———

Old Talbott Tavern

107 West Stephen Foster Road
Bardstown, KY 40004
(502) 348-3494
www.talbotts.com

It's been a rest stop for weary travelers since the late 1700s—a place that's played host to such guests as Abraham Lincoln, Daniel Boone, and even Jesse James. But this inn isn't known for all its distinguished guests. It's known more for the ones who never left.

There are numerous reports of guests waking up in the night to see a lady in a white gown hovering over their bed and of diners watching their forks move on their own. The haunted happenings even inspired one employee, Patti Starr, to trade in her timecard for a taste of the supernatural. She's now a professional "ghost hunter" and conducts tours here for those in search of some mysterious friends. That's where we caught up with her for our *Best Of Food Frights* show . . . .

Patti showed up equipped like MacGyver, complete with a tape recorder, a digital camera, an EMF to measure electrical energy, an Electro Sensor to measure invisible radio waves, and dousing rods to detect the presence of ghosts. Jill and crew set off on a mission with her to "see the light."

Keep in mind that Patti's not a ghost buster. She's not asking any of these spirits to leave. In fact, she considers them part of the family here. When ghost hunting, she believes you need to talk to them, which is why, if you saw the piece, she is repeatedly calling out in her high-pitched voice, "Hi guys, it's me, Patti," adding, "I just want to show everyone that you do exist. If you're here, send me a signal." With that she starts snapping pictures like crazy, then squeals in delight when the digital image is displayed. She points animatedly at the image, and explains to Jill that all those round circles that you *used* to think were lens flares are actually orbs. If that's true, then Jill's gang was surrounded by a bunch of curious ghosts who took particular interest in cameraman Dan Dwyer. Jill admits she did feel a chill in the air, but then again, she's always cold.

Kentucky

Kentucky

Beaumont Inn

638 Beaumont Inn Drive
Harrodsburg, KY 40330
(859) 734-3381 or (800) 352-3992
www.beaumontinn.com

At the Beaumont Inn, down here in bourbon and Bluegrass Country, you'll find a special style of Southern hospitality. The owners like to say it's a place to rest, relax, and relive the quiet elegance of yesteryear.

The historic inn dates back to 1845, when it was an exclusive school for young ladies. At one point it became a woman's college, which is where Annie Bell entered the picture. She went to school and even taught here. When it closed in 1916, Annie saw an opportunity and, in 1917, after she married and became Annie Goddard, she and her husband bought it. They weren't sure what to do with it, until they realized there was a steady stream of women coming back to show their daughters their alma mater. That's when Annie realized it would make a wonderful inn where these women could visit and reminisce.

In 1919, they opened up, and now, more than 80 years later, the same family still runs it. At the helm today is Chuck Dedman, the great-grandson of Annie. He and his wife, Helen, serve up a healthy helping of hospitality along with Kentucky favorites like their famous country ham. It's said to be the best in the state; some would argue the best in the South.

What puts theirs in a class above the rest is what happens in the ham house behind the inn. Chuck says that for a country ham to be classified as such, it has to age for at least 180 days. Here they age it anywhere from 18 to 27 months. He says that, like fine wine, it only improves with time. The sharp, salty taste is wonderful.

Save room for their General Robert E. Lee Cake. This orange-lemon cake is as big as the legend for which it was named. It was reportedly the general's favorite sweet treat, although here, they could feed an entire army with the amount they make.

Tennessee

Hog Heaven

115 27th Avenue North
Nashville, TN 37203
(615) 329-1234
www.hogheavenbbq.com

When you eat barbeque at this joint, you're not in pig purgatory, but rather hog heaven because what they smoke up is simply divine.

Owners Andy and Katy Garner took over this old cement building (complete with a screened-in porch) in 1989. The joint originally opened in 1986 and went through three owners in three years. Maybe it's "four times a charm," because after the Garner's appeared on the scene, Hog Heaven began to heat up.

Andy and Katy both worked other jobs in the beginning to stay afloat, and when Katy gave birth to their first child, Richard, he was kept in a cardboard box near the front window so Mom could still wait on customers and keep an eye on the little guy. Talk about being born into barbeque!

Although there isn't a lot in the way of indoor seating, the restaurant is right in Centennial Park, where there's seating for 3,000 in the great outdoors. All their meats are smoked on site, and all their sauces are mixed up here, too. While they have their delicious tomato-vinegar-based sauce, they also have a unique tangy, mayonnaise-based white sauce that customers drool over.

Jill with crew and the Hog Heaven family.

After 14 years, the Garners say they aren't going anywhere, which means this slice of heaven will continue to bestow its blessings upon those who love their barbeque.

———

Mirror

2317 12th Avenue South
Nashville, TN 37204
(615) 383-8330
www.eatdrinkreflect.com

Marc really likes what he sees in the Mirror. That's no surprise to those who know him, but in this case he's referring to a funky restaurant that rates as one of the most exciting and unexpected discoveries by *The Best Of*.

It's Miami-meets-Music City in a setting that almost didn't happen. Husband and wife chef/owners Michael DeGregory and Colleen Belloise-DeGregory came to Nashville from South Florida in 1997 with plans to open a restaurant. But their investors bailed at the last second, leaving the couple working odd jobs to make ends meet. They were literally packing to move to New York when a new investor stepped in.

There were other obstacles to overcome. Nashville is more comfortable with chain restaurants, so the couple had to keep their cutting-edge concepts a bit dull. Then there was the neighborhood, called 12 South. It was just so-so when they moved in, but it's since started to come alive. Nothing stopped these two, but then again, they're used to hard work. Michael hates using ingredients out of a can, so he makes everything on his own, including ketchup. The Duck Confit, with sweet potato gnocchi and seared duck breast, is his start to finish, as is Hawaiian Pork with sweet potato mash. Over at the bar, Colleen ferments her own Limoncello—just because.

When Marc and his crew first tasted the food here, they were blown away. At first, they questioned whether they were just really famished after a hard day's work. But when the plates were passed around and the initial hunger faded, the flavor still stood out. In short, Mirror left a lasting image.

Seared Scallop Ceviche

ADAPTED FROM MIRROR,
MEMPHIS, TENNESSEE

MAKES 6 SERVINGS

1 pound (20 to 30) scallops, muscles removed
1 tablespoon kosher salt
1 tablespoon ground black pepper
¼ cup extra-virgin olive oil, plus extra for cooking
1 red bell pepper, cut into small dice
1 jalapeño chile, seeded and finely diced
6 scallions (white and green parts), finely diced
6 tablespoons fresh lime juice
¼ cup fresh lemon juice
1 bunch fresh cilantro

Season scallops with salt and pepper, and toss with olive oil. Let stand for about 5 minutes.

Meanwhile, heat a flat-bottomed sauté pan over medium-high heat. Add about ½ tablespoon oil, and heat until it smokes lightly.

Add scallops, in small batches; do not crowd or scallops will boil instead of sauté. Sauté scallops until golden on each side, turning. Transfer to a baking pan to cool. Repeat until all scallops are done. You might have to clean the pan out in between as not to burn any pieces that have stuck to the bottom.

When scallops are cool, slice into quarters and toss in a bowl with red bell peppers, jalapeño, scallions, lime juice, lemon juice, and cilantro. Cover and refrigerate for 2 hours, stirring every 30 minutes. Adjust seasoning if needed, and serve in a nice martini glass.

Loveless Motel and Café

8400 Highway 100
Nashville, TN 37221
(615) 646-9700
www.lovelesscafe.com

After a half-century of old-fashioned Southern charm, the Loveless Café has entered the new millennium—or at least the 1990s. Either way, it's changed. The restaurant best known as a mandatory stop for locals, tourists, and road-weary country singers was recently taken over by

Tennessee

a new owner, who realized the Loveless needed a little TLC.

Named for its original owners Lon and Annie Loveless, the café is a Nashville landmark, famous for its aging neon sign, hams, jams, fried chicken, and biscuits. This place is so Southern it even has redeye gravy on the menu. Made from ham drippings, water, and coffee—for color—it's a side dish for dipping. Locals grew up on it, but Northerners may find it an acquired taste.

Thanks to countless articles and TV appearances, the Loveless became a legend. But its buildings were showing their age. In 2003, Tomkats Catering Company—best known as a caterer on movie sets—became only the fourth owners in the company's history. Tomkats immediately started updating the structures and the menu. More grilled items were added, as were desserts and a smokehouse. Over in the little-used motel area—space was made for an art gallery and a shop to rent bicycles, motorcycles, and kayaks. The idea is to give guests more to do while they wait for one of the always hard-to-get tables.

Purists will argue the Loveless has lost something, while others will say it's about time.

Of course, they'll be arguing about it over chicken, biscuits, and maybe even a little redeye gravy.

Potato Cakes

ADAPTED FROM LOVELESS CAFÉ, NASHVILLE, TENNESSEE

YIELD: 8 SERVINGS

4 cups mashed potatoes (better to use day-old mashed potatoes)
½ cup chopped onions
1 egg
¼ cup flour

Mix together potatoes, onions, egg, and flour. Use an ice-cream scoop to form patties and drop on an oiled grill or iron skillet. Cook until 1 side browns. Then flip it over and press down on patty. Cook other side until it browns. Cook on each side for 5 to 6 minutes.

Fat Mo's Burgers
13 locations throughout Tennessee
www.fatmos.com

You have to love a guy who calls himself "Fat." But more important, you have to respect "Fat Mo" Mohammed Karimy's pursuit of the American Dream. He grew up in Iran and escaped the regime of Ayatollah Khomeini to become Nashville's burger mogul. He now owns 13 Fat Mo's, which makes him both fat and happy.

Fat Mo's success comes from offering the largest burgers in Tennessee. The Super Deluxe—with three patties and all the toppings—weighs in at a remarkable 28 ounces. There are also single and double burgers for those with more modest appetites, but even those are impressive. The company's slogan is "Burgers like they were before fast food." Waiting in line at the drive-thru clarifies the catchphrase. Everything is made to order, so the process isn't exactly hurried.

Fat Mo says that when he was little Mo, he would often eat eight Big Mac–size burgers at a time—and still be hungry. All he ever dreamed about was opening a place where he could serve burgers that would satisfy his appetite. Judging from his physique and his success, Fat Mo got his wish.

Merridee's Breadbasket
110 Fourth Avenue South
Franklin, TN 37064
(615) 790-3755
www.merridees.com

It seemed a simple enough plan. Jim and Marilyn Kreider, a couple from Pennsylvania, went down to Nashville for a visit. Jim wanted to make contacts for his song-writing career and just in case they decided to move south, they hooked up with a realtor to see the area.

They ended up in the historic, charming town of Franklin, where they lunched at Merridee's Breadbasket. Later, when remarking on how good the food was, the realtor, who happened to be a childhood friend of Merridee McCray, told them that the woman was dying of cancer. She went on to say Merridee was hoping and praying someone would take over the bakery and carry on her legacy.

Jim and Marilyn had long debated the idea of owning a baking business and thought perhaps fate was at play. They decided to meet Merridee and her husband, Tom. When they sat and talked with them, the women realized they shared similar backgrounds: Both grew up on dairy farms and lived the "farm life" that often revolves around hard work, family, and good home cooking; both also had a family tradition of baking bread every Saturday for the week ahead. At the end of their conversation, Merridee told the Kreider's that God had answered her prayers. She said she felt so blessed that he had brought them all the way from Pennsylvania to carry on the bakery.

Call it divine intervention, but Jim and Marilyn were so touched by her and her faith, they decided to let destiny lead the way. In the following months, arrangements were made for them to buy the bakery. Shortly after Merridee passed away in 1994, the Kreiders found themselves packing up and moving south.

They didn't change much about the place, except for expanding the menu a bit and offering a few of Marilyn's family recipes. Everything is still made from scratch, the old-fashioned way. You won't find pre-made mixes in this bakery . . . just bags of flour, flats of eggs, and cases of real creamery butter. It takes a lot of loving care to transform these staples into the delicious pies, cookies, and breads you will find on their shelves every day. It's a place that feels like home and smells even better.

Molasses Sugar Cookies

ADAPTED FROM MERRIDEE'S BREADBASKET, FRANKLIN, TENNESSEE

MAKES 3 TO 4 DOZEN COOKIES

¾ cup combination of half shortening and half butter, melted
1 cup sugar, plus ¼ cup for rolling

¼ cup sorghum syrup (do not use molasses)
1 egg
2 cups all-purpose flour
1 teaspoon baking soda
½ teaspoon ground cloves
½ teaspoon ground ginger
1 teaspoon ground cinnamon
½ teaspoon salt

Grease a large baking sheet.

Combine shortening mixture, 1 cup sugar, sorghum, and egg in a large bowl. Beat well. Sift together flour, baking soda, cloves, ginger, cinnamon, and salt, and add all at once to egg mixture. Mix until well blended. Cover and refrigerate for at least 1 hour.

Preheat the oven to 375°F.

Form dough into 1-inch balls, roll in ¼ cup sugar, and place on a baking sheet, leaving room for the cookies to spread. Bake for 8 to 10 minutes. Cool on a wire rack.

NOTE FROM MARILYN KREIDER: During our second Christmas here in Tennessee, I was making my Grandma Hostetter's molasses cookies at home for a cookie bake-off with friends, only to discover that her recipe and Merridee's recipe were exactly the same!

Miss Mary Bobo's Boarding House

925 Main Street
Lynchburg, TN 37352
(931) 759-7394
www.jackdaniels.com (click on recipes)

The requirements for eating here: Reserve early, come on time, bring your appetite, and leave the diet at home.

Welcome to Miss Mary Bobo's Boarding House in Lynchburg, Tennessee, population 550. In this tiny town, you'll always know when it's lunchtime. Listen for the bell and look to the big white house, where you'll see hordes of people—all of whom planned ahead—streaming in. It can take two weeks to two months to get a reservation here!

Tennessee

Once in the door, expect a family-style feast complete with a hostess full of hospitality. Each table seats about 12 to 14 people along with the hostess, who is there to eat with you and to be sure those bowls and platters of fried chicken, country fried steak, fried okra, and collard greens are kept full.

Miss Mary Bobo started this Tennessee tradition back in 1908. Every day she offered country cooking to her boarders and locals. After she passed away in 1983, the Jack Daniel's Distillery bought it and hired Lynne Tolley (Jack Daniel's great-grandniece) as the proprietress.

There is usually one daily dish that is cooked with some Jack Daniel's Whiskey in it. Even though their county is dry, legally they're allowed to cook with it; they just can't sell it. The other ingredient you'll find in most of their food is lard; thus our advice to leave the diet at home. After all, lard never seemed to hurt Miss Mary. She lived to be 101.

Tennessee

Traditional Southern Fried Chicken

ADAPTED FROM MISS MARY BOBO'S BOARDING HOUSE, LYNCHBURG, TENNESSE

MAKES 4 TO 5 SERVINGS

1 (2- to 2½-pound) chicken
2 eggs
1 cup milk
1½ teaspoons salt
1 teaspoon ground black pepper
1½ cups self-rising flour
3 cups lard

Cut chicken into serving pieces. In a shallow bowl, beat eggs and then stir in milk, salt, and pepper. Soak chicken in milk mixture for 5 to 10 minutes. Roll chicken in flour, being sure to completely cover each piece. Set aside to dry.

In a large cast-iron skillet, melt lard over medium heat. When fat is very hot, add thighs and legs, and cook for several minutes. Add the other pieces, being careful not to overcrowd the skillet. Cook until chicken is golden brown on one side, about 5 minutes.

Turn and brown on the other side. Reduce the heat to medium-low. Cover the pan, and cook for 15 minutes. Turn the pieces, cover, and cook for 15 minutes longer. Uncover for the last 5 to 10 minutes so crust will be crisp.

Corky's Ribs and Bar-B-Q

5259 Poplar Avenue
Memphis, TN 38119
(901) 685-9744

1740 North Germantown Parkway
Cordova, TN 38018
(901) 737-1988

743 Poplar Avenue
Collierville, TN 38017
(901) 405-4999
www.corkysbbq.com

Corky's is no-frills but big business. It's a one-time East Memphis rib joint that's grown into a conglomerate, without losing its touch.

In 1984, Don Pelts opened a 1950s-style barbeque restaurant in a building where a similar concept had just failed. Only he did things differently, the biggest improvement being the addition of a drive-thru window. It was a novel idea back then for a place offering casual dining, and it was only the beginning. His son Barry joined the business in 1990, and the two went whole hog into the big time. Early on, father and son realized the value of Memphis-based Federal Express, making it possible to overnight orders anywhere. If the fax machine increased business, the Internet made it go hog wild.

At the same time, the company expanded through catering, concessions, and televised shopping channels. It has a frozen food line available in more than 1,000 supermarkets. Through franchising, the Corky's name has expanded to 11 states in the South and Midwest. "We don't wait for customers to come to us," says Barry. "We take barbeque to where they are."

Although the business has grown, the core products—ribs and pork shoulders—have never varied. The meat is cooked long and slow over hickory chips. In Memphis, it's normally served dry—meaning covered in a spicy seasoning that includes onion powder, paprika, cayenne, and garlic salt. But because this is Corky's, you can also order it wet, with plenty of tangy barbeque sauces to choose from. The selection keeps the customers happy and gives the company more products to sell. Because at Corky's, the emphasis is on both the inc. and the oink.

———

North Carolina

Biltmore Estate

One North Pack Square
Asheville, NC 28801
(828) 225-1333 or (800) 624-1575
www.biltmore.com

Can you imagine having a 175,000-square-foot house? How about 34 master bedrooms, 43 bathrooms, and 65 fireplaces? Hard to comprehend, right? Not if you were George Vanderbilt

photo courtesy of Jodi Langer

Photographer Dan Dwyer shoots Jill doing a standup in front of the magnificent Biltmore Estate.

back in 1895. It was on Christmas Eve of that year that he opened his newly completed "home" to Asheville's high society. It's been an awe-inspiring sight to see ever since. In brief, this incredible castle is at the heart of any trip to the Asheville area.

The estate is open year 'round for tours, as are their four restaurants, ice-cream parlor, and bake shop, all scattered around the property.

The holidays are one of the most "wonderful times of the year" at Biltmore, which is when Jill and crew shot at the Stable Café for *The Best Of Holiday Hot Spots*. The estate has the menu books the Vanderbilts used on Christmas Day 1904, and at the Stable Café they've devised a similar menu during the holidays in the restaurant. Obviously they've elevated it to twenty-first-century standards, like with the rotisserie duck—slow cooked in an oven rather than over an open flame.

If you have time and can afford it, stay in the recently built AAA Four-Diamond Inn. It's lovely and offers breathtaking views of the area. Plus, with 8,000 acres of forests, farmlands, and rivers, you'll never be at a loss for what to do.

———

The Market Place

20 Wall Street
Asheville, NC 28801
(828) 252-4162
www.marketplace-restaurant.com

Chef Mark Rosenstein likes to think of himself as a pioneer of sorts. He opened his first restaurant in rural North Carolina when he was just 19. It was just a seasonal business, and although it did extremely well, he wanted a year-round place to make his edible art.

Not to be deterred, less than 10 years later, at the age of 27, he moved to Asheville and began trailblazing in this sleepy southern town. In 1979, despite the fact that the downtown area was "dead" as he describes it, he opened up The Market Place. Rundown, vacant vintage buildings surrounded him. He didn't care. He had a vision.

Over the years, other businesses followed his lead—restaurants, coffee shops, boutique clothing and gift stores. Nearly 25 years later, his vision is a reality. Mark is credited with helping to revitalize this now-thriving hot spot.

Sleek and contemporary in design, The Market Place boasts an award-winning menu and wine list, not to mention an owner who is dedicated to a "fresh" approach in cooking. Almost all his ingredients are seasonally picked and locally grown. When he's not at his restaurant, you're likely to find him shopping at the local farmer's market and chatting with vendors. As he likes to say, "It's not what you cook, but how you cook it." This pioneer is proof his theory works.

Apple Upside-Down Cake

ADAPTED FROM THE MARKET PLACE, ASHEVILLE, NORTH CAROLINA

MAKES 1 CAKE

2 cups all-purpose flour
2 teaspoons baking powder
2 cups sugar
2 eggs
6 tablespoons butter, melted
1 teaspoon vanilla extract
1 cup water
6 large tart apples, peeled, cored, and cut into about ¼-inch cubes
Apple slices, for garnish
1 cup heavy cream lightly whipped with 1 tablespoon sugar

Preheat the oven to 375°F. To make batter, combine flour, baking powder, and 1 cup sugar in a large bowl; set aside. In another bowl, lightly beat eggs. Add eggs, butter, and vanilla to dry ingredients, and mix well.

Combine water and remaining 1 cup sugar in a heavy saucepan over high heat. Be sure any sugar grains sticking to the sides are washed down, as they will cause the mixture to recrystallize. Boil the mixture until water has evaporated and sugar begins to change from white to light tan in color; swirl the pan gently as sugar cooks. Be careful; the pan is very hot at this stage. If you splatter sugar, it will stick and burn. Cook, swirling, until sugar is a deep auburn color.

Working quickly, pour caramelized sugar into a 4-cup baking mold, coating the inside completely, and arrange a layer of apples on the bottom of the mold. (This layer will later be the top of the cake.) Mix together remaining apples with batter, and press into the mold, packing gently.

Place the mold in a baking pan that's at least two-thirds as deep as the mold. Pour enough hot water into the baking pan to come halfway up the mold. Bake for 1 hour, or until a bamboo skewer inserted into cake comes out clean. If cake adheres to the skewer, continue baking, checking every 5 minutes or so.

Allow finished cake to cool for 30 minutes, then unmold unto a serving plate. Garnish with apple slices, and serve warm with the lightly whipped cream.

CHEF'S NOTE: To clean hard caramel from the pan in which you cooked it, fill the pan with hot water and bring the water to a boil.

The Grove Park Inn Resort and Spa

290 Macon Avenue
Asheville, NC 28804
(828) 252-2711 or (800) 438-5800
www.groveparkinn.com

Some of the resorts we cover are high on atmosphere and food but low on substance and story. It's difficult at times to find a mega-resort where the chefs have dynamic personalities, the history of the place is interesting, and the food is top-notch. We found all that and a 40,000-square-foot spa at this place—which is where Jill and crew were lounging every chance they could get.

The inn was the brainchild of St. Louis pharmaceutical magnate Edwin Wiley (E.W.) Grove, who came to the Asheville area initially at the advice of his doctor. He felt the mountain air helped his chronic case of hiccups as well as his insomnia. He fell in love with his surroundings and bought hundreds of acres of land north of town where the resort is now located. Nowadays it is still a spectacular retreat nestled

Jill toasting to the fun bunch of chefs at the Grove Park Inn.

in a woodsy area with a breathtaking view of the Blue Ridge Mountains.

When it comes to cooking, there are never too many chefs in these kitchens (note: plural *kitchens*—they have seven of them in this enormous place). This was one of our more entertaining cooking segments. The chefs at this resort are far from stodgy. They're a hoot. They know how to have fun, and it translated on camera.

Aaron Morgan describes himself as "A fat little boy whose mother never bought him sweets." He says he learned to bake out of necessity. He's done that and baked himself right up to the title of Executive Pastry Chef—and recently lost 50 pounds while at it.

Besides making hundreds of sweet treats for the resort, Aaron also judges the annual Gingerbread House Competition held here every November, attracting hundreds of entries.

The resort's Executive Chef David Rowland is far from the stereotypical uptight corporate guy. As he whipped up his pumpkin ravioli specialty that he serves every Thanksgiving in the Blue Ridge Dining Room, he had champagne waiting in the wings for us, which we sipped as the sauce simmered.

Grove Park is a far cry from an impersonal mega-resort. The standard rooms are pretty basic, but you can't beat the view, the setting, the award-winning golf course, and the spa.

After spending a few days here, you'll understand why, when it was built in 1913, it was hailed as the "Finest resort hotel in the world." It was called a place "Built not for the present alone, but for ages to come." Today, we call that a AAA Four-Diamond Award, which the Grove Park has earned 11 years in a row. Enough said.

Cranberry-Pumpkin Bread Pudding

ADAPTED FROM THE GROVE PARK INN RESORT AND SPA, ASHEVILLE, NORTH CAROLINA

MAKES 6 TO 8 SERVINGS

4 cups milk
1 cup sugar
8 eggs
½ tablespoon vanilla extract
1 tablespoon ground cinnamon
1 teaspoon ground cloves
1 teaspoon ground nutmeg
1 (16-ounce) can pumpkin pie filling
Bread cubes (biscuits or croissants are best)
1 cup fresh cranberries

Preheat the oven to 350°F. Butter a 13x9-inch baking dish.

Beat milk, sugar, eggs, vanilla, cinnamon, cloves, nutmeg, and pie filling in a large bowl until combined; set aside. Use enough bread cubes to fill the prepared baking dish. Sprinkle cranberries over bread cubes. Pour egg mixture over bread cubes, being sure all cubes are submerged. Push down on cubes if necessary.

Bake for about 1 hour, or until pudding is set. Serve warm.

North Carolina

North Carolina

Stone-Ground Grits and Shrimps

ADAPTED FROM THE GROVE PARK INN RESORT AND
SPA, ASHEVILLE, NORTH CAROLINA

MAKES 4 SERVINGS

Grits:

2 cups whole milk
2 cups water
1 cup stone-ground grits
1 teaspoon salt
4 tablespoons unsalted butter
1 cup heavy cream
2 teaspoons freshly ground black pepper

Shrimp:

2 tablespoons vegetable oil
1½ pounds (21 to 25 count) shrimp, peeled and
    deveined
3 shallots, chopped
1 clove garlic, chopped
1 cup strong brewed coffee
¼ teaspoon dried thyme
½ teaspoon brown sugar
Salt and freshly ground black pepper to taste
2 tablespoons butter, cut into pieces

To make grits: Bring milk and water to boil in a
heavy saucepan over medium heat. Stir in grits and
salt. Reduce the heat to low, and simmer, stirring
occasionally, for 30 minutes. Add butter, cream, and
pepper, and simmer for 5 minutes. Keep warm in a
double boiler.

Meanwhile, to prepare shrimp: Heat oil in a large
skillet over medium-high heat. Add shrimp and shallots, and sauté for about 3 minutes. Add garlic, and
sauté for 1 minute. Add coffee, thyme, and sugar;
bring to a boil. Season with salt and pepper. Remove
from the heat, and add butter, a little at a time, stirring until melted. Serve over grits.

Lake Lure Tours

118 Proctor Road
Lake Lure, NC 28746
(828) 625-1373 or (877) FUN-4-ALL (877-386-4255)
www.lakelure.com

Just about 30 minutes away from Asheville,
North Carolina, is a place that's been luring in
fun-seekers for nearly a century. Picturesque
Lake Lure and the town that surrounds it are
nestled deep in the heart of the Blue Ridge
Mountains and is a nice day trip if you have the
time.

We shot here for *The Best Of Fun Foods* in
October, and although the town was still bustling,
it was apparently much less frenetic than in the
height of summer. You might want to take note
because we can't imagine how crowded it must
be during peak tourist times. You'd probably be
hard-pressed to find a parking spot or even find
room to maneuver the narrow sidewalks.

Our first stop in this charming town was
Laura's House (390 Main Street, 828-625-
9125) to try the Mud Pies. These no-bake cookies made with chocolate, peanut butter, and oat-
meal are extremely tasty and easy to take with
you—you might want to load up. They also have
a full-service restaurant that serves up regional
specialties.

Next we hit **Kristi's Cinnamon Rolls** (374
Main Street, 828-625-8123). As the name suggests, they sell—well, cinnamon buns. They
have this bun thing down, because if you come
at lunch, you can get the hot dog cooked inside
a delicious homemade bun (don't worry, no cinnamon on this one).

At **John Bull's Trading Company** (414
Main Street, 828-625-9005), you can sink your
teeth into fudge flavors like Pumpkin and
Jamaican Rum—all homemade, of course.

We ended our shoot with Lake Lure Tours.
They take you on and around the lake and tell
you the history of the area. It only lasts about an
hour, and you'll see some beautiful scenery and
also (drum roll please), the location where the
film *Dirty Dancing* was shot. They even give you
a piece of wood from Johnny's cabin. What you
do with it, we're not sure.

At the end of the day, if you're up for it, hike up to Chimney Rock. At the top of this rock face you'll get an incredible view of the area and work off all those calories you racked up.

———

Caro-Mi Dining Room

3231 U.S. Highway 176
Tryon, NC 28782
(828) 859-5200

At Caro-Mi Jill might have found the most over-looked star chef yet in Preston Vernon. With his big toothy smile, long black hair, and gentle demeanor, he doesn't offer up the bam of other star chefs. But sometimes slow and steady wins the race, and when it comes to his slow country cooking, this guy takes the cake—or fried chicken and country ham, as the case may be.

Caro-Mi, named after the original owner's love of both the Carolinas and Miami, opened in 1945 a few miles down the road. Business was okay, but not great, so in the 1950s, they moved to the current spot. They also hired a new dishwasher, who really put the place on the map. Huh?

You see, Preston started in 1959 washing dishes. A week later, when the chef quit, Preston got his big break. He tried his hand at cooking, and the place hasn't been the same since. In fact, when current owners Charles and Annette Stafford decided to buy Caro-Mi in 1990, they made sure Preston was worked into the deal.

The guy can cook. Every day he's at the helm keeping this ship cruising along. His co-workers, customers, and the owners alike revere him. On any given night you'll find long lines out the door waiting to bite into his southern specialties.

Take note: If you like to drink while you dine, pick up your own beer or wine on the way. No alcohol is sold here—it's a dry county. If you like ham, try theirs. They age it out back and it almost tastes like Italian proscuitto—it's that good.

There's nothing fancy about Caro-Mi; it's a rustic place in a wonderful rural setting. The menu is small—only about seven items each night. But if you're looking for a bit of "country bam" on your plate, then this is the place to come.

South Carolina

Jestine's Kitchen

251 Meeting Street
Charleston, SC 29401
(843) 722-7224

Even though Jestine Matthews lived to be 112, Dana Berlin Strange's fear was that no one would remember her or know what an impact she had made in this world. That's why she opened Jestine's Kitchen—to honor a woman she felt was like a mother to her.

Dana's grandparents, who owned a dry goods store, told Jestine that if she helped raise their child, they would take care of her the rest of her life. Not only did Jestine raise Dana's mom, Shera Lee, she also helped raise Dana and her siblings.

One of Shera Lee's distinct memories was of a time when she was 6 years old. She and Jestine got on a bus and the driver told them they couldn't sit together. (This was back in the late 1930s when segregation was still very much a part of the South.) Shera Lee threw a fit and planted herself on the bus floor until the driver allowed them to sit together. From that time on, whenever these two got on the bus, a form of desegregation took place. In that sense, Shera Lee was way ahead of her time.

Jestine not only ran the household, but also helped with the cooking. Although she had made southern food all her life, the challenge came in making it work for a Kosher Jewish household. She learned to make gefilte fish and matzo ball soup, as well as southern staples like red rice and okra gumbo—only without using pork.

For Dana, the turning point to open a restaurant came in 1996, when Jestine, at 110, became ill. Dana says she panicked and felt she needed to do something to pay homage to Jestine. Here you can find many of Jestine's specialties, including that red rice and okra gumbo—without the pork. They also offer regular items like collard greens and green beans cooked with bacon. Perhaps their most famous item is dessert: the Coca Cola Cake. The recipe dates back to World

War II, when people couldn't get sugar. To sweeten their cakes, they'd make a Coca Cola glaze, poke holes in the cake, and let the icing work its sweet magic through.

Luckily for these southerners, there is no shortage of sugar now, or they might be in trouble when it comes to "sweet tea." At Jestine's, they call this quintessential southern drink "table wine." Put it this way: There's enough sugar in there to keep you buzzing for a week.

When you walk in the door, look for the plaque on the wall. It's a tribute to Jestine and her lifelong devotion to one family that inspired a restaurant. Dana says she must be smiling, never knowing that all those years she made fried chicken, meatloaf, and gumbo that her specialties might appear on places like Food Network or in a book like this one. We're happy to help carry on her story.

Robert's

182 East Bay Street
Charleston, SC 29401
(843) 577-7565 or (866) 341-3663
www.robertsofcharleston.com

Every night is a celebration here with chef and owner Robert Dickson singing and sautéing. It's not unusual for him to make his debut into the dining room carrying plates of food, while belting out the chorus from *Oliver,* "Food Glorious Food." This melodious chef brings down the house and brings it to life with Broadway renditions ranging from *My Fair Lady* to *Oklahoma*.

In addition to song, each night he serves up a prix fixe menu with Roasted Chateaubriand taking center stage as the main course (fish is also an option). Robert's menu is classical French, and the setting is classic romance. Tables fairly close to one another make it an intimate space. So unless you want to talk to your neighbors, you'll have to snuggle up, whisper, and perhaps even smooch. Hey, people don't call dining here "romance at Robert's" for nothing.

Louis's at Pawleys and The Fish Camp Bar

Hammock Shop Village
10880 Ocean Highway (U.S. Highway 17)
Pawleys Island, SC 29585
(843) 237-8757
www.louisatpawleys.com

Show business has always been in Louis Osteen's blood. After all, he was born into a family of theater owners. But the show he puts on in South Carolina's lowcountry isn't on stage, but rather, in your stomach. This guy can cook—so well you'll find yourself dreaming of his famous crab cakes and fish dishes long after you leave his restaurant. Not bad considering he went to the school of hot stoves and hard knocks.

Louis originally set up shop in Charleston, which is where Jill and crew shot for *The Best Of New Trends*, showcasing Louis's lowcountry cooking techniques. He has since closed that restaurant and opened the current one on Pawleys Island—a quiet, oceanfront community that boasts of being the state's oldest family vacation resort.

To understand lowcountry cuisine, you have to look at South Carolina's geography. In the lower part of the state, where the river meets the ocean, the ground actually slants down lower and the water from the river runs slower. When it meets the ocean tides, it takes on a deep, dark, shiny black appearance and is an ideal spot to harvest fresh fish. In fact, in the inlets and estuaries around the area, you'll find an abundance of shellfish such as clams, oysters, and muscles. Louis is largely credited with using nature's bounty to make his cuisine, thus putting lowcountry cooking on the nation's culinary map.

McClellanville Lump Crab Cakes with Whole-Grain Mustard Sauce

ADAPTED FROM LOUIS'S AT PAWLEYS, PAWLEYS ISLAND, SOUTH CAROLINA

MAKES 12 (2-OUNCE) APPETIZER-SIZE CRAB CAKES OR 6 (4-OUNCE) DINNER-SIZE CRAB CAKES; ¾ CUP SAUCE

Crab Cakes:

1 cup best-quality mayonnaise
1 large egg white
¼ teaspoon cayenne
¼ teaspoon seafood seasoning, such as Old Bay
¼ teaspoon dry mustard, such as Colman's English mustard
2 tablespoons fresh lemon juice
3 tablespoons extra-fine cracker meal
1 pound lump crabmeat, gently picked over to remove any shell without breaking up the big pieces of crab, or ¾ pound crabmeat and ¼ pound lobster meat
1½ cups breadcrumbs, made in a food processor from fresh grocery-store white bread, crusts removed

Whole-Grain Mustard Sauce:

¼ cup dry white wine
2 tablespoons brandy
1 cup heavy cream
¼ cup whole-grain Dijon mustard
1-2 tablespoons fresh lemon juice or juice of ½ lemon
¼ teaspoon salt
Scant ¼ teaspoon freshly ground black pepper
¼ cup peanut oil
2 tablespoons unsalted butter

To make crab cakes: Whisk mayonnaise and egg white together in a small bowl until well blended. Add cayenne, seafood seasoning, dry mustard, lemon juice, and cracker meal. Whisk until well blended. Carefully fold in crabmeat.

Divide mixture into 12 equal parts of 2 ounces each, or 6 equal parts of 4 ounces each, and gently pat each portion into the round shape of crab cakes.

Gently coat cakes with the breadcrumbs. Place on a platter lined with waxed paper, cover with plastic wrap, and refrigerate for at least 1 hour or until ready to cook. Do not hold for more than 4 hours.

To make sauce: Combine wine and brandy in a small nonreactive saucepan. Boil over medium-high heat until only about 1 tablespoon liquid remains. Whisk in cream. Reduce the heat to medium, and briskly simmer until the mixture thickens slightly, 6 to 8 minutes.

Stir in mustard and bring the mixture back to just a simmer. *Do not boil it.* Add lemon juice, salt, and pepper. Keep sauce warm (on the back of the stove or over barely simmering water in the top of a double boiler) until ready to serve.

When ready to serve, heat oil and butter in a heavy sauté pan over medium-high heat. Sauté 4-ounce crab cakes for 1 minute 45 seconds on each side, turning once. Sauté 2-ounce crab cakes for 1 minute 15 seconds on each side, turning once. Crab cakes will be nicely browned on the outside but still very creamy and moist on the inside. When cooked, drain cakes briefly on paper towels. Serve immediately with mustard sauce or keep warm in a 200°F oven for up to 15 minutes. If crab cakes stay in the oven any longer, they will dry out.

CHEF'S NOTES: Be careful not to boil this sauce once you add the mustard or it will become bitter. If you want a more assertive sauce, use as much as ⅓ cup mustard.

South Carolina

Georgia

Georgia

Seeger's

111 West Paces Ferry Road
Atlanta, GA 30305
(404) 846-9779
www.seegers.com

Words that describe this restaurant: *Expensive. A Mobile Five-Star. Sleek. Contemporary.*

Words that describe executive chef and owner Guenter Seeger: *Bold. Tough. Disciplined. a Perfectionist.*

You would never use the words *warm and fuzzy* and *Guenter Seeger* in the same sentence. Nevertheless, this German-born restaurateur is one of Atlanta's most celebrated chefs. Meeting him is like meeting a drill sergeant (minus whistle and crew cut) who seeks perfection in every aspect of his restaurant. Critics describe his personality in early years as volatile and temperamental. However, after he became a father, many saw a softer side emerge.

He told Jill when shooting here for *The Best Of Top Tables* that to be the best, you have to start with the best. Whether it's the best ingredients, the best linens, or the best sous chefs, Seeger strives to control all components of his place. He does it like the master he is.

He doesn't like to characterize his cuisine (and believe us, this isn't a man you want to question), but we were able to gather up a few adjectives to describe it: *Elegant. Sophisticated. Intensely pure.*

His menu is strictly prix fixe. A five-course meal will run you around $69, not including wine. If that's not enough to please your palate, you can upgrade to the Chef's Menu, which includes eight courses, for $85.

No doubt about it, the man can cook. Whether or not you like his style, he'll leave a lasting impression on your palate.

Note: You can also visit a second Seeger's in South Carolina, where you'll find a Southern-inspired prix fixe menu. (**Seeger's at The Willcox,** 100 Colleton Avenue, SW, Aiken, SC 29801, 803-648-1898, www.thewillcox.com)

Bacchanalia

1198 Howell Mill Road
Atlanta, GA 30318
(404) 365-0410
www.starprovisions.com

Bacchus is the Greek and Roman god of wine and revelry, and Bacchanalia refers to a feast that was held in his honor. In Atlanta, Bacchanalia refers to one heckuva good restaurant. Give it a try, and you just might think you've experienced something godly.

The restaurant is the brainchild of Anne Quatrano and Clifford Harrison, who are rapidly becoming the stuff of legends around here. They're both chefs, they own restaurants together, and they're married. This dynamic cooking duo stormed onto Atlanta's dining scene in 1993, and the city hasn't been the same since.

The two met in culinary school in San Francisco in the late 1980s. They moved to New York, where they worked at top restaurants before moving to Atlanta to restore an old property that was in Anne's family. They turned their patch of land outside the city into an incredible farm, complete with pigs, horses, cows, goats, chickens, cats, and dogs.

Their Jersey cow provides milk to make their cheese and butter. They also grow a lot of their own produce on the property. It all comes together on the table at Bacchanalia, which has been rated by Zagat's as the city's top restaurant seven years in a row.

Adjacent to their restaurant is their store, Star Provisions—basically an upscale gourmet grocery. Here they sell hard-to-find foods like truffles and foie gras, so you can attempt to re-create your favorite menu items at home. However, we think you'll be hard-pressed to make the magic that these two create on your plate. We suggest planning ahead and making a reservation here.

Daddy D'z

264 Memorial Drive, SE
Atlanta, GA 30312
(404) 222-0206
www.daddydz.com

You couldn't get more different from Seeger's or Bacchanalia than Daddy D'z. Their slogan: "We Ain't Pretty, But We're Good." That they are. This finger-lickin' favorite is a self-proclaimed dive, and proud of it.

Ron Newman always loved to cook but got sidetracked on his career path and ended up as a wholesale jeweler. But in 1993, he got his dream back on track and traded in his jewels for this joynt (that's how it's spelled on the sign), and the people of Atlanta have never been luckier. Their house specialty is the barbeque spare ribs—tender, succulent, and as the menu states, "bad to the bone!"

Shortly after this piece aired on our *Best Of Barbeque* show, an e-mail was posted to the Food Network website. Actually, it was more of a manuscript. The diatribe was full of rants about how down and dirty Daddy D'z was, how the service was lousy, and the place a pit (and they weren't talking about the BBQ pit where the meats are smoked). We were pretty surprised. What did they expect? When the owner says it's a dive, you better believe it.

Make no mistake Daddy D'z is not fine dining. However, we found the service fast and friendly and the inside relatively clean. No matter what this disgruntled viewer/patron thought, we still stand by Daddy D'z and their barbeque.

———

Dante's Down the Hatch

3380 Peachtree Road, NE
Atlanta, GA 30326
(404) 266-1600
www.dantesdownthehatch.com

Let's see if we have this straight. There's a giant eighteenth-century Spanish galleon-style ship, docked *inside* a restaurant. Oh, by the way, it's surrounded by a moat, where six real crocodiles live. Let's not leave out the multi-level Mediterranean "fishing village" dining areas that overlook the port, and a décor that includes a giant ball of melted wax. All this just to eat fondue—a food you cook yourself? Yeah, when it comes to Dante's Down the Hatch, that sounds just about right.

Dante's isn't just a restaurant, it's an entertainment complex. Jazz bands play most nights. Menus come in 55 languages. When the house is full and the tables are aglow with fondue burners, Dante's offers a quick trip to Neverland without leaving Buckhead.

The man at the helm is Dante Stephensen, a retired Navy SEAL who travels the country in his own railroad car when he's not at the restaurant. He first set sail with Dante's in 1970, and it's been fairly smooth sailing since.

The menu—oh yeah, people actually do come here to eat—has been the same from the beginning. Select your fondue—beef, chicken, shrimp, and cheese are among the choices—stab it with a fork, and get cooking in a bowl of hot oil. Save room for chocolate fondue for dessert. In no time, the process becomes very social, with dinner companions sharing their food. Don't worry if you eat too much; just beware that in a restaurant with a giant ship, a moat, and crocodiles, it's wise not to go too far overboard.

———

R. Thomas Deluxe Grill

1812 Peachtree Road
Atlanta, GA 30309
(404) 872-2942
www.rthomasdeluxegrill.com

Richard Thomas spent a career selling fast food and then had a wake-up call. Unfortunately for his family, it required a year-and-a-half-long road trip that he failed to tell them about. One day, he simply climbed into his sports car and took off across the country. The only way his wife and son were able to track his whereabouts was through his credit card receipts and 17 speeding tickets. When he left, he had been the owner of hundreds of fried chicken restaurants, as well as a

Georgia

one-time honcho with another fast-food company. When he returned, he was R. Thomas, a healthier man who was about to create the most distinctive 24/7 restaurant in the country.

Opened in 1985, R. Thomas Deluxe caters to both vegetarians and carnivores alike. It's the kind of place where you can get fresh squeezed vegetable juice or a beer. There's Eggless Egg Salad or Free Range Chicken. The menu welcomes you to be as healthy as you like or order a burger. Nobody is going to shove it down your throat one way or the other.

Besides the food, what makes R. Thomas Deluxe unique is the psychedelic scene. The outside is covered in plants, exotic birds, and knickknacks including a partial *Statue of Liberty.* Inside, there's a patio topped with a parachute, a disco ball, and occasional visits from a table-hopping psychic. It's a family place by day, but the later it gets, the odder the crowd. It's worth the trip here just to people-watch. Of course, as R. Thomas can tell you, it's best to let your family know where you're going to be if you plan to visit for a while.

———

Elizabeth on 37th

105 East 37th Street
Savannah, GA 31401
(912) 236-5547
www.elizabethon37th.com

Don't be afraid to give the owners of this restaurant orders. Yeah, ask them for water, for food, for the bill—keep them busy. Sound a bit odd, especially at a fine dining establishment? Not when the owners are also *servers.*

Gary and Greg Butch worked here for 20 years waiting tables, so when Elizabeth Terry decided to sell the place, she looked no farther than the front of the house. The Butch brothers have always had a deep connection to the place and loved their jobs, so they simply took it a step further. Granted, these men are at the point in their careers where they could be *giving* orders instead of taking them, but they say that's not their style. They prefer a more hands-on approach.

This is fine dining at its best. Sophisticated Southern food served up in a beautiful old mansion. As for the service: impeccable. Would you expect any less?

Remember that when it comes to tipping time.

Potato-Crusted Red Snapper
ADAPTED FROM ELIZABETH ON 37TH, SAVANNAH, GEORGIA

MAKES 6 SERVINGS

6 (6-ounce) red snapper fillets
5 russet potatoes, peeled and grated
½ cup butter, melted
1 tablespoon salt
¾ tablespoon freshly ground black pepper
1 cup grated Asiago cheese
1 tablespoon finely minced lemon zest

Preheat the oven to 425°F. Lightly oil a baking sheet.

Bring a large pot of lightly salted water to boil. Add potatoes, boil for 30 seconds, and drain. Plunge potatoes into an ice bath and drain immediately. Spread potatoes on a plate or baking sheet to dry. When dry, toss with butter, salt, pepper, cheese, and lemon zest. Coat each fillet with potato mixture, lightly pressing with your fingertips.

Place fish on the prepared baking sheet. Roast for 15 to 20 minutes, or until slightly browned and cooked through.

Suzabelle's

102 East Broad Street
Savannah, GA 31401
(912) 790-7888
www.suzabelles-savannah.com

If life is indeed a stage, then Suzanne Coleman-Cone is making the most of her second act. This one-time aspiring actress left Savannah in the 1980s for New York City, but returned home when her mom became terminally ill. She ended up opening a restaurant that features her own form of Broadway, and she says this act is here to stay.

The curtain opens on bordello crimson walls, fitting customers' desire to "paint the town red." From there, every part of the performance at Suzabelle's is orchestrated with a combination of New York style and Southern charm. She sets the stage with the piano bar, which usually stars New York City transplant Diana Rogers all decked out and dressed up in dramatic costumes, belting out Broadway-style tunes.

But in the dining room, dramatic dishes take center stage. The menu, described as South Carolina lowcountry fare with an upscale flair, features their classic appetizer: the Plantation Wrap Lumpia. Rice paper wraps are stuffed with herbed ground pork and then fried up. Not to be upstaged are entrées that range from Black Grouper with Fresh Vegetable Slaw to Pork Tenderloin Marinated in Sweet Molasses Barbecue.

Suzanne likes to call it fine dining made fun, and from the looks of her production, it seems there's no shortage of people coming back for repeat performances.

Black-Eyed Pea Fritters
ADAPTED FROM SUZABELLE'S, SAVANNAH, GEORGIA

MAKES 4 SERVINGS; 24 FRITTERS

1½ pounds black-eyed peas, cooked
2 large eggs, beaten
½ teaspoon salt
½ teaspoon ground black pepper
½ cup all-purpose flour
1 small to medium onion, minced
¼ teaspoon baking soda
¼ teaspoon baking powder
Vegetable oil, for deep-frying

Drain peas and mash. Add eggs, salt, pepper, flour, onion, baking soda, and baking powder, and mix well. Form into balls. Heat oil in a deep-fryer to 350°F. Add fritters, in batches, and fry until golden. (Pan-frying, turning once, works well in home kitchens.) Drain on paper towels and let cool.

CHEF'S NOTE: You can substitute 3 (15-ounce) cans drained black-eyed peas for the dried peas.

Chef Joe Randall's Cooking School

5409 Waters Avenue
Savannah, GA 31404
(912) 303-0409
www.chefjoerandall.com

Chef Joe Randall likes to say he puts a little "South in your mouth." If you're looking for a fun dining free-for-all, then look no farther than his cooking school. Each week he holds a handful of classes in which you go, watch him cook, then gobble up all his hard work. For around $45, you get a 4- to 5-course meal, but instead of just eating it, you learn how to make it.

Chef Joe and his wife, Barbara, are eager to feed anyone with a hunger for knowledge and a love of down-home Southern cooking. The Southern Passage meal is a journey unto itself. Seems like the only way to get his students to stop talking is to feed them, so from fried green tomatoes and candied sweet potatoes to fried

Georgia

chicken, rice and peas, okra and mac and cheese, you'll be lucky if you can walk—or roll, better yet—out of there.

The room is set up so that students sit at a U-shape counter with Joe in the center cooking. It makes for fun, interactive dining—especially when the "students" bring their own booze. This teacher is happy to pour for you. At the end of the meal, everyone is given folders with all the recipes inside. He encourages all his pupils to do their homework and cook up a similar feast at home. No telling if they get high marks on this or not, but one thing is certain: When it comes to fun, down-home dining, this chef definitely makes the grade.

—

North Beach Grill

41-A Meddin Drive
Tybee Island, GA 31328
(912) 786-9003

Georges' of Tybee

1105 East Highway 80
Tybee Island, GA 31328
(912) 786-9730
www.georgesoftybee.com

If you ask George Spriggs and George Jackson when they first met, they'll tell you 1990. However, it seemed they were destined to meet much earlier than that. Both grew up in Washington, DC; both went to college in Durham, North Carolina; and both lived in the same apartment complex there. It wasn't until they were both working at the *same* restaurant in Hilton Head that they finally met. George Jackson was training George Spriggs. At the end of the day, they both walked out to the parking lot together and Jackson went to open his car. The key wouldn't work. That's when they realized they both drove the exact same vehicle: a 1988 Isuzu Trooper.

Once they put two and two together, they realized they had something else in common: a goal to own their own restaurant. So in 1993,

they opened North Beach Grill—a casual ocean-front joint where beachcombers can fill up on fresh favorites like Fish Tacos, Asparagus Crab Salad, and plantains with homemade salsa, all without taking off their flip-flops or swimsuits. This is the perfect beachfront spot. Cold beer and killer margaritas only add to the ambiance of this screen-door shack.

But their destiny together doesn't end here. Nearby they've also opened the island's first fine dining restaurant called, what else: Georges' (yes, that's plural) of Tybee, a romantic and inviting place featuring delicious dishes like duck, lobster, rack of lamb, and filets.

Tybee Island has long been one of Georgia's great getaways. It's still a part of the state, but it's a spot that puts you in an entirely *different* state of mind—one where waterfront relaxation and recreation are the orders of the day. While here, if you happen to have a hankering for a meal, there's no longer a need to leave the island. You can thank fate and two men named George for that.

Sautéed Shrimp

ADAPTED FROM THE NORTH BEACH GRILL, TYBEE ISLAND, GEORGIA

MAKES 2 SERVINGS

3 tablespoons olive oil
¼ cup minced garlic
1 pound (21 to 25) count shrimp, unpeeled
2 tablespoons fresh lemon juice
½ cup fish stock
2 teaspoons dried basil
2 tablespoons spicy seafood seasoning

In a large sauté pan, heat oil over medium heat. Add garlic, and sauté until it begins to soften. Add shrimp, and sauté for 1 minute. Add lemon juice, stock, basil, and seafood seasoning, and simmer until shrimp is cooked and the flavors combine, 4 to 6 minutes.

Serve with tortilla chips, pasta, or on its own.

Georgia

Florida

'Ohana

Disney's Polynesian Resort
Walt Disney World Resort
1600 Seven Seas Drive
Lake Buena Vista, Florida
(407) 824-2000
(407) 939-3463-Disney Dining Line
disneyworld.disney.go.com

Ohana means "family" in Hawaiian, and no place does family better than Disney. You can take the kids to have breakfast with Mickey, Chip, Dale, and Goofy (what they call a character breakfast around here), and you don't even have to go to the amusement park. Partial-day passes for the Polynesian Resort are handed out at the main gate. Enjoy a standard scrambled eggs, sausage, and potatoes breakfast, or waffles in the shape of Disney's famous mouse. (It's important to call the Disney Dining Line for reservations.)

The characters don't show for dinner, but there's singing, hula-hoop and coconut-rolling contests, along with an all-you-can-feast of Polynesian-style grilled meat and seafood on skewers. Guests are all called "cousin," so everyone is family, at 'Ohana.

———

Bubbalou's Bodacious BBQ

1471 Lee Road
Winter Park, FL 32892

12100 Challenger Parkway
Orlando, FL 32826

5818 Conroy Road
Orlando, FL 32835

1049 East Altamonte Drive
Altamonte Springs, FL 32702
(407) 423-1212 or 866-BUBBALOUS (866-282-2256)
www.bubbalousbbq.com

Owner Sam Meiner calls himself the Big Pig. What do you expect from a guy who included the word *bodacious* in the name of his restau-

rant? When you sell as much pork barbeque as this guy does, you can refer to yourself any way you want. Talk about pigging out, Meiner claims his four central Florida restaurants sell a hundred tons of pork ribs each year. With that kind of success, Meiner is certainly high on the hog.

Everyday at lunch, and again at dinner, there's gridlock in the parking lots at all the Bubbalou's. Traffic police often show up to help ease the congestion. Sam says he paid attention as a child when his mother told him the best restaurants were the places with the most cars. What's the fuss about? Besides some seriously good barbeque slow cooked over hard wood, Bubbalou's offers an enjoyably laid-back atmosphere, a reflection of the easygoing Big Pig himself. The parking challenge aside, people tend to share tables and talk up a storm. There's plenty of outside seating, especially at the Winter Park location, where Meiner has modestly named a picnic table area on a backyard bluff after himself, calling it "Sam Hill." Apparently, Big Pig Dining Area didn't have the same ring to it.

———

95 Cordova

Casa Monica Hotel
95 Cordova Street
St. Augustine, FL 32084
(904) 827-1888
www.casamonica.com

St. Augustine has been called the most romantic town in America. It's also both the oldest and most youthful, thanks to Ponce de Leon, who discovered the Fountain of Youth in 1513. It's no wonder that when Henry Flagler came here in 1885, he instantly fell in love with the area and dubbed it the "French Riviera of Florida."

When he took over a beautiful hotel and renamed it Casa Monica, St. Augustine began to boom. However, Flagler died in 1913, and shortly after that the town became sleepy once again. With the onset of the Great Depression, Casa Monica was forced to close and fell into disrepair. It was eventually turned into an apartment

photo courtesy of Dan Dwyer

Jill and producer Jodi Langer discover the Fountain of Youth . . . a little too late.

Florida

Sweet Success

When we shot at Casa Monica in April 2002, the pastry chef, Donald Gaul, appeared no different from any other person in the kitchen creating sweat treats. However, the difference with Donald is that he's deaf.

A local signer came to assist with the shoot. It was a huge help to have her doing sign language, but it was also eye-opening for me to see how well we could communicate just by taste, gestures, and facial expressions while cooking. Donald is vivacious, full of life and energy, so he made my job easy.

It just goes to show that you can share some of the best things in life with taste alone.

photo courtesy of Jodi Langer

Jill with deaf chef, Donald Gaul and his sign language interpreter at the Casa Monica Hotel.

building, and in later years, used as the county courthouse.

In 1997, Richard Kessler, a hotel developer from Orlando, happened upon the place and recognized its potential. He bought it for something north of $3 million and then put at least that amount back into restoring this beloved piece of old Spanish architecture.

If romance is on the menu, start in the Cobalt Lounge, where there are more than 40 different martini drinks to choose from. For dinner, their signature restaurant, 95 Cordova, is far from your run-of-the-mill "hotel dining." Chef Rene Nyfeler hails from Switzerland and brings a lot of European flair to his meals. Specialties include Sesame Seared Scallops in a saffron sauce; fire-grilled Chilean Sea Bass; and for an appetizer try the Cordova Escargot made with exotic mushrooms sautéed in a white wine cream sauce.

To finish off your romantic evening, the bellman will drive you around in one of the hotel's antique cars, giving you a glimpse into the history and beauty of America's oldest city. A ride like this can turn an average evening into an enchanted one.

Built in one century, perfected in another, the Casa Monica continues to lure in lovebirds—and anyone else—who wants to experience its "new" Old World charm.

Chef Rene's Shrimp, Mussel, and Scallop Orecchiette Pasta

ADAPTED FROM 95 CORDOVA, ST. AUGUSTINE, FLORIDA

MAKES 6 SERVINGS

1 cup extra-virgin olive oil
20 (26 to 30 count) shrimp, tail on
28 mussels
20 (20 to 30 count) scallops
28 kalamata olives
4 vine-ripened tomatoes, diced
20 baby broccoli florets
Salt and freshly ground black pepper to taste
4 tablespoons white wine
3 tablespoons fresh lemon juice

*20 ounces orecchiette pasta or your favorite kind,
    cooked al dente and drained*
4 tablespoons minced fresh basil
1 cup shredded Parmesan cheese

Heat olive oil in a sauté pan over medium-high heat. Add shrimps, mussels, and scallops, and sauté for about 2 minutes. Add olives, tomatoes, and broccoli. Season with salt and pepper. Stir in wine and lemon juice, scraping up any browned bits from the bottom of the pan. Add hot pasta, and toss with basil and cheese.

O'Steen's

205 Anastasia Boulevard
St. Augustine, FL 32080
(904) 829-6974

It's 11 o'clock in the morning in St. Augustine, and already a line is forming outside this famous Florida restaurant—one that doesn't take credit cards or reservations, doesn't serve alcohol, and doesn't advertise. So why do people come in droves?

One word: shrimp.

O'Steen's is an institution here famous for their battered, fried, shrimp. In fact, Jill claims she's never had better. Granted she is a bit biased because her mom grew up in this town and family vacations and holidays were often spent visiting her grandparents here. Every time she came down, O'Steen's was the first place they went. But her bias aside, the line outside speaks for itself. There is *always* a wait.

The restaurant started in 1965 when one man, Robert O'Steen, turned his misfortune into opportunity. O'Steen worked for the Florida East Coast Railroad, but in 1962 workers went on strike and the railroad ultimately went under. Instead of moving or finding another job, he decided to open a restaurant.

That same summer, the son of one of his friends, a 12-year-old boy named Lonnie Pomar, came looking for work. O'Steen became almost a second father to him, and over the years their friendship continued to develop. Lonnie worked for him through high school, and when graduation rolled around and his friends were going to college, Lonnie decided to stay here. Turns out it was the best education he could have had. In 1983, when O'Steen retired, he handed Lonnie the reins. That's about the only thing that has ever changed at this place.

They have all types of seafood specialties on the menu, but by far the most popular is their shrimp. They go through more than 200 pounds a day. The shrimp are salted, put in flour, dipped

O'Steen's Fried Shrimp

ADAPTED FROM O'STEEN'S, ST. AUGUSTINE, FLORIDA

MAKES 4 SERVINGS

36 extra-large shrimp
2 eggs, beaten
2 tablespoons water
½ cup all-purpose flour
1 cup cracker meal
1 teaspoon salt
½ teaspoon cayenne
Peanut oil, for frying
*Hot pepper sauce, preferably Datil Bottled Hell
    pepper sauce*

Peel and devein shrimp, leaving the tails intact. Slice lengthwise from top to bottom, being sure not to cut all the way through. Fan out shrimp. Mix eggs with water in a shallow dish. Place flour in another dish. Combine cracker meal, salt, and cayenne in another dish.

Pour 2 inches of oil into a large skillet; heat to 350°F. Coat shrimp, one at a time, in flour and shake off the excess. Dip in egg mixture, drain off the excess, and coat evenly with cracker mixture. Add to hot oil, in batches, so shrimp are not crowded. Cook until golden brown, 2 to 3 minutes, being sure not to overcook. Drain on metal racks and serve at once with hot sauce.

Florida

in an egg wash, then put in cracker meal, and deep-fried. Sounds simple enough (see recipe on previous page), but when Jill's mom tried it at home, they both agreed: It just wasn't O'Steen's.

A close second to the shrimp is their home-made hush puppies. They go through thousands a day, and they taste best when served alongside that shrimp with slaw and fries.

———

Outback Crabshack

8155 County Road 13 North
St. Augustine, FL 32092
(904) 522-0500

Joe Tuttle and Dave Sweat are self-proclaimed "crabbing dudes." Both dropped out of college and began to commercial fish, crab, and cook. Eventually, they set up shop on the banks of the St. John's River and ran a turkey shoot. To help keep their customers happy, they served up blue crabs and beer.

Before long, people were urging them to turn their fishing camp/turkey shoot business into yet another business: a restaurant. They followed the advice and, thus, evolved the Outback Crabshack. It sits amid the swamps and cypress trees on the brackish backwaters in North Florida's backcountry. In fact, the water here *is* a little backward. The St. John's River, like the Nile, flows north.

This place oozes ambiance. The restaurant is huge and sprawling, with lots of extraordinary seafood. They serve 1,500 to 2,000 meals a day. For starters, there are those blue crabs. The restaurant goes through 300 to 400 pounds each night.

The Swamp Platter is even more impressive. As the name suggests, basically the whole swamp is thrown on your plate. Nine pounds of shellfish—from crabs and clams to crawfish and shrimp—doused with their secret seasoning. Don't bother with a napkin when eating this, because you'll want to lick all that spice off your hands.

The Crabshack is 15 miles from St. Augustine, and although it might be a bit off the beaten path, these crab catchers extraordinaire wouldn't want it any other way. After eating here, neither will you.

———

Murray Bros. Caddyshack

455 South Legacy Trail, Suite E-106
St. Augustine, FL 32092
(904) 940-3673
www.murraybroscaddyshack.com

The shoot began with Jill sitting around a table with Bill Murray and his brothers. When asked, "Why open Caddyshack?" Bill replied, "Uh, we wanted to meet waitresses who wanted to meet drunks." Everyone cracked up.

And so commenced one of our most fun—and funny—shoots. You wouldn't expect anything less when you're sitting at the table with the six Murray brothers, each hilarious in his own right. In addition to Bill, there's Brian Doyle, Ed, Andy, Joel, and John.

Consider Caddyshack, located in the famed World Golf Village about 15 miles outside St. Augustine, a place where irreverence meets obsession. It clearly combines that with Murrays' love of the links. The flagship restaurant includes

photo courtesy of Dan Sitarski

Jill gets friendly with Bill Murray at the Caddyshack.

plenty of Murray memorabilia and, as expected, sight gags are part of the décor. You'll find lawn mowers on the ceiling along with beer kegs and, of course, plenty of gopher jokes.

Following Bill's enormous success on *Saturday Night Live* came *Caddyshack*, written by his brother, Brian Doyle Murray. The 1980 cult hit launched Bill's film career, and 20 years later inspired their "entrée" into the restaurant business.

If Bill's the star power behind the restaurant, younger brother Andy is the food force. The long-time chef and restaurateur put the menu together with food and beverage director, Ricky Gibson. They designed it to reflect the Murrays' Midwest upbringing.

That's why they serve dishes like Chicago-style hot dogs, Sausage Marinara, and Italian Beef. Other favorites include barbeque ribs, oversize onion rings, and, in keeping with the restaurant's theme, there's the "tee" bone steak. For dessert, try the Baby Ruth Cheesecake, named after that oh-so-famous (and infamous) scene in the movie.

Caddyshack is not a diet-friendly restaurant, but rather a place to come eat, drink, and be Murray. We think it's definitely a hole in one.

————

Bern's Steak House

1208 South Howard Avenue
Tampa, FL 33606
(813) 251-2421
www.bernssteakhouse.com

Bern's Steak House is the most famous family-owned steakhouse in the country, glorified for its dry-aged steaks and exalted for its enormous wine list. But mention Bern's to anyone who's been there, and the response is always the same, "Looks like a bordello."

Despite recent renovations, Bern's famous over-the-top décor still exists. Only now, it looks like a tasteful bordello.

Bern's slogan, "We do things differently," applies to a lot more than just the furnishings.

Things were different right from the start in

Cinderella Story—or Not

It's not every day that you get to serve lunch to a bona fide celebrity and, in this case, we decided to break the ice with Bill Murray by delivering him lunch on the golf course. And I guess he liked the sandwich I brought him because he invited me to hit a few golf balls with him and his buddies.

I have to confess that I don't know the first thing about golf, but I couldn't pass up the opportunity, especially because it would give us some good footage for our piece on his restaurant.

First, Bill showed me how to hold the club and how to swing. Seemed pretty straightforward, but on my first attempt, my club hit the green sending a divot—that's golf-talk for a flying chunk of sod into the air. Bill turned to his friends and remarked, "Oh, this is gonna be good."

It was now time to try to actually hit the ball.

I cautioned the crowd to move a safe distance away, took a deep breath, said a prayer, and swung. I might as well have been swinging with my eyes closed—perhaps they were. Another patch of grass was gone, but this time the ball had moved slightly. I remarked that the wind from the club had moved the ball, to which Bill replied, "No, I think that was the wind from your mouth." This guy already knew me too well!

He then advised me that the great thing about golf is you can decide after each shot if you want to continue playing. With that he asked me, "Would you like to continue?" I took this as my hint to bow out gracefully, adding, "I'm probably not a Cinderella story," an ingratiating reference to his autobiography, *Cinderella Story: My Life in Golf*. Bill replied, "No, but you look like you could clean the house."

1956. Depending on which story you hear, Bern and Gert Laxer's car either broke down while they were visiting Tampa from New York, or they ran out of money. Either way, they stayed. Eventually, the couple opened a small coffee shop. Bern, who's often described as a perfectionist, kept a list of customers' favorite jams and made sure they were stocked. It was just the beginning of several enormous collections.

Later, they moved to a larger place in a shopping center. There was an old sign above the door that read "Beer Haven." Bern liked it because it had almost enough letters to spell his name. All he had to do was buy an apostrophe and an "s."

Bern's started serving steaks but grew into something much more. There are eight dining rooms, plus an upstairs dessert room. Steaks are dry-aged for weeks, which means a third of its beef is lost to shrinkage. There are three pages of steaks to choose from on the menu. Prefer seafood? In the kitchen there are three 1,200-gallon fish tanks, fully stocked with the freshest catch. Vegetables are grown on Bern's own organic farm. Tours are a regular part of any visit.

Second to the décor, nothing gets mentioned more than Bern's wine list. It's 180 pages long, pared down from a recent high of more than 2,000. The wine room in the restaurant is stocked with more than 90,000 bottles, but if you can't find what you like there, there are 400,000 more in nearby storage facilities. It's the world's largest wine cellar.

As for the bodacious art pieces, many were collected by Bern at fancy auctions or flea markets. Most people can't tell the difference. Son David Laxer took over the business after Bern

was seriously injured in a car accident in 1993. The renowned restaurateur passed away in 2002. David has since worked on upgrading both the menu and Bern's famous décor, being careful to make sure one of the world's most famous steakhouses never loses its sizzle.

Red Fish Grill

9610 Old Cutler Road
Coral Gables, FL 33156
(305) 668-8788
www.redfishgrill.net

At Red Fish Grill, the food is good but it's not the only reason people come. It's the setting. Just 20 minutes south of Miami, and a little off the beaten path, you'll find this natural hideaway where locals and tourists alike can escape the grind of city life.

Set in Matheson Hammock Park, a haven for boaters, swimmers, picnickers, sunbathers, and hikers, the Red Fish Grill becomes the main attraction after the park closes at sundown. Tucked into the waterfront looking out over Biscayne Bay, it's quiet and isolated and has an atmosphere that harkens back to Old Florida.

The building housing the restaurant was originally erected as a WPA project in the 1930s. It's a squat, rectangle shape with a charcoal-gray coral exterior. Not a breathtaking piece of architecture to say the least, but the interior has been renovated into a warm space accented with dark wood and tropical touches.

Outside though, is really where you want to sit. Here you can cast your eyes on the prize: The view down the palm-shaded lawn, beyond the narrow stretch of beach and across the water as the sun falls into the horizon is worth the price of admission. Once the sun has set, you can enjoy the sparkling majesty of downtown Miami in the distance, the star-filled sky, the sounds of lapping water, and the smell of salt water in the air.

As the name suggests, freshly grilled fish dishes dominate the menu. Favorites include Sautéed Snapper with shallot-mashed potatoes and a red wine sauce; Dolphin Provencal with artichokes, black olives, and tomatoes; and Grilled Salmon with a honey-mustard glaze.

———

Versailles Restaurant and Bakery

3555 SW 8th Street
Miami, FL 33135
(305) 445-7614

To call Versailles an institution might be an understatement. It's not uncommon to see satellite trucks and news reporters here. Nor is it unusual to see politicians shaking hands and schmoozing the crowd. Anytime there's a news event that is pertinent to Miami's Cuban community, this is where everyone comes. And if you're looking for a taste of Cuba, this is the place you should come.

Felipe Valls Sr., like many Cubans, fled his homeland in 1960 shortly after Fidel Castro won the revolution. He left everything he owned behind, bringing only his wife, kids, and the shirts on their backs. In 1971, he opened up a small cafeteria where the Cuban community could converge here in Little Havana. It's since grown into a 400-seat restaurant where people—including those politicians—come from all over for a taste of authentic Cuban cuisine.

So why is a Cuban place called Versailles? Well, the guy who designed it had a thing for mirrors and the French style of architecture so it ended up looking like France's famous hall of mirrors in the palace of Versailles . . . well, sort of. With all the chandeliers and candelabras, we kind of think it looks like the Vegas version of Versailles—minus the slot machines.

The restaurant serves just about any Cuban dish you can imagine, from Ropa Vieja, which is shredded beef seasoned with spices, to the Plantain Pie with Picadillo. But if you're just in the mood for a buzz, grab a shot of Cuban coffee from their walk-up window. No doubt you'll be cranked up the rest of the day.

Then with all that energy from the caffeine, you can explore the Calle Ocho neighborhood—the heart of Little Havana that is home to the largest population of Cuban Americans in the country.

Mandarin Oriental Miami

500 Brickell Key Drive
Miami, FL 33131
(305) 913-8288
www.mandarinoriental.com

There are two great restaurants to check out inside this incredible hotel set on beautiful Key Brickell, overlooking Biscayne Bay. The first is Azul, which in Spanish means "blue."

This AAA Five-Diamond restaurant is a hot spot in Miami and so is the chef. Miami native and Executive Chef Michelle Bernstein brings amazing shellfish and seafood in from all over the world. She also brings her own Latin touch to the table, along with a mix of Asian and French influences. She says the secret to her success is she cooks with lots of amore. You'll find plenty of it on every plate.

The second restaurant, Café Sambal, is where the foods of the Far East are fused with the beauty of Biscayne Bay. The restaurant overlooks the water, and it's the perfect place to lounge away your lunch hour. Do this while sitting outside and soaking up sunshine, eating sushi, and drinking sake. If you're into feng shui—the ancient art of placement—you'll find plenty here in the décor.

Lots of positive chi flows in and out of the kitchen, with Asian-inspired menu items like Duck Shu Mai Dumplings, Sugar Cane Roasted Barbecue Salmon, and Singapore Curried Noodles.

Singapore Curried Noodles

ADAPTED FROM CAFÉ SAMBAL, MIAMI, FLORIDA

MAKES 4 SERVINGS

16 ounces egg noodles
2 eggs
Salt and freshly ground black pepper to taste
2 tablespoons peanut oil
4 ounces rock shrimp
2 teaspoons sliced garlic
2 fresh chiles, minced
3 tablespoons curry powder
4 ounces calamari, cut into ½-inch rings
4 ounces tofu, cut into medium dice
½ cup shredded napa cabbage
¼ cup bean sprouts
2 scallions, sliced
3 tablespoons soy sauce
1 bunch fresh cilantro, chopped, 4 sprigs reserved
    for garnish
2 limes, cut into wedges

Cook noodles until tender to the bite, and set aside.

Beat together eggs and a pinch of salt and pepper. Preheat a nonstick skillet or wok; add eggs, swirling the pan to make a thin omelet. Cook until set, then slide from the pan. Cool, roll, and thinly slice.

Heat oil in a wok over medium-high heat. Add rock shrimp. Stir-fry until pink, about 2 minutes; add garlic, chiles, and curry powder. Add calamari, and stir-fry until white, about 2 minutes. Add noodles, and toss to combine. Add tofu, cabbage, bean sprouts, scallions, soy sauce, and chopped cilantro, and toss to combine. Garnish with omelet slices, reserved cilantro sprigs, and limes.

Conch Flyer Restaurant and Lounge

Key West International Airport
3495 South Roosevelt Boulevard
Key West, FL 33040
(305) 296-6333

There's an interesting malady in these parts known as Key's Disease. Symptoms include a newfound laid-back attitude and a general lack of desire to return home after a Key West vacation. Sufferers can often be found in the Conch Flyer at the Key West airport, trying to decide if a few more days here might just be the cure.

The Conch Flyer is the most distinctive airport restaurant in the country. Given the category, that's usually not saying much. Located at the far end of the terminal and just a few miles south of reality, it used to be known as the Great Escape. There were only a few flights a day then, and after the last one left, the restaurant would change into a strip club. You don't find that in many airports. The Great Escape went up in the flames under mysterious circumstances in 1976 and sat empty until 1984 when a former pilot, John Richmond, bought the location and built the Conch Flyer.

The restaurant's slogan "Whatever", taps into Key West's laid-back attitude. And there are a lot of local favorites on the menu, like Conch Flyer Conch Chowder, Conch Fritters, and Key Lime Pie—without conch. Running late? There's the $5 "I Only Have 5 Minutes" Special. It's a bag of chips and a shot of schnapps. But most people prefer to linger, especially out back on the "beach" patio—made with 50 tons of imported sand. The problem is, the setting only contributes to the whole "I don't want to leave" theme. In fact, many sufferers of Key's Disease arrive at the Conch Flyer only to miss their planes after too many Bloody Marys. Hey, what's another day or two going to hurt? Okay then, make it a week.

Conch Flyer Conch Chowder

THIS RECIPE IS PRESENTED EXACTLY AS SUBMITTED BY CONCH FLYER RESTAURANT AND LOUNGE, KEY WEST, FLORIDA

YIELD: PLENTY

10 pounds—ground or mixed conch meat
2 quarts—diced clams
1—crushed tomato concentrate
1—can tomato sauce
8—large carrots
2—bunches celery
6—large onions
6—large green peppers
8—large potatoes
½—chopped garlic
2 tablespoons—beef base
2 tablespoons—chicken base
15–20 bay leaves
2 quarts—water
1 cup—hot sauce
1 cup—Italian seasoning
1 tablespoon—cayenne

Put all this stuff into a pot, and cook it for a couple hours. *Note:* These directions require the skill of a professional chef and should not be attempted by the novice cook.

Alabama

Bottega

2240 Highland Avenue South
Birmingham, AL 35205
(205) 939-1000
www.bottegarestaurant.com

"**L**et me put it to you like this: If I were on death row, this is where I'd want to have my last meal." Talk about an extreme endorsement. This was a first for us, but that's exactly what a woman told Jill when she was shooting here. Although we hope you're never faced with that scenario, you get the picture. The food here is "to die for."

Following on the success of his fine French restaurant, Highlands, owner Frank Stitt decided to open a second spot that combines the many flavors of the Mediterranean. His food will take your taste buds on a ride. One bite and you might think you're in Tuscany; another bite and you might be dreaming of Greece.

His signature dishes include lamb shanks marinated in basil, garlic, rosemary, and olive oil for 24 to 48 hours, then braised until beautiful; pappardelle with rabbit, bacon, and artichokes; and his signature sensation, the Parmesan Soufflé.

The historic building was Birmingham's premier clothing store in the 1920s. When Frank opened the restaurant in 1988, he divided it into two eateries. One half is upscale; the other half is Café Bottega—a more casual area where wood-fired pizzas are the specialty.

When you walk up to the building, you'll see an inscription on the stone archway above the columns. It reads: *Bottega Favorita*, which means "a favorite shop." However, judging by what customers say, it's now thought of as one of Birmingham's favorite restaurants. A place to literally take your breath away; that is, if you only had one last breath to take.

Alabama

Highlands Bar and Grill

2011 11th Avenue South
Birmingham, AL 35205
(205) 939-1400
www.highlandsbarandgrill.com

Highlands is Frank Stitt's first restaurant, which he opened in 1982. Located in the historic Five Points South District, you'll find the flavors of France creatively combined with the tastes of Dixie. He uses simple, local ingredients to make elegant dishes like Live and Kickin' Soft Shell Crabs and Grilled Venison Leg. Highland's is definitely upscale, but it's also warm and relaxed, without pretension.

Of course in any French restaurant there's a requirement to save room for dessert. From Strawberry Buttermilk Cake to Lemon Chiffon Mousse, this is one course you don't want to miss. Consider it research into a region renowned for its food. Plus, it's much cheaper than a flight to France.

___

Hot and Hot Fish Club

2180 11th Court South
Birmingham, AL 35205
(205) 933-5474
www.hotandhotfishclub.com

The restaurant's name doesn't suggest fine dining, but part of it suggests romantic dining, as in "hot and hot," or should that be "hot and heavy"? Well, whatever the term, this place is perfect both for reeling in romantics and for those who love fine food.

After working at top establishments around the South, chef/owner Chris Hastings opened Hot and Hot in 1995, naming it after his great-great grandfather's fishing club where the freshly caught fish was always brought out "hot and hot."

On most days you'll find Chris cooking his unique creations in his open exhibition kitchen, where southern specialties meet contemporary American fare. Delectable dishes like Shrimp Risotto with Saffron and Spring Onions, Black Grouper on Vegetable Couscous, and Grilled Beef Sirloin on Bitter Lettuces with Potato Galette. He even takes down-home foods like southern pork and beans and elevates them to a sophisticated palate.

His dishes are works of art—literally. The food is served up on plates and bowls made by local artists. It's tough to decide which looks better—your plate or what's on it. But after one taste, there'll be no question. If you're looking for a hot date with some oo-la-la, this is one y'all won't want to break.

Creamy Shrimp and Grits

ADAPTED FROM THE HOT AND HOT FISH CLUB, BIRMINGHAM, ALABAMA

MAKES 6 SERVINGS

Grits:
1 tablespoon butter
½ teaspoon finely chopped garlic
1 teaspoon chopped fresh thyme
1½ cups chicken stock
1½ cups heavy cream
¾ cup stone-ground grits
Salt and freshly ground pepper to taste

Shrimp:
1 tablespoon butter
6 tablespoons finely diced carrots, celery, and
    onions (a mirepoix)
½ tablespoon finely chopped shallots
½ teaspoon chopped fresh thyme
60 large shrimp, peeled and deveined
1 tablespoon cider vinegar
1 tablespoon fresh lemon juice
Salt and freshly ground black pepper to taste
6 tablespoons finely diced tomatoes
1 tablespoon chopped fresh parsley
1 tablespoon chopped fresh chives
6 tablespoons julienned prosciutto

To prepare grits: Melt butter in a nonreactive pot. Add garlic and 1 teaspoon thyme and sauté briefly, being careful not to burn garlic.

Add stock and cream. Bring to a boil. Whisk in grits. Reduce the heat to low, and cook grits, stirring,

4 to 5 minutes. Season with salt and pepper. Keep warm.

To prepare shrimp: In a saucepan, melt ½ tablespoon butter. Add mirepoix, shallots, and ½ teaspoon thyme, and sauté for 30 seconds. Add shrimp, and briefly sauté. Stir in vinegar and lemon juice, scraping up any browned bits. Boil until almost all the liquid is gone; whisk in remaining ½ tablespoon butter. Season with salt and pepper. Top with tomatoes and parsley. Divide grits among the plates; spoon shrimp over grits. Garnish with the chives and prosciutto.

Irondale Café

1906 1st Avenue North
Irondale, AL 35210
(205) 956-5258
www.irondalecafe.com

*F*ried Green Tomatoes, the hit movie, based on the novel by Fannie Flagg, made the vegetable (or is it really a fruit?) famous, and Irondale is the restaurant that inspired the book. Got it?

You know you're at Irondale Café, called "The Whistle Stop" in the movie, when you look up from your lunch and see nonstop freight trains out the window and nonstop lines of people coming in the door. Not bad for a place that began in 1928 as a hot-dog stand. Mary Jo McMichael and her husband, Bill, bought the café in 1972, after the original owner, Bess Fortenberry, decided to retire. They never had any idea what this career move would entail and what kind of success would follow them.

For decades they worked tirelessly to turn a profit. In 1979, when the county health department told them the building was out of date and they'd have to tear it down, they did. Bill, who worked on the railroad from 7 A.M. to 3 P.M., spent many a night working on the new site to save money on construction costs as they expanded their space from 31 to 100 seats.

In 1990, when the hardware store next door went up for sale, they bought it and expanded further. Good thing, because after the movie *Fried Green Tomatoes* came out in 1992, all semblance of order went out the window. The lines were out the door with people wanting to try their fried green tomatoes and hear about Miss Bess Fortenberry. If you've seen the movie, the character Idgie Threadgoode, played

Alabama

Fried Green Tomatoes

ADAPTED FROM THE IRONDALE CAFÉ,
IRONDALE, ALABAMA

MAKES ABOUT 4 SERVINGS

About 4 large green tomatoes
1½ cups all-purpose flour
½ cups cornmeal
½ teaspoon salt
½ teaspoon ground black pepper
Milk
1½ cups vegetable oil

Select the greenest tomatoes available. Wash, remove the stem, and slice into ¼-inch-thick slices; place in a bowl or platter. Mix flour, cornmeal, salt, and pepper with just enough milk to make a thick batter (the consistency of pancake batter).

Heat oil in a deep skillet over high heat, reduce the heat to medium-high. Dip tomato slices into batter, wiping against the bowl to remove any excess batter, and place in hot oil. When browned on both sides, remove from oil and place in a colander to drain (this will keep tomatoes from becoming soggy). To serve, stand up tomatoes like wheels in a serving bowl.

CHEF'S NOTE: Another way to batter the green tomatoes is to dip them into beaten egg or buttermilk, drain off the excess liquid, and dip them into a mixture of flour and cornmeal. Fry in bacon drippings or hot oil; drain in a colander before serving. If you have a deep-fryer, you can also cook them that way and then drain in the colander.

by Mary Stuart Masterson, was loosely based on Bess, who happened to be Fannie Flagg's aunt.

Jill shot here in 1999 and had the privilege of meeting Mary Jo and Bill before they retired and handed the reins to Jim Dolan. It seems that Jim is keeping this hometown hit true to its core, as he continues to carry on the tradition of serving up southern specialties like roast beef, turnip greens, black-eyed peas, fried pork chops, and cornbread. In the South, they often call menus like the one here a "meat and three." Usually the daily special gives you a choice of one meat and three vegetables. Of course, one vegetable you should order is the fried green tomato. There's a reason they go through 60 to 70 pounds a day—and it's not just because of the movie.

Mississippi

Madidi
164 Delta Avenue
Clarksdale, MS 38614
(662) 627-7770
www.madidires.com

Ground Zero Blues Club
0 Blues Alley
Clarksdale, MS 38614
(662) 621-9009
www.groundzerobluesclub.com

You don't think of fine dining and blues in the same sentence, but if you're Morgan Freeman and you're in Clarksdale, Mississippi, you do.

This small town, which is known as the birthplace of the blues, has also given birth to a fine French restaurant, Madidi, owned by actor Morgan Freeman and his friend, Clarksdale native Bill Luckett.

The two met when Luckett did some legal work for Freeman in 1999. After getting to know each other, they came to realize they both loved to eat. However, pickins were slim in this sleepy delta town, so the two decided to open their own restaurant. Technically they serve Southern

Star Struck

Interviewing a celebrity like Morgan Freeman can be a nerve-wracking experience. Is he going to be nice to me? Will he give me more than a 5-minute interview? What if I get food stuck in my teeth or spill my wine on him? But Freeman put me at ease from the moment I met him. For being an Academy Award–winning actor, he's a very down-to-earth guy.

Freeman grew up not far from Clarksdale and, like many African Americans from the segregated South, he came from very humble beginnings. The son of a sharecropper, he joined the Air Force at age 18 and was sent to California. Once out of the military in 1959, he followed his dream—taking what he calls the "long, heavy, hard, tacky road" from the heart of the Delta to the heart of Hollywood.

It took him years to break into show biz—and much longer to attain superstar status.

But he's tried to live his life following two guiding principles that his mother imparted to him: "Do unto others as you would have them do unto you," and "Pride goeth before a fall."

His advice for aspiring actors is equally simple: "Learn it from the ground up. Learn the nuts and bolts of it and then Hollywood will come looking for you."

After we finished shooting at Madidi, we headed to Ground Zero for a night of dancing—the perfect way to end the day with a gentleman of taste and talent.

cuisine with a French twist—but whatever you call it, it's good. No, make that delicious. From beautiful beef fillets to fresh halibut to Freeman's favorite: the herb-crusted rack of lamb, this ranks up there with the best of them.

After you've filled up, head down the street to another Freeman-Luckett venture: Ground Zero Blues Club. It's not unusual to find Morgan and his friends dancing the night away here. They get some great acts in, as they should, considering

Morgan Freeman with Jill's crew at Madidi.

this town was built on the blues. In fact, it's at the crossroads of Highways 61 and 49 that Robert Johnson was said to have sold his soul to the devil so he could play the guitar like no other. Although that might be legend, it is a fact that many blues greats put this town on the map. Morgan Freeman is helping to keep it there.

———

Ajax Diner

118 Courthouse Square
Oxford, MS 38655
(662) 232-8880
www.ajaxdiner.com

When owner Randy Yates opened Ajax in 1997, his goal wasn't to make it a fine dining restaurant or even the hippest restaurant in town. He just wanted to open up a diner that served, at the very least, barbeque and beer. Well, you can find that—and a whole lot more—here.

Located on the Oxford town square, Ajax Diner dishes up true down-home comforts like fried catfish, homemade meatloaf, gravy-cheese fries, and deep-fried pickles.

It's all made under the watchful eye of *cook* Amy Crockett. You won't find anyone boasting the title of *chef* here. They proudly call themselves cooks, and they say that without chefs, there's a lot less yelling in the kitchen.

If you get the fried pickles, be sure to dip them in their Comeback Sauce, which is kind of like Thousand Island dressing, but with curry

and chili powder to spice it up. Ya know why it's called Comeback? Because one bite and y'all will be "coming back" for more.

———

Bottletree Bakery

923 Van Buren Avenue
Oxford, MS 38655
(662) 236-5000

Mississippi is a state steeped in superstition. Many say it starts deep in the Delta, where stories of spirits have spread like ripples in the water to reach every corner of the state. At the Bottletree Bakery in Oxford, superstition is taken seriously. You can see it—even smell it—in the air.

One whiff of this place and you know those sweet spirits are lured in and leaving their mark here. All those bottletrees owner Cynthia Gerlach has around are apparently working to keep the good in and the bad out.

You see, down here, people put glass bottles in trees to keep away evil spirits. The idea is if you have a bottletree in your yard, the spirit is caught in it before it gets into your house. Cynthia has small bottletrees all over her café for that very reason.

She also has lots of freshly baked pies, cookies, and cakes, along with soups, salads, and sandwiches.

For those of you who don't believe in superstition, consider this: Shortly after the piece Jill did on Bottletree hit the air, Oprah's producers called Cynthia to get her pies on the show. One of her employees, Twinkle Van Winkle (her *real* name!), actually drove from Mississippi to Chicago with 300 apple pies for the audience to try. On television! With Oprah!

———

Shack Up Inn

001 Commissary Circle
Clarksdale, MS 38614
(662) 624-8329
www.shackupinn.com

They say one man's trash is another man's treasure. If that's true, then Bill Talbot has taken recycling to a whole new level. He likes to call the Shack Up Inn "a hobby gone awry."

Welcome to Mississippi's first B & B—not bed and breakfast, bed and *beer*.

For starters, there's the outdoor martini pool. One day, Bill got an urge to start digging a small hole out front. Two and a half months later, he found himself with a crater in the front yard. Not sure what to do, he poured in cement, and stuck in fence posts from his family's cemetery to serve as decorations. It's now Clarksdale's first and only martini pool-or beer-drinking pool, as often the case may be.

Then there are the shacks. Real, refurbished sharecropper—also known as shotgun—shacks. Nicknamed because you can open the front door and shoot straight through the back with a shotgun.

While they remain rustic, they're restored with just enough modern amenities like indoor plumbing and air-conditioning to make your stay comfortable, yet still authentic. Each one also has a refrigerator, which is where the beer, as in *bed and beer*, comes into the picture.

Bill didn't want to mess with breakfast, so instead he puts a six-pack of beer in your fridge. That'll be about the easiest thing to find inside.

These shacks are littered with recyclables, antiques, and well, junk. Cotton-picker spindles to hold curtain rods, church pews nailed to the wall to hold books, and blues memorabilia everywhere you look.

Each shack pays homage to the various blues greats that came out of the area, like Robert Johnson, Muddy Waters, and Pinetop Perkins. And in keeping with that theme, the only channel you get on your television is a blues station.

Every Thursday night they have BBQ and even the smoker they cook it in is recycled—an old tractor that they've converted. Their pork is incredible—stuffed with pickled jalapeños and smoked all day until it's so succulent you won't even reach for the sauce.

So let the barbecue fill your belly and the blues fill your soul. We're pretty sure you'll be wanting seconds on both counts.

Taylor Grocery
County Road 338, #4A
Taylor, MS 38673
(662) 236-1716

To locals, it's known merely as "The Catfish Place."

Mississippians will tell you they've been fishing for—and frying up—catfish for as long as the mighty Mississippi has run through the South. And if you're gonna put catfish on the menu in these parts, you better know how to do it right. In fact, they proudly proclaim their state the "Catfish Capital of the World."

For those wanting to experience some real Mississippi catfish, head 9 miles south of Oxford to the town of Taylor, and a population of less than 300. Blink and you might miss it.

No frills here. Checkered tablecloths, graffiti all over the walls, and lots of brown bags on the tables. Why you ask? Well, it's just the law-abiding folks of Lafayette County following the "Brown Bag Law." It's a dry county, so to drink beer or wine, you have to BYOB (bring your own bag).

Back in the early 1900s it was a grocery—one that thrived for more than 70 years. In the 1970s, when the owners needed to bring more business in, they set up tables in the back and started selling catfish. It worked—people came. They're still hooked today.

But if you dine here, mind your manners, which are spelled out for you on signs, like the one that says "No Spitting on the Porch," or Jill's favorite, "Eat Here or We Both Starve."

That was good enough reason for us to dig in, albeit politely.

A sign of the times at Taylor Grocery.

photo courtesy of Jodi Langer

Mississippi Catfish and Hushpuppies

ADAPTED FROM TAYLOR GROCERY,
TAYLOR, MISSISSIPPI

MAKES 4 SERVINGS

Hushpuppies:
2 cups yellow cornmeal
1 cup all-purpose flour
1 tablespoon sugar
1 teaspoon salt
1 egg, lightly beaten
4 green onions (white and green parts), chopped
About 1½ cups buttermilk
Peanut oil for deep-frying

Catfish:
Peanut oil for deep-frying
2 cups yellow cornmeal
¼ cup all-purpose flour
2 tablespoons coarse black pepper
1 tablespoon lemon pepper
1 teaspoon sweet paprika
1 teaspoon granulated garlic
1 teaspoon salt
4 catfish fillets
2 cups whole milk
Dash hot pepper sauce

To make hushpuppies: Combine cornmeal, flour, sugar, salt, egg, and onions in a mixing bowl. Stir in buttermilk as needed until batter reaches a thick, mashed potato–like consistency. Refrigerate for 45 minutes to 1 hour before using.

Heat about 2 inches peanut oil in a large skillet to 350°F. Dip a small ice-cream scoop in cold water. Using the scoop, dip out about 1 tablespoon batter at a time and drop carefully into hot oil. Cook hushpuppies until golden brown, about 4 minutes. Hushpuppies should roll over in oil by themselves. If they do not, turn them over.

To prepare catfish: In a separate skillet, heat about 2 inches peanut oil to 350°F. Combine cornmeal, flour, black pepper, lemon pepper, paprika, garlic, and salt in a large plastic bag. Seal and shake until well mixed. Cut catfish in half lengthwise. Pat dry with paper towels. Mix milk and hot sauce in a shallow bowl. Dip catfish into milk bath, place in the bag with cornmeal mixture, and shake until covered.

Add catfish to hot oil, and cook until brown and firm, 3 to 4 minutes.

The Little Dooey

100 Fellowship Street
Starkville, MS 39759
(662) 323-6094

127 Highway 12 West
Starkville, MS 39759
(662) 323-5334

701 Highway 45 North
Columbus, MS 39701
(662) 327-0088

708 Alabama Road
Columbus, MS 39702
(662) 245-1382

802 Highway 50 West
West Point, MS 39773
(662) 495-1111
www.littledooey.com

The local saying goes, "A Little Dooey is good, a lot of Little Dooey is great."

Owner Margaret Ann Woods's mother and her two friends coined the phrase; anyone who was coming over to their house for dinner was served a "Little Dooey." It meant something they put a lot of thought and love into—in other words, something unique and special.

At The Little Dooey, what they serve up is unique all right. Just when you thought barbeque couldn't get any better and Southern food couldn't get any more rich, the Woodses have taken it to a new level.

Their brainstorm was to take two of the best things about Southern cooking—ribs and deep frying—and put them together. Yep, their ribs are dipped in batter, coated in flour, then deep-fried to a luscious golden brown. Eating them is a dose of decadence and then some.

To be fair, they do have traditionally barbequed meats, too, along with catfish, hushpuppies, and all sorts of Southern delights.

But if you want to send your cholesterol—and your taste buds—skyrocketing to the high heavens, then bite into a Little Dooey deep-fried rib. These little devils are a divinely delicious experience.

Mississippi

Louisiana

Mother's Restaurant

401 Poydras Street
New Orleans, LA 70130
(504) 523-9656
www.mothersrestaurant.net

Marc, Jill and crew making merry in the French Quarter.

photo courtesy of Dan Dwyer

They don't want you holding up the line here trying to decide what you want. That's why at this casual, cafeteria-style restaurant in the New Orleans business district they put the Mother's Dictionary on the back of their menu. Take it as a cue to figure out what you want while you're waiting in line—and believe us, you will wait. This wildly popular place has been around since 1938 and has an almost cultlike following. To give you a head start on your eating decision, here's a small cheat sheet so you can one-up your dining companions.

Not sure what *etouffée* is? First learn how to pronounce it: *AY-too-fay*. Try it a few times, and it will begin to roll off your tongue. In French it means something that's smothered or cooked in a tightly closed pot with little or no liquid. The type of meat used in this dish varies from place to place. Some put in sausage and chicken, others use duck and shrimp—any combination will work, and everyone thinks theirs is best. At Mother's, the dish consists of smothered crawfish in a roux with vegetables, including tomatoes to give it a nice red color.

Gumbo is a spicy stew, usually thickened with okra. In fact, it's named after the African Bantu word *gumbo*, which means "okra." It's made with a variety of ingredients, like andouille sausage, chicken, shrimp, or crawfish, and vegetables. The distinguishing characteristic is the dark roux, which adds a rich flavor to the dish, and the filé powder, which is ground up sassafras leaves. At Mother's, they make a seafood gumbo with shrimp, crabmeat, and oysters.

Jambalaya's origins are found in the Spanish dish paella, which is traditionally made with rice, stock, and a variety of meats such as pork or ham, seafood, and vegetables. But the root of its name is found in the French word *jambon*, which means "ham." Jambalaya is made with chicken, sausage, fresh herbs, and a light tomato sauce. It's usually pronounced *JUM-ba-LIE-ya*, if you ask for *JAM-ba-LIE-ya*, you're sure to be given that "tourist" look.

Po' Boys, also called *Poor Boys*, are huge sandwiches made out of whole French loaves, split down the middle, hollowed out, then filled with a variety of ingredients. On most menus, including Mother's, you can order a Po' Boy with everything from roast beef and gravy to ham and cheese, to turkey, shrimp, and even oysters. These supersize sandwiches are said to have come about during a streetcar strike back in 1914. A couple of Cajun "poor boys," Benny and Clovis Martin, created the sandwich and sold them for 10 cents apiece to the thousands of "poor boys" who couldn't afford a regular meal. If you order one "dressed," that means with everything on: mustard, mayo, lettuce, and tomatoes. At Mother's, they add Creole mustard to the mix.

Now the question remains: What do you order? We can't help you there. It's all good—especially on a hangover, which most people have when hanging out in the French Quarter. The only advice we can give you is not to hem and haw here. Do your homework, get in line, and be ready to order when it's your turn.

Louisiana

Camellia Grill

626 South Carrollton Avenue
New Orleans, LA 70118
(504) 866-9573

Only in New Orleans is a restaurant beloved for both its quaint Southern charm and its ability to cure hangovers. Tourists flock to the Camellia Grill because it's wholesome, college students come because it's hip, but everyone is here for the same reason: the incredible comfort food.

This isn't a place where you'll find "heart-healthy" icons on the menu. The hamburgers have just the right amount of grease, and the waffles come dripping in pecan sauce. The Camellia opens early and closes late and offers breakfast all day long. You probably won't find omelets this fluffy anywhere else. (The secret is in whipping the eggs in a mixer.) One of the most popular omelets is served with chili and cheese, with fries on the side to soak it all up. Most people can't leave here without either a milkshake freeze or the renowned pecan pie. It's cheap eats for families, a fantastic splurge for visitors, and the right potion—and portion—for those who suffer from an overabundance of the French Quarter.

The Camellia doesn't look like it's changed a bit since it opened in 1946. There are just 29 stools that wrap around a curved counter, which means there's usually a line. Once you do sit down, your bow-tied waiter offers a handshake or some other personal greeting. If it's headwaiter Marvin Day, you get a fist-bump and an enthusiastic "Word!" Unless, of course, Marvin senses you're recovering from a rough night. Then he tries to keep it down, at least until your food kicks in.

Chef's Special Omelet

ADAPTED FROM CAMELLIA GRILL,
NEW ORLEANS, LOUISIANA

MAKES 1 LARGE OMELET

3 eggs
½ cup diced potato, boiled until tender
½ cup diced onion
½ cup diced ham
½ cup diced bacon, cooked
1 slice Swiss cheese
1 slice American cheese
1 cup meat or bean chili, heated

Put eggs into a blender, and mix on high until they are almost white.

Sauté potato, onion, ham, and bacon in a large skillet over medium-high heat for 30 seconds. Pour eggs over vegetables and meat. Let eggs cook until slightly firm around the edges. Add Swiss and American cheese slices. Gently roll eggs over into an omelet shape. Cook until firm, about 2 minutes.

Turn out the omelet on a plate, and pour chili over the top.

Pat O'Brien's

718 St. Peter Street
New Orleans, LA 70116
(504) 525-4823 or (800) 597-4823
www.patobriens.com

In a city world-renowned for good times, Pat O'Brien's is party central. It's one of the largest, busiest bars in America, renowned for a strong drink called the Hurricane, a flaming fountain on its signature Garden Patio, and a simple slogan that says it all: "Have Fun!"

P-O-B's, as it's often called, is really about a half-dozen bars packed into one giant building. Among them, there's the Piano Bar, where the crowd sings along with dueling entertainers. The Main Bar offers more of an intimate setting—well, as intimate as this place gets. And the centerpiece of the 4,000-square-foot Garden Patio is the famous fountain, which has witnessed so

Louisiana

many shenanigans, P-O-B's website actually has a page titled "If the Fountain Could Talk, We Would All Be in Trouble."

There are more than 70 specialty drinks on the menu, but it's the fruity, rum-based Hurricane that will blow you away. It's served in a 26-ounce pear-shape glass that often becomes a souvenir if, after a few drinks, you remember to take it with you. Once home, it's said to hold $10 in pennies.

Pat O'Brien was a local character who owned a famous speakeasy during Prohibition. The password to get in was "Storm's brewing." When liquor became legal, he opened a bar with his name on it, and eventually moved it to the current location. The Hurricane was invented during World War II, when there was plenty of rum from the tropics but little imported liquor. So why not capitalize on what was plentiful? Today, the bar sells more than a million Hurricanes a year.

———

Napoleon House

500 Chartres Street
New Orleans, LA 70130
(504) 524-9752
www.napoleonhouse.com

When you walk inside this Big Easy landmark, look to the perch among the whiskey bottles, behind the mirrored bar. That's where you'll find the bust of the little general himself, Napoleon Bonaparte. It's a modest, dusty tribute to the French Emperor who, at the age of 51, was supposed to spend his final days in the place that bears his name.

In 1821, when Napoleon was living in exile on the island of St. Helena, Nicholas Girod, a former mayor of New Orleans, offered him his residence here in the French Quarter. Girod wanted the general to live out his final days in peace. Napoleon spoiled the plan by dying before he ever made it to North America.

In 1914, the Impastato family bought the building and has owned it ever since. Around 1920 they converted it into a bar and restaurant,

naming it the Napoleon House. For most of the twentieth century, it's been a famous haunt for artists and writers. Maybe it's the familiarity that attracts them to this place. After all, the décor has literally not changed in nearly 100 years. Peeling paint on the walls, yellowing pictures with the corners turned up, water stains on the ceiling—it's all part of the charm.

One reason you should go is for their famous Muffuletta—a sandwich of such generous proportion you might never look at sliced bread the same way again. This bread is round and nine inches in diameter. Stuffed inside: ham, Genoa salami, pastrami, Swiss and provolone cheeses, along with an olive salad consisting of celery, capers, and artichokes. It should almost be called a sink sandwich because you'd be better off eating it hunched over a sink.

Have a Pimm's Cup to wash it all down. This legendary and signature drink, made with Pimm's alcohol, lemonade, and 7-Up, is garnished with a piece of cucumber. Drink it at the bar, and give a toast to the general and the place that bears his name.

———

Bistro Maison de Ville

727 Rue Toulouse
New Orleans, LA 70130
(504) 528-9206
www.maisondeville.com

It's called the smallest kitchen in New Orleans, but what Bistro Maison de Ville's kitchen lacks in size is made up for in the food that comes out of it. Chef/owner Gregory Picolo's French *centric* bistro—as in French and eccentric—is located in the historic Hotel Maison de Ville, in the heart of the Vieux Carre, or French Quarter.

Chef Picolo was born and raised in New Orleans and stays close to his culinary roots by cooking up Creole dishes, all of which have a distinctly French flair. When you're talking food, Creole is a blend of French, Spanish, Italian, and African-Caribbean tastes that have been adapted over the years. Typically it's a more upscale style of cooking compared to Cajun, which is what you'll usually find in the bayous and the countryside outside the big city.

For starters, some Picolo favorites include his Bistro Crawfish Remoulade and his Louisiana Oysters, Escargot, and Grilled Portobello Mushroom Caps topped with Spinach Pernod Cream. For dinner, you can't beat the Grilled Louisiana Shrimp served with Roasted Pepper and Cheddar Hominy Cake, or the House Smoked Breast of Duck, served with a Leek, Roquefort, and Pecan Corncake.

If you're looking for history on the menu, he has that, too. In the hotel, room number 9 was the favorite home away from home for Tennessee Williams. It was here he wrote *A Streetcar Named Desire*.

Before coming here, there's a word you should know: *lagniappe* (*LAN-yap*). It's frequently used in Louisiana and means "a little something extra." Picolo might have the smallest kitchen in the city, but when it comes to putting food on your plate, he serves it up with some big doses of lagniappe.

Acme Oyster House

724 Iberville Street
New Orleans, LA 70130
(504) 522-5973
www.acmeoyster.com

Acme Oyster House is home to some bad mothershuckers. That's what the guys who open oysters at the raw bar call themselves. What did you think? They're bad because they're so good, prying apart the shell, slicing the slimy sucker free, and serving it up on the half-shell in seconds flat.

They have to move fast because Acme sells more than 7,000 raw oysters a day. And that's just in the French Quarter restaurant. There are three other locations, but the one downtown is pretty much the original. Acme opened in the Quarter in 1910 and moved around the corner to its current building in 1924. Located barely a block off Bourbon Street, Acme isn't some kind of high-priced tourist joint. As many locals eat here as out-of-towners.

In N'awlins, the proper way to eat an erster is to top it with a shot of Tabasco sauce and then suck it right off the shell. You can also bathe it in cocktail sauce, but in these parts, you're supposed to mix that yourself with ketchup, horseradish, Worcestershire sauce, and a little lemon juice. All the condiments are next to your place at the raw bar.

Of course, if you're not ready for the fresh stuff, there are plenty of fried oysters and clams. Acme also offers it in sushi. The menu is loaded with other New Orleans standards, like Po' Boys, gumbo, and jambalaya.

But raw oysters are the specialty. Its popularity is helped by its reputation as an aphrodisiac. The legendary eighteenth-century Italian lover Casanova supposedly ate several dozen a day. That's chump change at Acme. The restaurant's record holder is a guy named Boyd Bullot of Hammond, Louisiana, who polished off 42 and a half dozen not long ago, along with a full meal. Do you know what the bad mothershuckers here call him? A big eater.

Brennan's Restaurant

417 Royal Sreet
New Orleans, LA 70130
(504) 525-9711
www.brennansneworleans.com

Touristy? Yes.
Famous? Yes.
Pricey? Yes.
Worth it? At least once.

If you want the best Bananas Foster anywhere, then you have to come to this landmark restaurant in the heart of the French Quarter. Brennan's is known for top-notch Creole cuisine, and it also lays claim to inventing this fabulously famous and favorite dessert. No surprise that it's the most requested item on the menu. You can try it at home, but chances are it won't taste as good. On an up note, it also won't cost you as much, either. Here expect to pay between $7 and $8 for this decadent delight.

Louisiana

Louisiana

Bananas Foster

ADAPTED FROM BRENNAN'S RESTAURANT, NEW ORLEANS, LOUISIANA

MAKES 4 SERVINGS

¼ cup butter
1 cup packed light brown sugar
½ teaspoon ground cinnamon
¼ cup banana liqueur
4 bananas, cut in half lengthwise, then halved
¼ cup dark rum
4 scoops vanilla ice cream

Combine butter, brown sugar, and cinnamon in a flambé pan or skillet. Place the pan over low heat either on an alcohol burner or on top of the stove. Cook, stirring, until sugar dissolves. Stir in banana liqueur; add bananas to the pan. Cook until bananas soften and begin to brown; carefully add rum. Cook sauce until rum is hot, then tip the pan slightly to ignite rum. (If using an electric burner, ignite rum with a long match.) When the flames subside, lift bananas out of the pan and place 4 pieces over each portion of ice cream. Generously spoon warm sauce over the top of ice cream, and serve immediately.

Café Du Monde

800 Decatur Street
New Orleans, LA 70116
(504) 525-4544 or (800) 772-2927
www.cafedumonde.com

This is perhaps one of the most heavily tourist-trafficked places in New Orleans. It's open 24 hours a day, closed only on Christmas, and if an occasional hurricane gets in their way. However, you should go here at least once, if for nothing else than to say you did. But when you do, remember: This ain't Starbucks. Forget the latte or the mocha or ordering it skinny. Here you get their coffee two ways: Café au Lait, made with whole milk, or straight up, as in black.

So what makes it unique? For one, the way they make their coffee. It's flavored with chicory root—a tradition that started back when Café

Du Monde opened in 1862. French settlers first introduced the idea, using the root to add flavor and body to their brew. Chicory is the root of the endive plant. The root is roasted and ground up and is said to soften the bitter edge of dark coffees. The French developed the technique during their civil war when coffee was scarce.

The other specialty here is the beignets, a French-style donut. These divine delights are deep-fried and coated in gobs of powdered sugar. Although they'll leave a mess on your mouth and your clothes, they are worth every bite.

Located across from the popular Jackson Square, this is the perfect place to sit, sip, linger, and people-watch. However, expect to stand in long lines. It's not called a French Quarter favorite for nothing.

Commander's Palace

1403 Washington Avenue
New Orleans, LA 70130
(504) 899-8221
www.commanderspalace.com

The River Café in Brooklyn (see page 34) is known as the restaurant that launched 1,000 chefs. Commander's Palace can take that badge of honor up a notch. This is the place that launched one very famous chef: Emeril Lagasse. Just a kid out of cooking school when he started here, the owners of the legendary Commander's Palace took him under their wing, nurtured his talents, and in many ways get partial credit for helping springboard him to stardom. But despite Emeril's fame, his legacy is not what makes this restaurant famous. It's the food.

Commander's has always been a place for renowned chefs and culinary masterpieces. Before Emeril there was Paul Prudhomme, often called the Father of Creole-Cajun cooking and arguably one of the best chefs in the world. And after Emeril came the critically acclaimed Jamie Shannon, who sadly passed away of bone cancer in 2000.

Nowadays it's Executive Chef Tory McPhail making his mark on the scene and continuing the tradition of churning out some of Louisiana's hottest dishes. One legendary must-try dish is the Turtle Soup au Sherry. Begin with that and then move on to any number of specialties. There's the Pecan Crusted Gulf Fish made with champagne-poached jumbo lump crabmeat; the Grilled Veal Chop Tchoupitoulas, tender Wisconsin veal with goat cheese, stone-ground grits, and a brandied wild mushroom demi-glace; or Louisiana Seafood Courtbouillon, made with wild fish, shrimp, and briny oysters.

No matter what you eat, save room for the Bread Pudding Soufflé, called "The Queen of Creole Desserts." This is one rich and royal concoction passed down from the French. Although the origins of this dish come from using day-old bread, you could say they've taken the notion of waste not, want not up a notch.

Bam!

Uglesich's Restaurant and Bar

1238 Barrone Street
New Orleans, LA 70113
(504) 523-8571

A regular patron of Uglesich's told Marc this quintessential story: He stopped by the restaurant to savor a last lunch before a long trip out of town and then headed to the airport. As his plane took off, a fellow passenger noticed the distinctive scent coming off his clothes, smiled as he turned to him and asked, "Uglesich's?"

This New Orleans seafood joint sure makes a lasting impression. Open just for lunch, it's housed in a rundown building in an iffy neighborhood near the Garden District. There's always a wait, because there are only ten tables inside, plus a few more outside. They don't take credit cards or reservations, nor do they serve coffee or dessert. Normally, you would call this kind of place a dive, except it's too good.

Anthony and Gail Uglesich, who start each day cooking in their own house because the restaurant is so small, have attracted the attention of other New Orleans chefs, who come here to eat.

The Fried Green Tomatoes in Shrimp Remoulade could pack this place on its own. Order a Fried Oyster Po' Boy, and the oysters will be shucked fresh right then and there. If the dish you order isn't fried, then it comes swimming in a rich butter sauce like the Barbecue Shrimp.

Don't rush through your food, but don't linger, either. Someone is waiting for your table. But fear not, you'll remember your Uglesich's experience throughout the day, and most likely, so will the guy next to you.

Windsor Court Hotel

300 Gravier Street
New Orleans, LA 70130
(504) 523-6000 or (800) 262-2662
www.windsorcourthotel.com

New Orleans is a town known for three things: parties, parties, and, well, parties. But the type of party we're talking about inside the Windsor Court Hotel probably isn't what first comes to mind. In a city famous for its raucous revelry, we found this to be a quiet oasis, but also an establishment that likes parties—especially the type steeped in tradition. Their party pays tribute to the style and sensibility of England and one of its most royal rituals: the tea party.

Each day at 2 and 4:30, you'll see Southern ladies dressed to the nines, sitting primly and properly, sipping on tea and munching daintily on English tea sandwiches, scones, salmon, and caviar. You don't need to be an aristocrat to take part in this ancient custom. However, when Jill shot here for *The Best Of Tea* show, the Windsor Court enlisted an etiquette consultant to give her a few pointers on proper protocol.

For starters, the etiquette maven insisted that when putting a napkin on your lap, be sure the fold is flush with your waistline, and when using it, don't wipe it across your mouth, rather simply blot the napkin from side to side.

Although it's customary to have the hot tea poured into your cup for you, it's up to you to get a handle on drinking it, and that involves the way

Louisiana

Louisiana

you handle your cup. For anyone who thinks your pinkie finger should be in the air, think again. Consider it a major tea faux pas. The proper way to hold it is with your three fingers underneath the handle, your thumb on top and your pinkie resting just beneath.

When it comes to nibbling, tea sandwiches are eaten first—their saltiness is said to "blunt" the appetite. Surprisingly it *is* acceptable to pick up these babies with your fingers and pop the whole thing in your mouth—just don't talk with your mouth full, lest you get banished to the tea drinker's hall of shame—or worse yet, thrown into the debauchery of the French Quarter— and that's no place for a lady. Following the sandwiches are the semi-sweet scones, usually served with lemon curd, strawberry jam, and clotted cream. Put a dab on for each bite. In other words, don't smear the whole scone with jam and then eat it.

If taking tea isn't your thing, you can enjoy a delicious meal at the hotel's four-star, four-diamond restaurant, The New Orleans Grill. In fact, no matter where you are in this elegant hotel, you'll find it a quiet haven from the madness outside. They even have an extensive English art and antique collection valued at $8 million for guests to enjoy. So even amid the craziness of New Orleans, inside these walls you can find a place where food, art, and the art of etiquette still reign supreme.

———

Mulate's

201 Julia Street
New Orleans, LA 70130
(504) 522-1492 or (800) 854-9149
www.mulates.com

Mulate's boldly tackles the pressing question: Is alligator seafood or meat? It's an issue most restaurants don't have to decide. But then, few places are as authentically Cajun as this one.

That's about as serious as things get at Mulate's, a giant restaurant and dance hall known for its partying good times. Open seven nights a week, it welcomes large crowds who

Marc jammin' Cajun-style at Mulate's, New Orleans.

come to catch up on their Cajun. There are bands nightly, and after a few beers, the dance floor fills with people, some of whom actually know the proper moves.

When it comes to its Cajun food, Mulate's definitely takes the right steps. There are plenty of familiar dishes, like grilled catfish and crawfish. But the restaurant also offers its share of unique eats. Ever have Boudin? It's spicy pork and rice dressing, stuffed into a casing that you don't eat. Instead, you ease the filling out with your teeth—eating it as if it's a pork-sickle.

Then there's that whole alligator issue. At Mulate's, it's listed as seafood, right there on the menu in the same section as the fried crawfish. Sure, it might taste like chicken, but that doesn't make it poultry.

Maybe he should just use the spoons to eat?

When we taped at Mulate's, the band quickly realized I was slightly Cajun-impaired. After watching me try to dance to their upbeat music, they took pity and invited me to join the band and play the washboard and spoons. After a song or two, they realized they should have left well enough alone while I was out on the dance floor.

Angelo Brocato Ice Cream and Confectionary, Inc.

214 North Carrollton Avenue
New Orleans, LA 70119
(504) 486-0078
www.angelobrocatoicecream.com

Like you need yet another temptation in New Orleans. Relax. What are a few harmless Italian desserts going to hurt?

Brocato's is as much a part of the Big Easy as Mardi Gras—and nearly as much fun. It's been around for a century and still prepares spumoni—Italian ice cream—and Italian ices with the same recipes that founder Angelo Brocato brought from Sicily.

When Angelo first started in the French Quarter in 1905, there were seven other places nearby selling the same sweet treats. He was the only one to last. It wasn't easy. When he died, it took three of his sons to take his place, and they had a hard time keeping pace. Angelo's grandson Arthur is now in charge, and together with his family and staff, he prepares everything from scratch. The only place you'll find fresher spumoni is in Italy. The overall best-seller is lemon ice, which is made daily from fresh lemons, sugar, and water. That's it. It doesn't have to be complicated to be good. In addition, there are cases of pastries.

In 1979, Brocato's moved from the French Quarter to a residential area called Mid-City.

Customers moved with it. It's a good bet half of New Orleans was raised on Brocato's, coming here to celebrate special occasions. After all, what are a few harmless desserts going to hurt?

Lafitte's Landing at Bittersweet Plantation

404 Claiborne Avenue
Donaldsonville, LA 70346
(225) 473-1232
www.jfolse.com

You'll find this hidden gem deep in the heart of bayou country on the west bank of the Mississippi River. With just 9,000 people who call Donaldsonville home, it's also a haven for those who are hungry for history. For a short time, during the 1830s, this town was the capital of Louisiana. After it lost its prestigious title, it became just another river town, but one that was bustling with commerce. However, like many small towns, when the interstate was built on the east side of the river, the traffic moved away from the town center, and it began to shrivel up. Buildings were boarded, businesses went bankrupt, and Donaldsonville was on the verge of becoming a ghost town.

Enter John Folse, a man who many say helped put Donaldsonville back on the map. He opened his original Lafitte's Landing in 1978, bringing the secrets of his Cajun cooking to the table—and into the hearts of many. From cookbooks and cooking tours, he set out on a worldwide mission to tell people around the globe about rural Louisiana's rich culinary history. He did it so well that in 1988 he was named "Louisiana's Culinary Ambassador to the World" by the Louisiana legislature. People began driving from miles away to dine at his restaurant. The town began to experience a rebirth.

But alas, history has a way of repeating itself, and just like the town's disappearance, one night in October 1998, John's restaurant went up in smoke. It was completely destroyed by fire. However, John says there was no doubt he would rebuild. And the place he found to rebuild was, ironically, his own home.

The residence that is now Lafitte's Landing at Bittersweet Plantation dates back to 1859. It was John's wife's original family home and their home for 20 years. After the fire, John and his wife decided to turn it into a restaurant and a bed and breakfast. Nowadays, you either have to be an overnight guest here to enjoy the food, or get yourself invited to a party or reception. They no longer have a regular restaurant. But if you are lucky enough to dine here, take note of the plates on your table. After the first restaurant burned down, a fireman pulled a charred plate from the rubble. John had exact replicas made so everyone who comes in is given a bittersweet reminder that good can come from misfortune—no doubt, a good reminder to us all.

Louisiana

White Chocolate Bread Pudding

ADAPTED FROM LAFITTE'S LANDING,
DONALDSONVILLE, LOUISIANA

MAKES 6 TO 8 SERVINGS

3 (10-inch) loaves French bread
4 whole eggs
6 egg yolks
4 cups heavy whipping cream
1 cup milk
1 cup sugar
9 ounces Baker's white chocolate

Preheat the oven to 300°F. Slice French bread into ½-inch-thick round slices, and set aside. In a large mixing bowl, combine eggs and egg yolks. Using a wire whisk, blend well and set aside.

In a large saucepan, combine cream, milk, and sugar. Bring the mixture to a low simmer over medium heat. Add chocolate. Using a wire whisk, stir until chocolate is completely melted. Remove from the heat and, stirring quickly, add eggs to cream mixture. Blend thoroughly to keep eggs from scrambling.

Arrange bread slices in 2 to 3 layers in a 13x9-inch baking dish. Pour half of the cream mixture over bread, allowing it to soak up most of the mixture before adding the rest. Using your fingertips, press bread gently, allowing cream mixture to be absorbed evenly into bread. Pour remaining cream mixture over bread, and repeat the process. Cover the dish with aluminum foil, and refrigerated for a minimum of 5 hours prior to baking. Bake, covered, for about 1 hour; remove the foil and bake 45 minutes or until top is golden brown.

This bread pudding is actually better if chilled in the refrigerator overnight, then cut into squares and heated in individual portions in the microwave.

You might want to create a white chocolate sauce for topping the bread pudding by combining 8 ounces melted white chocolate and 3 ounces heavy whipping cream. This can be done in a double boiler or microwave.

CHEF JOHN FOLSE'S COMMENT: Bread pudding is considered the "apple pie" of South Louisiana. Because of our heavy French influence, crusty French bread is in abundance here. Our German population gave us a good supply of milk and eggs, and when combined with leftover bread, one of our premier desserts emerged.

Eggs à la Crème

ADAPTED FROM LAFITTE'S LANDING,
DONALDSONVILLE, LOUISIANA

MAKES 6 SERVINGS

¼ cup butter, melted
⅛ cup minced onion
⅛ cup minced celery
⅛ cup minced red bell peppers
⅛ cup minced green bell peppers
½ tablespoon all-purpose flour
1 cup heavy whipping cream
Salt and freshly ground black pepper to taste
Creole seasoning to taste
12 eggs
1 teaspoon chopped fresh thyme
2 tablespoons chopped fresh basil
1 tablespoon minced garlic
2 tablespoons chopped fresh parsley, plus extra
    for garnish
2 tablespoons sliced green onion tops
¼ cup vegetable oil
1 cup crawfish tails
Toast to serve
Sweet paprika for garnish

In a cast-iron skillet, heat butter over medium-high heat. Add onion, celery, and red and green bell peppers. Sauté until vegetables are wilted, 3 to 5 minutes. Stir in flour, blending well into vegetable mixture. Add ½ cup cream, stirring until a thickened white sauce is achieved. Season with salt, pepper, and Creole seasoning. Remove from the heat, and set aside.

In a large mixing bowl, combine eggs, thyme, basil, garlic, parsley, green onions, remaining ½ cup cream, and prepared white sauce. Using a wire whisk, beat until frothy. Season with salt, pepper, and Creole seasoning.

In a large cast-iron skillet, heat oil over medium-high heat. Add crawfish tails, and sauté until pink and curled, 2 to 3 minutes. Add egg mixture and, using a spatula, stir eggs gently until well scrambled but not dry and overcooked. Spoon eggs into a stemmed champagne goblet, and serve with toast. Garnish with chopped parsley and paprika.

CHEF JOHN FOLSE'S COMMENT: I've been served many exotic egg dishes in my travels, including the thousand-year-old eggs of China. However, I can think of no better egg dish or one more beautifully presented than these eggs from T'Frere House in Lafayette. With a cup of hot black Cajun coffee, nothing more is needed to start the day!

Strawn's Eat Shop

125 Kings Highway
Shreveport, LA 71104
(318) 868-0634

The middle of the workweek is sort of an unofficial holiday at Strawn's Eat Shop. Around here, it's known as Chicken Wednesday. We did say it was unofficial. Still, Chicken Wednesday is a big deal, due to the popularity of the daily special that includes a full plate of Strawn's fried chicken, rice, gravy, black-eyed peas, and salad. Never mind that the same dish is served Saturdays and Sundays; at Strawn's, you don't mess with tradition.

Down home and very casual, Strawn's has been serving its classic diner-style food since 1944. Mondays features Meatloaf, on Tuesdays it's Chicken and Dumplings, Thursday has Chicken Fried Steak, and Friday offers Roast Beef. With that kind of menu, owner Buddy Gauthier calls Strawn's a "very good greasy spoon." We're glad he said it. Gauthier is a straight-shooter who is famous in Shreveport for having won the restaurant in a card game. The story isn't true—Buddy says he doesn't even play cards—but the legend lives on even despite his denials. Then again, he could be bluffing.

No one's bluffing about the impact of Strawn's whipped-cream-topped strawberry pies. They're so popular, Buddy says he's often stopped in distant airports by travelers who jokingly wonder if he's got an extra pie on him. Sorry, he doesn't. You actually have to go to Strawn's for a slice. Just be sure you come early if it's Chicken Wednesday.

Strawn's Fried Chicken

ADAPTED FROM STRAWN'S EAT SHOP, SHREVEPORT, LOUISIANA

YIELD: 4 SERVINGS

4 chicken breasts, skin on, bone in
1 gallon cold water
2 tablespoons granulated garlic
2 cups all-purpose flour
1 tablespoon cayenne
1½ tablespoons seasoned salt
½ teaspoon salt
1½ tablespoons Accent (flavor enhancer)
Vegetable oil for deep-frying

Soak chicken breasts for at least 10 minutes in cold water to which 1 tablespoon granulated garlic has been added.

Mix together flour, cayenne, seasoned salt, regular salt, remaining 1 tablespoon granulated garlic, and Accent in a paper bag. Add breasts, one at a time, and shake each thoroughly to coat.

Heat oil to approximately 315°F in a deep-fryer. Fry breasts approximately 15 to 20 minutes or until golden brown and cooked through. Drain on paper towels, and serve.

Louisiana

Arkansas

McClard's Bar-B-Q

505 Albert Pike
Hot Springs, AR 71913
(501) 623-9665 or (866) McClards (622-5273)
www.mcclards.com

Can you guess which president went from eating at this white house to the one in DC? If you said Bill Clinton, you're right. Apparently, he and Hillary were both regulars; they even dined here right before jetting off on their honeymoon. During Clinton's years in office, it wasn't uncommon for owner Joe McClard to get the call that *Air Force One* was stopping in town. Sometimes it would require the Secret Service to sweep the place before the president came in; other times, the McClards just sent bags of Bill's BBQ favorites to the plane. Evidently the press corps was a well-fed bunch when Arkansas was on the schedule.

They have a saying here about their BBQ: "Best in the state since '28." In a nutshell, that sums up this Arkansas institution. You'd be hard-pressed to find anything better. It began back in the 1920s in an unusual way. Alex and Gladys McClard owned a motel in the area called the Westside Tourist Court. One summer a traveler came through and stayed with them for two months. Upon checkout, he told them he had no money and couldn't pay his $10 bill. In exchange he offered them a recipe that he claimed was the world's best BBQ sauce. Thinking they had nothing to lose, the McClards bid the traveler farewell, took the recipe, and whipped up a batch. That's when they realized the traveler wasn't feeding them a line.

In 1928, the Westside Tourist Court became the Westside Bar-B-Q with goat as the meat of choice. Thus, an Arkansas legend was born. Business boomed, and in 1942, they changed the name to McClard's and moved into a whitewashed stucco building just a few blocks from the original location. To the delight of most customers, the goat has been replaced with pork and beef, but the barbeque sauce has remained the same.

Now, the second, third, and fourth generations of the McClard family operate the restaurant. In fact, every morning—or should we say middle of the night—you'll find 'ol J.D. McClard in the joint just after 1 A.M., making the sauce and baking the beans as he has done for more than 50 years. He told Jill that at 80 years old, he still considers himself a "spring chicken." If only we can all be so lucky . . . .

Each week, McClard's serves about 7,000 pounds of hickory smoked beef, pork, and ribs. They're also famous for their homemade tamales and something called the Whole Spread, which consists of the meat from two tamales spread on a plate, topped with corn chips, beans, chopped beef, BBQ sauce, onions, and cheese. It's so incredibly tasty and greasy you can't help but love it. But do realize you can't eat one every day or else you wouldn't live long enough to finish reading this book—or even this chapter, for that matter.

As for the barbeque sauce recipe, it's locked away in a safe-deposit box at a Hot Springs bank. Not a bad return on a $10 investment.

photo courtesy of Jodi Langer

Joe McClard, a third generation BBQ'er at McClard's.

photo courtesy of Jodi Langer

Arkansas

Making fried chicken livers and gizzards with Louise White at Mrs. Miller's.

Mrs. Miller's
4723 Central Avenue
Hot Springs, AR 71913
(501) 525-8861

Okay, we think it's fair to call this an acquired taste: pan-fried chicken livers and gizzards. At least it was for Jill—one she still hasn't quite gotten used to. However, everyone around here raves about them, so we feel compelled to mention the place where we stumbled across this largely Southern delicacy.

Luckily, there are many other food choices on their menu, such as fried catfish, jumbo shrimp, and quail. Mrs. Miller's is true Southern cooking—the kind your mom or grandma used to make—in the setting of an old home so you feel like you're going to someone's house for dinner. In many ways you are.

Mrs. Miller and her sister Edna, who both loved to cook, opened the restaurant in 1937. The recipes became so legendary that people soon began calling Mrs. Miller "Mom." Today, Mrs. Miller's great-niece and husband run the restaurant, carrying on her tradition of good food . . . including those chicken parts that people cluck over.

Maggie's Pickle Café
414 Central Avenue
Hot Springs, AR 71901
(501) 318-1866
(Open March–November)

For most people, getting your name on the front of a restaurant is the result of a lot of hard work and sacrifice. Not so for Maggie Clement of Maggie's Pickle Café. You could say she leads a dog's life. That's right. When this Dachshund isn't busy manning the front door, she's at home napping. After all, she does work limited hours, which is why there's also Pickles, her playmate and co-worker, to help out when the going really gets tough.

Both dogs kind of resemble in shape the signature treat here: fried pickles. This fried side is simple: Dill or sweet pickles are battered in breadcrumbs and egg wash, then deep-fried.

To accompany the fried pickles are sandwiches, salads, burgers, and dogs (the kind you eat—what, you thought we were talking about Maggie and Pickles? Shame on you). It's pretty basic and pretty cheap. Just what the *other* owners, Jennifer and Louis Clement, wanted when they left Texas for Arkansas.

One word of advice: If you can't finish your meal, including your pickles, instead of getting a doggy bag, you can just give them to the dogs. As you might have guessed, Maggie and Pickles eat pickles, too.

——

Café 1217

1217 Malvern Avenue
Hot Springs, AR 71901
(501) 318-1094

After you've properly eaten your way through all the fried foods in this chapter, head to this café for what Jill and her producer Jodi Langer refer to as "clean food"—freshly roasted vegetables, gourmet lasagna and enchiladas, beautiful salads, and scrumptious desserts. Nothing here is too heavy . . . on the stomach or the wallet.

When owner Diana Marez-Bratton moved here, she knew she wanted to open a gourmet deli store/restaurant. What she wasn't sure about was how it would be received. Apparently the bank wasn't sure, either. Although she and her husband put together a business plan, bank after bank turned them down. That's when they turned to their credit cards.

They maxed them out, and on a wing and a prayer, opened Café 1217 in 1997. Luckily for them—and their pocketbooks—it was an instant success. In just 2 months, the staff grew from 4 employees to 14.

Nowadays you'll regularly see long lines of people waiting to fill up on her gourmet deli

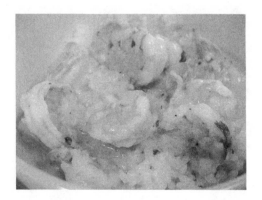

delights such as one of our favorite "clean" dishes, the shrimp tossed in a toasted garlic aïoli sauce. We liked her food so much that in our two short days in Hot Springs, we went there twice—once was after we finished shooting at a different restaurant. No offense to the heavy fried-food places we shot, but hey, when you're looking for clean food, this is as spic and span as it gets.

Spicy Toasted Garlic Aïoli Shrimp

ADAPTED FROM CAFÉ 1217, HOT SPRINGS, ARKANSAS

MAKES 6 SERVINGS AS AN ENTRÉE, 12 AS AN APPETIZER

Shrimp:
1½ quarts water
5 bay leaves
Juice of 3 lemons, lemon halves reserved
1 cup white wine
2 teaspoons cayenne
3 tablespoons kosher salt
2 pounds shrimp, deveined, peeled, and tails left intact

Aïoli:
4 tablespoons chopped fresh garlic
2 tablespoons sweet paprika
1 teaspoon cayenne
½ teaspoon ground black pepper
1 tablespoon kosher salt

½ cup mayonnaise
2 teaspoons Dijon mustard
2 tablespoons red wine vinegar
Juice of 2 lemons

To cook shrimp: Bring water, bay leaves, lemon juice and lemon halves, wine, cayenne, and salt to a low boil in a large pot over medium heat. Add shrimp, and cook until pink, about 5 minutes. Drain well, and remove bay leaves.

To make the aïoli: Mix together garlic, paprika, cayenne, pepper, salt, mayonnaise, mustard, vinegar, and lemon juice in a bowl. Add shrimp, and toss to coat.

NOTE: Jill likes to substitute scallops for the shrimp and serve warm over linguine, with pine nuts on top. If using scallops, cook only until no longer translucent, or they will be tough.

David Family Kitchen
2301 Broadway Street
Little Rock, AR 72206
(501) 371-0141

Seems like every place Jill did in Arkansas had some sort of odor—not necessarily a bad odor, but just strong food smells in general: the BBQ pit at McClard's; the deep-fryer at Maggie's Pickle Café; the pan-fried chicken livers and gizzards at Mrs. Miller's. But the one place where the smell really surprised her and her crew was at the David Family Kitchen. If you've never smelled chitterlings (commonly known as chitlins), then you're in for quite an awakening.

Jill and crew arrived here on a Sunday morning, still sleepy-eyed from the night before, but the moment they walked in, they all suddenly became bright-eyed and bushy-tailed. It was the smell of those chitlins simmering on the stove. Chitterlings, the intestines of a freshly slaughtered pig, have a smell that can best be described as somewhere between ammonia and raw meat. Not an easy stench to stomach at 10 A.M.

However, this is a Southern specialty that hundreds of places make and thousands of people enjoy—just not Jill and gang—or at least not yet. She concluded it's another one of those acquired tastes.

They shot at David Family Kitchen for *The Best Of Soul Food Sensations,* and perhaps with the exception of the chitlins, it's a place that will certainly feed your soul. The restaurant came about after owner Pearl David had a dream. In it, her living room was full of hungry children whom she needed to feed. This dream had such an impact on her, she told her husband, the Reverend David, that she felt it was God's calling for her to open a restaurant. He didn't take her epiphany lightly, and less than a month later, on October 1, 1998, the restaurant opened its doors.

Ever since, they've been feeding the hungry souls of this community. Reverend David feeds customers spiritually, regularly offering counseling and prayer, while Pearl feeds them with her divine delights like oxtail stew, collard greens, sweet potatoes, and smothered steak.

So even if chitlins aren't your thing, there are plenty of other foods to choose from. By the way, Jill is happy to report that by the time the restaurant opened around noon, those chitlins had boiled down and the smell had largely disappeared. Either that or her Yankee nose had gotten used to it.

Arkansas

The Midwest

Ohio, Indiana, Illinois, Michigan, Iowa, Missouri, Wisconsin, Minnesota

NEW YORKERS AND Californians sometimes smugly refer to the Midwest as the "fly-over states," best visited at 30,000 feet on the way to the other coast. Midwesterners know better. And so do we!

On our numerous forays into the middle of the country, we found some of our favorite meals and some of the greatest people you'll ever meet.

So be prepared to have those beer-and-cheese stereotypes about Wisconsin dispelled. We found mysterious fish rituals in the northern part of the state and a spy's hideout in the south. Take a trip to sweet home Chicago for visits with America's greatest chef and the world's greatest blues guitarist. Not to mention getting down and dirty for "cheezborger,

cheezborger, cheezborger!" And who knew that Minnesota, land of 10,000 lakes, also happens to be home to some fantastic cuisine. From homemade chocolates to down-home Kurdish cooking, our journeys to America's northern states always left us feeling fine.

And that's just a taste of it! After reading this chapter, you'll want to make the Midwest a destination. Because if you fly over these states, who knows what you might miss!

Ohio

Thurman Café

183 Thurman Avenue
German Village
Columbus, OH 43206
(614) 443-1570

The old adage that less is more never really caught on at Thurman Café, especially when it comes to its signature hamburger, the Thurman Burger. In this case, less isn't even in the vocabulary.

It starts with 1 pound of beef. Let's repeat that: *1 pound!* Then they add (follow closely) sautéed onions, green peppers, grilled mushrooms, banana peppers, ham, Mozzarella and Provolone cheese, lettuce, tomato, and mayonnaise. When the Thurman Burger is assembled on a roll, it stands at least half a foot tall.

This isn't some gimmick. Thurman's sells hundreds of these burgers every day and goes through 1,000 pounds of ground beef every week. (Another big seller, the Salsa Burger, is so loaded with the homemade spicy sauce it should come with antacid.)

Eating the messy burgers is treacherous. You can try using your hands or go with a fork and knife. Most people settle on a combination attack, but there's no proven method. Thurman's would make a fortune if it charged for napkins.

In fact, price is one area where the term *less* applies. Thurman's is very reasonable.

It's also small. With only 50 seats, this local favorite in the historic German Village neighborhood, is always crowded.

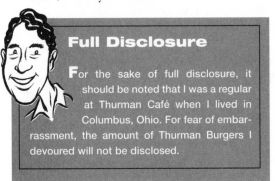

Full Disclosure

For the sake of full disclosure, it should be noted that I was a regular at Thurman Café when I lived in Columbus, Ohio. For fear of embarrassment, the amount of Thurman Burgers I devoured will not be disclosed.

Another item in the "less" category is the décor. The walls are littered with pictures, beer coasters, and assorted knickknacks, which co-owners Mike and Paul Suclescy call the look early "Ohio State dorm room." But this only adds to the unique dining experience. Anything more elaborate would be less. And we can't have that here.

Thurman's Salsa Burger
ADAPTED FROM THURMAN CAFÉ, COLUMBUS, OHIO

YIELD: 4 SERVINGS

1 (10-ounce) can diced tomatoes
1 (10-ounce) can tomato sauce
2 large onions, chopped
12 jalapeños, chopped
1 cup diced green peppers
4 tablespoons seasoned salt
12 ounces crushed red pepper
4 tablespoons taco seasoning
12 ounces cayenne
2 tablespoons granulated garlic
8 tablespoons dried cilantro
4 (12-ounce) beef patties
Mozzarella, Texas Toast, lettuce, sour cream for garnish

Mix together tomatoes, tomato sauce, onions, jalapeños, green peppers, salt, red pepper, taco seasoning, cayenne, garlic, and dried cilantro in a larger container. Chill.

The Thurman Café uses the salsa on a 12-ounce burger that has been fried and topped with 3 ounces mozzarella cheese and served open-faced on Texas Toast on a bed of lettuce. Add a side of sour cream, and you have the Thurman Salsa Burger.

Ohio

Nancy's Home Cooking

3133 North High Street
Columbus, OH 43202
(614) 265-9012

Thursdays are legendary at Nancy's. As almost anyone in Columbus can tell you, it's Chicken and Noodle day. The dish isn't just the daily special; it's the only thing on the menu. It leads to a remarkable sight; a counter packed with people from every walk of life, eating the same dish.

Located near Ohio State University, Nancy's is the kind of place you think exists only in Mayberry. Around here, you help yourself to more coffee. You might as well grab a piece of pie as long as you're up. And don't wait for the check. At Nancy's, you pay on the honor system. Cash only. And it never costs more than $5, unless you get dessert. Then it's $6.

Other days feature other specials: Ham and Scalloped Potatoes on Tuesdays, Meat Loaf on Wednesdays. But for some reason, no one ever wants to miss Chicken and Noodle Thursday. Breakfasts are just as crowded, with plates loaded with giant omelets and home fries.

To give you an idea just how down-home Nancy's is, if owner Cindy King is ever late showing up for work, a number of neighborhood regulars have keys to the front door. They come in, turn on the grill, and get the coffee going.

Mayberry should be so lucky.

By the way, there is no "Nancy." Cindy thought it was too much aggravation to change an old sign out front with the name on it when she bought the place in 1970.

———

Schmidt's Restaurant und Sausage Haus

240 East Kossuth Street
Columbus, OH 43206
(614) 444-6808

It doesn't matter what month it is; every day seems like Octoberfest at Schmidt's. The waitresses dress in authentic Bavarian costumes, and the crowd loads up on sausage and beer. German bands play at the end of the week.

Family owned since 1886, Schmidt's was a meatpacking plant for most of a century. It became a restaurant in 1967 and has since grown to landmark status along the cobblestone streets of historic German Village.

The menu features Old World favorites like Weiner Schnitzel (lightly coated veal cutlets) und Gravy, and Saurbraten (marinated roast). But Schmidt's real fame comes from its sausages and links, primarily the spicy Bahama Mama, a plump, hickory-smoked beef and pork sausage.

The best deal is the buffet. It offers a variety of Schmidt's sausages, meat loaf, German potato salad, and other fantastic sides.

Just to make things difficult, Schmidt's displays its enormous half-pound Cream Puffs in a case near the entranceway, so you think about them the entire meal.

———

Maisonette

114 East 6th Street
Cincinnati, OH 45202
(513) 721-2260
www.maisonette.com

Cincinnati is home to one of the most honored restaurants in the country. Maisonette has been named a Mobile Five Star recipient every year since 1964, the current North American record.

Francophiles will love Maisonette. It's très French, very formal, and requires jackets and reservations. Opened in 1949 by Nathan Comisar and run by the same family ever since, Maisonette has had only five Executive Chefs in its history. The most recent, Bertrand Bouquin, joined in 2001 and has kept the Five Star streak going.

———

Zip's Cafe

1036 Delta Avenue
Cincinnati, OH 45208
(513) 871-9876

Legend has it that Zip's started off in the 1920s as a bookie parlor. Gamblers needed a code to

Ohio

get in the back room, where all the betting was taking place.

These days, you don't need a password to get into Zip's, just patience. As one of the most popular neighborhood hangouts in Cincinnati, it's usually crowded. There's an open seating policy, which means you share your table with others. Gone are the old phone lines that used to handle the action, replaced with TVs, jukeboxes, and a toy train that circles the restaurant to keep the kids entertained.

In terms of favorites, the big money is on the juicy Zip Burgers. They're not large or fancy, but they've become required eating for generations of Cincinnatians.

After more than 70 years, Zips is still a good bet.

———

Indiana

Joe Huber Family Farm and Restaurant

2421 Scottsville Road
Starlight, IN 47106
(812) 923-5255
www.joehubers.com

It's hard to describe in words what Joe Huber's Family Farm is all about. Sure it's about good— no, make that great—homemade food. As the name suggests, the restaurant is part of a working farm, which means most of the vegetables and fruits on the menu were picked right outside the back door. But this is much more than *just* a place to eat. That's why they keep the word *family* in the restaurant's title.

The Huber story dates back to 1843, when Simon Huber migrated from Baden-Baden, Germany, to Starlight with his precious cargo of apple trees ready to plant. Seven generations later, the Hubers still live and care for the land, growing everything from apples and strawberries to pumpkins and beans. In fact, it was the bean crop that inspired the restaurant. One year, fifth generation Joe Huber, Jr. had such a huge crop of beans he knew he couldn't harvest

them all himself. So he took out an ad asking people to come pick their own. People came from all over, and the picking of produce became so popular a tradition was born. There was only one problem. All these hungry farmhands needed a place to eat. Joe's wife, Bonnie, was an excellent cook, so she started whipping up some hearty Huber home cooking. Her food became so legendary, customers urged her to open a restaurant. In 1983, the Hubers did just that, and it's been going strong ever since.

When you drive on the winding road to the restaurant, you'll pass fields and farms, rolling hills, and pastures. You'll think you're lost. But rest assured: Eventually you'll see an arrow for the place. Once you walk inside and see the 400-seat dining room, you're bound to ask yourself, *How in the heck do they feed so many people in such a remote spot?* We don't have the answer except to say Bonnie's recipes are that good and the Huber family spirit is that strong.

Nowadays it's Joe and Bonnie's daughter, Kim, who runs the restaurant, making sure her mom's time-honored recipes make the grade. Joe and Bonnie still live next door to the restaurant in the original farmhouse and are regular customers.

———

The Log Inn

Rural Route 2 (one mile off Highway 41)
Haubstadt, IN 47639
(812) 867-3216

When Jill and her crew pulled up to The Log Inn, they went into a panic. They had read that this was supposed to *look* like a log cabin, but this was just a big gray building covered with aluminum siding. You might have the same reaction, but before you get too worked up, remember that you shouldn't judge a book by its cover, nor should you judge a restaurant by its exterior—even one with gray siding.

Once inside, you'll understand the reason for this restaurant's seemingly illogical name: There are *lots* of logs at The Log Inn and it's the interior walls that show them off. In fact, some of

Indiana

the logs date back to the 1820s. And therein lies the reason for the siding, which is meant to protect this historic place from the outside elements. Originally opened in 1825 as a trading post and stagecoach stop, in 1844 a young lawyer by the name of Abraham Lincoln stopped in while campaigning for the Whig Party.

Fast forward to 2004, and you can actually eat in the room where Abe sat. True to their Lincoln legacy, they cook up good, honest food—Abe would be pleased. It's all served family style—fried chicken, German fries, and country ham, plus incredible homemade desserts.

Gene and Rita Elpers are the current owners, although it was Rita's father who originally bought the property in 1947, turning it from a tavern into a restaurant. Back then there weren't *any* logs visible on the exterior or interior. It wasn't until her dad began some renovations in the 1960s that he came across the log structure behind the walls. They had been covered up for nearly 100 years. Rita's parents painstakingly restored the inside to its original state, making the log cabin come to life. Ah, ye of little faith. Jill and gang readily admit they should have known better. Any place with Abe Lincoln in its history wouldn't pull a fast one on you.

German Potatoes

ADAPTED FROM THE LOG INN,
HAUBSTADT, INDIANA

MAKES 4 TO 6 SIDE SERVINGS

4 pounds potatoes, peeled
½ cup shortening
½ cup chopped onion
Salt and freshly ground black pepper to taste

In a large pot of salted water, boil potatoes until they are almost fork-tender. Do not overcook. Drain potatoes and cool. Cut potatoes into about ¼-inch-thick slices. Heat shortening in a large cast-iron skillet over medium heat. Add onion and potatoes, and cook until golden brown. Season with salt and pepper. Serve alongside fried chicken for a delicious country meal.

Iaria's Italian Restaurant

317 South College Avenue
Indianapolis, IN 46202
(317) 638-7706

This is a neighborhood joint known for its homemade Italian dishes, but it's also a story of how things evolve out of necessity. Pietro and Antonia Iaria emigrated from Italy and settled in Indianapolis in 1907. In 1912, as a way to make money, they fed and boarded other Italian immigrants who worked across the street at a rubber factory. Antonia's cooking became so legendary that they eventually turned part of their home into a deli and grocery store, and thus an Indianapolis institution was born. In 1933, it officially became a restaurant, serving up Sicilian delights like Lasagna, Chicken Marsala, and Eggplant Parmesan.

Now, the fourth generation of the Iaria family is keeping the tradition alive in this unassuming cinder-block building. Inside you'll find a family-friendly atmosphere along with a pretty extensive wall of fame. Just about every local celebrity has been here, and when national sports figures and actors are in town, this is where they come. The atmosphere is casual, and the food is pretty inexpensive, but served up with lots of amore. Classic Italian at its best.

Indiana

Chicken Piccata

ADAPTED FROM IARIA'S ITALIAN RESTAURANT,
INDIANAPOLIS, INDIANA

MAKES 4 SERVINGS

4 (6-ounce) chicken breasts
2 cups all-purpose flour seasoned with salt and
    pepper
¼ cup olive oil
¼ cup bottled lemon juice
2 cups chicken stock
1 tablespoon capers
⅓ cup unsalted butter

Dust chicken breasts with seasoned flour. Shake off any excess. Heat olive oil in a medium, heavy sauté pan over medium heat, and add chicken breasts. Sauté, turning, until golden brown on both sides.

When chicken breasts are browned, drain off oil and add lemon juice, chicken stock, and capers. Simmer until chicken is firm to the touch, about 5 minutes, turning chicken halfway through. Turn off the heat, add butter, and stir until melted. Put one chicken breast on each of four plates, and drizzle with sauce.

Big Fella's

3469 North College Avenue
Indianapolis, IN 46205
(317) 927-0076

When you think of soul food, you don't think fancy. Rather, you usually think of no frills or fuss and lots of muss. So it was to Jill's surprise when they showed up here to shoot for *The Best Of Soul Food Sensations* and were greeted with a different site: a dining room with tablecloths, flowers (albeit silk), and a grand piano in the center.

Welcome to Indianapolis's upscale soul food restaurant—one that is as much about serving your stomach as it is about serving the community. Dr. Gene "Big Fella" McFadden opened up his namesake restaurant in the 1970s, in a spot that seemed a bit risky—the area was rough, the building rundown. But this one-time teacher-turned-entrepreneur was convinced

that by opening a restaurant here, he could make a difference in the lives of young African Americans. He was right. His restaurant helped breathe new life into the neighborhood.

However, in 1993, McFadden tired of the businesses and shut it down to focus on other ventures. For ten years, different people tried to make a go of it, but it just wasn't the same. In 2003, at the urging of many in the community, McFadden re-opened Big Fella's, leasing it to a close family friend. Now, as he'll tell you, "it's back and better than ever," adding, "there's a new Big Fella in town." That new fella is Harry Dunn, who completely renovated the place.

On some days Big Fella's has a buffet in the dining room, but you are always given the option of ordering table service. The menu boasts of Southern specialties like Catfish Nuggets, Rib Tips and Wings, the Big Fella Burger, and Sweet Potato Pie.

If you're in the mood to dine in style, come to Big Fella's. A word of advice: Bring a big (fella) appetite.

———

Illinois

Charlie Trotter's

816 West Armitage Avenue
Chicago, IL 60614
(773) 248-6228
www.charlietrotters.com

Charlie Trotter wants to make the point that he's difficult. Standing in the immaculate kitchen of his Lincoln Park restaurant (it was the setting for the opening scene of *My Best Friend's Wedding*), the world-renowned chef complains about some press coverage from years ago.

It seems there once was an article in a local magazine that named him one of the meanest people in Chicago, behind Michael Jordan. Incredibly, Trotter isn't upset about being on the list. Instead, he's angry that he isn't number one.

"I told my staff that I'd have to work harder the next year," he says.

The Best Restaurant We Have Yet to Cover

After our experience at Trotter's, the crew and I were still hungry for a meal. Jill, who was also taping in Chicago, had joined us, arriving at Trotter's just in time to find the welcome mat rolled up tight.

Taking pity on us, a passerby on the street suggested we go to Sai Café, a popular sushi restaurant a few blocks down. The message may well have been sent from above (or maybe it was just that hare tenderloin talking again).

Sai Café owner James Bee couldn't have been more hospitable. He picked out our food, served more than anyone could possibly eat, then refused to take our money. We insisted, trust us. But no go. Then he gave everyone Sai Café T-shirts.

Among foodies, James Bee would never be mentioned in the same breath as Charlie Trotter. We have to say we agree with that assessment. Only in our case, we mean that as a compliment to Bee. (**Sai Café**, 2010 North Sheffield Avenue, Chicago, IL 60614, 773-472-8080, www.SaiCafe.com)

A short guy in an overstarched chef's coat, Trotter does a good job of living up to his reputation. During the shoot for *The Best Of,* he cursed at cooks, went from pleasant to abrasive in an instant, and at one point, stuck his hand over our cameraman's lens as if he were trying to avoid the crew from *Cops.*

But the man sure can cook. Trotter is generally considered one of, if not the best chef in America. Food critics write about him with something verging on religious fervor. It takes ten weeks to get a reservation at his restaurant; four months if you want to sit at the cramped chef's table in the kitchen. Once you're in, you don't even order off a menu. You just tell the waiter what you like and don't like, and the rest is up to the kitchen.

The truth is, watching Trotter prepare food is an incredible experience. Early during a demonstration, he's asked what he's going to make. "I don't know," he says. "We're going to figure that out as we go."

And the food seems to talk to him. At one point, he's so zoned in to a hare tenderloin that he appears to be channeling the rabbit itself. As he stares intently into the meat, he says to Marc, "With no offense to you, I'm not that interested in your being here right now."

Obviously in Trotter's world, coaxing the flavor out of a dead animal is much more important than social graces.

Coax he does. Forget about describing the taste of his dishes. It's beyond anything you've ever experienced. It would be easy to say the flavor jumps off the plate, but that wouldn't do it justice.

We'd like to tell you that Marc and his crew savored Trotter's cooking in one of his formal dining rooms, but the truth is they were forced to slam it down while hunched over a coffee maker in the bustling kitchen. Trotter served up several dishes but refused to invite the crew to sit down. Still, the experience was unbelievable, which we mean in a good way, mostly.

Even with all that, Trotter's makes our list of favorite restaurants. If the few scraps of food they threw at us are that impressive, imagine what a real meal tastes like. In this case, our imagination will have to suffice.

Trotter has his soft side. Several times a week, he invites local school children to enjoy a multi-course meal at the restaurant. They get tours and lectures about excellence from Trotter and his staff. Everything is free. The only requirement is that the students ask questions.

But as a final reminder of his charm, Trotter bids a chilly adieu to Marc and his crew as they wrap up their taping at his restaurant:

"Are you almost done?" the diminutive chef asked.

"Yes, we're just finishing and are about to leave," Marc replied.

"Good," said Trotter, disdain clinging to the

word. Then he disappeared through the door, without a handshake or good-bye.

———

Billy Goat Tavern

430 North Michigan Avenue (Lower Level)
Chicago, IL 60611
(312) 222-1525

The Billy Goat is dark, hard to find, and offers a very limited menu. But it might be one of the most famous taverns in the country.

Does this ring a bell? "Cheezborger, cheezborger, cheezborger! No fries; chips. No Pepsi; Coke."

Even if you didn't hear it firsthand, you probably know that famous refrain from *Saturday Night Live*.

And most likely you've heard of the "The Billy Goat Curse" against the Chicago Cubs.

This is home base for that, as well.

The Billy Goat was famously spoofed on *Saturday Night Live* in the 1970s. Show writer Don Novello, who went on to become Father Guido Sarducci, was a tavern regular in his pre-television days. He created the skits starring John Belushi and Dan Aykroyd as the Greek-accented cooks famous for their abbreviated service.

The cooks here really do yell "cheezeborger." Customers usually end up with at least a double—no matter what they order. No one seems to mind.

The Curse is another issue.

It was the work of founder Billy Sianis, a local character who never went anywhere without his pet goat. In 1945, he tried to bring it to Wrigley Field for a Cubs World Series game against the Detroit Tigers. But management had him tossed out, telling him the goat smelled. When the Cubs lost the series, he sent the team a telegram, asking, "Who smells now?"

Then he conjured up his curse. The Cubs, and most of Chicago, haven't been the same since (note the 2003 National League Championship Series).

Meantime, the Billy Goat Tavern has thrived, despite a rather blunt message on the way in that says "Enter at your own risk," and another as you exit that says, "Butt out." And don't forget all that yelling in between: "Cheezeborger, cheezeborger, cheezeborger. No fries; chips. No Pepsi; Coke."

———

photo courtesy of Phil Johnston

The Billy Goat Tavern, immortalized by Saturday Night Live.

Buddy Guy's Legends

754 South Wabash Avenue
Chicago, IL 60605
(312) 427-0333
www.buddyguys.com

Legend is a word that ought not be tossed around lightly. It's a description that few people receive and even fewer deserve. But if you're looking for a textbook definition of a true legend, you need look no further than Buddy Guy. Described by Eric Clapton as "simply the greatest guitar player alive," Buddy Guy has taken blues guitar to seemingly unimaginable heights.

The son of a Louisiana sharecropper, Buddy Guy came to Chicago in the late 1950s. He quickly became an integral part of what was

Illinois

then the country's most electrifying blues scene, playing with everyone from Howlin' Wolf to Muddy Waters. A half-century later, he's keeping the blues alive (and kickin') with Buddy Guy's Legends, one of Chicago's, indeed America's, premier blues clubs.

Naturally, you would expect to hear amazing music at a club owned by a blues legend. Let the music feed your soul, but be sure to save room in your belly for some pretty good food. Keeping true to Buddy's roots, Legends features a menu that follows the path of the blues. So you can find specialties from New Orleans Cajun and Creole to Memphis barbeque.

Executive Chef Jason Girard is careful to keep the food authentic, yet he manages to add his own touch as well. Take his signature dish, Legendary Jambalaya, a recipe that starts with chicken, andouille sausage, onion, celery, red bell pepper, and lots of garlic. Jambalaya purists say this is more of a jambalaya-gumbo hybrid. But one taste of it, and all you'll be calling it is "good."

Buddy Guy thinks so. It's one of his favorite dishes. And when you've got a legend on your side, who cares what anyone else thinks?

Legendary Jambalaya

ADAPTED FROM BUDDY GUY'S LEGENDS, CHICAGO, ILLINOIS

YIELD: 4 SERVINGS

2 tablespoons peanut oil
12 ounces smoked andouille or kielbasa sausage, sliced
2 boneless, skinless chicken breasts, cubed
1 medium onion, diced
2 stalks celery, diced
2 cloves garlic, minced
1 bell pepper, diced
1 (28-ounce) can peeled diced tomatoes
½ teaspoon hot sauce
1 teaspoon filé powder
1 tablespoon Cajun spice blend
Cooked steamed rice, for serving

Heat a large, heavy, dry stockpot or Dutch oven over high heat. Add 1 tablespoon peanut oil, and then brown sausage. Remove sausage from the pan, and reserve drippings. Add another tablespoon peanut oil and then brown chicken, adding more peanut oil, if necessary.

Return sausage to the pan with chicken, and add onion, celery, garlic, and pepper. Sauté until meats and vegetables are cooked through. Add tomatoes and hot sauce, and stir with a wooden spoon to combine. Add filé powder and Cajun spice, reduce the heat to low, and simmer for at least 1 hour. Serve over cooked, steamed rice.

Ed Debevic's

640 North Wells Street
Chicago, IL 60610
(312) 664-1707
www.featuredfoods.com

Ed Debevic learned how to sling hash at Lill's Homesick Diner in Talooca, Illinois. He opened his own place after Lill closed and moved to Florida.

Or not.

It seems no one has ever really seen Ed Debevic. Or remembers Lill's Diner. As for Talooca, Illinois—we're still searching for it on the map.

Not that we would question anything out loud in this campy 1950s-style diner. Not when the waitstaff specializes in service with a snarl. Garishly dressed waitresses snap their gum impatiently, toss straws at customers, and tell their tables they'll be back when they feel like it. Around here, the customer is *rarely* right. It's the *Happy Days* hangout off its Prozac. There's actually a sign that says, "Eat and GET OUT!"

Of course, it's all a joke . . . we hope.

Ed Debevic's does take its food seriously. It serves large portions of what you might expect from a diner: meatloaf, pot roast, burgers, and sandwiches.

And your waiter always throws in a side of lip, no extra charge.

Sugar-A Dessert Bar

108 West Kinzie Street
Chicago, IL 60610
(312) 822-9999

When you come to Chicago, you gotta find out what the buzz is all about . . . and at Sugar, it begins the moment you walk in the door. The black and yellow bristles that make up the wall represent the pollen-catching hairs of a bee's legs. Certainly not something you see everyday. No, at this outrageous dessert bar, everything is about the buzz—from the desserts to the drinks.

Sugar is the brainchild of owner Jerry Suqi, who opened up this candy-coated utopia in 2002 with two business partners. Jerry is a lover of literature, and at the same time, a tortured writer. Not able to complete his dream of writing a novel, he decided to combine his love of sugar with his love of words. What he's created is simply brilliant.

His masterful "menu-script" is based not only on classic desserts but also on the literary classics. Take the Marquis de Sucre—their signature dessert platter—named after the Marquis de Sade who's famous for saying that he liked everything all at once. That's what they give you: everything and all at once. The platter is made of hand-blown sugar. It's topped with just about

every decadent delight you can imagine and gives new meaning to the phrase "edible art."

The descriptions on the menu are about as imaginative as the creations. Temptation got the best of us and we had to share a few:

The Pound and the Fury
It is a tale told by a chef, full of poppy seed pound cake and furious
lemon curd and stewed rhubarb, signifying delight.
Enjoy the demise of this dessert as you lay dining.

The Papaya Mintafesto
Sadly, Marx was mistaken. It is not religion, but rather pineapple
sorbet wreathed by papaya-mint soup that is the true opiate
We supply upon demand—no Stalin.

Leaves of Lemongrass
Oh chef! My chef! The dreadful wait is done;
The lime soufflé has risen, and the prize we sought is won;
Lemongrass ice cream mans the starboard bow
Whilst anchored by a ginger anglaise

Illinois

The Stainless-Steel Dancers + 1

Every half-hour, Ed Debevic's waitstaff gets up on the front counter to perform. The Stainless-Steel Dancers, as they're known, put on quite a show. Except once.

For some reason, they invited me up to bust a move. But before I could join the act, they insisted I get into character. An apron, some goofy glasses, and a paper hat later, the Soda Jerk was born.

The name was appropriate, given the Jerk's dancing abilities. It was so bad the usually caustic waitstaff actually took pity on me. The whole thing probably violated corporate policy anyway—so don't tell Ed Debevic. If you ever see him.

Marc, aka "The Soda Jerk", joins the Stainless Steel Dancers at Ed Debevic's.

The list goes on and on. The Berry Wives of Windsor, The Unbearable Lightness of Brûlée, and Macdeath by Chocolate, which is far from any Shakespearean tragedy. The menu is a "novel" way for Jerry to express himself.

His favorite literary character is Hamlet. Why? Because he says his worst fear is not acting when it is time to act, and Hamlet was the ultimate procrastinator. No surprise Jerry's favorite dessert is The Yamlet—made with yam crème caramel and a pecan brown butter cake. Ahhh . . . sweets for the sweet.

Sugar—a restaurant by any other name would *not* taste as sweet.

Opera

1301 South Wabash Avenue
Chicago, IL 60605
(312) 461-0161
www.opera-chicago.com

If restaurants were like movies, this place would be PG-13, bordering on an R.

Opera is a delightfully risqué Chinese restaurant located in Chicago's developing South Loop neighborhood. And what makes it so sexy is a secluded area owner Jerry Kleiner playfully calls "the red light district."

At the back of the restaurant, behind a long wall, which is lacquered with suggestive Asian newspapers, there are several curtained, intimate dining nooks hidden from the main restaurant. They're dark and cozy and make you feel like you're doing something a little bit naughty just being there.

Don't worry, there's no chance anything could happen here, not with all the waiters and customers nearby. But it does stimulate the imagination.

Kleiner's imagination went into overdrive coming up with Opera. The owner of several successful local restaurants, Kleiner says he wasn't sure what he was looking for when he traveled to China seeking inspiration for a new place. He says he discovered his muse at a Chinese opera in Shanghai. People walked

photo courtesy of Ryan Roessler

Entrance to the "red light district" of Chicago's Opera restaurant.

around, ate and talked, even during the performance. He found it exciting.

He came back and opened Opera in 2002—designing everything right down to the velvet pillow-back chairs. Most descriptions probably start with the word *funky*. Other than those back rooms, this place is open, bright, and very loud. Just like the Chinese opera.

Executive Chef Paul Wildermuth's contemporary Chinese platters are every bit as spicy and provocative as the rest of the restaurant. The food is served family style—just right for sharing.

Only one suggestion: If you think you hear a fat lady sing at this Opera, don't look behind the curtains.

Illinois

Topolobampo and Frontera Grill

445 North Clark Street
Chicago, IL 60610
(312) 661-1434
www.fronterakitchens.com

Forget about the standard enchiladas and burritos at these two Mexican restaurants. Rather, it's menu items like Duck Breast with Velvety Apricot Mole or Pan-Roasted, Chipotle-Glazed Wild Alaskan King Salmon that will make your taste buds say "Arriba."

Oklahoma-born-and-raised chef/owner Rick Bayless has put Mexican food on the culinary map like no one else in this country. There's a reason critics rave about this superstar chef.

When dining at the more upscale Topolobampo, you might want to forget about watching your wallet—or at least be prepared to watch it drain. If you're not up for that, then check out Frontera Grill—no less delicious, but much less expensive. You'll also find some more familiar favorites on this menu, albeit with a gourmet spin, like crispy taquitos filled with chicken and poblano chiles, and tamales with various fillings. If you can't make it here, then look for his salsas and other Mexican specialties in your supermarket.

———

Mr. Beef

666 North Orleans Street
Chicago, IL 60610
(312) 337-8500

Forget about tables and chairs. In the windy city, when it comes to chowing down on Italian Beef at Mr. Beef, you want to be standing firmly on two feet. This sloppy, slurpy, messy, and meaty meal seems to taste better when you're standing up.

Chicagoans will tell you the Italian beef sandwich was born on the streets of this city. It was the perfect fare for the working man—or woman—who didn't have time to sit down for lunch.

What makes Mr. Beef stand out in a crowd is the slow-roasted, seasoned sirloin butts. They're cooled overnight, the pan juices are saved to make the gravy, and the fat is actually trimmed off by hand. Cook Todd Kruczek told us that although you may order it and get it fast, it's certainly not "fast food." People don't realize how much work goes into making one of these.

For those in the know, "juicy" is the best way to go. That means they submerge the entire sandwich in a bath of gravy. It's then finished off with a celery/carrot/pepper mix called Giardiniera. A word of warning: You might find yourself taking a beef shower. When this submarine goes down the hatch, expect the juices to run down your arms and get all over your clothes. That's why it's best to stay standing and lean over the counter to eat.

They have added what they call an "elegant dining room," as in a row of tables and benches, but we suggest you partake in the long-standing tradition and enjoy one of Chicago's most beloved "standup" routines.

———

Illinois

Twisted Spoke

501 North Ogden Avenue
Chicago, IL 60622
(312) 666-1500

3369 North Clark Street
Chicago, IL 60657
(773) 525-5300
www.twistedspoke.com

Co-owner Mitch Einhorn calls his restaurant a biker bar—for families.

Decorated with busted motorcycle parts and the occasional skeleton, Twisted Spoke has the look of an early Hell's Angels hangout. But that's more theme than mean. Like bikers themselves, the restaurant might seem rough and tough outside, but it's really warm and friendly inside. Tattoos are not a requirement. In fact, most people walk or drive a car here. The only thing big and burly you have to fear is the portion size.

The better-than-pub-grub food is homemade. Or as Einhorn says, "Just like Mom's if she was a biker babe from hell." Mondays feature all-you-can-eat Meatloaf, and on Thursdays there's limitless Pot Roast. Just to show you they're politically correct, the menu says the

hummus is made from "women peas, the peas formerly known as chick." See? What's to fear?

Bottom line at Twisted Spoke: You don't have to ride to a Hog to eat like one.

Twisted Spoke Pot Roast

ADAPTED FROM TWISTED SPOKE,
CHICAGO, ILLINOIS

YIELD: 10 SERVINGS

10- to 12-pound chuck or shoulder roast
Kosher salt to taste
Pepper to taste
1 pound mirepoix (⅓ pound small dice carrots, ⅓ pound small dice celery, ⅓ pound small dice onions sautéed in butter)
¼ cup flour
1 cup Carmelina tomatoes (tomatoes only, not the juice)
¼ bottle dry red wine
1 quart beef stock
⅛ cup black peppercorns
2 sprigs fresh thyme
3 bay leaves
½ cup garlic cloves
½ bunch fresh flat leaf parsley
7 pounds large carrots, cut in 2-inch pieces
7 pounds new red potatoes, cut in quarters

Trim chuck of extra fat. Salt and pepper chuck, then brown at very high heat, on both sides. Remove chuck from the pan, add mirepoix to the pan, and brown. Add flour, and cook until brown, 3 to 4 minutes. Add tomatoes and cook for 2 minutes. Add red wine.

Return chuck to the pan. Add beef stock, peppercorns, thyme, bay leaves, garlic, and parsley. Bring to a simmer, cover, and place in the oven at 300°F for 4 hours or until tender.

Add carrots and potatoes for the last 2 hours. When it's done, put meat, carrot, and potatoes in the steam table. Strain gravy, and skim fat.

To serve, slice ½-inch slices against the grain, put on a plate with carrots and potatoes, ladle gravy over the top of everything, and garnish with a little chopped parsley.

photo courtesy of Jill Littman

Riding with the owner of the Twisted Spoke, Mitch Einhorn, Chicago.

Illinois

Lou Mitchell's

565 West Jackson Boulevard
Chicago, IL 60661-5767
(312) 939-3111

If Wheaties is the "Breakfast of Champions," Lou Mitchell's in Chicago is the breakfast that champions *wish* they were eating. The consummate greasy spoon in the consummate American city, Lou Mitchell's is not to be missed.

The restaurant has been a Chicago institution since 1923, satisfying the breakfast crowd generation after generation. With juicy, cheese-oozing omelets and stacks of pancakes almost as high as the Sears Tower, you might leave feeling a bit guilty—that is, if you're worried about your waistline. But we encourage you to get past the guilt and indulge in a place that's as much a part of Chicago as the Cubs.

Outside Lou Mitchell's, a Chicago institution since 1923.

photo courtesy of Phil Johnston

One warning: We're not the first ones to sing Lou Mitchell's praises. The place is amazingly popular. Expect a line, especially on weekends. But the wait is actually part of the experience. Lou's friendly staff serves Milk Duds and home-made donut holes to the masses waiting for a table. It can't compare to the breakfast you're about to eat, but at least you won't have to listen to your stomach growling while you stand in line.

———

Lou Malnati's Pizzeria

6649 North Lincoln Avenue*
Lincolnwood, IL 60712
(847) 673-0800 or (800) LOU-TO-GO (800) 568-8646
www.loumalnatis.com

*Location of the original pizzeria. Check the website or call for other locations.

It's hard to say exactly why, but Chicagoans tend to have a *thing* with New Yorkers. They think New Yorkers are loud and rude, and when it comes to pizza, they say New Yorkers simply don't know what they're talking about. Because as any good Chicagoan will tell you, *real* pizza should be eaten with a knife and fork—and not for reasons of etiquette, but out of necessity. Chicago-style deep-dish ain't exactly finger food.

In Chicago, the name Lou Malnati is practically synonymous with deep-dish pizza. The Malnati family's history is steeped in deep-dish. Lou got his start working with his dad, Rudy Malnati, at Chicago's first deep-dish pizzeria in the 1940s. In 1971, Lou opened the first Lou Malnati's Pizzeria in the northern Chicago suburb of Lincolnwood. (There are now 21 family-owned Malnati's throughout Chicagoland.) Lou died in 1978, but his sons took over the family business and run it to this day.

If you've never tried Malnati's pizza, you should seriously consider changing that. It's just one of those things Americans ought to do—kind of like the culinary equivalent of seeing the Grand Canyon (although the pizza's not quite *that* deep).

Malnati's Chicago-style deep-dish pizza is actually the opposite of regular pizza. Literally. The

Illinois

mozzarella cheese is placed right on the dough. Then the other ingredients (sausage is tops in Chicago) are stacked on top of the cheese. The pie is topped with fresh tomato sauce. Toss a bit more cheese and some spices on top of that, and you've got a true slice of the American pizza dream.

Eat your heart out, New York. Or better yet, eat a slice of Lou Malnati's, and find out what you've been missing!

———

Ina's

1235 West Randolph Street
Chicago, IL 60607
(312) 226-8227
www.breakfastqueen.com

It's 6 A.M. and already Jill and her crew are watching the sun rise above Chicago. This is an early morning for the gang, who usually prefer to start around 9 or 10. But in the historic Randolph-Fulton market district, the early bird *really* gets the worm. If they had waited until 10 o'clock, they might have had nothing to shoot.

Since the mid-1800s, the Randolph-Fulton market area has been known as "the neighborhood that feeds Chicago," a hefty title to carry around. Many of the workers get here just after midnight to begin stocking their shelves and loading their trucks. At the break of dawn, they start pulling out to deliver their goods to restaurants, grocery stores, and markets around the city.

Ina Pinkney of Ina's also has a title that carries a lot of weight. She's known as the "breakfast queen of Chicago" and wants to be sure no one misses the most important meal of the day. Her restaurant, which also serves lunch and dinner, is right in the market area. She also begins bright and early, chatting with her purveyors and picking out the produce that make her morning meals reign supreme.

After the shopping's done, she heads back to the restaurant. Typically by 7 A.M., the place is already abuzz with caffeinated conversation, and the smells of a good gourmet breakfast permeate the place. Jill and crew couldn't help but liven up here.

This is when you realize why Ina rises with the sun—her food simply shines through. Her Heavenly Hots are thin sour-cream pancakes served with fresh fruit compote (you won't even need syrup!). Then there's the vegetable hash served with poached eggs and the French toast soaked in vanilla overnight, served with a caramelized cinnamon-sugar coating. Everything here is made with her special touch. Ina is just one of those women who lights up a room with her contagious smile and liveliness, and eating at her restaurant is a great way to start the day. You just better count on taking that afternoon nap.

Pasta Frittata
ADAPTED FROM INA'S, CHICAGO, ILLINOIS

YIELD: 4 SERVINGS

2 teaspoons olive oil
¾ cup chopped onion
2 garlic cloves, minced
¾ cup julienne red bell pepper
1½ cups sliced mushrooms
1½ cups julienne zucchini
1 teaspoon dried oregano
2½ teaspoons salt
2 teaspoons pepper
10 eggs
1¼ cups whole milk
1½ cups shredded sharp cheddar cheese
½ cup grated Parmesan cheese
1 pound cream cheese
3 cups cooked spaghetti
Lightly sautéed fresh tomato sauce (optional)

Preheat oven to 350°F.

Brush a 10-inch round cake pan lightly with oil. Cut a piece of parchment paper the same size, place in pan, brush again with oil, and set aside.

Sauté onions and garlic in olive oil until soft, then add red bell pepper, mushrooms, and zucchini and continue to cook until soft. Drain off liquid, and add oregano, 1 teaspoon each of salt and pepper. Set aside to cool.

In a large mixer bowl, beat eggs, milk, cheddar cheese, Parmesan cheese, and 1½ teaspoons salt and 1 teaspoon pepper on low speed. When combined, add cream cheese in small bite-size bits (pull pieces by hand).

Put cooked spaghetti into pan. Do the same with vegetables. Pour in egg mixture, and mix with your hands so all the components are equally distributed in the pan. Pat down so that as much of the solids as possible are covered with the liquid.

Bake for 30 to 40 minutes until firm to the touch and lightly brown. It will puff up and settle when cool. Serve immediately on a bed of lightly sautéed fresh tomato sauce (if desired).

Michigan

American Coney Island

114 West Lafayette Boulevard
Detroit, MI 48226
(313) 961-7758
www.americanconeyisland.com

In downtown Detroit, there are two legendary Coney-dog restaurants that sit side by side. They were opened by the same family and sell the same basic product, Coney dogs, covered with chili and topped with mustard. But that's about where the similarities end.

American Coney Island is the downtown dog stand that started it all, courtesy of Gus Keros, who immigrated to Detroit from Greece in 1903. He wanted to pay homage to his new home and knew Coney Island in New York City was a famous place for hot dogs. So he put two and two together, and in 1917 opened American Coney Island.

A few years later, his brother Bill opened his own Coney-dog restaurant next door, not to compete, but rather to build on the family fortune. He named his after the street: Lafayette.

For years, the businesses boomed, and Coney Corner grew into local legend. But tensions arose in the 1970s, when Lafayette was sold to company employees.

As for the American, the Keros family decided to modernize in 1989. They expanded, gave the American a face-lift, and started selling salads, soups, and desserts—in addition to the dogs. They even offer a menu so customers can keep it all straight.

No question about it, the American is not only brighter and more modern than Lafayette, it's open around the clock, 365 days a year, and it sells a special breed of dog. The recipe for the highly seasoned natural casing is top secret, as are the ingredients for the chili sauce with which they're slathered. Yellow mustard and chopped Vidalia onions top 'em off.

Loyal customers are very patriotic about American Coney Island. To them, this is *the* place to get a true Detroit delicacy.

Lafayette Coney Island

118 West Lafayette Boulevard
Detroit, MI 48226
(313) 964-8198

Lafayette might be the newcomer (opened in 1924), but in terms of appearance, Lafayette is the "before" picture to American Coney Island's "after." No flags, and no fancy decorations, just memorable hot dogs.

There are similarities between the two places. Lafayette gets its buns and mustard from the same company as American, and much like the place next door, it keeps its hot dog and chili recipes a secret.

But friendly competition this is not.

Lafayette wouldn't think of expanding its menu. The list of items is limited to the chili-dogs, hamburgers, and fries.

When it comes to loyalty, most Lafayette regulars are pretty intense. They won't even think about going into American, much less eating their hot dogs. You can't blame them, considering their parents brought them here, and they're now sharing the tradition with their children.

Jill and Marc didn't realize the intensity of the animosity between the two places until they asked a manager from Lafayette to shake hands on-camera with the owner of American.

He refused.

———

Buddy's Pizza

17125 Conant Street*
Detroit, MI 48212
(313) 892-9001
www.buddyspizza.com

*There are nine locations throughout metro-Detroit. This is their flagship store. Check out the web or call for other locations.

In downtown Detroit there's a slogan, "It's not the size that counts; it's the shape." Specifically, the shape of pizza you'll find at Buddy's. Here, it's hip to be square.

They began serving their famous square pizza in 1946. Nine locations later, they're still cranking it out. Pretty remarkable considering that both Domino's and Little Caesar's were founded in Michigan and have their corporate headquarters here. You gotta be good to compete with the big boys. We're here to tell you they are!

First, they spread the deep-dish dough in their seasoned square pans. Next the pepperoni, then the Wisconsin Brick Cheese, and last the sauce. As for the origin of the square, apparently the first workers were Sicilian immigrants who modeled the pizza after rectangular focaccia bread. The shape stuck.

Folks around here will let you in on a little secret. They claim that deep-dish pizza was invented here at Buddy's, *not* by the guys in the Windy City.

But perhaps their biggest secret is in the staff. Talk to just about any old-timer from the top corporate management on down and they'll tell you they started as a dishwasher or busboy years ago and worked their way up. This is a place that really treats its employees well, and it shows.

When we were there shooting, we met Irving Slosnick, who, at 89 years old, is still working 5 days and 50 hours a week. And it's not because he *has* to; it's because he *wants* to. He started here in 1978, a short-timer by some employee's standards.

Whether or not they invented deep dish is hard to say. But one thing we know is true: Buddy's Pizza is a place that doesn't cut corners—not on their pizza, and not on their people.

———

The Whitney

4421 Woodward Avenue
Detroit, MI 48201
(313) 832-5700
www.thewhitney.com

When making a reservation at The Whitney in Detroit, you might want to ask for an extra place setting because you never know when a special ghostly guest will decide to join you.

David Whitney Jr. made his fortune from wood in the mid-to-late 1800s. Once the largest lumber baron in the Midwest, he built this 40,000-square-foot mansion to showcase all his prized possessions. Unfortunately, he wasn't able to cherish it for very long because a few years after completing it in 1894, he passed away. However, many believe he still haunts the halls of his home.

On numerous occasions, guests have claimed to see apparitions in the various dining rooms. In fact, you could write a book about the visions seen in the library. And up the grand staircase, past the original Tiffany windows and light fixtures, is the grandfather clock that, on occasion, chimes randomly.

The elevator maintains the same mysterious schedule. It opens, but no one is there. (This happened to Jill during her interview with current owner John McCarthy when shooting *The Best Of Haunted Restaurants*. It's in the piece so there's proof.) Now whether it's just a mechanical malfunction, who knows . . . that'll have to be explored on the Do-It-Yourself Network.

Seems the chefs who cook here have something in common with the ghosts. Their food is out-of-this-world. From the Ginger Soy Braised Beef Short-Ribs to the Rack of Veal, you'll have a supernatural experience.

Michigan

So while at The Whitney, if there's a sudden chill in the air or you see a shadow dashing about, don't be afraid. It's just old man Whitney dropping down at dinnertime.

—

Roma Café

3401 Riopelle Street
Detroit, MI 48207
(313) 831-5940
www.romacafe.com

This is the kind of Italian restaurant where you feel like a regular even if it's your first visit. Spend a few minutes here and you'll find yourself fighting the urge to kiss people on the cheek and order a round for the house. It's just that authentic.

The sensation is even more remarkable considering the Roma Café is in the middle of nowhere. Officially, it's on the fringe of Detroit's historic Eastern Market, but that doesn't mean much when you're lost and calling from your car. The hostess actually spends much of her time giving directions.

But walk in the door, and you're home. It's like one big festive family reunion, complete with a crazy uncle or two.

Much of the credit goes to the waiters. These guys are serious professionals. In fact, they're unionized (hey, it's Detroit), which gets them health and dental benefits. But mostly, it means excellent service.

How good? Well, usually customers just let their waiters handle the ordering. All they have to say is that they're in the mood for veal (or pasta or whatever), and the waiter decides the actual dish. You're in his hands; he'll take good care of you.

This develops fantastic loyalty. Most regulars have their own favorite waiter and refuse to order from anyone else. Some customers actually keep track of their guy's schedule so they don't show up when he's off or on vacation.

The Roma Café dates its origins back to 1890 and claims to be Detroit's oldest restaurant. Nice tidbit, but it doesn't mean as much as the fact that it's been in the hands of the Sossi family for

Do We Cook? The Answer Is: A Definite Maybe

I'm often asked if I have a background in cooking. The answer is yes, if you count warming up a Swanson's Hungry Man meal as cooking. (Or is that baking?)

I got the job on *The Best Of* because Food Network liked my broadcasting experience. Learning to properly sear foie gras came later; probably about the time I learned how to pronounce foie gras.

But after hundreds of interviews with top chefs, I've learned a few things. Among them: Never salt your food in a restaurant. Chefs use enough (kosher or sea) salt back in the kitchen to empty the Dead Sea. Then there's the butter issue. It usually goes like this: A chef will say, "We're going to finish this sauce with a *little* butter." At that point, I hear beeps from a dump truck backing up toward the pan, preparing to unload several mountains of butter. Okay, a slight exaggeration, but you get the idea. Even I understand that fat is flavor.

Learning from the pros has made a big difference. I'm brave (and maybe even skilled) enough now to handle the recipes in this book. Usually, they even turn out right. But the one recipe that always works perfectly is the Veal Florentina from Roma Café, which is included here. It's fast, it's easy, and it edges out a Hungry Man meal *almost* every time. Good luck.

most of a century. If you're in with owner Janet Sossi Becoure, then you're set for life.

Interesting trivia: Long ago, Janet's grandfather *almost* went into business with an old friend of his. The idea was to package Italian food. Grandpa declined—but his friend Hector went on to great success. You probably know him by his professional name: Chef Boyardee.

Yes, the family missed out on a great fortune. But the Roma Café offers the kind of at-home authenticity you can't put in a can.

Michigan

Veal Florentina

ADAPTED FROM ROMA CAFÉ,
DETROIT, MICHIGAN

YIELD: 4 SERVINGS

4 (1-ounce) medallions of veal
2 slices prosciutto
2 slices fontina cheese
Flour for dusting
½ cup olive oil for sautéing
1 cup sliced mushrooms
½ cup marsala wine
Salt and pepper to taste

Lay out medallion of veal, and place 1 slice proscuitto and 1 slice fontina cheese on top of each piece of veal. Place a piece of veal on top of each to create a sandwich effect, and dust the outside with flour.

In a large sauté pan, heat olive oil on medium heat; add veal, and brown on both sides. Remove excess oil, add mushrooms and marsala wine, salt, and pepper to taste, and reduce for 4 to 5 minutes. Remove veal, plate, and spoon mushrooms and sauce over veal.

Under the Eagle

9000 Joseph Campau Avenue
Hamtramck, MI 48212
(313) 875-5905

Two words: food coma.

Under the Eagle serves some seriously hearty Polish food. Open since 1973, owner Theresa Peczeniuk never wasted her energy making the place fancy. Instead, she saved the heavy lifting for her cooking. You will not walk out of here hungry.

Located in Hamtramck, a city within a city, it's actually surrounded by Detroit. The platters are much the same. They're meals on top of meals. Case in point: A specialty called Chicken Susanna, named for Theresa's daughter, is a large chicken breast wrapped in potato pancakes. Most restaurants would consider that two separate entrées. But around here, they throw on sauerkraut and beets—as if you had room.

Then there's the combination platter: two pierogies, sausage, an applesauce blintz, sauerkraut, and mashed potatoes.

If you don't need a nap after that, you should see a doctor for insomnia.

Tribute Restaurant

31425 West Twelve Mile Road
Farmington Hills, MI 48334
(248) 848-9393
www.tributerestaurant.com

If you ask Executive Chef Takashi Yagihashi what he does, he'll tell you it's more than just cook. Think of him as a conductor and each night in his kitchen is a performance. His stage is Tribute, a restaurant that pays *tribute* to the art of fine dining. He creates a symphony of tastes and flavors composed to please even the harshest critics.

Located in an upscale suburb of Detroit, the restaurant was built in 1996 by the Wisne family, well-known suppliers to the auto industry. They wanted to have a top-notch place for auto executives to wine and dine their clients. In other words: No expense was spared in designing and decorating the dining room; from the signed

Michigan

The Encore

I love dessert. But you can hardly describe what pastry chef Michael Laiskonis at Tribute makes as "dessert." It's beyond that. Consider it the harmonious finale.

What I'm talking about isn't on the menu, but for those in the know, Michael always has a secret stash. It's called The Egg—a hollowed-out eggshell, filled with milk chocolate crème brûlée. It bakes. It cools.

Drops of caramel go on top along with cold, caramel custard foam, followed by a drizzling of maple syrup. Is your mouth watering yet? Well wait, it gets better.

He sprinkles a few grains of sea salt on top. Sea salt, you ask? I'll admit it: I, too, was skeptical. He told me to trust him. I did. So trust me. You'll never look at an egg the same way again.

Andy Warhol painting to the napkin rings studded with semi-precious stones. The price tag was more than $2 million. The goal was to put Detroit on the culinary map, and judging from the accolades, it has succeeded.

The *New York Times* called Tribute "One of America's top restaurants." It is regularly mentioned in the pages of *Bon Appétit* and *Wine Spectator* magazines. Chef Yagihashi was named "Best Chef in the Midwest" in 2003 by the James Beard Foundation.

The cuisine is described as contemporary French with an Asian twist. It's nothing short of spectacular. No matter what you order, it's bound to be a hit production.

And wait until you see the walk-through wine cellar. Encased in glass, you actually pass through and under it on your way to the dining room. Bottles, ranging from $30 to $3,500, are melodiously paired with your food.

Tribute is definitely a place that's in tune with life's little pleasures.

Ristorante Café Cortina

30715 West Ten Mile Road
Farmington Hills, MI 48336
(248) 474-3033
www.cafecortina.com

The setting is romantic, the food is romantic, and so is the story of how this place came to be.

For Rina and Adriano Tonon, opening Ristorante Café Cortina in 1976 was their dream come true. Both Adriano, an immigrant from Northern Italy, and Rina, the daughter of Italian immigrants, grew up in the restaurant business. They met, got married, and found this little piece of land in what was at the time a largely undeveloped area of suburban Detroit. All that stood on the property was an apple orchard and a small house.

They built a restaurant, created a garden, and named their gem after a popular ski resort town in the Italian Alps. Their goal was to be the best restaurant in metro Detroit. They were well on their way, winning all sorts of awards. Unfortunately, their love story took a tragic turn.

In the early 1990s, Adriano passed away. Rina was left with some tough choices. Should she continue the dream they began together on her own? After much soul searching, she told us, "I really rolled up my sleeves and thought 'I am going to make you [Adriano] very proud. I am going to continue the dream we had.'"

She did with the help of their son, Adrian, by her side.

In March 2003, Café Cortina was named "Detroit's Restaurant of the Year" by *Hour Magazine*. That same month we came and did a story on them for *The Best Of Pasta Places*. Rina says the accolades are a fitting tribute to her late husband and signify everything he wanted to achieve with the restaurant.

A stickler for rolling and cutting his pasta by

Michigan

hand, Adriano was also a believer in using the freshest possible ingredients; thus the garden out back. Now, Chef Jeffrey Hoffman, nicknamed "Hoffa," is giving the same care and attention to the food. His specialties include gnocchi with porcini mushrooms, sun-dried tomatoes, and truffle oil; and tortellini with a meaty ragu.

When asked why everyone calls him Hoffa, he said that in the early stages of cooking, he was always disappearing from the kitchen to run outside and pick herbs from the garden. Because of his "disappearing act," the staff started calling him Hoffa, and the name stuck.

The restaurant seats about 200, but the ambiance is still cozy and romantic. The best seats in the house surround the fireside pit, where people dine amid candlelight and the glow of the fire. From the moment you walk in until the time you leave, you are just about guaranteed to find amore in every corner. Perhaps it's Adriano checking in from above on the love he left behind.

The Grill

Ritz Carlton, Dearborn
Fairlane Plaza
300 Town Center Drive
Dearborn, MI 48126
(313) 441-2000
www.ritzcarlton.com

Ask a Ritz Carlton employee anywhere to show you their Credo card, and they'll reach into their pocket, their purse, sometimes even the lining of their shoe to produce a remarkable piece of work.

Credo cards are wallet-size reminders to employees that they work at a top-flight hotel chain and are required to provide the best service available. The card includes instructions as simple as smiling and maintaining eye contact with guests. But the overall theme, boldly printed on the card, is this: "We Are Ladies and Gentlemen Serving Ladies and Gentlemen."

The message has certainly taken hold at The Grill at the Ritz Carlton, Dearborn. Picked as the city's best restaurant (2003) by *The Detroit Free Press*, it's formal without being stuffy. You

---

An Official Card Carrier

I was so impressed with the sentiments on the Ritz Carlton's Credo card, I decided to carry one, too. Given that I don't work for the hotel chain, keeping it in my wallet pretty much certifies that I am indeed a nerd. But because the card reminds me to be professional and proud, I make sure I'm the biggest and best nerd I can possibly be.

---

can actually relax and enjoy yourself even though it's a sophisticated atmosphere.

The regional American cuisine is simple but excellent. Signature items include the Colorado Rack of Lamb scented with rosemary, or the Pan Seared Wild Striped Bass with Heirloom Tomato Fondue and Potato Purée. It's all done well, not overdone. Chef de Cuisine Stephen Jalbert avoids the pitfall of throwing too much into a recipe.

The service is on a par with the food. It's more notable for what you don't see than what you do. The waitstaff is polite (they call you by name), but not overbearing. Your glass is filled before you notice it's empty. Ask an employee where the pay phone is, and he'll walk you to it.

That's how things are done at the Ritz Carlton. It's their credo.

Zingerman's Delicatessen

422 Detroit Street
Ann Arbor, MI 48104
(734) 663-DELI (734-663-3354)
www.zingermans.com

You wouldn't think that waiting in line would be a welcome thing at most restaurants, but then again, Zingerman's isn't like most places.

For starters, there's pure menu madness. All their sandwiches are named after employees or customers. Some of them are numbered, some

Michigan

not. And although they have a numbering system of 1 to 100, some of the numbers are missing, and nothing is in numerical order. Add to the wackiness: They rotate the menu. Some sandwiches get retired and then come back; others go into retirement forever (but they keep lists of all the old sandwiches and will make them by request).

If it's all too overwhelming, you can play it safe and order the #2, the Zingerman's Reuben. This is the sandwich that started it all back in 1982 when owners Ari Weinzweig and Paul Saginaw opened the deli. Both were University of Michigan grads who were desperate for a deli in their own backyard. As Ari confessed, "We couldn't get good corned beef in Ann Arbor." They changed that, and now more than 20 years later, this place pulls rank. In fact, in January 2003, it was ranked the "Coolest Small Company in America" by *Inc. Magazine*.

Why is it called Zingerman's? Well, they say Ari's last name was too hard to pronounce and Paul's last name is Saginaw—enough said. So they made up a name . . . one that has quite a *zing* to it. Obviously it worked.

In no time the lines were out the door, and that was just the beginning. The delicatessen launched both a catering company and a coffee shop, and so on and so forth. It became such an entity that now all their businesses are under the ZCOB umbrella: Zingerman's Community of Businesses. At last count there were about seven of 'em, with more on the way.

Don't mistake this for a franchise, though. That's not part of their plan. In other words, there will be only one delicatessen. Sorry, die-hard deli fans, you'll have to come to Ann Arbor and stand in line with the rest of the Zingerman faithful.

At peak times the wait can tick on for an hour or more. When you finally do get to the front of the line, you're asked if you want the nosher or the fresher. For everyone out there who doesn't know Yiddish, *nosher* means "small eater" and *fresher* means "big eater." Take their Reuben, for example. The fresher has nearly a half-pound of corned beef. The nosher; a mere quarter-pound. No matter which you order, it's a mouthful. No wonder they go through about 2,000 pounds of corned beef a week. No skimping on portions here.

While standing in line, let us know if you can figure out their menu. We don't even think the owners have a method to their madness, but then again, that's part of the charm.

Michigan

Zingerman's Reuben Sandwich

ADAPTED FROM ZINGERMAN'S DELICATESSEN, ANN ARBOR, MICHIGAN

YIELD: 6 SANDWICHES

2 pounds very good but not too lean corned beef, sliced
1 loaf really good Jewish rye bread without seeds, unsliced
1½ cups Zingerman's Russian Dressing (see recipe below)
¾ pound sauerkraut
12 slices Swiss cheese
Butter or olive oil for grilling

Preheat oven to 350°F.
Sprinkle meat with a little water, then wrap it tightly in tin foil and place it in the oven.

At the same time, put the whole loaf of rye, unwrapped, into the oven. After approximately 15 minutes, remove bread from the oven. The crust should be crunchy but not overly hard or burnt. Set bread on the counter, and give it a few minutes to cool off for easier handling.

Prepare your plates by warming them in the oven or microwave.

As soon as bread has cooled enough to hold (about 5 minutes), place it on a cutting board. Hold the loaf on its side in your noncutting hand, with its top crust facing away from you. Hold the bread knife at about a 45-degree angle across the corner of bread and start slicing. You should end up with 12 slices.

Remove corned beef from the oven; steam should emerge when you open the foil. Spread each slice of bread with 1 ounce Russian Dressing. Pile on 5 ounces corned beef, 2 ounces sauerkraut, and 2 slices Swiss, then set the second slice of bread on top of sandwich.

Heat a heavy skillet. Brush the outside of each slice of bread with a bit of butter or olive oil. When the pan is hot (oil should sizzle a bit when it hits the pan), place sandwich in the skillet. Place a heavy bowl on top of sandwich to weigh it down. When the first side has been grilled to a golden brown, flip and repeat. Remove from the pan, cut diagonally, and serve it while it's hot!

Zingerman's Russian Dressing

YIELD: 2 CUPS

¾ cup mayonnaise
¼ cup plus 2 to 3 tablespoons chili sauce
2 tablespoons sour cream
2 teaspoons chopped fresh curly parsley
1 tablespoon plus 1 teaspoon minced Spanish onion
1 tablespoon plus 1 teaspoon minced dill pickle
½ teaspoon fresh lemon juice
½ teaspoon horseradish
¼ teaspoon Worcestershire sauce

In a medium bowl, combine mayonnaise, chili sauce, sour cream, parsley, onion, pickle, lemon juice, horseradish, and Worcestershire sauce, and mix well.

Iowa

Jacob's Table
121 West Green Street
Postville, IA 52162
(563) 864-7087

A rabbi and a Lutheran pastor walk into a kosher deli in a small Iowa farm town. The rabbi says, "I'll take a pound of hummus." The pastor says, "Two loaves of challah, please." What, you were expecting a punch line? There's no joke here. This is a scene that plays out daily in Postville, Iowa (population 2,273). And although Iowa is the nation's leading pork-producing state, it also happens to be that Postville is home to one of the world's largest kosher meat processing plants.

That explains the raison d'être for Jacob's Table, Postville's first—and likely small-town Iowa's *only*—kosher deli. Opened in 1998 to serve the ever-expanding Orthodox Jewish population, Jacob's is now a mainstay in downtown Postville—just as popular as the local café, where bacon and eggs are a specialty.

Owner Shulamis Jenkelowitz moved to Postville from Brooklyn, New York, as did many of the town's 200-plus Jewish residents. An unapologetic New Yorker, she'll be the first to admit the transition was a bit rough, but her food has proven to be something of a bridge linking the community's diverse population.

One slurp of her matzo ball soup and you'll understand why. At first, Jenkelowitz handed out samples of traditionally Jewish and Middle Eastern fare to encourage locals to try "foreign" foods like hummus and falafel. It didn't take long for natives to catch on, and to start snatching up her specialties. She says the deli sells 500 loaves of her rye bread a week and more than 100 pounds of homemade challah bread every Friday (mostly to non-Jewish residents).

Tucked away in the northeast corner of Iowa (the closest city with a population over 50,000 is La Crosse, Wisconsin, an hour away), you might say Postville is a bit off the beaten path. But if you're into witnessing firsthand the ever-changing complexion of America, we promise you won't be disappointed. Besides, where else are you going to find a bagel this good in the middle of the Midwest?

Matzo Ball Chicken Soup

ADAPTED FROM JACOB'S TABLE, POSTVILLE, IOWA

MAKES 12 TO 15 (1¼-CUP) SERVINGS; ABOUT 12 MATZO BALLS

Soup:
1 (3-pound) chicken, cut into quarters
12 cups water
3 carrots, peeled and chopped
5 stalks celery, chopped
1 sweet potato, peeled and chopped
2 small zucchinis, chopped
1 medium onion, chopped
1 tablespoon salt
¼ teaspoon freshly ground black pepper

Matzo Balls:
4 large eggs
¼ cup seltzer water
¼ cup vegetable oil
1 teaspoon salt
Pinch freshly ground black pepper
1 cup matzo meal

To make soup: Place chicken in an 8-quart pot and add water. Place carrots, celery, potato, zucchini, and onion in the pot, and add salt and pepper. Bring chicken to a boil, reduce the heat, and simmer for 2 hours. Pour soup into a strainer set in a large bowl. Cool chicken enough to handle, and discard skin and bones. Cut meat into bite-size pieces. Place vegetables, chicken, and broth in the refrigerator, and let cool completely. The fat will rise to top of broth.

To make matzo balls: Lightly beat eggs. Add water, oil, salt, and pepper, and mix well. Stir in matzo meal until thoroughly mixed. Refrigerate for 30 minutes to 1 hour.

Meanwhile, partially fill a large pot with water and bring to a boil. Moisten the palms of your hands with cold water. Form the mixture into balls ¾ to 1 inch in diameter, and drop into boiling water.

When all matzo balls are in the pot, reduce the heat to low. Simmer, covered, for about 30 minutes, or until done. Remove with slotted spoon to a large bowl.

To finish soup: Skim the fat off top of broth, and transfer to a large pot over medium heat. Add vegetables and chicken. Add matzo balls, and simmer for 15 minutes before serving.

Hotel Pattee

1112 Willis Avenue
Perry, IA 50220
(515) 465-3511
www.hotelpattee.com

"**J**ill, would you mind helping me out with something?" Chef David North called from behind the counter. Always one who likes to be involved in the cooking segments we shoot, Jill scurried next to the chef like a dutiful student. Her cameraman continued to roll tape as Chef North began to make an Iowa smoked pork tenderloin with fresh Iowa corn and roasted red peppers. Seemed like every other cooking segment we shoot, pretty straightforward.

Chef North dumped about 1 cup flour on the counter, handed Jill a butcher knife, and asked, "Would you mind chopping flour for me?" Jill, never one to doubt a chef's skill, replied, "Sure, no problem, although I've never been asked to chop flour before." As she chopped away, the chef specified his request, "I need it finely chopped, a little more than what you're doing." Aiming to please, Jill continued on, then played to the camera a little bit, shrugging her shoulders as if this were an everyday request. That's when she caught cameraman Dan Dwyer and soundman Tom Forliti cracking up. She realized she had been duped.

In this tiny prairie town sits one of the most distinctive hotels in the country. The hotel was founded in 1913, by the Pattee brothers. They built the hotel in honor of their father, David Pattee, one of the town's founders. However, over the years, it changed hands many times, fell into disrepair, and eventually ended up on the auction block. Enter Roberta Ahmanson, a woman who grew up in Perry, moved to California, and married a philanthropist. She always kept an eye on the welfare of her small town, so when the hotel went up for final sale in 1993, she anted up. For just $38,000, the hotel was hers.

Four years and $10 million later, the Hotel Pattee reopened its doors. But this is no average hotel. Walking in here is more like walking into a surreal art gallery. Each room is meant to reflect Iowa and the small towns that dot the landscape. The Louis Armstrong Room pays homage to the time the famous jazz musician stayed at the hotel in 1953. The Ragbrai Room—named for the famous annual bike ride across Iowa—has lampshades made out of bike seats and headboards in the shape of bicycle spokes. There's also a bowling alley in the basement that is part of the original hotel as well as a library and a spa. Amazing for a town of fewer than 3,000 people.

Then there's the food. David's Milwaukee Diner, named after the railroad that was once the heartbeat of the town, is far from any diner you're likely to eat in. And although Chef David North might be a prankster, he takes his cooking quite seriously. Pulled Pork Wonton's, Five Spice Salmon, and Petite Filet on top of a Poached Lobster Tail are just a few of his specialties.

There are surprises around every corner here. We won't give them all away, but we'll leave you with this: chopping flour isn't one of them, but it did make for one helluva segment on our blooper tape!

South Union Bread Café

1011 Locust Avenue
Des Moines, IA 50309
(515) 288-9232
www.centrodesmoines.com

Eating garlic before a date or a business meeting might not seem like a good idea, but at George Formaro's sandwich shop, customers don't seem to care. His food is so fresh and good that what-

Farmer in the Dell

It's not every day that one gets to ruin a farmer's freshly planted arugula. But on this crisp spring day in rural Iowa, that's exactly what I did.

We began the shoot at Larry Cleverly's farm in Mingo, IA for our *Best Of Farm Fresh* show on, well, a farm. Larry used to be an executive in New York and Chicago. But after nearly 25 years in the corporate world, he decided he'd had enough of the rat race. In 1996, he and his wife packed up 100 pounds of garlic and a bag of tomato seed and headed west, back to his family's Iowa farm.

In our attempt to make this piece for the show more folksy, I decided to temporarily shed my "TV Host" title and replace it with the title of "Farmer Jill." Larry had me digging up garlic, looking at his other crops, and helping him plant lettuce. But as an overachiever, even in my short-lived farming career, I wanted more. I wanted the tractor.

The crew and I eventually convinced Larry that having me till some of his land would make the piece more interesting. He picked an area where nothing was growing and put me to work. I was cruising along on the tractor, tilling away and having a great time, when I heard shouts from behind, "Stop! stop!" I went to brake, but instead hit the gas and went full force into a field of freshly planted arugula, churning up all kinds of dirt, seedlings, and tiny sprouts that were just coming up.

Finally, in a desperate attempt to stop, I turned off the ignition and the tractor came to a dead halt. But now, instead of hearing screams, all I heard was silence. I was scared to look behind for fear of seeing the damage I had done. When I finally turned around, Larry was slowly walking toward me while my crew stood in the far distance shaking their heads. He looked at me thoughtfully and said, "You're more a natural on television than you are on the tractor. I think you better stick to your day job." Point taken.

Luckily the lettuce did grow back, and we're happy to report that Larry's business is booming. But if there is ever a shortage of arugula in Iowa, blame me.

ever residual odors may linger are apparently worth every bite.

His garlic soup and foccacia bread, for which the dough takes 36 hours to ferment—along with his menu of meat-filled sandwiches—attract a legion of diehard regulars. He gets his free-range lunchmeat from local farmer Larry Cleverly, who gets it from Niman Ranch. As Larry likes to say, "The animals only have one bad day." Larry also supplies him with local produce and his famous organic garlic.

George is one of those guys who doesn't skimp on quality, even if it means paying more. His philosophy has paid off. He now owns a second restaurant, Centro (515-244-7033), right next door, where he cooks New York–style pizza in a coal-fired oven, as well as an array of authentic Italian dishes. His mother was Sicilian and practically raised him on garlic, which is why he puts it in everything. Half jokingly he told us that he's trying to make garlic ice cream. Knowing George, you might find it there when you visit.

Focaccia Bread

ADAPTED FROM SOUTH UNION BREAD CAFÉ, DES MOINES, IOWA

MAKES 2 (14-INCH) LOAVES

Starter:
2 cups bread flour
1 cup water
2 teaspoons active dry yeast

Dough:
2 cups warm water (78 to 85°F)
4 teaspoons sea salt, plus extra for topping
5½ to 6 cups bread flour
Olive oil for topping
Chopped garlic, to taste, for topping

To make starter: Mix flour, water, and yeast in a large bowl, cover, and let rest overnight at room temperature.

To make dough: Mix water, salt, and enough of flour into starter to make a soft dough. Knead dough

on a floured surface for about 5 minutes. Place in a bowl, cover, and let rise for 2 to 3 hours until doubled in size.

Divide dough into 2 pieces, shape into round balls, and let rise, covered, for 30 minutes.

Preheat the oven with a baking stone to 475°F.

Flatten dough balls as if making a pizza. Place on a floured pizza peel. Brush flattened dough with olive oil, and top with chopped garlic and sea salt. Place carefully onto the hot stone. Bake for 7 to 12 minutes, or until golden brown, popping any air bubbles that form during baking.

Missouri

Arthur Bryant's

1727 Brooklyn Avenue
Kansas City, MO 64127
(816) 231-1123
www.arthurbryantsbbq.com

You might think barbeque would be an innocuous enough topic of discussion. You might think it, but you would be wrong. In fact, there are few culinary subjects likely to inflame the kind of regionalist pride that barbeque does. Appropriately, it was in the middle of the country where we found ourselves in the middle of this debate.

Most anyone from Kansas City will tell you their town is tops when it comes to barbeque. And the undisputed king of the KC grill: Arthur Bryant's. Around here, *this* King Arthur rivals the guy with the knights and the round table.

Visit Arthur Bryant's restaurant, however, and you can expect a Formica table and cafeteria-style dining. While Bryant's is long on lines and short on décor, the minute you bite into a barbeque beef sandwich, you'll feel like royalty. It might be the only sandwich you'll ever eat with a fork.

The legend of Kansas City's King Arthur began in the 1930s, when Arthur's brother, Charlie, opened the restaurant. Arthur took over in 1946, and the place has been a destination restaurant ever since. Arthur Bryant died in 1982, but his ribs lived on, so to speak. *New Yorker* writer Calvin Trillin called it "The single best restaurant in the world."

Of course, ask anyone from Texas or Memphis or the Carolinas, and those would be fighting words. The people in these states are constantly ribbing each other for barbeque bragging rights. Seriously. Barbeque is not to be taken lightly, especially when you're talking about the sauce.

For those not entrenched in the debate, here's a basic primer: Texans tend to favor beef. Carolinians go for pork. In Kansas City the saying goes, "If it moves, we cook it." As for the sauce, Texas barbeque sauce is usually tomato based and tends to have a kick. Traditional Carolina sauce is more vinegar based. Kansas City sauce is somewhere in between—tomato based, slightly spicy, and a little sweet.

In terms of *quantity*, Kansas City wins, hands down. With more than 90 barbeque joints, KC boasts the most barbeque restaurants in America. Of course, Kansas City aficionados will tell you their town wins the *quality* battle, as well.

One trip to Arthur Bryant's, and you just might be convinced.

---

d'Bronx Deli

3904 Bell Street
Kansas City, MO 64111
(816) 531-0550

2450 Grand Avenue (in Crown Center shops)
Kansas City, MO 64108
(816) 842-2211

Say it like a New Yorker—"da Bronx." Okay, now you're talking. "Ya wanna pickle wid dat? Yes or no, c'mon, we don't haves all days here."

Consider d'Bronx Deli a slice of New York on Midwestern turf. Although the attitude here isn't really as rough as the stereotypical New York approach, the sandwiches and the pizza are the real deal. And they should be. Owner Janet Bloom's father Lou Moses is from "da Bronx," so

when she and her husband, Robert, decided to open this joint, they had Lou watching them every step of the way. From the lines that regularly snake out the door, seems like they got it right. Her father gives it a thumbs up and tells customers from the Big Apple to eat their heart out.

And yeah, I do's want pickles wid that. Got it?

Fritz's Railroad Restaurant

Crown Center Mall
2450 Grand Boulevard
Kansas City, MO 64108
(816) 474-4004

250 North 18th Street
Kansas City, KS 66102
(913) 281-2777

This is the little kid-friendly restaurant that could.

The main a-TRACK-tion is a toy train that actually delivers meals to the tables. It circles the restaurant overhead, food in tow, and automatically stops at the right booth. (Customers first have to order from a phone at their table.) It then lowers the food on a platform to the hungry diners below.

The fun is in guessing if the latest express contains your order. It keeps children, and their parents, entertained for quite some time.

Founder Fritz Kropf invented the patented system in the 1970s, drawing on his experience as a Navy mechanic. It was his way of dealing with issues restaurants often face with workers. Other than a few mechanical problems, a train never quits unexpectedly or calls in sick.

Fritz's is mainly a burger joint. The unique flavor comes from pressing grilled onions into the ground beef as it cooks. One burger, the large Gen Dare, come with grilled hash browns right in the sandwich.

Everything is cooked to order, then delivered fresh to your table, right on track.

Plaza III

4749 Pennsylvania Street
Kansas City, MO 64112
(816) 753-0000
www.dineoutinkc.com

Kansas City is proudly known as a cowtown. From the rodeos to the ranches to the prize-winning cattle, this is where you'll find some of the best beef around. Of the two great steak joints we mention in this section, the first is Plaza III, located in the heart of Kansas City's famed Plaza—an area full of restaurants, boutiques, and hotels.

At this top-of-the-line steakhouse, all they serve is prime beef. What makes prime different from choice is first and foremost the price. Prime typically costs 60-70 percent more than choice. Second, the taste: There's more marbling in prime, i.e., fat, which is due to the steers being fed corn, not grass. Prime is so tender and tasty it simply melts in your mouth. Plus, at Plaza III, they cut and age their own beef, so they have a standard that is truly a cut above the rest.

Manager Joe Wilcox says that one customer claimed that you have to go to New York City to get the best steak. To which Joe replied, "Where do you think that meat is raised?" Good point.

No bones to pick here. Hands down, this cowtown is the place to meet for meat.

Hereford House

East 20th Street
Kansas City, MO 64108
(816) 842-1080
www.herefordhouse.com

Kansas City and steak are usually mentioned in the same sentence, along with the words *Hereford House.*

Opened in 1957, Hereford House gained national fame, in part, because of the city's rise as a convention center. Visitors would return home to brag about dining on authentic Kansas City steak, leading to the next set of convention-eers rushing to the restaurant.

But the Hereford House went into decline in the 1980s. Longtime employees helped keep the place afloat, but even they couldn't overcome the fact that the restaurant was serving instant mashed potatoes and steaks heated in a microwave.

Eventually, new owners stepped in and returned the Hereford House to prominence. It's since opened in several other locations—and once again people mention Hereford House and KC together, usually in that order.

Ted Drewes Frozen Custard Stand

6726 Chippewa (Old Route 66)
St. Louis, MO 63109
(314) 481-2652

4224 South Grand Boulevard
St. Louis, MO 63111
(314) 352-7376
www.teddrewes.com

There's the Gateway Arch in St. Louis. And then there's Ted Drewes. One landmark is glistening stainless steel. The other is renowned for its frosty Concretes.

photo courtesy of Jill Littman

Marc with Ted Drewes whose Concrete shakes are so thick you can turn them upside down without spilling a drop—of course, it helps if they're the souvenir variety made from real concrete.

Missouri

Concretes? We're not talking about cement, here.

Ted Drewes sells the most famous frozen custard shakes on either side of the Mississippi. They're called Concretes, because they're so thick that servers turn them upside down for a moment as they hand them to customers—and nothing spills out.

Ted Drewes has been a local favorite since 1930. That's 35 years longer than the Arch. There are two take-out stands these days, the most famous one on Chippewa, which is the old Route 66, where people start lining up even before it opens at 11 A.M.

During Marc's shoot at Ted Drewes, there were a couple former St. Louis residents who had come straight from the airport to get their fix, a salesman filling up a large cooler of Concretes to court favor with prospective customers, and busloads of eager students.

Sure, in St. Louis, the Arch is the Gateway to the West. But when it comes to Concretes, Ted Drewes is the gateway to the best.

———

Missouri Baking Company

2027 Edwards Avenue
St. Louis, MO 63110
(314) 773-6566

In an area of town called The Hill, located just west of downtown St. Louis, is America's *other* Little Italy. And, just like its New York counterpart, it's filled with Old World sights, sounds, and smells. It was on these streets where baseball legends Joe Garagiola and Yogi Berra grew up. It's also a place where in a 1-square-mile radius, you can get a true taste of Italy. One of the highlights of The Hill is picking up breakfast at the Missouri Baking Company.

Owned by the Gambaro family since 1926, all the breakfast breads and desserts are made by hand. Try a Cuccidati, which is a mix of fig, raisins, chocolate chips, pine nuts, and orange peel, all rolled up in an Italian cookie pastry. The Pan Tramvai means "bus bread" in Italian. It's what the immigrants used to take with them on the bus when they went to work. It's Italian bread loaded with raisins to sweeten it up.

———

John Volpi Company

5254 Daggett Avenue
St. Louis, MO 63110
(314) 772-8550

Another stop on The Hill is Volpi's, a small Italian meat and cheese market that has made its mark for more than 60 years. Actually, the John Volpi Company started selling their meats all over the world back in 1902. This retail shop, which came later, is just a small offshoot of their bigger business. It's not surprising to find more Italian spoken here than English. Luckily with food, you can break down any barriers, or at least that's what Jill found as she gobbled down prosciutto, salami, and Italian sausages.

———

Charlie Gitto's

5226 Shaw Avenue
St. Louis, MO 63110
(314) 772-8898
www.charliegittos.com

For those with a big Italian appetite, head to Charlie Gitto's, which lays claim to inventing a St. Louis specialty: Toasted Ravioli. The whole recipe came about by accident. Back in 1947, the chef was preparing boiled ravioli when he accidentally dropped it in breadcrumbs. He decided to fry it up and see how it tasted, thus toasted ravioli was born. They serve it with tomato sauce for dipping. It's true—some of the best things in life are born by accident.

Charlie Gitto's Toasted Ravioli

ADAPTED FROM CHARLIE GITTO'S, ST. LOUIS, MISSOURI

YIELD: 8-10 SERVINGS

Dough:
3½ cups flour
3 eggs
3 tablespoons salad oil
½ cup water
½ teaspoon salt

Meat Filling:
½ pound beef, cubed
½ pound veal, cubed
½ cup chopped onions
½ cup chopped celery
½ cup chopped carrots
Salt and pepper
1½ cups cooked, chopped spinach
4 eggs
1 cup grated Parmesan cheese, plus more for garnish
4 eggs, beaten
2 cups milk
4 cups seasoned breadcrumbs
Tomato sauce for serving

For dough: In a large mixing bowl, add flour, 3 eggs, oil, water, and salt, and mix until the ingredients come together to form a dough. Turn dough out onto a floured surface, and knead until smooth and elastic, about 10 to 15 minutes. Wrap in plastic wrap, and set aside.

Preheat the oven to 350°F.

For meat filling: Combine beef, veal, onions, celery, carrots, salt, and pepper in a roasting pan and roast until cooked through, about 1 hour. Let cool.

Add spinach, then grind ingredients in a meat grinder with a fine grind. Add 4 eggs and Parmesan cheese, and mix well to create a pastelike texture.

Roll out dough on a floured surface using a rolling pin. Make a large, very thin layer of dough. Spread out a thin layer of filling on half of one side of dough, using a spatula. Fold dough end over filling side of dough. Mark filled dough with a ravioli marker (ravioli rolling pin). Cut out ravioli using a ravioli cutter. Freeze until hard.

To bread ravioli: Make an egg wash by mixing together 4 beaten eggs and milk. Add ravioli to wash, then dip in seasoned breadcrumbs. Refreeze until ready to fry.

Preheat a deep fryer to 350°F.

Fry ravioli until golden brown. Serve hot on a plate sprinkled with freshly grated Parmesan on top and tomato sauce on the side.

BB's Jazz, Blues and Soups

700 South Broadway
St. Louis, MO 63102
(314) 436-5222
www.bbsjazzbluessoups.com

When the sun sets in St. Louis, the blues musicians on Broadway rise to the occasion. There's a handful of clubs in this area, but if you're looking for some music *and* food to stir your soul, we suggest checking out this joint. They serve up finger-lickin' favorites like ribs, fried chicken, and jambalaya. On nights when the Cardinals are playing, BB's actually does barbeque out front. As the name suggests, they also have soups. Each day a different one is made from scratch.

But they serve up more than just good food. Some of the best jazz and blues acts come here to play. This area is kind of like the hall of fame for St. Louis musicians. After all, legends like Miles Davis and Ike Turner got their start in St. Louis before going on to greatness.

Both the building and BB's have their own unique history. The building has been everything from a bordello to a boarding house to a mercantile shop. And since 1976, it's been BB's three times. Huh? Well, according to owner Mark O'Shaughnessy, he and his business partner first opened up the club in 1976. By 1977 they went under. Mark tried again in 1980. By 1982 they were out of business again. But three times a charm, right?

In 1996 he gave it one last shot, and this time

Missouri

his business stuck. No striking out. He says, they're here to stay.

———

Kopperman's Delicatessen

386 North Euclid Avenue
St. Louis, MO 63108
(314) 361-0100

Kopperman's specializes in what it calls "ungesh-tupt (*un-gah-shtup-ed*) sandwiches," which is Yiddish for "overstuffed." That might be a bit of an unge-statement, considering they are big but not immense.

Don't worry, you won't leave hungry. Kopperman's has been *the* name for Jewish-style delicatessen food in St. Louis since 1897. The original store was downtown, but the latest version has been a fixture in the trendy Central West End neighborhood since 1983.

It's famous for its all-day breakfast and for those specialty sandwiches (Pastrami, Corned Beef, Kopperman's Kombos, etc.). But the restaurant also prides itself on its variety. You can even have ham with your chopped liver. Chicken wings are as common as chicken soup. In fact, the most popular sandwich might be the curried chicken salad—certainly not your standard Jewish-deli fare.

Kopperman's is also a specialty store, with a large variety of wines, cheeses, and cakes.

———

Annie Gunn's/The Smoke House Market

16806 Chesterfield Airport Road
Chesterfield, MO 63005
(636) 532-7684

There's an old Irish saying at this restaurant in west St. Louis—one which owner Thom Sehnert has built a business around—"Cead Mille Failte." In Gaelic, it means "a hundred thousand welcomes," and it's what his great-grandmother Annie Gunn lived by.

Sehnert says that even though Annie had very little money, she always had a house full of people

and plenty to eat and drink. It was as if she was born with a halo of hospitality over her head.

When Thom decided to get into the restaurant business, the name came easy. And just like Annie's house, there's always lots of food to welcome you. Trust us when we say these portions are *huge!*

For starters, there's the jumbo smoked shrimp—huge, succulent, juicy shrimp smoked right out back in their smokehouse—along with other meats like sausage and ham. For dinner, consider ordering the veal chop with whipped potatoes and morel mushrooms. It's just one of their many larger-than-life portions. Their peppercorn-coated filet mignon is a mere 16 ounces, and the half-chicken topped with smoked tomatoes will leave you clucking.

Next door to Annie Gunn's, is The Smoke House Market. It is full of wonderful sauces and spices you can take home with you, should you want to bestow the same hospitality on your dinner guests as Annie Gunn did.

Although business booms here, it hasn't always been this good. The restaurant got completely wiped out/destroyed during the great flood in 1993 when the Mississippi and Missouri Rivers jumped their banks. Thom and his family were devastated. But once again, they turned to an old Irish proverb: "Everyone knows how to ride, one must learn how to fall," meaning that because they had done it once, they could do it again. Seven months later, they were back in business—this time bigger, and in many ways, Thom says, better.

Missouri

Grilled Peppered Beef Tenderloin

ADAPTED FROM ANNIE GUNN'S,
CHESTERFIELD, MISSOURI

YIELD: 4 SERVINGS

Morel Mushroom Sauce:

¼ cup pure olive oil
2 cups morel mushrooms
4 garlic cloves, minced
¾ cup cabernet sauvignon
¾ cup brown veal stock
2 tablespoons fresh thyme
4 tablespoons butter
Salt and pepper

Potatoes:

2 pounds Yukon Gold potatoes, peeled
4 cups heavy cream
2 cups unsalted butter
Salt and pepper

Tenderloin:

4 (10-ounce) beef tenderloin fillets
1 tablespoon kosher salt
3 tablespoons cracked black pepper
Extra-virgin olive oil

For mushroom sauce: In a skillet with oil, sauté mushrooms until tender. Add garlic, and brown lightly. Deglaze the skillet with cabernet sauvignon, and reduce by three-fourths. Add veal stock, and reduce by half. Add thyme, and finish with butter. Season with salt and pepper. Keep warm until ready to serve.

For potatoes: Place potatoes in a stockpot with lukewarm water to cover, and bring to a boil. Reduce to a simmer, and skim the foam off the top. Cook until tender. In a saucepot, heat cream and butter while potatoes are cooking. Drain water from potatoes and put potatoes through a sieve; add butter and cream, and season with salt and pepper. Whip vigorously.

Preheat the grill to medium high. Roll fillets in salt and pepper. Massage meat with olive oil. Grill to desired degree of doneness, about 130°F for medium when taken on an instant-read thermometer.

Wisconsin

The Safe House

779 N. Front Street
Milwaukee, WI 53202
(414) 271-2007
www.safe-house.com

Finding The Safe House, an unmarked clandestine cocktail bar, is the easy part. Getting in is another matter. But if you're looking for a drinking (and dining) adventure, this is one place you don't want to miss.

The term "safe house" literally means a spy's hideout, which is why such places remain unmarked. The purported existence of real safe houses—and anything even remotely James Bond–ish—has fascinated owner David Baldwin for years.

The first hint in the search for this murky underworld is to look for the "International Exports, Ltd." sign out front. Find that and you're one step closer to your destination.

But here's where it gets tricky. At the front door, the bouncers will ask you for the secret pass code. If you don't know it, you have to earn your way in. You might be reduced to quacking like a duck, doing a cheer of their choice, or acting out some scenario they think up—all of which is put on television screens in the main bar area for all the "agents" who *did* do their homework to see. When your ego is sufficiently reduced to rubble, you're allowed to go up to the bar, where most of those agents will greet you with jeers and a hearty round of applause. In other words, leave your ego behind and bring your sense of humor.

When Jill shot here, she sleuthed around ahead of time and found out the pass code. It's ████ - ████. (What, you think we'd make it that easy on you? A good spy never puts that kind of information in writing.)

Inside you'll find gags and gimmicks, secret escape routes, and surveillance equipment, not to mention some crafty cocktail concoctions. There's the 007 Martini, shaken not stirred. The bartender actually pours the drink, then puts it

The great chili debate is probably something that will never be settled in our lifetime. Who invented chili, and whose is the best? Try telling a Texan that there's better chili anywhere else, and you might find yourself in a Wild West shootout. Those in New Mexico often differ with those in Mexico as to who has the hottest batch around—no doubt this is one heated argument. However, when it comes to the rise in popularity of chili, there's one theory that has a lot of substance. It's said to come from chuck wagon chefs in the early nineteenth century, whose cooks were limited to the ingredients they could carry on the trail. Cattle were butchered along the way to add the meat to the mixture. Over the years, chili became a staple in the American Southwest, and its popularity spread throughout the country.

Wisconsin

in a container that shoots it through hundreds of feet of tubing that runs along the ceilings through every room in the house (at least the rooms you know about it), before ending up back at the bar.

Here's an insider's tip: On the Propaganda Sheets, they list their house specialty drinks. If you're a guy, order the Hail to the Chief. For you gals, order Her Majesty's Secret Service. Then sit back and watch what happens. Intrigued? You should be.

The Mission Impossible might be impossible to finish. As for the ingredients in the Spy's Demise drink: They're classified, as are those in the Top Secret. Even Jill couldn't crack the code. When pressed, Baldwin told her some of the recipes were smuggled out of wartime China. He said that if he told her he'd have to "terminate her with extreme pleasure."

Hey, this job's great, but not that great.

Real Chili

1625 West Wells Street
Milwaukee, WI 53233
(414) 342-6955

419 East Wells Street
Milwaukee, WI 53202
(414) 271-4042

The later it gets, the hotter this place becomes, literally and figuratively. To put it mildy—err, maybe

not so mildly—when talking about a no fuss, lots of muss, sloppy, saucy, and steaming hot joint, Real Chili is the real deal.

At 2 A.M., this place could be described as a zoo—or a big after-bar party. We called it a *Best Of Delicious Dive*, at which some restaurants might cringe, but not owner Aaron Upton and his dad, Dan Helfer. They took our title as a badge of honor: Real hot, real rowdy, and best at being a real dive.

Their chili is similar to Cincinnati Red Chili—served over spaghetti—with or without beans and topped with onions, cheese, and sour cream. When it comes to the spicy meaty mixture, the more you have them put on, the hotter it is. In other words: more meat, more heat.

Late at night, after the taste buds have numbed from lots of drinking, it becomes almost a rite of passage to go for the hottest, then douse it with hot pepper oil and pepper flakes. Jill took on the challenge—sober. From her first bite, a bunch of inebriated customers chanted, "Hotter, hotter, hotter" as she earned her right to be called a "Chili Head." One fire-eater told her that it's only a good meal if you start to sweat—and sweat she did as Jill's cameraman will testify when her forehead became shiny enough to bounce the lights off of.

But if you're looking for some high-octane chili before hitting the hay, check out their slogan: Real Chili—it's not *just* for breakfast anymore.

Sciortino's Bakery

1101 East Brady Street
Milwaukee, WI 53202
(414) 272-4623

In the heart of this Italian enclave, you'll find Sciortino's, pronounced *shore-tino's*. This Italian bakery was founded by Peter Sciortino, who came to America in 1911. He learned how to bake in Brooklyn, before meeting his wife and moving to Milwaukee in the late 1930s. He opened the bakery in 1948. When Peter retired in 1997, he handed it over to the Vella family, who continues to run the thriving business today.

If you go early in the morning, you're likely to see a rookie from the nearby fire department making his morning rounds, buying homemade cannoli, chocolate and vanilla bonbons, and pecan fingers for the guys back at the fire station.

If you order biscotti, say it the right way, the Italian way. The "o" is long, so it's pronounced *bis-coat-i*, not *bis-cot-i*. There you go. Now you're sounding like a *real* Italian, and can fit right in.

Glorioso Brothers Grocery

1020 East Brady Street
Milwaukee, WI 53202
(414) 272-0540

Just down the street from Sciortino's is a wonderful neighborhood grocery called Glorioso Brothers that's been around since February 14, 1946. Owner Joe Glorioso opened on Valentine's Day and says he's been in love with his business ever since. At 81 years old, he still works 7 days a week.

Joe's dad came to the United States from Italy in 1905 and peddled fruit out of a pushcart. Joe used to help him out because his dad didn't speak any English. When Joe got out of the service following World War II, he opened the store.

There are lots of Old World favorites here, from fresh mozzarella and Parmesan cheeses to imported olives and aged prosciutto. In fact, it was Joe who first introduced this aged meat to Milwaukee. He says it wasn't until the 1970s

that the government would allow him to import it and that he was the first person in the state of Wisconsin to do so. He describes his Italian customers as being "overjoyed" when he brought it in.

At Glorioso's, there's a sign that hangs proudly on the wall: "Quality is remembered long after price is forgotten," words that in many ways, both the old and new in this neighborhood live by.

Speed Queen Bar-B-Que

1130 West Walnut Street
Milwaukee, WI 53205
(414) 265-2900

Smoke it, and they will come. At least here at Speed Queen.

Betty Gillespie (known to everyone as "Mrs. G") started Speed Queen in the 1950s in the back of a storefront. She and her husband, Leonard, took their family's recipe for barbeque and set up shop right next to Milwaukee's undisputed king of barbeque: The Black King. As word spread about Mrs. G's hickory-smoked meats, her succulent sauces, and her speedy service, she was dubbed the "Speed Queen." She has reigned over this town ever since.

After making two more moves, the couple settled in 1975 on 12th and Walnut Streets.

Italian Enclave

Brady Street is one of those unexpected finds in a city known more for beer than biscotti. Yet this is a neighborhood where Milwaukee's Italian population has solidly set its roots.

There are plenty of new kids on the blocks around Brady Street, too. You'll find cute boutiques and art shops, trendy restaurants, and bars. Check it all out, but just remember it was families like the Vellas and Gloriosos that made this Italian haven "hip."

For more information on Brady Street, check out www.bradystreet.com.

wisconsin

Today, Betty and her children run the business, proudly producing "Milwaukee's Finest Barbeque Meats," as the sign suggests.

Thick, chewy, morsels of tender-yet-crunchy pork are crisp from the grill. The catch of the day is usually perch or catfish, crusted in cornmeal and deep-fried. Beef brisket, slowly cooked and thinly sliced is slathered with your choice of regular or hot sauce. All dinners come with a slice of Wonder Bread and a container of coleslaw.

This old barbeque joint is on the edge of a rough part of town and even boasts a bulletproof drive-up window, just in case someone decides to pack heat while picking up their smoked special. The toilet paper in the bathroom is actually padlocked to the wall.

You wouldn't think a messy meal would be a take-out favorite, but here at least 90 percent of their business is to-go, thus the line of cars that snake around the building. And although they serve it up fast, we suggest you eat it slow, savoring every bite. It's one way to pay homage to the "Queen."

—

Leon's Frozen Custard

3131 South 27th Street
Milwaukee, WI 53215
(414) 383-1784

Think of it as a place that's been frozen in time since 1942, with the only major change since Leon Schneider first opened up being the disappearance of carhops. Now you have to order your custard from the walk-up window, then hang out in the parking lot to savor your creamy cone.

For those of you who think ice cream and custard are synonymous, think again. Any custard connoisseur will tell you that one lick is all it takes to distinguish between the two. Custard is made from cream, egg yolks, and sugar and has much less air added to it, which makes it denser. Also, it never freezes solid, but chills out at 23°F, making it softer and creamier than ice cream.

Leon's son Ron is now in charge here and is what some would call a product purist. This guy doesn't cut corners when it comes to his custard. He's never changed the machinery or the way he makes his delight. He serves food, but not fried food. Says he never will. Just hot dogs with or without chili and a Spanish Hamburger, which is sort of like a Sloppy Joe.

So if you're looking to *chill out* in Milwaukee with a sweet taste of nostalgia, rev up your engines and head here. Turn the clock back and pay homage to a place that has stood the test of time and the challenges of *not* changing. Call it comfort in a cone.

—

O & H Danish Bakery

1841 Douglas Avenue
Racine, WI 53402
(262) 637-8895 or (800) 227-6665 for mail order
www.ohdanishbakery.com

If you've never had a Kringle, we're tempted to tell you not to try it. That's because they're so good, you might find yourself at a Kringles Anonymous meeting someday. But if you are going to indulge, O & H is the place to do it.

This Danish delight is an oval-shape ring (about 13 inches in diameter) and consists of 32 layers of a flaky pastry with a sweet filling. The list of filling flavors is extensive: pecan, raspberry, cream cheese, and cherry, to name a few.

The art of making Kringles began in nineteenth-century Denmark when a bunch of Danish bakers went on strike. Bakery owners brought in Austrians to replace them. The Austrian bakers had a technique of rolling lard in between layers of dough to create a flaky pastry. When the strike ended, the Danes continued

Eating the Seven Sisters

I love Kringles from O & H, especially the cherry. But there's yet another Danish delicacy I feel compelled to mention, in case you want multiple addictions in your life: The Seven Sisters Coffee Cake. It, too, takes its name from Danish sailors, who used to navigate the seas by using the seven visible stars, known as the Seven Sisters of Pleiades. The delicacy is made with seven sweet rolls that are strategically placed in a round pan with almonds and custard poured in before baking.

You might just find yourself starry-eyed after eating it.

to use that layering technique, but instead of lard, they used butter.

Originally, the Kringle was in the shape of a pretzel, or sailor's knot, which in Denmark is a symbol for a bakery (they put a crown on top of it).

And while the shape has been Americanized, there are still plenty of reminders of Denmark in this town.

In fact, Racine has one of the largest Danish populations in the United States. One such Dane, Christian Olesen, and his business partner, Harvey Holtz, opened O & H Bakery in 1949, bringing a taste of their homeland to Wisconsin.

In 1963, Holtz got out of the business and the Olesen family took over entirely. Now Christian's three grandsons, Michael, Dale, and Eric run the place with remarkable dedication: Michael gets in at midnight to start baking, followed by Dale at 3 A.M., and Eric at 6 A.M. True baker's hours.

So if you feel like you need an addiction in your life, check 'em out. Just be forewarned it might be a hard one to break. They ship their Kringles all over the country, so there's no escaping this Danish pastry.

Little Sister Resort

360 Little Sister Road
Sister Bay, WI 54234
(920) 854-4013
www.littlesisterresort.com

In Door County, Wisconsin, something fishy is going on. Just as the sun starts to set, a crowd

gathers around a 20-gallon cauldron that is filled with boiling water over an open fire outside the Little Sister Resort. A man emerges from the restaurant and pours in 5 pounds of salt and 150 new potatoes. He checks his watch. Exactly 8 minutes later, he adds 210 small white boiler onions. Then, exactly 8 minutes after that, 70 pieces of Wisconsin Whitefish go in (they call it poor man's lobster in these parts). The crowd watches and waits. For those who say a watched pot never boils, we've got news for you . . . it does here.

Welcome to one of Wisconsin's oldest traditions: a fish boil.

Every summer you'll find a handful of restaurants putting on a show like this one. Owners Greg and Sue Sunstrom, who began working at Little Sister as a newly engaged couple in the 1970s have raised their two children here and have seen generation after generation return to watch the fish boil.

The final stage in this production is the "boil over," in which Greg literally adds fuel to the fire in the form of kerosene. The great burst of flames causes the oils in the top of the pot to boil over as the crowd bursts into a round of applause. At this stage, everyone heads into the restaurant, where the work of Sue and her staff begins.

On a typical summer night, they dish up about a hundred plates of steaming hot fish along with those tender potatoes and juicy onions. For those who don't like fish, you can substitute chicken, although we recommend you go for the fish.

The meal is traditionally finished off with a slice of homemade cherry pie.

Attending a fish boil is a great family tradition

Wisconsin

in these parts and is something you should experience if you find yourself visiting this pristine peninsula.

Not a Tall Tale

The shoot at the Little Sister fish boil was going smoothly. The water boiled right on cue, the crowd was enthusiastic, but then, just as I was gearing up to take my ceremonial bite for the camera . . . tragedy struck. Okay, not tragedy really, but something resembling it. It started with a little cough following that fateful first bite.

"What's wrong?" my producer, Jodi Langer, asked.

I didn't know. I coughed again. My eyes started to water. The coughing became more pronounced. My face turned red. I saw my life flash before me as I mustered the courage to whisper, "I . . . think I have a fish bone caught in my throat."

Fully accustomed to my heightened sense of drama, Jodi rolled her eyes. But as my coughing continued and my discomfort became apparent, she relented.

"Come here," she said.

She pulled me aside and looked down my throat, then gasped in horror. I knew it was bad. Then she started digging in her purse. By now, my hacking was out of control—not dissimilar to a cat trying to eject a big hairball. Using the last rays of the setting sun as her only source of light, Jodi got to work.

"Say aah," she told me as she approached my throat with a rusty pair of eyebrow tweezers. (This should officially dispel any thoughts anyone has of television being glamorous.) After several painful minutes, Jodi emerged with the culprit: An inch-long whitefish bone that had lodged itself squarely in my uvula.

My coughing ceased, my tears dried up, and I knew then that I would live long enough to take another bite. Hey, it's a tough job, but somebody's gotta do it . . .

Smoked Fish Paté

ADAPTED FROM LITTLE SISTER RESORT, SISTER BAY, WISCONSIN

YIELD: 4 SERVINGS

1½ cups boned smoked fish (any species of fish works well)
1 cup sandwich spread (not mayonnaise)
1½ tablespoons Worcestershire sauce
1 tablespoon diced dried onions
1 teaspoon pepper
1 teaspoon garlic powder

Mix together fish, sandwich spread, Worcestershire sauce, onions, pepper, and garlic powder, with electric beater (a little chunky is okay). Serve with crackers or bread chunks.

The Blacksmith Inn

8152 Highway 57
Baileys Harbor, WI 54202
(920) 839-9222 or (800) 769-8619
www.theblacksmithinn.com

For innkeepers Joan Holliday and Bryan Nelson, home is where the heart is. And home for them is also a home away from home for others. The Blacksmith Inn is nestled on the shores of Lake Michigan in this picturesque part of Door County—all of which has a distinctly Cape Cod feel.

As the name suggests, there is a blacksmith shop on the premises, which dates to 1904, when August Zahn came here from Germany and opened the business. He and his family lived above the shop for 7 years while he built the house next door, which is now the inn. There are relics of his blacksmith days all over the place, like candle holders, horseshoes, sconces, and Zahn's original tools. It's truly a preserved piece of history, but with modern amenities. Joan and Bryan did an incredible job remodeling the inn and even adding on another building for guests. That homey feel is apparent the moment you walk in.

Breakfast is simple: freshly baked muffins, scones, freshly squeezed juices, and homemade granola. Sit outside on the deck overlooking the lake, and soak up your surroundings.

This is a place where history meets hearth and home, so if you're ever in Door County, here's hoping there's room at this inn.

Rhubarb Walnut Muffins

ADAPTED FROM THE BLACKSMITH INN, BAILEYS HARBOR, WISCONSIN

YIELD: 8 SERVINGS

1½ cups flour
¾ cup brown sugar
½ teaspoon baking soda
½ teaspoon salt
⅓ cup vegetable oil
1 egg
½ cup buttermilk
1 teaspoon vanilla
1 cup chopped rhubarb
½ cup chopped walnuts

Topping:
½ cup brown sugar
¼ cup chopped walnuts
½ teaspoon cinnamon

Preheat oven to 325°F. Combine flour, sugar, baking soda, and salt. Add oil, egg, buttermilk, and vanilla, mixing only until moist. Fold in rhubarb and walnuts. Put a scoop of the mixture in muffin tins. Combine sugar, walnuts, and cinnamon, and sprinkle over muffins. Bake for 20 to 25 minutes.

Dried Cherry Scones

ADAPTED FROM THE BLACKSMITH INN, BAILEYS HARBOR, WISCONSIN

YIELD: 8 SERVINGS

2 cups flour
⅓ cup sugar
2 teaspoons baking powder
¼ teaspoon salt
⅓ cup chilled butter, cut into pieces
1 egg
⅔ cup whipping cream
1 teaspoon vanilla extract
1 teaspoon almond extract
1 cup dried cherries
Egg wash: 1 egg and 1 teaspoon water, beaten
Sugar and sliced almonds, for sprinkling

Preheat oven to 325°F.
Combine flour, sugar, baking powder, and salt. Cut in butter with pastry blender. Combine egg, cream, vanilla, and almond extract, and mix into dry ingredients just until moistened. Add cherries. Mixture will be very sticky. Turn onto floured surface, and knead 4 to 5 times with floured hands. Pat out to ½-inch thick, and cut into circles. Brush tops with egg wash. Sprinkle tops with sugar and sliced almonds. Place on greased baking sheet, and bake for 15 to 18 minutes.

Canoe Bay

W16065 Hogback Road
Chetek, WI 54728
(715) 924-4594
www.canoebay.com

"**Y**ou will never see and there never has been a child on the property. Children are not allowed under any circumstances," says Canoe Bay owner Dan Dobrowolski. "Neither are groups," he adds.

Here, they cater only to couples and singles.

Sound a bit extreme? Not to Dan and his wife, Lisa.

If you are looking for the epitome of peace and quiet, look no further. This Relais and Chateaux property is a place for you weary workaholics to unwind. Forgot what your spouse looks like? You *both* will remember here. Married to your cell phone? Not here you're not. It won't work.

Besides "no kids and no groups," the one rule they have at this resort: Relax—even if they have to force feed it to you. Two hours from Minneapolis and nine miles from the nearest freeway, Mother Nature helps them out in the nurturing department.

Dan and Lisa themselves led hectic lives in Chicago. He was a meteorologist on a local news station there; she was in marketing. When they decided to look for a less-frenetic lifestyle, they didn't have to look far. Around the turn of the century, Dan's grandfather had owned this land—about 6 hours outside Chicago. In the 1960s, it was sold to a religious organization that sold it back to the family in the 1990s. Dan and Lisa came up with a plan to preserve it while at the same time preserving their sanity.

If you come in the summer, you won't see or hear any Jet Skis or motorboats. If you come in the winter, you won't see or hear any snowmobiles. All you will hear is the sound of silence and your feet making fresh tracks in the snow.

It's easy to relax when you're staying in Frank Lloyd Wright–inspired cottages with tubs for two, flaming fireplaces, and in-room spas. Of course it comes with a price. Rooms range from $300 to $1,700 a night.

When it comes to the cooking, no detail is overlooked. Executive Chef Scott Johnson makes sure everything in the kitchen—down to the butter and the milk—is organically and locally produced. Each night he puts on a four-course prix fixe meal. If he's searing char, it'll be flown in that day. If beef tenderloin is on the menu, chances are he got it within a 30-mile radius.

Because people are stressed out all the time, Dan has a fair amount of job security in this endeavor. But more than any business decision, he says he feels strongly about getting couples to spend more quality time together—without the kids and the hassles of daily life. It's what his Wisconsin wilderness is all about.

Minnesota

Just Truffles

1326 Grand Avenue
St. Paul, MN 55105
(651) 690-0075 or (877) 977-9177
www.justtruffles.com

You won't find them making any old chocolate, caramel, or toffees in this quaint shop in the charming Summit Hill neighborhood of St. Paul. No, like the name suggests, they make "just truffles." And although they do sell a small amount of other people's candy like Asher's chocolate-covered pretzels, their main focus is the truffle. But mind you, these aren't just any old truffles. You'll be singing their praises after popping one in your mouth. At least that's what Luciano Pavarotti did, which is why one of their truffles, made with rum and coconut, is called the Tenor Temptation.

The story goes like this: Owner Kathleen Ohehir-Johnson got a phone call in 1991 telling her that Pavarotti was slated to perform at the Civic Center. She was asked to prepare a special truffle for his dinner party. Whatever she made hit the right note, because at the concert she noticed he was wearing the gold elastic stretch bow from the box of truffles around his wrist! She later found out he often wears something for good luck. To this day, he still orders the truffles whenever he's in town.

Kathleen and her husband Roger began the truffle business in a roundabout way. She started making them out of her home one Christmas season and gave them away as gifts. Gradually people starting calling and asking her if they could order them for parties and presents. She and Roger set up shop in a commercial kitchen and filled orders at night after they got off work. Word started to spread about how good they were, and eventually they opened a shop. Roger quit his full-time computer sales job to run the business. Kathleen still works full-time at the airport ticket counter for Northwest Airlines but does truffle making at night.

The reason for *just* truffles? Each one takes

time. They are all handmade—from the mixing to the shaping, to the delicate dipping.

In February 2003, I got a call from Oprah Winfrey's producers to appear on one of her "only the best" shows, when she features guests who talk about some of the best products available—jewelry, cars, or what have you. When I was asked about the best chocolate places we had featured on *The Best Of*, Just Truffles and a few others came immediately to mind. Next thing I know, I was on my way to Chicago. At the same time, owner Kathleen Ohehir-Johnson was being asked to send 350 truffles to the show for the audience to sample.

When the show aired, all chaos broke out at Just Truffles. Being mentioned on Oprah is a big deal—and that little plug she got was enough to send business out the door—literally. Moments after the show ran, the phones started to ring and a line formed outside. The mayhem lasted for days. People were coming out of the woodwork to try the truffles. Even travelers on a layover at the airport were hitching cabs to take them here.

It was so crazy, the shop finally put a message on their voicemail saying they were backed up on orders and couldn't answer the phone.

Kathleen and Roger estimate in that one week alone they sold 15,000 truffles. It took them five weeks to get caught up on orders. But they are the first to acknowledge that having Food Network and Oprah Winfrey mention your business is a good problem to have.

Barbary Fig

720 Grand Avenue
St. Paul, MN 55105
(651) 290-2085

Some people will go to great lengths for true love. In fact, they might even cross the globe to follow their passion. That's exactly what Brahim Hadj-Moussa did. In the 1970s, while living in France, he fell in love with an American woman who was an exchange student there. They married, and he followed her here to the United States.

For this native Algerian, going from the sun and sand of North Africa to the snowy streets of St. Paul, Minnesota, was a shock, to say the least. When we asked him about it, his eyes got wide, his hands began to fly around, and he said, "I had no idea, no idea, no idea it was going to be like this. There was so much snow I could not *believe* my eyes."

But he braved the cold, and in 1989, brought the flavors of his homeland to the historic Summit Hill neighborhood of St. Paul, where he's been given a very *warm* welcome. He bought an old Victorian mansion, painted the inside with bright colors and murals, and started making his Mediterranean specialties and fulfilling his dream to run a restaurant.

His dream was slow going at first—not just because of the slow economy—but because many Minnesotans weren't used to eating exotic, ethnic foods like this. He calls it peasant food, and menu items include unique couscous, exotic stews, and Tagines. The Chicken Tagine is his most popular: Chicken with zucchini and leeks over basmati rice, topped with a tomato-ginger chutney.

Barbary Fig is closed Tuesdays. When we asked Hadj why, he told us it's because in France, all the museums close on that day, and in keeping with tradition, he decided that would also be his day of rest.

Minnesota

Minnesota

Chicken Tagine with Tomato Chutney

ADAPTED FROM BARBARY FIG, ST. PAUL, MINNESOTA

YIELD: 4 SERVINGS

Tomato Chutney:

5 cups water
4 cups chopped Roma tomatoes
½ cup red wine vinegar
½ cup sugar
2 teaspoons grated fresh ginger
1 teaspoon cayenne
Salt to taste

Basmati Rice:

2 tablespoons finely chopped onion
1 tablespoon olive oil
1 cup Basmati rice
¼ teaspoon black pepper
¼ teaspoon turmeric
1½ cups chicken broth
Salt to taste

Chicken Tagine:

⅓ cup chopped onion
1 tablespoon olive oil
2 boneless, skinless chicken breasts, cut into strips
1 teaspoon ground ginger
1 teaspoon cinnamon
2 cups chicken broth
1 zucchini, cut into julienne strips
1 leek, cut into julienne strips
Salt and pepper to taste
1 teaspoon black caraway seeds, for garnish

For chutney: Bring water, tomatoes, vinegar, sugar, ginger, cayenne, and salt to a boil in saucepan for about 10 minutes. Then reduce heat and simmer until water has completely evaporated and sauce has thickened into a jamlike consistency. Reserve.

For rice: Sauté onion in olive oil for about 5 minutes. Add rice, pepper, and turmeric, and mix well. Add broth, salt and pepper, and bring to a boil for 2 minutes. Reduce heat to low, cover tightly, and cook for 20 to 25 minutes.

For chicken: Sauté onion in olive oil. Add chicken strips, and sauté until almost golden. Add ginger, cinnamon, and broth, and bring to a boil. Reduce heat and cook for 15 minutes. Add zucchini and leek, and cook for 5 minutes. Remove from heat and season with salt and pepper to taste.

Serve chicken and vegetables over rice. Top with a dollop of tomato chutney, and garnish with black caraway seeds.

Babani's Kurdish Restaurant

544 Saint Peter Street
St. Paul, MN 55102
(651) 602-9964
www.babanis.com

Rodwan Nakshabandi is a survivor.

After being forced to join Saddam Hussein's army in the 1980s to fight the Iran-Iraq War, he decided to flee his country when the Gulf War broke out. He, like thousands of Kurds, took to the mountains in a desperate bid to reach Turkey. Braving 14 days of treacherous terrain and near starvation, Rodwan finally made it to a Turkish refugee camp.

Once there, he found conditions weren't much better. Contagious diseases ran rampant, and the hygienic conditions were horrific. But one thing was different: There was hope. And the compassion he found from one woman was not only extraordinary, but life-changing.

Tanya Faud is half Kurdish. She says when her family immigrated to Minneapolis in the 1950s, they were the only Kurdish family in the state. People thought Kurds were from someplace in Africa.

Tanya is a true humanitarian, spending many of her adult years working in refugee camps in the Middle East. In 1991, she went to Silopi, Turkey, to work at a U.N. refugee camp for Iraqi Kurds. She was one of two health coordinators for about 7,000 refugees living in the camp. One of those refugees was Rodwan. At the camp, he cooked for the single men, and his cuisine became one of the few bright spots in the severe environment. Before long, Tanya got to know him and his tent mates through sharing one of the most basic human necessities: food. "He would make these unbelievable elaborate dishes at the camp on one little stove," Tanya recalls. A friendship was forged.

Tanya went back to Minnesota and sponsored Rodwan to immigrate to America. Sponsorship is not a legally binding agreement like adoption, but it is a written agreement of responsibility for that person for a term of three years. Basically Tanya made a three-year commitment to help Rodwan get on his feet.

Rodwan Nakshabandi, whose dream came true at Babani's Kurdish restaurant.

photo courtesy of Dan Dwyer

In 1993, after spending two years in the refugee camp, he arrived in the Twin Cities, and Tanya was there to greet him.

First, she helped him get a job. But for Rodwan, that wasn't enough. He wanted more. He wanted "The Dream." In 1997, with a handful of investors and a big gamble, Tanya opened Babani's restaurant. You can guess who was the chef.

The dream is now a reality. Rodwan now owns the restaurant. He bought it from Tanya, who now is a regular customer. They both say Babani's is the first—and nearly only—Kurdish restaurant in America. (Apparently there are a few deli establishments in the country.)

Rodwan describes Kurdish cooking as a mix of Greek, Turkish, Lebanese, and Indian. One of the most popular dishes is the Sheikh Babani—named after a Sheikh from the Babani tribe. The dish is made with eggplant stuffed with ground beef and seasoned with an array of spices, then topped with a tomato sauce. The Dowjic Soup, a staple in the region, is a mix of chicken, yogurt, basil, and lemon.

Besides the good food, what makes Babani's a notch above wonderful is the story behind it and the man who traveled so far to find freedom and his life-long dream.

Minnesota

Sheikh Babani

ADAPTED FROM BABANI'S KURDISH RESTAURANT, ST. PAUL, MINNESOTA

YIELD: 4 SERVINGS

2 medium eggplants
Vegetable oil, for frying
1½ pounds lean ground beef
¼ cup olive oil
3 tablespoons chopped fresh parsley
½ tablespoon freshly ground pepper
½ tablespoon salt

Red Sauce:

2 eggplant cores
½ green pepper, chopped
1 jalapeño pepper, chopped
¼ cup olive oil
2 teaspoons salt
1 teaspoon black pepper
½ cup water
1 tablespoon beef base
4 cups crushed tomatoes
Parsley for garnish

Cut eggplant in half lengthwise and width wise, and "stripe" the skin with a peeler. Core eggplant, leaving at least ⅓-inch outer layer. Reserve cores for red sauce (recipe follows). Sauté eggplant until all sides are brown.

Lightly brown beef in a fry pan, and drain oil. Blend beef in a food processor and then return to fry pan. Add oil, parsley, pepper, and salt, and cook over medium-high heat for 4 minutes. Reduce heat to medium, and continue to cook for about 10 minutes.

For red sauce, blend eggplant cores, green pepper, and jalapeño until smooth in a food processor. Place in saucepan with heated olive oil, and sauté until it boils and melts together. Season with salt and pepper. Add water, beef base, and tomatoes, and boil until it thickens and oil appears at top.

Then stuff eggplant with prepared beef, and top with red sauce. Garnish with parsley and serve with rice.

Café Latte

850 Grand Avenue
St. Paul, MN 55105
(651) 224-5687
www.cafelatte.com

Forget the whole thing about saving room for dessert. At this classy cafeteria-style restaurant, they don't save the best for last. Rather, when you take your tray down the line, they invite you to start with the sweets and then see if you have any room left over for lunch! Black Forest Cheesecake, Mocha Tortes, and their famous Turtle Cake topped with fudge, caramel, and pecans, will beckon you from behind the glass. Their salads and sandwiches shouldn't be missed either, but as one customer told us, "Life's uncertain. Eat dessert first." That's one philosophy we can all live by (at least in moderation)!

Café Latte's Turtle Cake

ADAPTED FROM CAFÉ LATTE, ST. PAUL, MINNESOTA

MAKES 1 (9-INCH) THREE-LAYER CAKE

Cake:

1 egg
⅔ cup vegetable oil
1 cup buttermilk
2 cups flour
1¾ cups sugar
½ cup good-quality cocoa
1 tablespoon baking soda
1 teaspoon salt
1 cup hot coffee

Frosting:

½ cup milk
1 cup sugar
6 tablespoons butter
2 cups good-quality semisweet chocolate chips
1½ cups toasted pecans
¾ cup caramel topping

Preheat the oven to 350°F. Grease 3 (9-inch) cake pans. Cover the bottom of each pan with a sheet of parchment paper.

For cake: In a medium bowl, combine egg, oil, and buttermilk. In another larger bowl, mix together flour, sugar, cocoa, baking soda, and salt. Gradually add wet ingredients to dry ingredients until well mixed. Gradually add hot coffee. Scrape batter into prepared pans. Bake cakes for 25 to 30 minutes, or until a toothpick inserted in the center comes clean. Let cakes rest in pans for 10 minutes. Turn out onto wire racks to cool completely.

For frosting: Mix milk and sugar together in a saucepan. Add butter. Bring to a boil and then remove from heat. Add chocolate chips to pan and, using a wire whisk, mix until smooth. (*Note:* If frosting is too thick, add 1 or 2 tablespoons hot coffee.)

Place 1 cooled cake layer with the top side down on a cake plate. Spread with one-third of frosting, pushing it out slightly from edges to make a ripple or petal effect. Sprinkle with ½ cup pecans and drizzle with ¼ cup caramel. Add the next layer, again top side down. Repeat layers. Place top layer with the top side up. Repeat layers.

Bar Abilene

1300 Lagoon Street
Minneapolis, MN 55408
(612) 825-2525
www.barabilene.com

If you're looking for the hip, trendy area of Minneapolis, look no farther than the area known as Uptown. Here you'll find unique boutiques and bars, artsy theaters, and some of the hippest hangouts around. You'll also find a restaurant that seems to belong deep in the heart of Texas rather than deep in the heart of the Midwest. Sure, Texas may be about 1,000 miles away, but there is a lot to get fired up about here.

At Bar Abilene, the Southwestern food sizzles, the margaritas run wild, and the grill is definitely on fire, making it one of the *hottest* places in town. In fact, Chef Tom Gladbach will gladly throw just about anything on the grill—from steaks and salmon to fajitas and fruit. He calls

his food "cowboy fusion," and it's basically traditional Southwestern cooking combined with flavors from the Far East and Europe.

If that doesn't dazzle you, their signature shots will. You can "take flight" at the bar—not with wine flights, but rather tequila flights. Some of their shots shoot up into the $50 range. We're talking aged, smooth tequila—not your dorm-room variety.

So belly up to the bar, swagger over to a table, and enjoy the best of the West here in the Midwest.

———

Wuollet Bakery

3608 West 50th Street*
Minneapolis, MN 55410
(612) 922-4341
www.wuollet.com

*There are five Wuollet Bakeries in the greater Twin Cities area. For a list of their locations, check out their website or call them at the West 50th Street location.

Longtime baker Reino Wuollet began his baking business in 1944 with a $1,000 loan and a lot of flour and sugar. Nearly 60 years later, and 4 generations in the baking, Wuollet's is a staple in this town. Even though over the years they've expanded and now have computers and high-tech machines, the majority of their stuff is still done by hand, and they remain dedicated to using the finest ingredients.

Walking into Wuollet's, you won't see a lot of fancy tables. This is more like your old-fashioned bakery with a table or two and someone behind the counter waiting to sell you some of their famous tortes, pastries, and unique breads. They also make the most exquisite wedding cakes in the Twin Cities. (Jill can attest to this because they made her wedding cake, but then she has to admit to being somewhat biased.)

It's a place with a lot of sweet history and sweet success.

Minnesota

Minnesota

I Do

The best thing about this job is witnessing the generosity of the people in the food business. And I am happy to report that being the recipient of this largess is a nice perk of the job . . .

We featured Wuollet's in two shows: a special called *Wedding Feasts* and in *The Best Of Bakeries*. At the time of the wedding special, I happened to be planning my own nupitals.

So of course, during the shoot, I was picking owner Jim Jurmu's brain about wedding cakes. And because I considered Wuollet's the best in town, after the shoot was over, I set up a cake tasting. Ultimately we decided on a five-tier cheesecake, drizzled with white chocolate and topped with fresh berries.

Come wedding day, everyone raved about the cake. But the Wuollet family refused to take any payment from us. They simply wished us a sweet wedding and a happy marriage.

What can I say? I know free food can be a perk of the job, but I'm still forever amazed at the generosity out there and am truly indebted to so many people. One downside: The cheesecake was so good we couldn't wait the traditional year to eat the top tier. We ate it the day after.

Wuollet's Brownie Enormous

ADAPTED FROM WUOLLET BAKERY,
MINNEAPOLIS, MINNESOTA

YIELD: 4 SERVINGS

¾ cups melted butter
4 squares unsweetened baking chocolate
2 cups sugar
3 large eggs
1 teaspoon vanilla
1 cup flour
1 cup large walnut pieces mixed with chunks of
   premium-grade bar chocolate

Preheat oven to 350°F. Microwave butter and chocolate on high about 2 minutes until melted. Add sugar, eggs, vanilla, and flour, stirring after each addition. Gently fold in walnuts and chunks of chocolate. Pour into a 13x9-inch buttered baking dish, and bake for 30 to 35 minutes, until toothpick inserted in center comes out with fudgy crumbs. Do not overbake! Cool and cut into squares.

B.T. McElrath Chocolatier

2010 East Hennepin Avenue
Minneapolis, MN 55413
(612) 331-8800
www.btmcelrath.com

Even Willy Wonka would be hard-pressed to come up with chocolate truffle flavors like Red Zinfandel-Balsamic Vinegar, Lavender Black Peppercorn, and Kaffir Lime and Ginger. But deep down in the depths of an old food research lab in the industrial section of Northeast Minneapolis, a chocolate genius is making this very magic.

Brian McElrath started out as a chef but always had a yearning to make chocolate. Tired of the restaurant world, in 1996 he convinced his oh-so-patient and understanding wife, Christine, to help him set up shop in their house and "experiment." As Christine told us when we shot there for *The Best Of Chocolate Makers*, "We got started in the dining room . . . . [He] then turned a walk-in closet into a cooler where he kept his chocolates chilled. We had chocolate on the walls, chocolate on the curtains, everywhere . . . "

That's when they decided to move their operation to the basement of the research lab. Here, they and their 11 employees crank out 10,000 to 12,000 handmade chocolates a week. And it's more than just mouthwatering. Each piece is a *masterpiece*. They've won top honors year after year at the Fancy Food Show (the equivalent of the Oscars for specialty foods) among other top-notch accolades.

You can't visit this chocolate shop, but you can buy their artisan chocolates on the web and at specialty stores around the country. (Check their website for details.)

Victor's 1959 Café

3756 Grand Avenue South
Minneapolis, MN 55409
(612) 827-8948
www.victors1959cafe.com

It's a breakfast joint that boasts of being one of the country's only revolutionary cafés, one where you can sit in the left wing or the right wing; although owner Victor Valens chuckles and says most people wait to sit in the left wing . . . .

Victor is a rare breed in this country—he's a proud, *pro*-Castro Cuban American. In fact, Victor's 1959 Café is named after the year of the Cuban Revolution, 1959. Not a popular day for many politicians or Cuban Americans—that's when Castro marched into Havana, forever altering the landscape of the island country.

No surprise that Victor regularly stirs up the politically incorrect pot. He's been called a Communist (among many other things) and has been all but banned by the Little Havana community in Miami. He regularly gets hate mail, but it doesn't bother him. After all, he says, that's what makes America so great. It's a free country; you can believe what you want. Hallelujah, brother!

Whether or not you agree with his politics, you'll definitely agree with his cooking. To start your day, try the Dia Y Noche. Cuban black beans served with eggs, topped with a Cuban Creole sauce and sweet plantains on the side. Yum. For lunch, try the Bay of Pigs Sandwich with pork, sautéed onions, and mojo—a citrus Cuban sauce.

However, if you want to get on this chef's good side, don't ask for cheese or sour cream to go along with your dishes. He says that too many of us mistake Cuban food for Mexican. Although he has a few Mexican dishes on the menu as a gesture of diplomacy, he begs you to please try it his way . . . the revolutionary way. He jokes that if he's ever out of yucca or plantains, he tells his customers it's on the embargo list and suggests they write their local congressperson or senator. He jokingly says eating here is like "eating with the enemy." Victor doesn't call it forbidden food for nothing.

Ranchero Cubano

ADAPTED FROM VICTOR'S 1959 CAFÉ, MINNEAPOLIS, MINNESOTA

YIELD: 2 SERVINGS

4 eggs
Butter for frying
4 corn tortillas
½ cup shredded cheddar
Canned or homemade black beans
Creole Sauce (recipe follows)

In a large pan, cook eggs in butter sunny-side up or over easy. When eggs are just about done, divide tortillas between 2 plates, and top with cheese. Heat in microwave until cheese is melted. Top each tortilla with 1 egg, and top the whole thing with black beans and Creole Sauce.

Creole Sauce:
5 garlic cloves, chopped
½ green pepper, chopped
½ red pepper, chopped
½ onion, chopped
¼ cup olive oil
1 teaspoon chopped fresh oregano leaves
½ teaspoon ground cumin
1 (#10)* can tomato sauce
1 (#10)* can water
Salt and pepper

Saute garlic, green and red peppers, and onion in olive oil until translucent. Add oregano, cumin, tomato sauce, water, salt, and pepper, and simmer for about ½ hour or until all the flavors have blended to your liking. You'll have extra sauce to use for other recipes. It only gets better with age!

*#10 can is approximately equal to 5 (28-ounce) cans.

Bryant Lake Bowl

810 West Lake Street
Minneapolis, MN 55408
(612) 825-3737
www.bryantlakebowl.com

Bryant Lake Bowl boasts of being a bowling alley, a wine bar, and a theater—all under one roof. Yep, this place can certainly satisfy a lot of tastes.

The bowling alley has been around since the 1930s, but it wasn't until owner Kim Bartmann took it over that things really became eclectic.

When Kim decided to buy Bryant's in 1993, this area did not enjoy the repuation as the hip, grunge, or retro part of the city it has today. It was run down and rough. Her friends told her she was truly crazy—that an upscale bowling alley-slash-theater would never work. She went for it anyway and threw a strike.

Nowadays, Bryant Lake Bowl is one of the hottest hangouts in the city. The place is nearly always packed. Come early if you want to claim a lane. Feast on items like organic smoked trout and roasted garlic on a baguette, fresh ahi, or steak while sipping down a Belgian, French, or even local beer. If beer and bowling isn't your

thing, check out their fairly extensive, yet completely reasonable wine list. No gutter balls on this menu.

And when you want to get away from the loud lanes, step into their theater for a play.

It has been said that the origins of bowling trace back to 3200 B.C. If that's the case, then Bryant Lake Bowl continues to carry on this long-loved tradition. They've just taken it to a whole new level.

Peppermint Twist

115 Babcock Boulevard (on Highway 12)
Delano, MN 55328
(763) 972-2572
(Open from mid-April to mid-October.)

This is a place you can't miss, literally. As you drive west from the Twin Cities on Highway 12, you'll eventually pass a bright pink building. So pink you might need your sunglasses to reflect the glare.

Vicki and Mike Mirenda bought the place in 1982 after the brown and orange A&W in this same spot had gone under. Things were going

Minnesota

Minnesota Home

When asked why we have done so many shoots in Minnesota, I have two answers. The first: Like all great cities, Minneapolis and St. Paul have their fair share of delicious dives, five-star favorites, and ethnic eateries, not to mention those ten thousand lakes. Okay, so you want the real answer? Love. I know it's sappy, but true.

When I first started hosting *The Best Of,* my fiancé at the time, Phil Johnston, was a television reporter at the NBC affiliate here. We had met in Omaha, Nebraska, where I was the morning anchor and he was a reporter. When my contract was up, I moved to Minneapolis to join him. One of the biggest bonuses to our job is that Marc and I can live wherever we want, as long as there is an airport. However, there are times when it's nice to shoot the pieces and go home to your own bed, thus, my push to always shoot at least one week a season in Minnesota. My crew didn't mind because most of them are based in Minneapolis.

Fast forward five years and six seasons later, and now my husband and I live in New York City due to his change in career. And, because New York is a city the show hits every season, I still get my one week of shooting without having to board a plane. That also means once a year I can bring home my leftovers.

okay until 1988, when another fast-food joint moved into the area and the Mirendas immediately suffered a drop in business. They knew they needed to do something to stay on people's radar. So they painted their building the brightest pink they could find, forcing people to take notice.

For those of you who can't resist the draw of the hot pink building, you have two options. You can sit in your car and have the carhops wait on you, or you can grab a seat at one of the 25 picnic tables in the yard. (We suggest the latter if you are traveling with kids because there's all kinds of toys for them to play with outside.)

If you're really hungry, order the Delano Burger, a half-pound burger, made up of three patties, topped with fresh, sautéed mushrooms, onions, Swiss cheese, and their special sauce. Wash it down with their incredible raspberry shakes, which match the color of the joint.

By the way, they're still thriving in spite of the competition, so maybe the corporate bigwigs should take a look at their clever marketing with the pink. After all, they say you eat with your eyes as well as your stomach. Pink never tasted so good.

The Mountains and The Great Plains

Kansas, Montana, Idaho, North Dakota, South Dakota, Wyoming, Nebraska, Utah, Colorado,

WHO DECIDES TO open a restaurant in the middle of nowhere? And the bigger question, who *goes* to a restaurant in the middle of nowhere? Well, we did—to lots of them—and, boy, the stories we could tell . . . Oh wait, we *will* tell them—right here in this chapter!

Just like the pioneers who settled these parts, the restaurateurs who work in the Great Plains and Rocky Mountain regions are bold, resourceful, and innovative. So what if you might have to wade through a herd of livestock to get to some of these places? It's worth it. From a 3-pound prime rib to a Pheasant Napoleon, you might be surprised by the diverse cuisine we found in this rugged country. We were, but we certainly weren't disappointed!

Kansas

WheatFields Bakery and Cafe

904 Vermont Street
Lawrence, KS 66044
(785) 841-5553

Selling bread in Kansas is the equivalent of carrying coals to Newcastle. Offer an inferior product in the nation's breadbasket, and you can end up toast.

But around here, WheatFields is outstanding in its field. (That's a Kansas joke.)

The bakery sells nearly a thousand loaves a day, offering more than a dozen varieties. One popular specialty, the Kalamata Olive sourdough, is so tasty that it rarely makes it out the door untouched.

The heart of WheatFields is an enormous wood-fired brick oven imported from Spain that was installed by a master craftsman from Barcelona. At 25 tons, the oven is so large the front of the bakery had to be built around it.

An in-store café also offers breakfast, lunch, and dinner, because no one can live by bread alone. But if they had to, WheatFields would be the way to go.

Tuna and Artichoke Salad on Kalamata Olive Bread

ADAPTED FROM WHEATFIELDS BAKERY AND CAFÉ, LAWRENCE, KANSAS

YIELD: 2 SANDWICHES

4 slices bread (preferably Kalamata Olive Bread)
Tuna and Artichoke Salad (recipe below)
Fresh Herb and Garlic Aioli (recipe below)
2 slices provolone cheese
Sliced red onion

Albacore Tuna and Artichoke Salad:

1 cup tuna
⅓ cup chopped artichoke hearts
2 tablespoons sliced roasted red peppers
1 teaspoon minced lemon zest
½ teaspoon dried oregano
2 teaspoons chopped fresh parsley
Salt and pepper to taste

For tuna salad: In a bowl, combine tuna, artichoke hearts, red pepper, lemon zest, oregano, parsley, salt, and pepper, then refrigerate.

Fresh Herb and Garlic Aioli:

*NOTE: MAKES MORE THAN 2 SERVINGS, SO REFRIGERATE LEFTOVERS.

3 egg yolks
1 whole egg
2 tablespoons Dijon mustard
2 tablespoons roasted garlic
Juice from 1 lemon
2 cups olive oil
1 cup canola oil
1 tablespoon minced fresh sage
1½ teaspoons minced fresh thyme
1½ teaspoons minced fresh rosemary
Salt and pepper to taste

For aioli: In a food processor, combine egg yolks, egg, mustard, garlic, and lemon.

Turn on processor, and slowly add oils for emulsification. Add sage, thyme, rosemary, salt, and pepper.

Method for sandwich: Spread aioli on 1 slice of bread (preferably Kalamata Olive Bread). Top with tuna salad, sliced red onion, provolone cheese, and another slice of bread. Grill on stove for 2 to 3 minutes, flip, and grill other side.

Kansas

LumberJill

When the crew first showed up at Guy's Steakhouse to shoot, you could tell Guy wanted nothing to do with us. He had never been on camera before, much less on national TV. He was leery from the start of us "city folk." But what really warmed him up was my logging skills—or, should I say, lack thereof.

He told us he chops the wood to fire his pit out back, so I asked him if he'd take us there and do some chopping for us on camera. We thought it would make for good b-roll, a term used in television that means your basic footage that will help cover the piece. You could tell he wasn't at all keen on the idea—he had very little interest in even being on TV—and finally just flat out refused. So instead, the crew and I went out and decided I'd do some chopping on camera. At the time, it seemed like an easy enough task, but I was quickly proved wrong.

After several takes where I was trying to talk to the camera and hit the axe to the wood simultaneously, the crew was getting weary. They didn't know if I'd ever get it right, and on each take they were holding their collective breath, waiting for me to lose my grip on the axe and find it flying wildly through the air toward them.

Finally, after numerous tries, I did hit the wood. However, I was so excited by the fact that I had made my mark that I forgot what I was supposed to say, prompting yet another take. After nicknaming myself "LumberJill" on camera, and at last getting something that would work, Guy was so amused by the whole thing—and impressed by our determination, I think—he bought us all steaks that night. Seemed we really had earned our keep on this shoot.

Montana

Guy's Steakhouse at Lolo

6600 Highway 12 West
Lolo, MT 59801
(406) 273-2622

There are millions of acres of wild forest land throughout Montana—a rugged, yet beautiful landscape that is home to self-reliant people who live alongside nature and aren't afraid of a hard day's work. They are people like Guy Leibenguth, who owns this classic Montana steakhouse. You'll find him and his log cabin restaurant just 8 miles south of Missoula, through the craggy peaks of the Bitterroot Range, in the tiny town of Lolo.

Even though this guy had never worked in a restaurant, he did know how to construct one. A former lumberjack, he felled more than 40,000 board feet of logs and built his business from the ground up.

And even though he doesn't do the grilling, he does know how to make a good fire for his steaks. They're cooked on an open flame, in an open kitchen of sorts. The pit, which is called a "Western barbeque," is in the dining room and is built with bricks and fueled by wood. The flavor the steaks soak up from this form of grilling is remarkable. There's the 10-ounce sirloin called "Lolo's," the 16-ounce "Missoula," and for those with a really carnivorous appetite, a 24-ounce sirloin called the "Montana." It actually looks like the shape of the state. And is just about as big.

Here in Big Sky Country, sometimes bigger is better, at least for those with an insatiable appetite for meat.

Two Sisters

127 Alder
Missoula, MT 59802
(406) 327-8438

They have a slogan here: "Two sisters are better than one." Granted, the two sisters who own this place are a bit biased, but most everyone who works and eats here also agrees with the motto.

Beth and Susan Higgins grew up all around the world. Their father was in the military, so the family moved frequently. However, these two had a dream. They wanted to own a restaurant together. So they decided to open shop in, of all places, Missoula, Montana. Why? Well, both are members of the Black Feet Tribe. Their dad was a Native American, born on the reservation about a 4½-hour drive from the restaurant. So opening here in this part-Western, part-hippie, part-college town was the perfect way to bring their eclectic experiences together and get back to their roots.

What's great about this place is the variety of food, as well as the diversity of customers. You'll see a cowboy in one corner, a college student in another, and someone with orange hair in the middle. As far as food goes, they are known for having great chicken dishes like the organic chicken pot pie, and baked chicken with chipotle sauce, served up with spicy black beans and cornbread. They also make homemade soups daily, great salads, and incredible pies from scratch. If you like a big breakfast in the morning, this is the place to come. No matter what time of day you dine here, you'll know why the old adage is true: Two heads really *are* better than one.

———

Idaho

Rider Ranch
South 4199 Wolf Lodge Road
Coeur d'Alene, ID 83814
(208) 667-3373
www.riderranch.com

Imagine riding horseback through meadows filled with wildflowers and pristine pine forests. The mountain air is so crisp it makes you heady. No traffic, no paved roads, just you and the wilderness that surrounds you. Well, this dream can be yours at a hidden gem in Coeur d'Alene,

photo courtesy of Tom Forliti

Jill and producer Jodi Langer heading out to ride the range at Rider Ranch.

at the Rider Ranch—a great getaway for anyone in search of some true solitude.

Don't let the name of the place fool you—it's not just a riding ranch. It's a true working ranch that has been in the Rider family for more than 50 years. But it wasn't until 1986 that Linda and Rob Rider decided to share their 1,000 acres of nature with others.

They'll hitch up their horses and take you and your family or group on a trek through miles of their beautiful countryside. When it's over, the Riders don't let their riders just "mosey off into the sunset" on an empty stomach. For the evening dinner ride, they rustle up an authentic chuck wagon feast in a spectacular outdoor setting. Grilled sirloin steaks and potatoes are cooked on an open flame. Baked beans and even homemade chocolate cake are cooked in a Dutch oven over an open fire. To serve you, they rig up an outdoor table, complete with a tablecloth and centerpiece of huckleberries collected in the area. You savor your meal, knowing you've left the modern world behind.

Unfortunately, at the end of your dinner ride, you gotta get back in the saddle and head into the real world with the honking of horns and ringing of cell phones. Fortunately for the

Idaho

Riders, they simply need to make sure their horses—just like their guests—are well fed and taken care of before getting ready for another day in God's country.

Hot Fudge Cake

ADAPTED FROM RIDER RANCH,
COEUR D'ALENE, IDAHO

MAKES 12 SERVINGS

First Mixture:
2 cups all-purpose flour
4 teaspoons baking powder
½ teaspoon salt
1½ cups sugar
2 tablespoons unsweetened cocoa powder
⅓ cup powdered milk

Second Mixture:
2 cups packed light brown sugar
½ cup unsweetened cocoa powder
¼ cup butter or margarine
2½ cups water

To make the first mixture: Combine flour, baking powder, salt, sugar, 2 tablespoons cocoa powder, and milk in a bowl or self-sealing plastic bag.

To make the second mixture: Combine brown sugar and ½ cup cocoa powder in a bowl or self-sealing plastic bag.

Preheat the oven to 350°F. If making over an open fire, the rule of thumb is 25° per charcoal briquette, so will you need a total of 14 hot briquettes. Arrange some on the lid and some underneath the Dutch oven.

To prepare cake: Melt butter in a 12-inch Dutch oven over medium heat on the stovetop or open fire. Add 1½ cups water and the first mixture. Stir to make a cake batter. Sprinkle the second mixture over the top (do not mix or stir). Pour remaining 1 cup water over the top and around the edges.

Bake for 45 to 55 minutes (see cook's note). If using the charcoal, check after about 35 minutes.

COOK'S NOTE: This recipe is specially created for camping and cooking over an open fire. The dry ingredients can be easily packed and carried in plastic bags, and the butter can be packed in a recycled yogurt cup with a lid. This container can be your measuring cup. Include a spoon or something to stir with in one of the plastic bags, and you'll be ready to go. This is a good starter recipe, because if it isn't quite cooked you have hot fudge sauce. If it bakes too long, you have a brownie cake. If it is just right, the hot fudge is bubbling up through the cake. It is especially good with vanilla ice cream.

Beverly's at the Coeur d'Alene Resort

115 South 2nd Street
Coeur d'Alene, ID 83814
(208) 765-4000
www.cdaresort.com

For a laid-back, luxurious escape, check out the Coeur d'Alene Resort. It has just about anything you'd want, and then some. Situated on the banks of beautiful Lake Coeur d'Alene, surrounded by pine forests, the resort features spacious suites, great shops, a wonderful fine-dining restaurant, an awesome pool, and, most important—drum roll please—the world's only movable floating golf green.

Now Jill's not a golfer, but this floating green even had her intrigued, at least for the first nine balls she attempted to hit on camera. You tee off on the fourteenth hole, but because the floating green is hooked up to underwater cables, it's moved every day, so you'll never have a monotonous game. From the women's tee, you're looking at a range of anywhere from 85 to 100 yards. The men's tee is slightly farther. Not an easy feat even for the avid golfer, much less for someone with Jill's skill (or should we say lack thereof). For her, the challenge was just trying to hit the ball and not her photographer's head or his camera.

After finishing up unscathed (Jill, that is, not the putting green; she tore that up pretty badly), the crew headed inside to Beverly's to showcase their potato dishes for the *Best Of Potato Plates*

photo courtesy of Jodi Langer

The hopeless golf lesson at Coeur d'Alene Resort.

show. Never mind that they don't *grow* potatoes in northern Idaho—a minor geographical oversight that the owner of the resort kindly pointed out during the interview. No worry, luckily the restaurant does *serve* potatoes—and in unique ways, too.

Some of our favorites: the Dungeness Crab Crusted Halibut with a Potato Soufflé; Salmon with Lobster-Mashed Potatoes; and the Idaho Potato and Portobello Wellington. If you're not sure what kind of wine you're supposed to match with your potato plate, ask Sam Lang, the sommelier. He's great and tends to recommend really good, local Northwest wines that go with a lot of their dishes. On their catering menu, and occasionally in the restaurant, they'll serve up a dessert that looks like a baked potato. It's ice cream rolled in cocoa powder, garnished with white mousse to look like sour cream, chopped pistachio nuts to resemble green onions, little chocolate ball "bacon bits," and yellow candy "butter."

No visit here is complete without checking out their first-rate spa. Jill loves getting massages and convinced the crew to do the same. Her claim was sore arms from swinging the golf club in vain; her crew claimed their eyes were sore just from watching her fail time and again.

In short, everyone had good reason to get rubbed down, and by the time they were done, they all felt as mushy as mashed potatoes.

—

North Dakota

Georgia's and the Owl
Highway 85 and Main
Box 524
Amidon, ND 58620
(701) 879-6289

Seems like the world is getting more and more crowded by the minute. Take New York City, for example. There are more than 26,000 people per square mile. In Detroit, you'll find more than 6,800 people per square mile. Now take the entire state of North Dakota, where you'll find there are only about 9 people per square mile, with the eastern side considered the most populated. Okay, now let's break it down further. Slope County on the far southwestern side of the state only has an average of .6 people per square mile (yes, that's less than 1 person). That's also

North Dakota

An Encounter with Cujo

A few notes on North Dakota: At 3,500 feet, White Butte is the highest point in the state, and an alleged tourist attraction. You'd think it would be an easy spot to find, considering there are signs on the highway with arrows pointing out the direction to follow. Not so. We drove around in circles for an hour, searching through pastures and the few ranches that are in the area. But to no avail. It's not like there's anyone around for you to ask, either. At last, we found what we thought might be White Butte. On the way up this dirt road, you pass a ramshackle house. There's a sign asking you to give a $5 donation. Apparently the "landmark" butte is on this rancher's property, and he wants some compensation for the occasional idiot tourists, like ourselves, driving on his land. But even with all the best intentions of making a donation, there is no guarantee that things will go smoothly.

When my producer Jodi Langer approached the farmer's door with money in hand, she was met by "Cujo," the attack poodle, who almost ripped off her pant leg. Apparently no one was home and, because we didn't feel like having Jodi permanently maimed, we just put the money on the seat of the beat-up pickup truck and took off for our destination. We're still not 100 percent sure we found it. We climbed a bluff that looked pretty high and decided it looked like a "white butte" to us.

But our epic didn't end there. In the course of shooting my standups, a herd of about 50 cows took a liking to our SUV, which was parked at the base of the butte.

If you saw the piece, you saw me running down the rocky hill, attempting to shoo them away. That was no joke. That was reality TV at its best. A lot of people, particularly "urban snobs," turn up their noses when you mention places like North Dakota, but we gotta tell you, it was one of our *best* adventures.

North Dakota

where you'll find the smallest county seat in America: Amidon. Population 24. It's such an out-of-the-way place, you won't find it indexed in a road atlas; yet this tiny town boasts of one of the best restaurants in the Great Plains.

Georgia's and the Owl, named after owner Marie Lorge's daughter Georgia and their pet owl (now deceased), is Marie's life-long dream. She'd always wanted to own a restaurant. As a young girl, she would check out cookbooks from the library and make copies of recipes from *Gourmet Magazine*. After graduating from college, she didn't have the money to buy a restaurant, so she decided to teach school, knowing her dream would somehow work out. She was living in California, teaching at a parochial school, and was transferred to, of all places, North Dakota. But fate was at play, for it was here she met her husband, L. K., a welder by trade. They settled in Bismarck, but would always drive through Amidon when traveling the state, and time and again, she would remark that this one building sitting on Highway 85 would be

perfect for a restaurant. One day she called the owner of the building to see if he wanted to sell it. At first, he wasn't interested, but eventually he came around and they bought it.

Marie, a no-nonsense woman, will be the first to tell you her food isn't fancy or froufrou. She calls herself a food facilitator, not a food manipulator. That means she takes her cut of prime rib, seasons it a tiny bit, then leaves it alone on the grill to cook in its own juices. One word of advice: If you order the large prime rib, you better be hungry. It weighs nearly 3 pounds. The petite cut is a mere 1½ pounds. On average, she goes through about 200 pounds of prime rib a week, which means reservations—especially in the summer—are recommended. Hard to believe, considering Marie can have the entire town over for dinner and still have room for more.

So forget the crowded cities and life in the fast lane. Head to North Dakota and check out life in the *vast* lane. We think you'll find it has some pretty tasty rewards.

Hunter's Table and Tavern

Highway 12
Box 241
Rhame, ND 58651
(701) 279-6689

A lot of tall tales about Wild West adventures have come out of the wide, open country of North Dakota. One legend that still gives folks something to chew on is the tale about some tough-as-nails women who built one of the most successful businesses in the area.

Once upon a time a woman named Rae Getz and her husband went out for a drink to the only bar in town. A nasty brawl broke out and ruined their evening, so she vowed to open a restaurant where people could go for more quiet conversation. She gathered up about a dozen women, friends, and relatives, and before they knew it, a female revolution had swept through this tiny western town.

These women poured their blood, sweat, and tears into the project, along with logs, cement, and bottles—beautifully colored glass bottles were inserted between the log layers to let the light shine in. The roof is made of seven layers, consisting of plastic (okay, so that's a twentieth-century addition), sod, flax, and scoria. They opened up in April 1983.

Rae Getz eventually moved out of the area, and now Donna Graham rules the roost. She serves up hearty, home-cooked meals like mashed potatoes covered with beef gravy, smothered pork chops, fried chicken, and juicy steaks. She has her work cut out for her. Her task is to fill the bellies of all the ranchers and hunters in the area, thus the name, Hunter's Table and Tavern.

Rhame is a town of fewer than 200 people, yet this restaurant is quite the success story and gives new meaning to the term "female power." It's a frontier fairy tale that we hope will live happily ever after.

———

Pastime Club and Steakhouse

14 Main Street
Marmarth, ND 58643
(701) 279-9843

If you have found a reason to be in this part of the world and are able to find this place, then your battle is more than half over. But just because you've arrived on the doorstep of the Pastime Club and Steakhouse in Marmarth, North Dakota, doesn't mean your journey is complete. Once your eyes adjust to the swirling cigarette smoke that engulfs the place, you might look around this rough and tumble bar and find some wary ranchers and oil rig workers eyeballing you. Not to worry; it's just their way of welcoming in an outsider. After all, this isn't a major tourist destination.

Your first instinct might be to turn around and run out the door, hop into your car, and drive away. You'll think we steered you wrong. Don't. And we didn't. You know the story about the ugly duckling and the beautiful swan? Well, the beautiful swan is straight through the curtains at the end of the bar.

Once you make it into the restaurant proper, you're bound to shake your head in wonderment.

North Dakota

Don't Call Me for Lunch

If you're looking for lunch in North Dakota, you might be fighting hunger pains for a long time. That's because they don't call it "lunch" here. They call it "dinner," and what many of us call dinner is referred to as "supper" in these parts. The ranchers typically eat their big meal of the day around noon, which is why it's called dinner (apparently lunch doesn't sound filling enough). Got it? We hope so, because it's 33 miles from Rhame to the Montana border . . . but we have a sneaking suspicion they don't have "lunch" there, either.

You'll be baffled at how a fine-dining steakhouse could exist in such an out-of-the-way place. Even more amazing are the rave reviews it's received, including one from the *Los Angeles Times,* which states that Pastime is a "Steakhouse of such repute that, despite its remote spot in the state, reservations are recommended." Once you have dinner here, you, too, will know the secret.

In its heyday, the Milwaukee Railroad was the heartbeat of Marmarth. The trains would stop and the people working on them would stay in the town's bunkhouses, giving local businesses a boost. But when the railroad was sold to the Burlington Line, it no longer stopped in Marmarth, and many of those businesses shut their doors. Nowadays, the town is struggling. It has a lot of crumbling buildings and not many signs of life—but there are some, like Laurie Reichenberg's Pastime Steakhouse. She has one of just a few businesses left on Main Street.

White linen tablecloths and candles give Pastime a romantic, homey feel. The food isn't necessarily gourmet, but it is really good and draws people from all over. Laurie was originally from this area, and after becoming disillusioned with the cost of living in California, moved back. She'd always worked in restaurants and decided she'd open one of her own. She knew she'd have to make a pretty good meal to survive in a town of fewer than 150 people. Pastime is the perfect testimonial to her love of cooking—and why California's loss is North Dakota's gain.

She serves specialties like battered jumbo shrimp, walleye amandine, and of course, the biggest thing on her menu: steaks. She cooks with choice meat, and grills 'em however you like. Her signature steak, a 16-ounce rib eye, is served either plain or smothered in her secret spicy sauce.

So why open a steakhouse in the middle of nowhere? Laurie has two reasons. First, she says she wasn't doing anything at the time and figured she didn't have a whole lot to lose. She was just as surprised as everyone else when it took off. Second, and perhaps most important, she says small-town people deserve good food, and they shouldn't have to drive two hours to get it. We couldn't agree more.

Onion Butter Steak Sauce

ADAPTED FROM PASTIME CLUB AND STEAKHOUSE, MARMARTH, NORTH DAKOTA

MAKES ENOUGH SAUCE FOR 4 STEAKS

1/4 pound butter
1/2 cup sliced green onions
1 tablespoon crushed garlic
1/4 cup Worcestershire sauce
1/2 cup beef broth
1 tablespoon brown sugar
2 tablespoons chopped fresh parsley
2 tablespoons all-purpose flour
3 tablespoons water
1 teaspoon ground black pepper

Melt butter in a pan over medium heat. Add onions and garlic, and sauté for 5 minutes. Stir in Worcestershire sauce, broth, sugar, and parsley. Bring to a boil.

Mix flour and water in a small bowl until smooth. Stir into the boiling mixture, and cook, stirring, until thickened. Remove from the heat and add pepper.

Pitchfork Fondue

P.O. Box 198
Medora, ND 58645
(800) 633-6721
(Open summer only—early June to end of August)
www.medora.com

When you think of fondue, you think of dainty little forks and bite-size pieces of food. So here's a heads-up: The kind of fondue you'll find at the Pitchfork probably isn't what the French had in mind.

High atop a bluff overlooking the North Dakota Badlands, your cowboy cook takes an 11-ounce steak, sticks a pitchfork in it, and drops it into a vat of extremely hot oil. After frying it on the fork for 3 to 4 minutes, he pulls it out and plops it on your paper plate. It's no wonder forks fly fast and furious here—these guys are feeding up to 1,300 people a night.

After you've eaten all the meat you can, head down to the seven-story escalator, said to be one of the longest outdoor escalators in the United States (do they really have someone who keeps track of this stuff?), and into this 2,900-seat outdoor amphitheater. Here you'll enjoy North Dakota's number-one attraction: the Medora Musical, a Broadway-style production that traces the history of this Wild West town.

Medora is an interesting place. During the off-season, fewer than 100 people live here. But come summer, the town takes on a life of its own. During the high season, more than 350,000 tourists come to see what Teddy Roosevelt supposedly once called the "romance of his life." It is a ruggedly beautiful place, stark and stunning at the same time.

Founded in 1883 by a 24-year-old French nobleman, Marquis de Mores, Medora was named after his wife, Medora Von Hoffman, daughter of a wealthy New York City banker. The Marquis set out to literally make a town. He built a meat-packing plant, a brickyard, several stores and saloons, a hotel, and a Catholic church. Despite his vision, all his various enterprises had ended in financial failure by the fall of 1886. With their son and daughter, the Marquis and Marquise returned to France, and soon after, the town went bust.

Around the same time, another colorful character was drawn to the area. A young New York politician named Theodore Roosevelt first arrived here in September 1883 to hunt buffalo. He immediately fell in love with the land and eventually bought two ranches nearby.

In 1901, Roosevelt, at age 42, became the youngest president in U.S. history. He often credited his experiences in Medora with giving him the resolve and self-confidence needed for the awesome responsibilities he faced as president.

After all, you have to be tough to live in this land of extremes, enduring hot summers and frigid winters where the mercury sometimes dips to 70 below. It wasn't easy for those first frontiersmen, but you'll see by the beauty of the Badlands why a select few decided to stick it out and why today, many more come here to visit. It's a rough yet radiant place where the adventurous spirit of the West is still very much alive and well.

As for that fondue, we'd like to think the Marquis would be pleased that they continue to hold on to some element of his homeland, even though it's not exactly the French way of doing it.

———

South Dakota

Jakes

At The Midnight Star
677 Main Street
Deadwood, SD 57732
(605) 578-1555 or (800) 999-6482
www.themidnightstar.com

When you visit Deadwood, South Dakota, you will think you have stepped into a Hollywood movie set—but you're in for a surprise, because these wonderful Old West buildings are neither backdrops nor façades. This is an authentic Western town set against the beautiful backdrop of the Black Hills.

Deadwood first became famous during the gold rush era in 1876. But with the gold came vices, like gambling and prostitution. This is where Wild Bill Hickok was shot and killed by the infamous Jack McCall during a poker game. Look out for someone impersonating him; just be careful not to get too close. The blanks he shoots are a bit loud, so your eardrums will appreciate that you keep your distance. This is also where two famous frontierswomen really made their marks. First came Calamity Jane and later, Poker Alice. Both were cigar-smoking, gambling, rough-and-tumble women, each with a keen eye and a good shot.

Gambling came and went over the years, but Deadwood's houses of ill repute were another story. Although "officially" illegal, these houses flourished for more than a century. It wasn't until 1980 when officials finally cracked down that the "ladies of the evening" had to leave. But gambling *is* back, and this small town is once again famous—not only for its mini-Vegas feel,

South Dakota

but for one movie star who really helped put this whole area on the map: Kevin Costner.

Remember the beautiful landscapes—the sweeping prairies, the gorgeous pine forests, the big blue sky—in *Dances With Wolves*? Apparently Kevin fell deeply in love with South Dakota when shooting here in 1989. He and his brother Dan Costner wanted to put something permanent here, so the two brainstormed and came up with an idea for a fine dining restaurant in Deadwood.

When you walk into The Midnight Star, the first thing you'll notice (and hear) is the noise from the slot machines. Both the first and second floors are gambling halls. The next thing that'll catch your eye is the movie paraphernalia. Scenes from Kevin's stardom are all over the place. Check out his kitsch and costumes from *Field of Dreams, Bull Durham, Silverado*, and *Dances With Wolves,* to name a few.

On the third floor, you'll find their casual restaurant, Diamond Lil's Bar and Grill. Head up to the top floor and now, instead of feeling like you're on a gaming movie set, you'll feel like you're in a fine New York City restaurant.

Jakes might be named after the character Kevin played in *Silverado*, but nothing here says "Wild West." Rather, *opulent* and *elegant* are the adjectives that come to mind. This dining spot, which has been given the AAA Four-Diamond award several times, is for high rollers. But just because it can be an expensive meal doesn't mean jeans are out. Allow us to explain. In these parts, a well-dressed Westerner will have on starched and newly pressed Wranglers (note: they're not called jeans out here), a white shirt with a tie and jacket, and an expensive Stetson hat. The sophistication of this look has no equal in New York or San Francisco.

The food is upscale American regional.

Because they are in steak-and-potatoes country, you'll find those staples on the menu—but cooked up in a gourmet fashion. One of the favorites: Elk served with Yukon mashed potatoes and topped with a blackberry Coca-Cola reduction sauce. The Pheasant Napoleon with roasted red peppers, wilted spinach, and shiitake mushrooms could probably garner an Oscar if food were a category.

Although you're a long way from Tinseltown, after hanging out here you might find you prefer the more laid-back pace. We'd like to think the bright lights in this small city are worth their weight in gold.

Full Circle

I got my start in television in Rapid City, South Dakota, as a reporter at KEVN. Keep in mind that many television journalists start in small markets, so my situation was pretty typical.

My father is from a long line of ranchers who make their living on those windswept prairies of western South Dakota. So when I got my first break and drove with my dad and two cats to Rapid City from the east coast, my rancher relatives welcomed me with open arms.

Deadwood is only about 45 miles from Rapid City, so on nights off at KEVN, my colleagues and I often headed here to grab a beer and put a quarter or two in the slot machines. We hoped to win enough to buy another drink or even dinner. But for most of us underpaid reporters, dining at Jakes was never an option. It was unthinkable to spend $50 to $100 on dinner. That's a month's worth of groceries or a couple new outfits.

When I returned to shoot in Deadwood for the Food Network, I felt in many ways that my career had come full circle. It was serendipitous that now, after nearly 10 years, I'd finally have a chance to taste some of the food that had eluded me on my limited budget as a small-town reporter. It was worth waiting for.

South Dakota

Pheasant Napoleon

ADAPTED FROM JAKES, DEADWOOD, SOUTH
DAKOTA

MAKES 2 SERVINGS, ABOUT ½ CUP SAUCE

Pheasant Sauce:

1 quart water

Bones and trimmings from 1 pheasant

1 bay leaf

2 tablespoons sherry or Madiera

About ¼ cup each chopped carrot, onion, and celery

½ tablespoon cornstarch mixed with 2 tablespoons water

Salt and white pepper, to taste

2 (about 5-inch) squares puff pastry dough

1 egg beaten with 1 tablespoon water, for egg wash

Freshly ground black pepper

Clarified butter

1 pheasant breast, boned, quartered, and pounded slightly

1 cup all-purpose flour, seasoned with salt, white pepper, and dried sage

4 (½-inch-thick) red bell pepper rings

6 shiitake mushrooms

½ cup fresh spinach

To make sauce: Combine water, bones, bay leaf, sherry, carrot, onion, and celery in a large saucepan. Simmer for about 1 hour. Strain and boil liquid until reduced to about ½ cup. Stir in cornstarch mixture, and cook, stirring, until slightly thickened. Season with salt and pepper.

Preheat the oven to 400°F. Cut dough from corner to corner to get 4 triangles. Brush with egg wash, and sprinkle with pepper. Prick dough slightly with a fork, and place on a baking sheet. Bake about 15 minutes or until golden brown.

To a very hot saucepan over medium-high heat, add a small amount of clarified butter. Coat pheasant in flour, and sauté until slightly browned. Remove pheasant and keep warm.

Add bell pepper rings and mushrooms to the saucepan, adding more butter, if necessary, and sauté until vegetables are softened. Add spinach, and cook for a few seconds, just until wilted.

To serve: Cut pheasant on the diagonal into about 6 pieces. Place one pastry piece in the center of each plate, then a piece of pheasant, then 1 bell pepper ring, then pheasant, then 1 mushroom, then pheasant, then spinach, and so on. Top with puff dough, and 1 red pepper ring. Garnish plate with remaining mushrooms, and drizzle with sauce.

State Game Lodge and Resort

Custer State Park
East Highway 16A
Custer, SD 57730
(800) 658-3530 for Resort Reservations
(605) 255-4541 for Game Lodge Reception Desk
www.custerresorts.com

Across the prairies of western South Dakota, in a land many call one of the last of our great frontiers, is Custer State Park and the Game Lodge. It's literally a home where the buffalo roam and the deer and the antelope play—and it's quite a playground they have. There are 73,000 acres of pristine, untamed land that make up the park. It's set up so you can drive through it on your own or take one of their Buffalo Safari Jeep Tours. (We liked this option because you learn so much more about the area, plus you ride in the open air.)

There are about 1,500 buffalo roaming about and, although they might look like gentle giants, these wild and wooly animals are amazingly agile, and they *will* charge you.

To see the antelope, you'll have to be quick. Known as the speedsters of the prairie, they can run up to 45 miles per hour. And they also have incredible eyesight. We were told they're able to see a fly on a fencepost a mile away.

After your excursions, relax in the Pheasant Dining Room and enjoy some of their game dishes. Although it might seem sacrilegious to eat buffalo right after watching them roam free, Braised Buffalo Shortribs soaked in a port wine sauce are one of the highlights on the menu.

South Dakota

Do as I Say, Not as I Do.

In the piece we did for our *Best Of Game* show, I did the "open" out in the park with a herd of buffalo behind me. Now, visitors are *not* supposed to get out of their vehicles. However, I felt an obligation to photographer Dave Dennison, who wanted to get a good picture, so I broke that rule. We got what we wanted, but as we were doing the final shot, the buffalo on a bluff behind us started coming in our direction, necessitating the crew take a speedy exit. We'd like to think we were just doing our jobs and taking one for the team, but in reality, we were probably being just plain stupid. Good thing we're still around to tell our tale.

South Dakota

Another specialty is the pheasant that is sometimes stuffed with boursin and montrachet cheeses and covered with a blackberry brandy–dried currant sauce; other times it's smoked and served over pasta.

The lodge dates back from 1920 and has been a stomping ground for a few famous politicians. Teddy Roosevelt reportedly hunted bears in nearby Custer National Forest years before he became president, and Dwight D. Eisenhower came to the park for several days in 1953. The lodge's most famous guest, however, was President Calvin Coolidge. He spent the summer of 1927 here and called the Game Lodge his "Summer White House." You can now stay in the very room from which he ran the country and sit at the desk he used. With all the beauty around, you can hardly blame him for not high-tailing it back to Washington. No wonder the summer of 1927 was such a peaceful one.

Wall Drug

510 Main Street
Wall, SD 57790
(605) 279-2175
www.walldrug.com

According to the signs, it's 5,397 miles from Amsterdam, a mere 5,160 miles from London, and only 4,404 miles from the Leaning Tower of Pisa. What is it? Wall Drug of South Dakota, also known as "the Drugstore."

Okay, so it's a little hokey, but it's one of those places where you have to stop if you have the chance. After all, it came about completely *by chance* and has quite a tale to tell.

In 1931, in this dusty, drought- and depression-ridden prairie town, Ted and Dorothy Hustead bought the area's only drugstore. Ted was a pharmacist and wanted his own business. Problem was, the godforsaken town of Wall was in the middle of nowhere, with only about 300 people, most of whom were poor as church mice during the depression.

They attempted to make a go of it, but after five years of scraping by during the "dirty thirties," they were faced with yet another hot, dry, miserable summer. One day in July, Dorothy went to take a nap, only to notice the noise of tourist traffic motoring westward to the cooler Black Hills. It was at that moment their fate changed. She reasoned that if they could get the people off the highway and into the store, they might just be able to make ends meet. She had Ted put up signs on the highway advertising free ice water at Wall Drug. Her idea worked. Throngs of travelers began to stop in, and after they drank the ice water, they'd usually buy some ice cream or a soda.

The Husteads haven't been without customers since.

Eventually the drug store took on a life of its own, and instead of just selling prescriptions, soda, and ice cream, they began to sell just about everything under the sun, from weird and wacky souvenirs to authentic Western wear. You'll need a few hours, to get through this "drugstore." Be sure to check out the lifelike cowboy orchestra and chuckwagon quartet, along with the store's $2.2 million art collection. Their cafeteria-style

photo courtesy of Jill Cordes

Road signs show the way to Wall Drug.

restaurant seats 520 people, and it's where you can find free ice water and five-cent coffee, for which they're also famous. Even though the town's population hovers around 800, about 20,000 people come through each day in the summer. (Yes, it's incredible, but true!) Most of the visitors have a hankering for a hearty meal, which is why the joint goes through thousands of pounds of roast beef a season and more than 3,000 donuts a day.

As for those mileage signs, well, during World War II, a friend of the Husteads took a sign over to Europe and put it up, advertising how far it was to Wall Drug. Somehow this gimmick caught on, and more people started placing mileage signs around the country and the world. It became a joke that created curiosity for those who didn't know about this place and effectively turned into a brilliant form of free advertising. They also started giving out free bumper stickers with slogans like: "Have you dug Wall Drug?" and "Where the heck is Wall Drug?" Carry on the tradition, and grab a few to put up at some faraway place.

And in the future, be on the lookout for those worldly signs now that you're "in the know." That way, the next time you're on Easter Island, you'll find comfort in the fact that Wall Drug is only 5,541 miles away—a short journey, especially for those in Antarctica who have 10,645 miles to go.

South Dakota

Branded for Life

When you get here, look at all the ranch brands on the wall. All told, there are about 1,500 of them, signifying the important role—culturally and economically—that cattle ranchers play in this area. Here's a challenge: Try to find the XL brand. That was my great grandfather's brand that has now been passed down to my uncle, Kirk Cordes, a local rancher. So why use brands? Well, each rancher has his own unique brand to make it easy to tell which cattle belong to whom. It is also there for anyone who is a little less than honest to think twice before licking their chops about a potentially juicy steak from someone else's ranch. A rancher's brand also becomes the source of a larger identity. For example, instead of the Cordes ranch it may be simply called the XL-Ranch. Yep, these ole cowboys were way ahead of their time with their own version of vanity license plates. They just chose to put the message on cows rather than cars!

Wyoming

Wooden Knife

Junction Highways 44 and 377
Interior, SD 57750
(605) 433-5463 or (800) 303-2773
www.woodenknife.com

You might be hard-pressed to find a reason to go to Interior, South Dakota, but if the spirit moves you there, be sure to stop into the Wooden Knife and buy a box of Ansel Wooden Knife's slice of heaven: his Indian fry bread.

We originally did a story on the Wooden Knife Café, a place where Ansel sold both his boxes of fry bread and his famous Indian Tacos. After we shot *Best Of Roadside Dining,* Food Network's other popular show, *Food Finds,* paid him a visit. Ansel and his wife, Teresa, got so overwhelmed by the responses from both shows, they decided something had to go. They closed down the café, and now strictly sell the boxes of fry bread. People from as far away as Moscow, Guam, and Kuwait e-mail him their orders.

——

Wyoming

Million Dollar Cowboy Bar

25 North Cache Street
Jackson, WY 83001
(307) 733-2207
www.milliondollarcowboybar.com

Rowdy cowboys are known to down their share of whiskey at this legendary Old West watering hole, but one beloved regular really liked his spirits here. When he died in 1991, his ashes were put into a Jack Daniel's bottle, which is kept in the office of co-owner Hagen Dudley. Every so often, family members visit and toast him with a shot of the hard stuff.

The Million Dollar Cowboy Bar seems just the place to drink into perpetuity. Opened in 1937 right on Jackson's Town Square, it's been a hangout for gunslingers and city slickers alike. In the early days, it was a honky-tonk known for booze, betting, and bands. There are even a few old bullet holes around the bar—or at least that's what the bartenders claim. But long ago, pool tables replaced the gambling tables, and the Western atmosphere became a little less wild.

Still, you don't belly up to the bar around here as much as you saddle up, atop 38 stools made from authentic horse saddles. It's a gimmick that often leaves newcomers squirming, at least until they down a few drinks, or sit sidesaddle. Another trademark is the 624 silver dollars inlaid in the bar. Yes, it's a few bucks short of a million dollars, but the expensive moniker actually comes from an earlier owner who wanted to distinguish this place from all the other cowboy bars in Wyoming. The acres of strange-looking tumorous pine wood that runs the interior also helps the place stand out, as well as the giant neon sign outside.

Some of the biggest names in country music have taken to the stage, and there's plenty of two-stepping on the dance floor most nights. Spurs are optional, but as that guy in the bottle of Jack would have told you, good spirits are mandatory.

——

Mangy Moose Restaurant and Saloon

3285 West McCollister Drive
Teton Village, WY 83025
(307) 733-4913
www.mangymoose.net

A waitress had the perfect line when Marc noticed the overwhelming number of Generation Extreme males hanging out in the Mangy Moose. For women, who are seriously outnumbered around this ski resort, the joke is, "The odds are good, but the goods are odd."

This quirky bar/restaurant seems the ideal hangout for odd goods. It sits at the base of the Jackson Hole Mountain Resort in the Grand Teton (quick guys, look up the translation of that French term) National Park. The slopes outside feature the longest vertical drop anywhere in the United States, more than 4,100 feet from top to bottom. Sure it's a rush, but braving that kind of hill requires something a little out of the ordinary. And it's definitely worthy of a few drinks afterward.

Opened in 1967, the Mangy Moose is often picked by sports magazines as the best après ski bar in the land. Decorated T.G.I.F.–style, with signs, placards, and odds-and-ends, its center-piece is an actual (and anatomically correct) stuffed moose suspended from the ceiling. Those who check will discover it's yet another male who hangs out here. With drinks flowing and the socializing underway, the mood is as laid back as it gets. In fact, the easy-going atmosphere led the current owners David Yoder and Jeff Davies to buy the place virtually on a whim, even though they were barely acquainted at the time.

The Moose is open from breakfast through late night, with bands booked most evenings. There's an extensive menu in its restaurant next door and plenty of bar food. Bloomin' onions and wings make up a good part of the orders, but there's also prime rib, seafood, and a hearty buffalo meatloaf to help the scores of mountain jocks build enough strength to tackle the slopes and still have enough energy left over to throw back the odd brewski at the bar.

Mangy Moose Buffalo Meatloaf
ADAPTED FROM MANGY MOOSE,
TETON VILLAGE, WYOMING

MAKES 10 SERVINGS

5 pounds ground buffalo, well drained
½ cup chopped fresh garlic
2 red bell peppers, chopped
1 large yellow onion, chopped
½ cup each chopped fresh basil and parsley
8 ounces Grey Poupon mustard
⅓ cup steak sauce
¼ cup Worcestershire sauce
6 eggs
6 cups fresh breadcrumbs
3 tablespoons puréed canned chipotle chile in adobo sauce

Add buffalo, garlic, bell pepper, onion, basil, parsley, mustard, steak sauce, Worcestershire sauce, eggs, breadcrumbs, and chiles to a heavy-duty mixer bowl. Turn the mixer to low speed, and mix until all the ingredients are blended. (Don't turn on the mixer until all the ingredients are in the bowl, but be careful not to overmix.) Make into a loaf in a large shallow baking pan.

Bake at 350°F for 40 minutes or until cooked through. Do not overcook. Use pan drippings for gravy.

The Wort Hotel
50 North Glenwood Street
Jackson, WY 83001
(307) 733-2190 or (800) 322-2727
www.worthotel.com

In this remote mountain area originally known as Jackson's Hole, locals realized they needed two things: a nice hotel for visitors and a less amusing name.

The name change came first. The moniker honors Davey Jackson, an 1800s fur trader who traveled these hard-to-reach parts in Northwest Wyoming. The "Hole" refers to the low-lying area in the middle of several mountain ranges. Over time, the possessive was dropped, and the name shortened to the less-giggle-inducing Jackson Hole.

The hotel didn't come until 1941, when brothers John and Jess Wort opened their large luxury facility in downtown Jackson. (The town is called Jackson; the area is Jackson Hole.) At the time, the cost was a staggering $90,000—a

photo courtesy of Marc Silverstein

Bud McHugh and Larry Deal high atop Jackson Hole, Wyoming.

Wyoming

real crapshoot considering the area was mostly known for cowboys and elk. Fortunately, other people around here were gambling, too, at blackjack and poker tables conveniently located inside the hotel. Even though betting was officially illegal, it helped establish the Wort, with games continuing into the late 1950s. These days, tourists come for the incredible variety of outdoor activities and shopping.

A few years after opening, the hotel added its now-famous Silver Dollar Bar, with 2,032 uncirculated silver dollars imbedded in the bar. It remains the perfect place to meet, have a few drinks, and then mosey over to the Silver Dollar Grill, a Western-style chophouse offering the area's best steaks, game, and seafood.

In 1980, a fire nearly destroyed the Wort. Within days, a sign went up saying "We Will Be Back." The restoration took nearly a year but resulted in more luxurious rooms and suites. Still, there is the matter of the name. Spelled like a growth on your skin, it's pronounced *wirt*. Funny, yes, but given the hotel's success, no one around here is laughing.

Nebraska

Sioux Sundries
201 Main Street
Harrison, NE 69346
(308) 668-2577

photos courtesy of Tom Forliti

Jill serves Bill Coffee his namesake Coffee Burger, and then dives into her own....

Something *big* made this tiny town famous. Something *really big*. Something people have come to enjoy from as far away as Australia and Japan. What is it? Here's a hint: It's part of Delores Wasserburger's last name. No, not the first part of her last name, the *last* part: burger. She's the woman who owns Sioux Sundries in Harrison, Nebraska, and invented the nearly 2-pound Coffee Burger. Yep, two 14-ounce burgers slapped together and slowly cooked on the grill.

Dolores created this meaty masterpiece back in the 1980s after local rancher Bill Coffee kept bringing his ranch hands in for lunch (called "dinner" in these parts). These big, strong men constantly complained to Delores that her 1-pound burger wasn't filling them up. Always one to please her customers, she slapped together two 1-pound patties on the grill. Those ranch hands haven't complained since.

It looks ridiculous when it comes to your table because she uses a regular size bun to wrap this huge burger! When we asked her why, she replied, "Because it's *where's the bun* not *where's the beef*." Guess you could say here in Harrison, big burgers come in small packages.

Smoke and Mirrors

For the record, I didn't eat Delores's Coffee Burger all by myself. It just looks that way in the piece we shot for our *Best Of State Plates.* We felt her burger showed off Nebraska beef like no place else. As for my eating it, that was all sneaky camera moves and edits created by photographer Chris Peterson. He had me take a few bites on camera, then he'd stop the tape and we'd tear some burger off and feed it to producer Todd Vaske and soundman Tom Forliti (they're like our versions of "Mikey" from Life cereal—they'll eat anything). I would then proceed to take another bite and so on until the burger eventually whittled down to nearly nothing. When Chris edited the piece together, he made it look as if I, in fast motion, was eating the whole thing.

One of the questions I always get asked on the road is how I stay in shape and if I really do eat everything that's on my plate. The answer is yes, and nearly yes. I love food and have a hearty appetite, but I also work out. Plus, I've got a crew that's only too willing to help clean those plates.

The Ranch House

445 Second Street
Crawford, NE 69339
(308) 665-1231

When you're the wife of a rancher, you typically work long, hard hours holding a household together. You cook for the hungry ranch hands and your own family, take care of the normal household duties of laundry and cleaning, and work hard to be a good mother and a partner to your rancher-husband. But that is just the beginning. As ranch wife you probably pay the bills, serve as bookkeeper for the ranching business, and help with outside chores and work—fixing fence, putting up hay, and making sure baby calves don't freeze to death during a late spring blizzard. And, oh yes, when you need to get groceries or take your child to the doctor, you can plan on driving more than 100 miles on dirt and gravel roads.

In short: You gotta be a strong woman to handle this profession. Becky Sellman was all that and more. But once the kids were grown, she wanted to step down from the hard life of ranching and make a new—and easier—career for herself. She decided to open a restaurant.

Opening a restaurant is like telling yourself that training for the Olympics is an easy, risk-free task. It is one of the toughest professions in which to survive. Nearly 80 percent of all restaurants fail

within the first year. Most chefs work 80 hours on a good week and still end up in the red. Becky will be the first to admit she had no idea what she was getting herself into. She didn't even know how to run a cash register.

She found an historic 1907 building in Crawford. It had been everything from a hardware store to a mortuary. Despite its morbid past, she says she didn't sense impending doom. Rather, she dove right in, buying a historic bar from the 1880s, building a kitchen, and hiring a small staff. As for the cooking, well, she figured she had cooked beef for ranch hands all those years, so that would be the easy part. It might have been what saved her.

On the menu, she has about five different cuts of choice Nebraska beef (some from her own ranch) that she'll cook however you like. Her trick is to not mess with the meat too much. Flip it once and let it cook in its own juices. No salt, sauces, or seasoning needed on these big boys. She also serves up a true Western specialty: rocky mountain oysters, also known as bull testicles. They're deep-fried and served with a dipping sauce. It's definitely an acquired taste.

When Becky opened in 1999, business was slow, not because the local townspeople didn't support her, but because Crawford (population 1,000) is kind of in the middle of nowhere. The closest big city is Denver, 220 miles away. However, as word spread about her sizzling

Nebraska

steaks, the number of people coming in began to swell.

When asked which is easier, being a ranch wife or owning the Ranch House, she laughed and said, "Probably being a ranch wife, but this [the restaurant] is so much fun. I'm honored to be here." And from the looks of it, the town of Crawford is honored to have her.

Lovers Leap Vineyards

432 2nd Street
Crawford, NE 69339
(308) 665-2712
www.loversleapvineyards.com

If someone were to say Nebraska is the next Napa, you'd probably tell them to go take a flying leap. But here at Lovers Leap Vineyards, they've already gone off the cliff. Actually, that's how this remote winery got its name. It sits in the panhandle of Nebraska, surrounded by beautiful buttes. Legend has it that two Native Americans from warring tribes fell in love but were forbidden to marry. So they jumped off a butte to their deaths to ensure they would spend eternity together. That butte, which is right behind the vineyard, is called Lovers Leap.

Justin Moody, a dentist by trade, took a trip to Napa Valley in 1996 and was inspired to take on another job: winemaking. He reasoned that summer in Western Nebraska is similar to Napa Valley. In late spring and early fall, the temperatures dip into the 50s, which helps concentrate the sugars in some grapes and makes them ripen a bit faster. The biggest difference between his area and Napa is the wicked winters. He knew he needed a hearty grape to survive the cold and found a hybrid he thought would hang on. His dad, Dave Moody, is a rancher and knows better than any Ph.D. how the seasons and the soil work together. They figured that between the two of them, they had enough chemistry to make a go of it.

The vines were planted in May 1996, and their first harvest came in early fall of 1999. They have about 24 different varieties, everything from dry reds to sweet whites along with fruit and honey wines. They've put in a tasting room next to the production area so you can stop by, have some sips, and see for yourself how it's done.

High Plains Homestead

263 Sandcreek Road
Crawford, NE 69339
(308) 665-2592
www.highplainshomestead.com

According to Merlin Kesselring, when spring hits this corner of northwest Nebraska, things get a little wild out here. That's when he and his wife, Roberta, gather around on the porch and watch the grass come up and grow. When shooting here, Jill remarked to Merlin that watching grass grow wouldn't seem that exciting. Merlin told her, "That's about as exciting as we want it. Our motto is how the West was won . . . quietly."

And so it was, at least out here on the windswept prairie where the High Plains Homestead sits. Stepping into this surreal world is like stepping back in time. Merlin has made an entire town on part of his land. For starters, there's a blacksmith shop, a schoolhouse, and a post office—all modeled after ones he went to as a kid. A jail and sheriff's office are in the works, so be careful to abide by Merlin's laws out here. When you step into the Badlands Mercantile store, listen for the squeaky screen door. It will bring back memories of your grandmother's house. There are lots of antiques, like the pie pan your mom used to bake with and the anvil your dad or grandpa might have had.

Drift on into the Drifter Cookshack, and you'll find Roberta cooking up her delicious Indian Tacos, burgers, steaks, and homemade pies like pecan and sour-cream raisin. Most days of the week she serves lunch and dinner, but you're advised to call ahead just to be sure.

After dinner, if you feel like a drink, mosey down about four steps from the restaurant to the Dirty Creek Saloon. Important note: You are your own bartender. They don't sell alcohol

A Slice of Serenity

It was just a few weeks after September 11, 2001, that I journeyed out to High Plains. It was my first trip after the terrorist attacks, and I was nervous, not only about flying, but also about leaving my husband at home in New York. But I, like so many others, knew life needed to go on and jobs needed to get done. When I was here interviewing Merlin, I asked him what it was like to live in such an isolated place. No television, no cell phone reception. He said, "I'm close to God's creation. I don't think you call that isolation." As I stood outside that night and watched the moon rise over the prairie and listened to the sound of silence, I thought about what he had said. Serenity and solitude surrounded me, and I felt alone, but not lonely. That's when I realized the High Plains Homestead isn't just a place off the beaten path. It seems quite close to the heavens, too.

here, so bring your own. You'll find the saloon is straight out of a Clint Eastwood movie except that it's not for rough-and-tumble types. As Merlin told us, "We had a curfew here at 9 at night when we started, but we quit because nobody was up to hear it."

If you can stay the night, we suggest you do it. For one, there's not a regular hotel around for miles. But more to the point, it's an experience. They have a handful of cabins, four of them completely authentic and dating back more than 100 years. They were old homesteads Merlin put back together and refurbished. Although they don't have phones or televisions, they do have modern indoor plumbing and you are just about guaranteed to get one of the best night's sleep you've ever had.

Utah

Rico Mexican Market

779 South 500 East
Salt Lake City, UT 84102
(801) 533-9923

The motto at Rico Mexican Market is "Beans are our beansness." It all started with a few humble beans. In 1985, when Jorge Fierro was just 24 years old, he left his Mexican homeland and headed north for a better life. Eventually, he ended up in Utah, working temporary jobs

like construction and dishwashing. One day, while living in his tiny apartment, he went to the grocery store to buy some pinto beans. He was disgusted with what he found. The beans at this place were nowhere near the quality of the beans he got at home. It was there in the aisle that he had an epiphany.

Determined to produce a better product, he started selling bags of cooked beans at the farmer's market in 1997. Before he knew it, his beans became a booming business (or should we say "beansness"). With a small loan from the bank, he and his wife, Karen Palle, opened the Rico Mexican Market.

photo courtesy of Karin Palle

Jill with Jorge and crew at Rico Mexican Market.

Utah

Not only can you buy just about every Mexican cooking product under the sun here, but they also have Mexican pottery and other unique gifts. Recently they added a dine-in area where you can eat their tacos and tostados fresh out of the oven. They also do a huge take-out business, selling bags of their handmade flour tortillas and freshly made enchiladas, burritos, and tamales. After eating Jorge's food, you might never buy frozen Mexican food from your grocery store again.

In Spanish, ¡Qué rico! is a way of saying something is tasty, thus the name, Rico. We think it's fair to say this place is the big enchilada, and we guarantee you'll find a lot of "que rico" inside this Mexican market.

Shrimp Ceviche Tostadas

ADAPTED FROM RICO MEXICAN MARKET,
SALT LAKE CITY, UTAH

MAKE 4 SERVINGS; 8 TOSTADAS

6 to 8 limes
2 pounds (30 to 40 count) tiger shrimp, peeled
    and deveined
½ yellow onion, finely chopped
4 small tomatoes, diced
1 jalapeño chile, finely chopped
1 bunch fresh cilantro, leaves only, finely
    chopped
Salt to taste
2 (8-ounce) packages guacamole
8 tostada shells
Fresh cilantro leaves, for garnish
Hot sauce

Squeeze limes into a large bowl. Cut shrimp into about 4 pieces each. Place shrimp and onion in lime juice, cover, and let marinate in the refrigerator for at least 2 hours, stirring occasionally. Remove shrimp mixture from the refrigerator, and add tomatoes, jalapeño, chopped cilantro, and salt.

Drain lime juice from shrimp mixture. Spread guacamole on top of tostadas, and top with shrimp and vegetables. Garnish with cilantro leaves and hot sauce.

The Point Restaurant

2000 Circle of Hope
Salt Lake City, UT 84112
(801) 585-0616
www.thepoint.hci.utah.edu

When you think of top dining spots, a hospital cafeteria is probably on the bottom of your list. But here, inside the Huntsman Cancer Institute in Salt Lake City, the chefs have taken heart healthy, low-fat, "institutional" food to new heights. The restaurant is on the sixth floor of this world-renowned research facility, dedicated to treating and finding a cure for cancer. Nothing about it says "illness" or "hospital." It's light and airy and serves up one of the best views in the city. The room has been designed to come to a point at one end, hence the name.

The Point initially opened as a place for researchers and features food that is low in fat and sodium, even low in price, but *not* low in flavor. Their food gets such rave reviews, you'll see as many locals here as patients and staff.

One of their specialties is buffalo, a meat that is lean and low in cholesterol. It's shipped in from an Idaho ranch owned by Dr. Marlow Goble, an orthopedic surgeon. They create some meaty masterpieces from it like buffalo chili, buffalo pot stickers, buffalo burgers—even buffalo tortellini with a sun-dried tomato and artichoke sauce.

This place is a prescription for those who have a healthy appetite for life. That's the point. Get it?

Buffalo Pot Stickers with Asian Napa Cabbage Slaw

ADAPTED FROM THE POINT RESTAURANT,
SALT LAKE CITY, UTAH

MAKES 4 SERVINGS; 20 POT STICKERS

Pot Stickers:
1 fresh portobello mushroom, finely diced and
    blanched
1 teaspoon grated fresh ginger
¼ cup well-drained thawed frozen spinach
1½ teaspoons Asian sesame oil

Utah

1 egg, lightly beaten
½ tablespoon cornstarch
½ teaspoon cayenne
1 tablespoon chopped fresh cilantro
¼ teaspoon kosher salt
8 ounces ground buffalo meat
20 (½ package) round wonton wrappers
1 egg beaten with 2 tablespoons water for egg
   wash

Napa Cabbage Slaw:
¼ cup Asian sweet chili sauce
½ cup citrus soy or sweet soy sauce
½ head napa cabbage, shredded
1 carrot, shredded
1 tablespoon black sesame seeds

To make pot stickers: In a medium mixing bowl, combine mushroom, ginger, spinach, sesame oil, egg, cornstarch, cayenne, cilantro, and salt. Mix until cornstarch is well absorbed.

Slowly add meat, and mix until all ingredients are combined and uniform in consistency. (This should be like a moist meat loaf).

Place meat mixture in the refrigerator until chilled.

Place 4 wonton wrappers on a flat surface. With your fingertip, lightly moisten the edge of each wrapper with egg wash.

Place a small amount of meat mixture in the center of each wonton wrapper. Fold over wrapper to form a half moon. Press down firmly on the edges to seal. Repeat until all the filling is used.

As pot stickers are formed, place them on a baking sheet that has been lightly dusted with cornstarch. Preheat the oven to 200°F.

Bring a large pot of water to a boil. Gently drop pot stickers, in batches to avoid crowding, into boiling water. Simmer pot stickers for about 5 minutes; remove them from water with a slotted spoon to another baking sheet. Place in the oven to keep warm until all pot stickers have been cooked.

To make slaw: Mix together chili sauce, soy sauce, cabbage, carrot, and sesame seeds in a large bowl.

Serve slaw on the side with pot stickers.

Colorado

My Brother's Bar
2376 15th Street
Denver, CO 80202
(303) 455-9991

My Brother's Bar is the best-kept secret in Denver. Unlike restaurants that are famous for things they offer, this place is renowned for what it doesn't have, most notably a sign. There isn't one. As regulars like to say, "If you can't find the place, you shouldn't be here." People do locate it, usually by checking for the address or listening for the crowd.

Once inside, there are several other things you might notice missing, items that are usually important at bars, like bottled beer, a jukebox, a television, and plates. But it's not like the place is suffering. My Brother's Bar has been a hit in Denver since it opened in 1970.

Regarding the lack of a sign, the management says no one ever got around to putting one up. And as for beer bottles: There's a large assortment of suds (mostly microbrews) on tap. (To be perfectly accurate, the bar does serve low-alcohol beer in bottles.) A TV? A jukebox? No way. My Brother's Bar only plays classical music. This place is strictly Beethoven and burgers.

Which gets us to the plates. Or lack of them. Tradition here calls for burgers and sandwiches to be served on top of a condiment tray, surrounded in deli wrap. (Tip: Go for the signature Johnny Burger: a third of a pound of beef, grilled onions, Swiss and cheddar cheese, covered with jalapeño cream cheese.)

This is a very family-friendly place. So if you ask, they will serve your food on a plate. But come on! Why would anyone do that? This is a *bar* after all, just like the sign would say . . . if they had one.

The Fort

19192 Highway 8
Morrison, CO 80465
(303) 697-4771
www.thefort.com

The Fort didn't get off to a good start. During its first Thanksgiving dinner in 1963, the restaurant ran out of food, with several hundred reservations still to go.

Yet from this inauspicious beginning, The Fort has grown into a Denver-area landmark, a destination for locals, tourists, and business events.

It really is an Old West–style fort. The enormous building houses 9 dining rooms with seating for 3,500. It's designed to look like a fur trading post. Inside the towering adobe walls, a campfire burns in the courtyard. Waiters use tomahawks to uncork champagne bottles. Occasionally, cannons are fired. And in the center of the action, there's owner Sam Arnold, in frontier garb, growling his mountain-man toast, "Waugh!"

Arnold claims he never intended to open a restaurant. He says the castle-like building was supposed to be his family's home, until he realized he needed to pay for it. With no experience in the food industry, Arnold got a small business loan and opened a restaurant downstairs. His family moved in upstairs, along with their pet black bear, Sissy.

Fast-forward 40 years, and The Fort has become the world's largest seller of buffalo steak (50,000 entrées a year).

Buffalo (or "buffler," as Arnold likes to call it) is low in fat and cholesterol. Some say it's sweeter than beef. For those who really appreciate the exotic, there's also buffalo tongue, buffalo sausage, and Rocky Mountain Oysters. (For the uninitiated, those oysters are buffalo testicles—and, no, they don't taste like chicken.)

The menu also features one of Marc's favorite dishes: buffalo bone marrow, which used to be called prairie butter. Made from the marrow of the animal's large, Flinstone-size femur bones, it is cooked until it becomes creamy soft. Spread on toast and topped with a shot of green Tabasco sauce, Arnold says it's better than your first kiss.

If you're not interested in Marc's bone marrow dish, there are other delicacies like peanut-butter-stuffed jalapeños, rattlesnake, and the "Incorrect Steak"—a heart attack on a plate. The latter dish is a medium-rare New York strip steak, topped with red chili sauce, grated white cheddar cheese, and a fried egg, sunny side-up. (Defibrillator not included.)

Arnold, who developed most of these dishes, studied worldwide and is now a renowned gourmet chef and author. All that, plus he makes sure The Fort never runs out of food.

It Didn't Happen If It's Not on Tape

Our story on The Fort for the first season of *The Best Of* almost never made it on the air. We'd spent many hours at the restaurant and thought we had a pretty good story, until the tapes disappeared into the hands of an unnamed shipping company. Because The Fort was one of our favorites, we made it a point to return and re-tape everything during a later visit to Denver. Although we'll never reveal the freight company, there is a scene in the movie *Castaway* that caught my attention. In it, Tom Hanks' character opens a shipping box that washed up on his deserted island. Inside, there are several videotapes. I could swear the tapes were labeled "The Fort," but I could be wrong.

On the other hand, the same loss was good news for Jill. Another tape in the missing package was from one of her shoots at a medieval-themed restaurant in Las Vegas, where a producer had somehow talked her into dressing up like Princess Guinevere. Why, we'll never know. Jill denies any involvement in the disappearance of those tapes.

Buckhorn Exchange

1000 Osage Street
Denver, CO 80204
(303) 534-9505
www.buckhorn.com

Denver's oldest restaurant is proof that if you include the word *Shorty* in a guy's nickname, he's going to overcompensate, especially in the days of the Wild West.

The handle in question belonged to the pint-size Henry "Shorty Scout" Zietz, who founded Buckhorn Exchange in 1893. He was a longtime cohort of Buffalo Bill Cody and a good friend of Chief Sitting Bull, who came up with the moniker.

If "Shorty Scout" was big on anything, it was his guns. An avid hunter, he proudly displayed his large collection of mounted trophy heads on the walls of his restaurant. Barely a space was left uncovered—deer, lions, bears, there's even a two-headed calf. The collection was so vast, if PETA had been around in those days, its members would have had a cow (or whatever it is that PETA members can properly have).

Any remaining space was filled with displays of Zietz's gun collection—presumably the same weapons he used to help create the décor. The look fit. Buckhorn Exchange was pure frontier, a hangout for cattlemen, miners, gamblers, and politicians.

Little has changed over the past century-plus, especially those mounted trophy heads. Zietz's buddy Buffalo Bill hangs out here, too, in a sense. Every February, the restaurant celebrates his birthday with a look-alike contest. The whole Buckhorn Exchange experience makes you feel as if you're in a saloon in the Wild West—only with better food.

No shocker: The restaurant features game meat. The most popular dish is the combination buffalo and elk platter. But there's also quail, rattlesnake and alligator tail.

It's also known for a bean soup that's been on the menu since the beginning. On Wednesdays, they serve something called Buffalo Red Eye Stew, made in part with buffalo meat, bourbon, and coffee.

Primarily, Buckhorn Exchange is a steakhouse. The Supper Menu even offers giant New York strips—up to 4 pounds—obviously for sharing. Finish off one of those, even with help, and there's no way anyone would dare call you "Shorty."

Buckhorn Exchange Bean Soup

ADAPTED FROM BUCKHORN EXCHANGE, DENVER, COLORADO

MAKES 6 SERVINGS

1 pound dried great northern beans
½ cup diced onion
3 ounces diced ham
2 tablespoons chicken bouillon base
½ teaspoon seasoned salt
1 teaspoon liquid smoke flavoring
1 teaspoon granulated garlic
1 teaspoon white pepper
2 quarts water
3½ tablespoons cornstarch
½ cup water

Preheat the oven to 250°F. Combine beans, onion, ham, chicken base, seasoned salt, liquid smoke, garlic, pepper, and 2 quarts water in a large dutch oven. Cover and bake for 6 hours, or until beans are tender.

Remove the pan from the oven, place over medium heat, and bring to a boil. Mix cornstarch and ½ cup water in a small bowl. Stir cornstarch mixture into beans, and cook, stirring, until thickened. Reduce heat and simmer for 15 minutes.

DeLeo's Park Theatre Café and Deli

132 Moraine Street
Estes Park, CO 80517
(970) 577-1134

Where else can you eat a *Shakespeare in Love* or a *Babe?* Nowhere we know of, except here at DeLeo's Park Theatre Café and Deli, with owner Tom DeLeo directing the show. At his café, right next to the oldest working movie theater west of

Colorado

Colorado

the Mississippi, he produces some of the best sandwiches you'll ever sink your teeth into.

Shakespeare in Love features a mix of mayo and Italian dressing slathered on a piece of light rye with imported Swiss cheese, romaine lettuce, black olives, banana peppers, and ham piled on—and then piled on again. The *Babe* is heaped high with ham and your choice of cheese. One sandwich called *The Gobblefather*—is piled high with turkey and then gives you a choice of what bread and cheese you want. Get it? A choice. *The Big Reuboni* is an "Italian-ized" Reuben, made the DeLeo way with marble rye instead of pumpernickel. Ya gotta problem wid dat? Take it up with Tom who says, "It's my way or the highway."

It's no wonder that every week in this small town, he goes through more than 50 pounds of ham, 30 pounds of turkey, 45 pounds of beef brisket, and 50 pounds of sliced roast beef. His sandwiches are huge, so ya gotta have a big mouth to eat here and a loud mouth to compete with Tom.

This former insurance exec, a full-blown Italian East Coaster, is quite a character, but one who will make you smile. He's loud, likes to shout, will give you his opinion even if you didn't ask him for it, and will be the first to say when you walk in, "You get a slice of me whether you like it or not." He'll also make your stomach hurt—not from his deli delights, but from making you laugh. Appropriately enough, he grew up in Sandwich, Massachusetts. Must have been destiny for him to dive into the deli business.

So forget popcorn at the movie. Come to DeLeo's. It beats theater snacks, and Tom will put on quite a show of his own.

The Stanley Hotel

333 Wonderview
Estes Park, CO 80517
(970) 586-3371 or (800) 976-1377
www.stanleyhotel.com

If it scared the "king of horror," author Stephen King, then you know there's something spooky about this place. However, it did much more than frighten him. The Stanley Hotel in Estes Park, Colorado, became the inspiration for one of his most terrifying books, *The Shining*.

In 1973, King was suffering from writer's block. He came to Estes Park to clear out the cobwebs, checked into room 217, and within 48 hours had the whole storyline to the book sketched out in his head. However, there are many other tales reported to have taken place at this haunted hotel that appear to be the works of nonfiction. . . .

Take room 401: In the early 1990s, a newly married couple was staying at the Stanley. Before falling asleep, the husband took off his wedding band and put it on the nightstand. A few hours later, the couple suddenly woke up to find an elderly man standing in the corner. Mysteriously, he walked over to the nightstand, picked up the wedding ring, went into the bathroom, and tossed it down the sink. He then disappeared into the wall. Thinking she was imagining things, the woman became restless and went down to the bar for a drink. When she walked in the door she let out a bloodcurdling scream, for there in front of her she saw the portrait of Lord Dunraven, an Englishman who owned the property from 1872–1884. Near tears, she explained to the bartender that the

man in the painting was the man who had haunted her room. The now-hysterical woman demanded an explanation. The hotel didn't give her one, but a maintenance man did fish the ring out of the pipes.

You'll find many more chilling tales at this 138-room hotel, but you'll also find that it is rich in history and full of old-world charm and elegance. The Cascades Dining Room serves up a hauntingly mean menu: Colorado rack of lamb, steaks, and fresh trout caught in a stream nearby.

F. O. Stanley of Stanley Steamer Automobile fame built the hotel in 1909. He came to Estes Park in 1903 to help cure his tuberculosis. At the time, the town wasn't much, but Stanley changed all that. He built much of the infrastructure of Estes Park, including his beloved hotel. On opening day, June 3, 1909, he gave a gift to his wife, Flora: a piano that still sits in the music room. Just about every desk clerk and night watchman has claimed to see and hear that piano playing but with no one at the keys.

As for King's stay, he is said to have told the hotel that nothing out of the ordinary happened. We're grateful the ghosts left him alone, because who knows how much scarier *The Shining* might have been!

Gateway Café

432 Main Street
Lyons, CO 80540
(303) 823-5144
www.gatewaycafe.com

When James Van Dyk was a young boy, he used to go to the local café in his small town in central Vermont, eat cherry pie, and spin on the stools at the soda fountain. Four decades later, he's doing the same thing. Except now the stools are his, he's selling the pies, and he's doing it all at the foot of the Rocky Mountains.

Lyons, Colorado, is the epitome of small-town USA, complete with a café. The only thing that's different from the Gateway and the one James grew up with in Vermont is the food. This is far from a run-of-the-mill menu. For starters, all his meat is grass fed and locally raised. His vegetables and fruits are almost all organic and from local producers. What he does with buffalo meat will make even a vegetarian think twice.

The chokecherry braised buffalo shortribs taste heavenly. The main challenge is getting the wild cherries that add such an intense flavor to dishes. However, as James said, "It's always a race between who will pick them first, you or the bears." Fortunately, there's usually enough for both species.

His café is quaint, rustic, and classy. In his previous life, before he became a chef, he taught at the Colorado Institute of Art. He's got a cool art collection on the walls, and it's all for sale.

You'll also notice that in some of the décor and food there's an Asian influence. This comes from his wife, Noriko, who he met while doing a four-year stint as a cook in Japan. Thus the smoked tofu with teriyaki glaze and the Noriko's Gyozas (Pork Dumplings) and Japanese Mussels that appear on the menu.

When he first stumbled upon this place, it was a rundown breakfast joint that the owner was looking to sell. James immediately knew this was the restaurant for him—after all, it had the stools. He gutted nearly the whole place, but the stools were his inspiration.

Colorado

Now, along with all his excellent food, you can sit at the soda fountain and eat some of his delicious homemade pies, like sour cherry, blueberry-ginger, or pecan. Reminisce and let the experience evoke the memories of your childhood. And don't forget to spin.

Braised Buffalo Short Ribs

ADAPTED FROM GATEWAY CAFÉ, LYONS, COLORADO

MAKES 4 SERVINGS

4 (1½-inch) buffalo or beef short ribs
2 onions
2 cups red wine
1 tablespoon crushed juniper berries, or 1 sprig
    rosemary
2 bay leaves
1 teaspoon dried thyme
1 sprig rosemary
½ cup canola oil, plus 1 tablespoon
1 cup all-purpose flour
2 cups veal or beef stock
½ cup chokecherry or cherry preserves
Salt and freshly ground pepper to taste
4 medium mushrooms, sliced
16 pearl onions, peeled
Mashed potatoes and freshly grated horseradish,
    to serve

Place ribs in a nonreactive bowl. Slice onions, and place on top of ribs. Cover with wine. Make a sachet with juniper berries, bay leaves, thyme, and rosemary, and place in liquid. Marinate in the refrigerator for 24 hours.

Remove ribs and onions from marinade, reserving marinade. Heat ½ cup oil in a medium stockpot over medium heat. Lightly coat ribs in flour. Add ribs to the stockpot, and brown on all sides. Remove ribs, and add onions; sauté until golden brown. Pour off excess oil. Add ribs to onions, and add reserved marinade. Simmer for 10 minutes. Add stock and preserves. Simmer, covered, for about 2 hours, or until ribs are tender. Season with salt and pepper to taste. Before serving, remove sachet.

Heat 1 tablespoon oil in a large sauté pan. Add mushrooms and pearl onions, and sauté, stirring occasionally, until onions begin to brown, about 15 minutes. Season with salt and pepper and serve alongside short ribs with mashed potatoes and horseradish.

CHEF'S TIP: In the morning, put all the ingredients in a slow cooker on low. When you get home after work, your dinner should be done, and your house will smell heavenly.

The Little Nell

675 East Durant Avenue
Aspen, CO 81611
(970) 920-4600
www.thelittlenell.com

Known by regulars as a "legendary" hotel, not only because it's been around forever, but because of the top-drawer service, The Little Nell is nestled at the base of Aspen Mountain. It is legendary all right, especially if you're talking about the price. Just stepping foot into this five-star, five-diamond Relais and Chateau luxury hotel will cause your money to disappear. This is a quintessential Aspen place for the rich and famous. Star sightings are frequent, and for many who stay here, money is no object. When we were there (just shooting—not staying—as it's beyond our budget), we were given a glimpse into some of their suites. During the high season, they can go for more than $4,000 a night with a 4- to 7-day minimum stay required.

The dining room, Montagna, which means "mountain" in Italian, is big on elegance and price. Entrées range from $20 to $60 a dish and are delectable. If you compare it to the cost of the rooms, meals are a downright bargain!

You won't have to lift a finger here if you don't want to. They'll unpack your luggage, clean your clothes, and do your shopping and your "gift purchasing." They even have a set of ski concierges who will wax your skis and warm your boots.

Originally this land was the summer hunting ground of the Ute Indians. When explorers

Colorado

came in 1879 to search for silver, many claims were staked in the area. One was from a man named D. D. Fowler, who called his claim "The Little Nellie." Some say he named it after a "lady of the evening"; others say "little Nellie" was one of his long-lost loves. At any rate, he opened a silver mine on the property, but it was short lived. By 1893, the town went bust and Aspen basically fell off the map. It wasn't until the 1940s that the town began to rebound. The Little Nell opened in 1989 and is built on this former silver mine site. Apropos considering you'll need a silver spoon to eat or stay here.

Pine Creek Cookhouse

Castle Creek Road
Ashcroft, CO 81611
(970) 925-1044
www.pinecreekcookhouse.com

This is one dining adventure where you're almost guaranteed to work up an appetite. Although Pine Creek Cookhouse is not that far from civilization (the town of Ashcroft is 12 miles outside of Aspen), in winter there are no roads to drive on, which means you cross-country ski—unless you wimp out and insist on taking the horse-drawn sleigh. Although it's only about a mile and a half from the parking lot to the restaurant, not only are you starting at an extremely high altitude of 9,750 feet, but you have to ski uphill 300 more feet.

Once you get here, indulge. This isn't some ski lodge serving up the burgers and brats; rather, this menu boasts of wild boar and buffalo. The skiers' banquet lunch is buffet style, with lots of fresh salads, pastas, and dishes like Chilean Sea Bass over a wild mushroom risotto. You can have a cocktail here, but beware—a drink can have a fast and furious effect at a high altitude.

Every morsel is brought in by snowmobile, and every leftover is carried out the same way. Just keep in mind as you're chowing down that *you* also have to go out the same way you came, so you might want to think twice before over-stuffing yourself. That afternoon nap isn't an option here.

Down and Out

The shoot at Pine Creek Cookhouse wasn't exactly one of my more glamorous ones. I was making an attempt to cross-country ski for the first time and ended up with more than I bargained for. First, it took me considerably longer than more seasoned cross-country skiers to get up to the restaurant. Why? Because I had to keep picking myself up time and time again. But the worst of it was that I was suffering from altitude sickness.

I felt nauseated and sluggish and just wanted to sleep, but I did my best to rally. I figured if I willed my body hard enough, it would adjust to the altitude. I quickly realized I was wrong. By the time I got around to putting on my skis, I felt completely exhausted. However, I pushed on and managed to start my trek. We didn't get far before I broke into a sweat and had to sit down in the snow. Gasping for air, our guide—clearly prepared for these eventualities with newbies—brought on the oxygen. So there I sat on the side of the trail, breathing into an oxygen mask as my somewhat bemused crew looked on. I'm the first to admit I have a lot of hot air; so running out wasn't something I'd counted on. It was a fine television moment, albeit for the blooper reel.

Colorado

Where's Oklahoma?

Unfortunately, the Sooner state has to come later. We mean no disre-
spect to our Okie friends. In fact, we think Rogers and Hammerstein got
it wrong in their legendary musical. To us, Oklahoma is more than OK. It's just
that we haven't taped there yet.

Not that you haven't been on our schedule, as recently as January 2004. We were really looking forward to sampling some of Oklahoma's famous—well, whatever dish you're famous for. And
we were eager to imbibe in the state-mandated, drink-to-get-a-headache 3.2 beer. If nothing else,
we couldn't wait to see the only oil well in the world that sits on the grounds of the State Capitol in
Oklahoma City and laugh aloud as we spelled Tulsa backward. (Try it.) But sadly, schedules change.
Topics shift. And the home state of Brad Pitt, Garth Brooks, and Mickey Mantle got blown off the
schedule faster than an Oklahoma twister. To borrow a line from native son Paul Harvey, now you
know the rest of the story.

But consider this our promise. We're saving the best for—well—later. And after our long-over-
due visit, we plan to paraphrase another famous Oklahoman, Will Rogers, when we declare, we
never met an Oklahoma restaurant we didn't like. Ay yippy yi ki yea.

The Southwest

Arizona, Nevada, New Mexico, Texas

IN THE SOUTHWEST, the food influences come from all directions. There's country cooking from the South, seafood from the Gulf of Mexico, and spicy delights from south of the border. The land is rich in agriculture, and historically, cowboys rustled up plenty of steaks. The variety of restaurants is as plentiful as the sunshine.

And then there's Vegas, baby. Next stop, the Southwest.

Arizona

Los Dos Molinos

8646 South Central Avenue
Phoenix, AZ 85040
(602) 243-9113

900 East Main Street
Springerville, AZ 85938
(928) 333-4846

260 South Alma School Road
Mesa, AZ 85210
(480) 969-7475

119 East 18th Street
New York, NY 10003
(212) 505-1574

They say it's not the heat; it's the humidity. Whoever *they* are have obviously never been to Los Dos Molinos—a restaurant that's all about the heat! Another thing *they* say is if you can't take the heat, get out of the kitchen. But trust us, this is one kitchen you don't want to miss, which is why there's typically a 2- to 3-hour wait at their Phoenix flagship location.

Victoria Chavez, the family matriarch who started the business in the mid-1970s, starts her day in the Phoenix store at 3 A.M., making her homemade tortillas that are then served in all their Arizona restaurants.

As a young girl growing up poor in the New Mexico desert, Victoria's mom taught her to make authentic Mexican meals using home-grown vegetables and home-raised meat.

Following the death of her 17-year-old son in a car crash, Victoria began re-creating the meals of her childhood and found that it helped take her mind off her tragedy. Soon she was selling burritos out of her house in Springerville, Arizona, and eventually decided to open a restaurant there. Twenty-eight years later, she oversees all the restaurants, which are run by her daughters: Sandy in New York, Antoinette in Springerville, and Cheryl in Phoenix and Mesa.

As for the heat . . . If you want hot, order a dish with the New Mexico green chile sauce, like the Green Enchilada Dinner, topped with an egg. We also suggest the Adovada Pork Ribs baked in a red chile purée. Be sure to wash it down with one of their Kick-Ass Margaritas (yes, that is the official name of the drink, made with Cuervo Gold and Cointreau). You'll need one handy because we're not kidding about the heat. If you are even remotely leery of spicy foods, tell your server to tone down your dish. They'll do it (begrudgingly), but your lips will thank you for it. (Note: We did find that dishes at the New York restaurant tend to be milder than their Southwestern counterparts . . . perhaps a concession to diners' sensibilities!)

For the brave souls who like it hot, we say burn, baby, burn. You won't regret it.

Crocodile Tears

The first time I ever cried on camera was during the taping of our *Best Of* segment on Los Dos Molinos. But I'm not the only diner ever to be brought to tears. It's not at all uncommon to see people tearing up, maniacally (and futilely) fanning their mouths. The food here can be *that* hot.

But I have to confess to a bit of theatrics on my part. In one of our previous shows, I had a particularly ugly run-in with a scotch bonnet pepper—tears, gnashing of teeth, and so on. So when my producer Paul David suggested I try something at Los Dos Molinos hot enough to make me cry, I chickened out. More to the point, I cheated.

I had the chef cut up an onion, which I then proceeded to sniff. Behold the tears, which in the edited segment appeared to be a result of the peppers I had supposedly eaten. Move over Meryl Streep!

Michael's at the Citadel

8700 East Pinnacle Peak Road
Scottsdale, AZ 85255
(480) 515-2575
www.michaelsrestaurant.com

It's said one of the most dangerous places to stand is between Marc Silverstein and a camera. The risk multiplies considerably when Michael DeMaria enters the picture.

Chef Michael is a fixture on Phoenix television. Once a week, he hosts a segment on the local FOX-TV evening newscasts recommending good restaurants.

The TV assignment is part-time, but it takes on a new meaning when you consider DeMaria's first career as the owner of Michael's at the Citadel, a stylish gourmet restaurant that features DeMaria's contemporary American cuisine.

So basically, Chef Michael goes on local television and tells viewers to dine at his competitors. That takes confidence. But DeMaria doesn't seem like someone who needs to get over his shyness.

The restaurant itself isn't known for understatement. It features a two-story sandstone waterfall, nine fireplaces, and a glass-enclosed chef's table where diners can watch Michael at work.

As if that's not enough, there's also a fully equipped in-house cooking studio where Michael holds classes. Just in case you miss anything, the segments are taped on a state-of-the-art television system that includes two cameras.

But even with all the distractions, Chef Michael's food is the real star. Specialties like his Olive-Roast Chilean Sea Bass "In the Style of Niçoise," or the Veal Osso Buco on Shropshire Risotto with Braised Root Vegetables usually get most of the ink. Still, if you eat at Michael's, keep an eye out for a camera. And try to stay out of the way.

Arizona

Seared Olive-Rubbed Chilean Sea Bass "In the Style of Niçoise"

ADAPTED FROM MICHAEL'S AT THE CITADEL;
SCOTTSDALE, ARIZONA

MAKES 4 SERVINGS

Tomato Vinaigrette:
4 Roma tomatoes
1 tablespoon chopped shallot
1 teaspoon minced garlic
1 teaspoon minced fresh parsley
1 teaspoon minced fresh oregano
3 tablespoons red wine vinegar
Olive oil
Salt and freshly ground black pepper to taste

Sea Bass:
2 tablespoons canola oil
4 (4-ounce) sea bass fillets
4 teaspoons black olive tapenade
Pinch kosher salt
Freshly ground black pepper to taste
¼ cup chopped red tomato (see chef's note below)
¼ cup chopped golden tomato (see chef's note below)
¼ cup green beans, cut in ¼-inch slices, cooked until crisp-tender and drained
¼ cup diced potato, cooked in boiling water until just tender and drained
Fresh herbs for garnish

Preheat the oven to 375°F.

To prepare vinaigrette: Place whole tomatoes in the bowl of a food processor fitted with the metal blade. Process tomatoes until smooth. Strain through a fine mesh sieve; discard the solids. Add shallot, garlic, parsley, oregano, and vinegar to tomato purée. Slowly whisk in oil until you reach the desired consistency and flavor. Season with salt and pepper.

To prepare fish: Heat a nonstick skillet over medium heat until very hot and add oil. Place fish in the skillet, add tapenade, and season with salt and pepper. Cook until fish begins to look cooked around the sides. Turn fish, and place the pan in the oven for 3 to 6 minutes, depending on desired doneness. Set aside.

Place 1 tablespoon each of tomatoes, beans, and potato on each plate. Place 1 fish fillet on top. Drizzle vinaigrette around the plate, and garnish with fresh herbs.

CHEF'S NOTE: To peel tomatoes: Use the blanch and shock technique: Core the tomatoes, make an X on the top with a paring knife, and place the tomatoes in boiling, salted water for 10 to 20 seconds. (This time can be longer or shorter, depending on the ripeness of the tomatoes.)

When the skin starts to peel back, remove the tomato from the boiling water and shock it in ice water. Leave it in the cold water until the tomato is cold. The skin should slip off easily. Using a paring knife, remove all the skin and place the tomato on a paper towel–lined pan to absorb all the excess liquid.

Old Town Tortilla Factory

6910 East Main Street
Scottsdale, AZ 85251
(480) 945-4567
www.oldtowntortillafactory.com

Tortilla might be in the name, but tequila is in this restaurant's soul. The place is so dedicated to the Mexican firewater, there's a separate building just for making drinks. Called the Tequilaria—easier to say on the way in than on the way out—it features more than 100 premium tequilas, along with a large selection of Mexican beers and liquors. If you're daring, go for the Millionaire's Margarita. It's made from Jose Cuervo Reserva ($75 a bottle), 150-year-old Celebration Grand Marnier ($130 a bottle), and fresh-squeezed citrus juice (cheap). Hopefully, it will loosen you up before the tab arrives, because the drink costs a whopping $18! One should just about do it.

Tucked away in the art district of Old Town Scottsdale, the Tortilla Factory features Southwestern cuisine with Native American

photo courtesy of Old Town Tortilla Factory

This way to the tequila.

influences. As the name indicates, tortillas are a staple. They're offered in two dozen different flavors, including red chili, raspberry, and even piña colada.

The Tortilla Factory's centerpiece is the 1,200-square-foot flagstone outdoor patio, which accommodates 200 diners. It accounts for 70 percent of the restaurant. Don't worry about rain, because Scottsdale boasts 320 days of sunshine each year. But there is also indoor dining in an old converted adobe house just in case.

Arizona

No Objections

The margaritas weren't the only thing offering an interesting mix on the night our crew taped at the Old Town Tortilla Factory. At one end of the patio, a group from what looked like a modeling service entertained their escorts, while on the other end Supreme Court Justice Sandra Day O'Connor dined with her husband and friends. Now there's a restaurant that has a wide-ranging appeal.

Cheese Tortilla

ADAPTED FROM THE OLD TOWN TORTILLA
FACTORY, SCOTTSDALE, ARIZONA

MAKES ABOUT 30 TORTILLAS

Tortillas:
2 pounds (8 cups) all-purpose flour
1 tablespoon salt
1 tablespoon baking powder
1 cup lard
½ cup vegetable oil
1 pound cheddar cheese, shredded
1 pound Monterey Jack cheese, shredded

Sun-Dried Tomato Butter:
1 cup sun-dried tomatoes
3 cups warm water
1½ pounds unsalted butter at room temperature
1 tablespoon salt
2 cloves garlic, minced

To make tortillas: Mix together flour, salt, and baking powder in a large bowl. Stir in lard and oil, then cheddar and Monterey Jack cheeses. Mix together until a dough forms. It should look stretchy, yet firm. Portion dough into about 30 (1½-ounce) balls. With a rolling pin, flatten the balls on a lightly floured surface until thin and round.

Preheat a dry medium nonstick pan over medium heat. Place 1 tortilla in pan and cook until golden brown spots appear on the bottom. Flip and cook on the other side; be careful not to burn tortilla. Repeat with remaining tortillas.

To make tomato butter: Soak tomatoes in water for 10 minutes. Drain tomatoes; reserve soaking water. Process half of the tomatoes in a food processor until puréed, adding a little reserved water a few drops at a time. Add butter, salt, and garlic to tomatoes, and process until combined. Finely chop remaining tomatoes. Transfer butter mixture to a bowl, and stir in chopped tomatoes. Cover and refrigerate or make into a log and roll in plastic wrap. Refrigerate until firm. Serve butter with tortillas.

Ristorante Sandolo

Hyatt Regency Scottsdale Resort at Gainey Ranch
7500 East Doubletree Ranch Road
Scottsdale, AZ 85258
(480) 991-3388
www.scottsdale.hyatt.com

Nobody is going to confuse arid Arizona for the Venice canals, but Ristorante Sandolo offers its own unique take on romantic gondola rides.

Sandolo is one of several popular restaurants at the Hyatt Regency Scottsdale Resort at Gainey Ranch. It's a casual Italian bistro offering indoor/outdoor dining and the occasional singing waiter. Many of the regulars are locals, and up to 70 percent of the customers come from outside the resort. All in all, pretty high praise.

As an added attraction, Sandolo provides customers with a complimentary post-dinner gondola ride through the resort's 7-acre lake, complete with a singing gondolier. These guys can handle both an aria and an oar, giving them at least one advantage over Pavarotti.

Technically, the boats are called sandolas, because they're smaller than gondolas. The name comes from their shape: similar to sandals. Made in Venice and costing up to $25,000, they're shipped to the resort in water-filled crates so the wood doesn't dry. (We know these details aren't all that romantic, but it gives you something to talk about if the boat ride isn't going well.)

Keep in mind, you will be floating by the resort's amazing 2½-acre/10-pool water playground on one side, while on the other bank, golfers putt on the ninth hole of the Hyatt's championship golf course. If that doesn't give you something to sing about, then you just don't know romance.

The Coffee Pot

2050 West Highway 89A
Sedona, AZ 86336
(928) 282-6626

If you're one of those people who like to try everything on the menu, well, let's just say we've got a

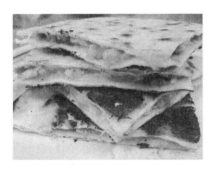

challenge for you! Take a trip to The Coffee Pot in Sedona, Arizona, and it'll take you 3 months of breakfasts just to get through their omelet selection. And if you want to try everything on the menu, be prepared to strap on the feedbag for a solid year. This place is known as the "home of the 101 omelets" and has a menu that brags of more than 300 selections. They crack more than 1,000 eggs a day. But if breakfast isn't what you're after, they also have great lunches and dinners, focusing on Mexican and American food.

Around in various incarnations since the 1950s (long before Sedona became New Age central), The Coffee Pot is almost as famous in Sedona as the rock it's named for. Coffee Pot Rock is just one of the stunningly gorgeous red rock formations surrounding this bustling town a couple hours north of Phoenix. Every year, millions (they average 4 million a year) of tourists flock to Sedona's vortexes—four rocks believed by some to have healing powers—to soak up some spirituality.

When we visited, however, it was to check out the omelets. We didn't make it through all 101, but we give a thumbs-up to their corned beef hash and the chorizo sausage omelets. At this place, if you name it, they'll make it. Even something as strange as a peanut butter and jelly omelet (listed as 101 on the menu) can be found here. Jill has an admittedly adventurous palate and couldn't pass up the chance to try it on camera with owner Marius Daher. However, we'll let you in on a secret: They appeared to "grin and bear it" on television, but both agreed off the record that it's better to stick with the first 100 omelets on the menu.

There's a great redwood patio outside where you can sit and stare at Coffee Pot Rock while debating if you have the nerve or desire to go for #101.

Yavapai Restaurant

Enchantment Resort
525 Boynton Canyon Road
Sedona, AZ 86336
(928) 282-2900
www.enchantmentresort.com

When you name a place Enchantment, you're automatically setting some pretty high expectations. It's safe to say, Enchantment Resort lives up to its name, meeting our expectations, and then some.

Humbled by the soaring red rock walls of Boynton Canyon, Enchantment is a 70-acre luxury resort, whose design is influenced as much by the stunning landscape as it is by the local Native American culture. Boynton Canyon is the birthplace of the Yavapai Apache Indian tribe and home to the 900-year-old Sinagua cliff dwellings.

The Yavapai Restaurant at Enchantment strives to reflect the beauty of the canyon. Literally. *Yavapai* actually means "people of the sun." If you eat inside, the massive windows give you a 180-degree view of the sun hitting the red rocks. If you sit outside, not only is the view incredible to behold, but the windows behind you actually reflect the canyon. That way, if you pull the short straw and have to sit facing the restaurant, you can still see that breathtaking crimson canyon. The setting is truly incomparable, and the food at Yavapai is almost as impressive.

The fare is upscale Southwestern with specialties such as seared elk loin with a blackberry compote or grilled Chilean sea bass with a chile rub that's topped with a papaya-mango salsa.

The view during the day is astonishing, but we also recommend a nighttime visit. The infinite stars in the high desert sky put on an absolutely extraordinary show. It's no wonder

Arizona

the Native people long ago saw this as a sacred place. If you go to Enchantment, use that age-old wisdom and allow the experience to cast its spell on you. We guarantee you'll have an enchanted evening.

———

L'Auberge de Sedona

301 L'Auberge Lane
Sedona, AZ 86336
(928) 282-1661 or (800) 272-6777 for reservations
www.lauberge.com

L'Auberge serves a brunch so satisfying that it's become a destination for many a Sunday driver in the area. We met a couple who drives from Phoenix once a month for this experience. But if you can't make it on the weekend, come any day of the week. This great getaway will transport you to another place, namely France.

L'Auberge in French means "small inn," and its diminutive size is part of its charm. Although the property is neither huge nor sprawling (the main lodge has about 21 rooms), the way it's designed you'll feel like you're in your own little world. But you'll have to be prepared to splurge if you want to stay in one of the cozy cottages on the property.

Sedona is surrounded by the Coconino National Forest, famous for all those red rocks. So after you've stuffed yourself with fine French food, go get lost in nature. You can hike, mountain bike, or even take a bracing dip into one of the natural artesian-water swimming holes. Then again, if you really are full, a nap in your fluffy bed might be in order. Bottom line: You have lots of choices at L'Auberge, and none of them are bad.

———

El Tovar

Box 699
Grand Canyon, AZ 86023
(928) 638-2631
www.grandcanyonlodges.com (click on dining)

Jill first experienced the dining room at the El Tovar Hotel years before she started with *The Best Of*. The meal followed a staggeringly beautiful 11-mile hike into the depths of the Grand Canyon, and even then, she knew this was no ordinary restaurant. Her return visit for *The Best Of Historical Landmarks*—while somewhat less grueling—was no less magnificent. Trust us, there's a reason 5 million people come to the Grand Canyon each year. It is an experience not to be missed.

El Tovar sits on the edge of the South Rim. And although it's impossible to compete with one of the seven natural wonders of the world, the restaurant just might be the perfect complement to it. The hotel (named for the Spanish explorer who first came across the Grand Canyon, Don Pedro de Tovar) was built in 1904, fashioned after a European hunting lodge. The stones used in building it are actually from the canyon—one of the reasons why the subdued, rustic architecture blends in beautifully with the majesty that surrounds it.

Despite having to compete with the view, the food in the dining room still manages to stand out. Most of the menu is infused with a Southwestern flare. The Roast Half Duckling with a prickly pear jalapeño glaze is amazing, as is the flame-broiled Beef Tenderloin coated in a

Arizona

garlic peppercorn sauce. After a long day of hiking, the food here will definitely hit the spot.

The Grand Canyon is an inspiring experience. If you've been, you know it's difficult finding words to describe the way it makes you feel. If you get the chance, you should make El Tovar part of that experience. Between the view and the food, you might even find the words you're looking for. And we bet *wondrous* will be one of them.

Tortilla-Crusted Salmon with Fire-Roasted Corn Salsa

ADAPTED FROM EL TOVAR RESTAURANT, GRAND CANYON NATIONAL PARK, ARIZONA

MAKES 4 SERVINGS

Fire-Roasted Corn Salsa:

4 ears fresh corn, roasted under broiler and kernels cut off

6 tomatillos, husked, rinsed, and cut into small dice

1 jalapeño chile, oiled, broiled until blistered, seeds removed, and cut into small dice

1 tomato, cut into medium dice

1 red bell pepper, cut into small dice

1 green bell pepper, cut into small dice

1 ounce (¾ cup) finely chopped fresh cilantro leaves

½ cup fresh lime juice

2 cloves garlic, minced

Hot pepper sauce to taste

Salt and freshly ground black pepper to taste

Tortilla-Crusted Salmon:

½ pound blue corn tortillas

4 (6-ounce) salmon fillets

2 cups all-purpose flour, seasoned with salt and freshly ground black pepper

6 eggs beaten with ¼ cup milk for egg wash

Canola oil for pan-frying

To make salsa: Mix together corn, tomatillos, jalapeños, tomato, red and green bell peppers, cilantro, lime juice, garlic, hot pepper sauce, salt, and pepper in a medium bowl. Let stand for 4 hours. Preheat the oven to 325°F.

To prepare salmon: Arrange tortillas on a non-stick baking sheet. Bake for 5 to 10 minutes or until crisp. Leave the oven on. Let tortillas cool. Grind tortillas in a blender or food processor until very fine crumbs.

Place salmon, skin side up, into seasoned flour, then dip into egg wash, and finally coat in tortilla crumbs, coating only one side. Heat oil in a large skillet over medium heat. Place salmon, tortilla side down, into hot oil. Pan-fry until crust sets and a little browning occurs. Drain off oil and flip salmon. Bake salmon for 8 to 10 minutes or until desired doneness.

Heat salsa in a skillet until hot, and spoon over salmon before serving.

Nevada

Bellagio

3600 South Las Vegas Boulevard
Las Vegas, NV 89109
(702) 693-7111
www.bellagio.com

It's been called one of the grandest hotels ever built, and the cost of $1.6 billion bought its owners a lot of grandness. As of the writing of this piece, it's the largest hotel-casino in the world to receive the AAA Five-Diamond award. It consistently makes the top of the nation's best and the world's best lists in hotels. With more than 3,000 rooms and 15 restaurants, a gallery of fine art, botanical gardens, 6 outdoor pools, 4 spas, and 40 private cabanas, Bellagio oozes opulence.

Then there are the casinos.

There are more than 100,000 square feet of gaming areas inside. You can find everything from Blackjack, Craps, and Mini-Baccarat to Three Card Poker, Sic Bo, and European Roulette, not to mention all the slot machines and video poker at your fingertips.

In a city where hitting the jackpot is usually the goal, if you're staying here, then you've probably already hit it.

So Many Choices, So Little Time

If you're only at the Bellagio for a few days, or in our case a day or two, you simply can't explore everything the hotel has to offer. On my brief visit, we covered both Café Bellagio and Café Gelato. Our focus was on desserts. And get this: They make 20,000 a day. It's mind-boggling.

No matter what restaurant you choose here, you'll most likely find a winning menu. It's really just a matter of what you have in your wallet. If you dine at Aqua for seafood or Le Cirque for French food (both Mobil Four-Star restaurants), or Prime for steaks, you better be sure you're holding a full house.

Osteria Del Circo

Bellagio
3600 South Las Vegas Boulevard
Las Vegas, NV 89109
(702) 693-8150

If scary clowns, a circus tent décor, and high prices are your idea of fine dining, then Osteria Del Circo is for you. It wasn't exactly our style, but food critics such as John Curtas from the local NPR radio affiliate call Circo the best restaurant in Las Vegas.

Based on the original Circo in New York, it's operated by the next generation of the Maccioni family, whose father Sirio created Manhattan's world famous Le Cirque. There's also a Le Cirque outpost next door to Circo. Partner/son Mario Maccioni told us the Bellagio wanted the restaurant in the hotel so much, it paid the several million dollars it took to design and open the place.

Diners get a treat long before the meal starts, as much of the restaurant faces the Bellagio's enormous lake and dancing fountains.

Circo specializes in homestyle Tuscan food. One chef showed us how detail makes the dif-

ference. For one popular ravioli-like dish, he regularly hand stamps each piece of round pasta with his own family crest even though the indentations are covered once the chef added sauce to the dish.

Top of the World

Stratosphere Hotel and Casino
2000 South Las Vegas Boulevard
Las Vegas, NV 89104
(702) 380-7711
www.stratospherehotel.com

Everyone knows high rollers rule in Las Vegas. And in true Vegas form, the Stratosphere has taken that notion to the most extravagant extreme. The Stratosphere is where you'll find the High Roller, an appropriate name for a roller coaster that whips around the outside of the 1,149-foot Stratosphere observation tower. Needless to say, acrophobics probably aren't going to dig this scene.

Here's a lesson we learned when visiting: Eat *after* riding the High Roller. Because when you dine at Top of the World restaurant, the last thing you'll want to do is lose your lunch (or your dinner, as the case may be).

Top of the World puts you 800 feet above Las Vegas, a few hundred feet *below* the High Roller. But the panorama of the city is equally stunning, if somewhat more subdued. And because the restaurant revolves 360 degrees every hour and a half, you'll never feel like the guy at the next table is getting a better view.

The menu is also impressive. Signature dishes include the Colorado Rack of Lamb, Maine Lobster, and Chilean Sea Bass. Be sure to save room for dessert, too. The crème brûlée is heavenly, but if you really want to remember where you are, order the Chocolate Strastosphere, done in the shape of the tower itself. It might not be as exhilarating as the ride, but it comes close.

Top of the World has everything you need for a perfect, romantic dinner. But we can't stress enough the importance of strategizing at the Stratosphere. Ride first; eat later.

3950

Mandalay Bay Resort and Casino
3950 South Las Vegas Boulevard
Las Vegas, Nevada 89119
(877) 632-7800 Resort
(877) 632-5300 Restaurants
www.mandalaybay.com

You can get in deep at Mandalay Bay, and we're not just talking about gambling losses.

For one thing, the resort has an enormous 11-acre wave pool that generates 6-foot waves.

Then there's Shark Reef. (Don't worry; it's not near the pool.) The $40 million aquarium is home to more than 100 different types of sea creatures, including some pretty mean-looking sharks.

For a long time, about the only thing missing at this wet and wild wonderland was a place to feed the whales.

Then they opened 3950.

A "whale" is a Vegas term for a high roller, a gambler who's able to part with tens of thousands, even hundreds of thousands of dollars or more at a sitting and not flinch. Sometimes they even win.

In short, a whale is every casino's favorite species of guest. As repayment, the establishments treat their prized customers lavishly, offering travel, top-notch accommodations, and of course, fancy meals.

3950 is just the place for that. It's glitzy and elegant at the same time. Designed to look like a twenty-first-century version of a 1950s-era supper club, it's rich with plush red velvet booths, suede walls, and leather seats. In a nod toward the sharks (the swimming variety, not the ones who play cards), there's a large screen with a live televised feed from Shark Reef.

The food is what they call contemporary classic. People who aren't whales will call it expensive. But ironically, with its top-notch food and excellent service, 3950 is the one place at Mandalay Bay where you don't have to worry about getting soaked.

The Bootlegger Bistro

7700 South Las Vegas Boulevard
Las Vegas, NV 89123
(702) 736-4939
www.bootleggerlasvegas.com

The woman entertaining the breakfast crowd is having a hard time getting the song going. Normally, Lorraine Hunt can belt out a tune. She is, after all, a veteran entertainer who worked all the big rooms during the heyday of the Las Vegas lounges.

Hunt usually takes the stage at The Bootlegger Bistro weekend nights, but she's working the crowd this morning at the request of the TV crew from *The Best Of.* And the tune just isn't working, probably because it's early and Hunt has been busy with her day job. Turns out that when she isn't performing at The Bootlegger, Lorraine Hunt is Lieutenant Governor of the state of Nevada.

It doesn't get any more "Vegas" than that.

The Bootlegger Bistro is pure Vegas. It's open 24/7. It has pleather booths and video slot machines. And it's packed with locals who keep this gem a secret from all the tourists.

Hunt's parents, Maria and Al Perry, opened what was then called "The Bootlegger" in downtown Las Vegas in 1972. It became a hit for its Italian and American food (the 80-something-ish Maria still runs the kitchen) and a well-known hangout for show business types. Lorraine and her family moved the restaurant to the south end of the Las Vegas strip in 2000 and added the word *Bistro* to the name. It's all of 5 minutes from Mandalay Bay, and not far from the schmaltzy Vegas of yesteryear.

Lorraine got her show business start in that golden era of 1960s showrooms. It was while teaming with a song-and-comedy troupe called "The Characters" that she met her husband, Charles "Blackie" Hunt. Later, she got interested in business affairs, which led to a career in politics. But "Blackie," with his rubber face and razor-sharp timing, keeps performing. These days, he and his show-biz partner Sonny King are the weekend headliners at The Bootlegger. Lorraine often joins them on stage to belt out a sultry torch song or two. That is, when she's not busy with affairs of the state.

This is Vegas, baby.

———

Eiffel Tower

Paris Las Vegas
3655 Las Vegas Boulevard
Las Vegas, NV 89109
(702) 948-6937
www.parkplace.com

A few reasons why the Eiffel Tower in Las Vegas is better than the original in Paris:

1. It has gambling.
2. From the top of the original, you can see Paris. From the top of the one in Vegas, you can see all the way to New York, New York (the hotel down the street).
3. While the original is nearly twice as high (1052 feet to 540 feet), the one in the good old United States was much more expensive ($1.3 million for the original in 1889, $28 million for the one with the casino).
4. Better French food here.

The Paris Las Vegas Resort is a smaller, more condensed version of the City of Light, with replicas of the Arc de Triomphe, the Eiffel Tower, and other French landmarks. Opened in 1999, it must have seemed like a good idea at the time.

The featured restaurant is eleven-stories up in the Eiffel Tower. While not sky-high, few places offer a more breathtaking view of the neon and excitement of Las Vegas Boulevard. The Bellagio fountains are right across the street, so people sitting along the front windows get a free show every fifteen minutes.

In a bit of a surprise, customers riding the elevator up to the restaurant discover their first view is not of Las Vegas, but of the bustling kitchen. That shows you where the emphasis is here. Only after guests see the battalion of chefs

and bakers at work are they escorted to the dining room.

The food is Classical French, with highlights like the Grand Seafood Platter with lobster, shrimp, crab, oysters, and clams; the beef tenderloin Rossini with foie gras and truffle sauce; and the braised salmon.

A few more advantages for visitors to this Eiffel Tower: No passport is needed and you won't come down with jet lag. It's everything good about Paris, sans the attitude.

———

New Mexico

The Daily Pie

Highway 60, Milepost 56
Pietown, NM 87827
(505) 772-2700
www.dailypie.com

When we shot at Pietown in fall 1999, we did a story on the Pie-o-neer café, owned at the time by Kathy Knapp. It was one of our favorite shoots: a town that sits 8,000 feet above sea level in the middle of the Continental Divide with more pies than people. The place was intriguing, especially because the Pie-o-neer seemed to have a constant buzz of activity, despite the slim population (fewer than 20 people live here). In writing this book, we were saddened to learn that the little restaurant, which served up delicious homemade pies, is no more. However, there is a new kid on the block.

We can't vouch for it because we haven't been, but we will tell you this: It's called the Daily Pie and is owned by Michael and Peggy Raw. They opened in May 2001 just down the street from the now-closed café. Locals tell us their meals are delicious. As for those pies, well, Peggy bakes them all herself, and they sound scrumptious. She usually has eight different pies on the menu at a time, from peanut butter to apple, cranberry, peach, coconut cream, chocolate cream, and pecan. Her husband does the regular cooking, which includes steaks, burgers on homemade buns, catfish, shrimp, and lasagna.

Although we're bummed the Pie-o-neer closed its doors, we can rest easy knowing Pietown isn't pie-less. Plus, they left us with this slogan: "Life goes on, days go by, that's why you should stop for pie." Thank goodness you still can.

Texas

Celebration Restaurant

4503 West Lovers Lane
Dallas, TX 75209
(214) 358-0612
www.celebrationrestaurant.com

At Celebration, you come in to load up on "groceries." No, not the kind of groceries you usually get at the supermarket. Around here, it's what they call the giant portions of home cooking served for lunch and dinner. And get this: At dinnertime, Celebration serves seconds!

That's right, if you're not full after one portion of pot roast, fried chicken, meat loaf, or broiled salmon (not to mention the soup, salad, or fresh fruit that start the meal, along with the three vegetables that come with your entrée), you can have another large serving! And you're not limited to what you just ate. You can get any of the other "groceries" on the menu, just as long as it costs the same or less than the entrée you originally ordered.

That's a lot of "groceries," certainly worthy of a Celebration.

Sautéed Squash

ADAPTED FROM CELEBRATION RESTAURANT, DALLAS, TEXAS

MAKES 2 SERVINGS

2 to 3 tablespoons olive oil
¼ pound yellow squash, sliced
¼ pound zucchini, sliced
1 bunch green onions, chopped
2 teaspoons chopped fresh garlic
Salt and freshly ground black pepper to taste
2 to 3 Roma tomatoes, diced

Heat a large skillet over high heat for 2 minutes. Add oil, yellow squash, zucchini, green onions, and garlic, and sauté, stirring occasionally, until tender, about 2½ to 3 minutes. Do not overcook. Remove from the heat. Season with salt and pepper. Stir in tomatoes, and serve.

Gennie's Bishop Grill

321 North Bishop Avenue
Dallas, TX 75208
(214) 946-1752

It's nearly 11 A.M., and there's already a long line in front of Gennie's Bishop Grill. It's not a bad way for the owners of this small, lunch-only cafeteria to start their day. Better yet, it seems this is a daily ritual.

But Gus and Rosemarie Hudson are way too busy to stop and marvel at their success. They awake each weekday morning at 3:30 A.M., and after a stop at the local market, are at the restaurant by 6. Gus handles most of the Texas-style home cooking, creating Gennie's famed chicken fried steak, pork loin chops, liver and onions, and baked garlic chicken. Rosemarie does the baking; producing a dozen or so pies, along with assorted cakes, cobblers, and pudding.

With the line in place, the doors are opened and lunch is served. You better move fast, because Gennie's closes at 2 P.M. Most days, everything sells out, sometimes a little too early.

Even more impressive, Rosemarie knows a little something about most of the customers. She's able to greet them by name and ask about family members, their business, or their golf scores without missing a beat.

The restaurant was started in 1971 by Rosemarie's late mother, Virginia (Ginnie) Purcell. Legend has it that she hired a sign painter of questionable intelligence, who misspelled her nickname as Gennie (the "Bishop" in the name refers to the street). At the time, there wasn't enough money to have the sign repainted.

The name is still pronounced *Ginnee*, but regulars don't really care what it's called just as long as you don't call them late for that 11 A.M. line.

Damn Yankee

There was a little good-natured North versus South ribbing when we taped at Gennie's. But co-owner Rosemarie Hudson won the battle hands down after I asked if she considered me a "damn Yankee."

"No," she replied, "You're just a Yankee. A damn Yankee is someone who doesn't have a return ticket."

Rosemarie's Peanut Butter Pie
ADAPTED FROM GENNIE'S BISHOP GRILL, DALLAS, TEXAS

MAKES 8 TO 12 SERVINGS

Pastry:
1½ cups sifted all-purpose flour
½ teaspoon salt
2 tablespoons sugar
½ cup shortening
2½ to 3 tablespoons ice water

Filling:
3 egg yolks
Pinch salt
2½ cups milk
¾ cup sugar
½ cup all-purpose flour
1 teaspoon vanilla extract
½ cup smooth peanut butter
1 cup heavy cream, whipped
½ cup peanuts, roasted

To make pastry: Sift together flour, salt, and sugar. Cut in shortening until the mixture resembles cornmeal. Add water, 1 tablespoon at a time, tossing with a fork until moist enough to hold together. Shape into a ball; wrap in waxed paper. Refrigerate for 1 hour.

On a lightly floured board, roll out pastry to an 11-inch circle. Dust the top lightly with flour, and use to line a 9-inch pie pan. Prick all over with a fork. Flute the edges. Place in the freezer for 15 to 20 minutes. Preheat the oven to 450°F. Bake pastry for 12 to 15 minutes, until golden. Cool on a wire rack.

To make filling: Combine egg yolks, salt, and milk in a heavy saucepan. Mix well. Cook over low heat, stirring constantly, until warm. Combine sugar and flour in a small bowl and gradually add to milk mixture. Cook, stirring constantly, until thickened. Boil for 1 minute. Remove from the heat. Stir in vanilla and peanut butter until blended. Let cool slightly.

Pour filling into pie shell. Chill thoroughly. Garnish with whipped cream and peanuts.

Babe's Chicken Dinner House

104 North Oak Street
Roanoke, Texas 76262
(817) 491-2900

Ever have a hard time deciding what to order at a restaurant? You won't have that problem here. Babe's keeps the choices to a minimum. You can either have fried chicken or chicken fried steak. How's that for simple?

For a place with such a limited menu, this Forth Worth–area restaurant sure packs in the crowds. There are long lines at both lunch and dinner, especially on weekends. The reason is due to the enormous servings. An order of chicken comes with a thigh, leg, breast, and wing. The chicken fried steak hangs over the edge of the plate. In addition, you get cut corn, mashed potatoes, gravy, biscuits, and salad. Once again, you don't have to make a choice, because all those side dishes are included. If you leave Babe's hungry, it's your own fault.

Marc with owner Dave Ross up yonder at the Ponder (aka The Ranchman's Café).

photo courtesy of Bud McHugh

front door creaks, there are old wooden booths, and aging newspaper clippings cover the wall. One prominent article recalls the biggest event to hit these parts, the filming of a scene in the movie *Bonnie and Clyde*. That was way back in 1966.

But the trip is worth it. Owner Dave Ross renders his own steaks in the back. (He also makes soap from the remnants, which he sells by the register.) The steaks are grilled to perfection and then served with an enormous potato—but only if you've made your reservation.

Ranchman's Café

110 West Bailey
Ponder, TX 76259
(940) 479-2221
www.ranchman.com

This is probably the one restaurant in America where you have to call ahead and reserve your potato.

It seems odd, yes, but there's not a lot of room in a place often called "the best little steakhouse in Texas." Most of the space in the small kitchen is dedicated to the main product, steak. Because the menu doesn't offer potato soup, or other dishes often made from leftovers, they like to keep a close accounting of the spuds.

Despite the quirky side-dish obsession, Ranchman's is pure Americana. Part of its charm comes from the location, "up yonder in Ponder," a sleepy town more than an hour outside both Dallas and Ft. Worth. The restaurant, which is also known as The Ponder Steakhouse, hasn't changed much since it opened in 1948. The

Fogo de Chao

4300 Beltline Drive
Addison, TX 75001
(972) 503-7300

8250 Westheimer Road
Houston, TX 77063
(713) 978-6500
www.fogodechao.com

Two words: *Texans-meat.*

What could make more sense?

Fogo de Chao and similar chains have spread across the country. But this Brazilian-based company got its U.S. start in Dallas. Good thinking.

Where better to launch an all-you-can-eat steakhouse with a distinctive style that hearkens to the Brazilian roots of its founders?

The restaurant has introduced what is known as Churrasco (pronounced shoo-rás-ko), or Brazilian barbeque, and it works like this: Waiters dressed as gauchos patrol the restaurant, armed with skewers loaded with various cuts of meat. Each customer holds a chip that's green on one side, red on the other. Anytime you want more

Texas

food, turn the chip to green, and the gauchos converge, slicing large portions onto your plate.

There are about 15 different cuts of beef, lamb, pork, or chicken. You can have a little or a lot. It's one price fits all.

The meat has been gently seasoned with coarse salt and then slow cooked over an open fire. The key is in cooking times. The name Fogo de Chao means, "fire in the earth," or simply, "campfire."

There's also a giant salad bar offering about 30 items. Actually, the term "salad bar" doesn't do it justice. Many restaurants would be lucky to consider this their entire menu. One tip: Go easy. There's so much meat to consume, you don't want to fill up too early.

Consider dining at Fogo de Chao a marathon, not a sprint. It's perfect for those on the Atkins diet. And Texans. And anyone else who's hungry.

Irma's

22 North Chenevert Street
Houston, TX 77002-1302
(713) 222-0767

To hang with Irma Galven, you gotta be an early riser, have a lot of energy, have patience, and be a good listener. Every day at the crack of dawn, Irma is up and off to Canino's market in Houston, picking out the produce she needs to make her authentic Mexican meals. She knows nearly all the vendors by name, and you can tell they love seeing her in the morning. She actually boasted that she could drive to the market with her eyes closed, although we didn't push her to show us.

She's back at the restaurant by 8 and open for her customers by 8:30 A.M., cooking up her specialties: huevos rancheros, chorizo, breakfast enchiladas—all made from scratch—along with her fresh pico de gallo.

When the clock strikes 11, she quickly switches gears into lunch mode. This is when Houston's business crowd, politicians, and anyone else who is craving her authentic food start to line up. That's when patience comes into play.

Irma's is such a popular place, it gets crowded quickly. Irma and her three grown children, who work alongside her, do the best they can, but everyone should expect to wait a bit.

You'll see Irma running around the floor, reciting the menu at one table and then bussing the next. Remember that listening skill we mentioned earlier? If you don't, then you're already in trouble because there is no paper menu at this restaurant. It's all in Irma's head. She tells her servers at the start of the day what's being offered, and they tell you. Expect to have about 12 different dishes to pick from, such as chiles rellenos, chicken mole, pork in an ancho chile sauce, or stuffed poblano peppers.

While you're waiting for your meal, there is plenty to keep you occupied. Irma is a collector of anything and everything, and people tend to give her stuff. Knickknacks, business cards, newspaper articles, and the like are stuck on the walls and shelves. In fact, you'll be hard-pressed to find a blank spot to leave your mark—but you'll want to try. After all, it's the only proof to show you've got what it takes to hang with Irma—a woman whose energy is amazing, whose enthusiasm is contagious—and whose food is downright delicious.

Chiles Rellenos Topped with Ranchero Sauce and Garnished with White Cheese and Cilantro

ADAPTED FROM IRMA'S, HOUSTON, TEXAS

MAKES 4 SERVINGS

Ranchero Sauce:
⅓ cup vegetable oil
1 onion, chopped
1 clove garlic, chopped
2 green or red bell peppers, chopped
4 fresh tomatoes, diced
1 (14.5-ounce) can chopped tomatoes, drained
Dash ground cumin

12 poblano chiles
⅓ cup canola oil
2 pounds lean ground beef round
1 cup chopped yellow or green onions
1 clove garlic, chopped
2 cups diced fresh tomatoes
1 teaspoon salt
½ teaspoon ground cumin
1 teaspoon freshly ground black pepper
8 eggs, separated
2 cups all-purpose flour
3 cups vegetable oil for deep-frying
Queso blanco, shredded, for garnish
Chopped fresh cilantro for garnish

To make sauce: Heat oil in a skillet over medium heat. Add onion, garlic, and bell peppers, and cook, stirring occasionally, until onion is transparent. Add fresh and canned tomatoes and cumin, and simmer until vegetables are tender but sauce has some texture, about 10 to 15 minutes. Set aside.

Roast chiles over a gas flame, turning until blistered and slightly charred all over. Put them into a heavy plastic bag, and set aside to steam for 10 to 20 minutes. Peel off skins. Carefully make a lengthwise slit in each chile and remove seeds and membranes. Rinse and drain well. Using paper towels, pat dry chiles.

Heat oil in a large skillet or saucepan over medium heat. Add meat, and cook until brown, stirring to break up meat. Add onions and garlic, and cook, stirring, for 1 minute. Add tomatoes, salt, cumin, and black pepper, and cook, stirring constantly, until meat mixture is dry, about 10 to 15 minutes. Set aside to cool.

Stuff chiles with meat mixture, and secure with a toothpick; set aside.

Beat egg whites until stiff and foamy in a large bowl. Add egg yolks to egg whites, and fold in to blend. Place flour in a separate bowl.

Heat oil in a deep skillet over medium heat to about 350°F or until a 1-inch bread cube turns golden brown in 65 seconds. Coat each stuffed chile with egg mixture, and lightly coat with flour. Carefully drop into hot oil. Fry, in batches, turning, until golden brown on both sides. Transfer chiles to paper towels to soak up excess fat.

To serve, top chiles with the sauce and garnish with queso blanco and cilantro.

Sambuca Jazz Cafe

The Rice Hotel
909 Texas Avenue
Houston, TX 77002
(713) 224-5299
www.sambucajazzcafe.com

As the name suggests, this is a place to get jazzed up. With live jazz musicians playing 7 nights a week, it's no wonder Sambuca is called the "supper club of the nineties." From the animal prints on the wall to the steel columns and the round booths, you'll instantly feel in the groove. Their food is definitely in sync with the décor: Modern and hip, but served with plenty of soul. Part Mediterranean, part comfort, and part Southern, their dishes don't miss a beat. Signatures include Honey BBQ Pork Chop, Pistachio and Dijon Encrusted Lamb, and a 14-ounce rib eye served with corn hash and Cajun crawfish. Whether it's the food, atmosphere, or music, this place is all that jazz, and more.

Texas

Texas

Maple Chicken with Cream de Brie Sauce

ADAPTED FROM THE SAMBUCA JAZZ CAFÉ, HOUSTON, TEXAS

MAKES 6 SERVINGS

Stuffing:

2 pounds ground chicken
1 teaspoon crushed red pepper
2 ounces chopped fresh sage
2 teaspoons chopped garlic
½ cup honey
½ cup packed light brown sugar
½ cup maple syrup
1 cup dried breadcrumbs
1 teaspoon salt
1 teaspoon coarsely ground black pepper

Cream de Brie Sauce:

1 cup white wine
2 tablespoons chopped garlic
2 teaspoons chopped shallot
4 cups heavy cream
4 ounces Brie, rind removed
4 ounces Dijon mustard
Salt and freshly ground black pepper to taste

6 (8-ounce) boneless, skinless chicken breasts,
    with a slit cut on the thick side for stuffing
Olive oil for sautéing
Flour for dusting
Chopped fresh parsley for garnish

To make stuffing: Place ground chicken in a large mixing bowl, add red pepper, sage, garlic, honey, brown sugar, and maple syrup, and mix thoroughly. Add breadcrumbs, salt, and black pepper. Place mixture in the refrigerator for 15 minutes to firm.

To make sauce: Combine wine, garlic, and shallot in a medium, heavy saucepan. Boil until reduced by half. Add cream, reduce the heat, and simmer for 10 minutes. Add Brie and mustard, and cook, stirring, until smooth; do not boil. Keep warm until needed.

Preheat the oven to 350°F.

Place meat mixture in a pastry bag with a wide tip. Pipe about one-sixth into the pocket of each chicken breast. Heat enough oil to cover the bottom in a large sauté pan over medium heat. Dust chicken with flour, and add chicken to the skillet. Sauté, turning, until browned on all sides. Place the skillet with chicken in the oven, and bake for 8 to 10 minutes or until cooked through.

Ladle some of sauce onto 6 plates. Slice each chicken breast into 6 or 7 pieces and arrange on top of sauce. Ladle more sauce over chicken. Sprinkle the plates with chopped parsley to finish.

Café Annie

1728 Post Oak Boulevard
Houston, TX 77057
(713) 840-1111
www.café-annie.com

It might sound odd: a filet of beef coated in a mixture of chocolate powder and ground coffee, covered with a pasilla chile sauce. But one bite and you'll be coming back for more. That's what the food is all about at Café Annie: Taking the usual and making it unusual. It's all done under the watchful eye of owner and executive chef Robert Del Grande. This guy has won just about every award under the sun and has cooked for notables like Julia Child and former President George H. W. Bush. No wonder he's known as Houston's "celebrity chef."

Filet of Beef Roasted with Coffee Beans with Pasilla Chile Broth and Creamy White Grits with Greens and Wild Mushrooms

ADAPTED FROM CAFÉ ANNIE, HOUSTON, TEXAS

MAKES 4 TO 6 SERVINGS

Filet of Beef:

1 (2-pound) filet of beef, preferably cut from the
    large end of the whole filet
1 teaspoon coarse salt
1 teaspoon freshly ground black pepper
2 tablespoons virgin olive oil
2 tablespoons very finely ground coffee beans

1 tablespoon unsweetened cocoa powder
⅛ teaspoon ground cinnamon

Pasilla Chile Broth:

1 tablespoon butter
½ large white onion, roughly chopped
4 to 8 cloves garlic, peeled
2 dried pasilla chiles (about ½ ounce total),
    stemmed, seeded, and torn into large pieces
1 thick white corn tortilla (about ¾ ounce)
2½ cups chicken stock
¼ cup heavy cream
1 teaspoon coarse salt
1 teaspoon brown sugar

Creamy White Grits with Bitter Greens and Wild Mushrooms:

4 cups water
1¼ cups coarse white grits
1½ teaspoons salt
1 tablespoon butter
½ yellow onion, minced
2 cloves garlic, minced
¾ pound shiitake mushrooms, stems removed and
    caps cut into quarters
4 ounces arugula or other bitter green, roughly
    chopped
Watercress sprigs for garnish

To prepare filet: Tie filet with butcher twine at ½-inch intervals. Rub filet well with salt and pepper, and rub with oil. Combine ground coffee, cocoa powder, and cinnamon in a small bowl, and mix well. Spread mixture over a work surface, and roll filet in mixture to evenly coat. Allow to stand for about 30 minutes.

To prepare chile broth: Heat a saucepan over medium-high heat. Add butter, and sauté onion and garlic until nicely browned. Add chiles and tortilla, and slowly sauté until ingredients are golden brown. Lower heat to medium-low if necessary. Add chicken stock. Bring stock to a boil, then simmer, lightly covered, for about 10 minutes. Remove from the heat and allow to cool. Transfer ingredients to a blender, and purée for about 1 minute or until smooth. Press sauce through a sieve to remove any unpuréed pieces. Add cream, salt, and brown sugar, and mix to combine. Sauce should not be too thick. (If it's too thick, add some additional chicken stock or water to correct to a very light consistency.) Reserve until ready to serve.

To roast filet: Preheat oven to 400°F. Place filet on a roasting rack in a roasting pan. Roast filet for 10 minutes at 400°F. Immediately lower the heat to 250°F. After 20 minutes, check internal temperature of filet (it should be 125°F for medium rare or 135°F for medium). If further cooking is necessary, return beef to oven (still set at 250°F), and slowly roast to desired temperature. Remove filet from oven and keep warm. Before carving, remove string.

To cook grits, mushrooms, and greens: In a 2-quart, heavy saucepan, bring water and salt to a boil. Gradually stir in grits. Bring water back to a boil. Lower the heat to a very low simmer. Cover the pot, but stir every 2 to 3 minutes until grits are thick. Grits will take about 20 minutes to cook. If grits become too thick, add a little water to adjust the consistency.

Melt butter until foaming in a skillet over medium-high heat. Add onion and garlic. Sauté until onion is translucent. Add mushrooms, and sauté until lightly cooked. Add greens, and briefly sauté until wilted. Remove from the heat.

To serve: Stir greens and mushroom mixture into grits and keep warm. Slice filet into ¼-inch-thick slices. Spoon some grits into the center of each dinner plate. Arrange the slices of filet around grits. Ladle some chile broth over filet. Garnish with watercress sprigs.

Driskill Grill

The Driskill Hotel
604 Brazos Street
Austin, TX 78701
(512) 474-5911
www.driskillgrill.com
www.driskillhotel.com

The Driskill Hotel is *the* hangout in Austin for politicians and poltergeists.

Politicians you can understand. The busy hotel, and its bar, are so close to the state Capitol Building, it's said there are more political decisions made here than at the legislature. For

Texas

years, Lyndon Johnson used the Driskill as his home away from home.

But poltergeists? While not as scary as the rough-and-tumble world of Texas politics, it's still pretty interesting.

The subjects converge when it comes to the haunting of the Driskill. The story goes that somewhere around the beginning of the 20th century, the hotel hosted a party for a prominent United States senator whose name has been lost in time.

Sadly during the event, the politician's young daughter fell to her demise chasing a favorite toy ball down the grand staircase.

It's believed her friendly ghost is still around, often heard laughing as she plays in the lobby. Sometimes she's so loud desk clerks have to ask her to lower her voice. With that, she disappears, leaving behind a chilly burst of air.

In addition, some guests say the elevator doors open to reveal the distant sounds of a long-ago party. It could be the one time they miss Muzak.

Cattle baron Jesse Driskill first opened the hotel in 1886, but financial problems forced him to sell within two years. Some say he's still around too, the smell of his cigar smoke is often sensed wafting through the lobby. Apparently, the lobby is very "in" in the afterworld.

One place here that is very real is the Driskill Grill, a sophisticated restaurant with top-notch food. Executive Chef David Bull, a graduate of the Culinary Institute of America, features dishes like Trio of Duck, Herb-and-Garlic Broiled Lobster, and Mustard Crusted Rack of Lamb. Like the ghosts, the memory of a fine meal at the Driskill Grill won't disappear.

———

Dorsett 221 Truck Stop

Interstate 35 South
Exit 221
Buda, TX 78610
(512) 312-0052
www.dorsett221.com

Unless you drive a rig, you probably don't pull into too many truck stops. But on the road of life, it's a mistake to pass by Dorsett 221.

Husband and wife co-owners Ronnie and Sandy Dorsett have incredible stories to tell. Like the time a pregnant woman went into labor. Nothing so unusual about that, except that she was traveling in a rig with her truck-driving husband and their three kids.

As the woman was being transported to the hospital, the crowd of regulars told her not to worry about her children because Ronnie and Sandy would take care of them. And they did—for four days. Even though they didn't know the parents' names. Pretty special.

Ronnie tells a sad story about getting a call from police in a distant state, and then having to tell a visiting trucker his family had met with tragedy. The Dorsetts bought the man an airline ticket and put him on the plane.

A trucker told Marc that months earlier, his visiting stepfather suffered a heart attack during a fill-up at the truck stop. The man said he felt like he was surrounded by family the way the Dorsetts responded. Fortunately, his stepfather recovered.

Moments after sharing the story, the driver was at the cash register when Ronnie Dorsett noticed him. The place may be busy, but it only took a moment for the owner to remember the incident and ask in his quiet Texas drawl, "How's your Pa?" Amazing.

Dorsett 221 is right outside Austin, and is known throughout the area for its chicken fried steak and meatloaf. (You were expecting maybe foie gras and sea scallops at a truck stop?) Recently, Ronnie Dorsett invented what he calls the taco omelet. Three-eggs filled with seasoned taco meat, lettuce, tomato, and cheese. People fill-up a lot more than their trucks here.

———

Hoover's Cooking

2002 Manor Road
Austin, TX 78722
(512) 479-5006
www.hooverscooking.com

The best way to understand the food they serve at this down-home restaurant is by taking a look at the drinks.

Well, one drink in particular. When you order lemonade, it comes in a large, one-quart pitcher—with a straw. That's it. The pitcher isn't for sharing around your table—it's all yours. You don't even pour it into a glass, that's what the straw is for.

The menu is full of what's called "Southern Pride" dishes like chicken fried steak, meatloaf, and fried or charbroiled catfish. Hoover's also has its own smokehouse where they pour the flavor on pork ribs, Jamaican jerk chicken, and Elgin sausage. All the portions are large. So come hungry. And thirsty.

O's Campus Café

University of Texas at Austin
201 East 24th Street and Speedway (ACES Building)
(512) 232-9060
www.aces.utexas.edu/ocafe

O's Campus Café is fine dining for college students. Located in the $30 million dollar ACES Building, where brainiacs study cutting-edge technology, a good restaurant was one of the requirements of the building's benefactor, Dallas millionaire Peter O'Donnell (he's the "O" in the Café's name).

Run by the same family that owns Jeffrey's, one of Austin's fancier restaurants, the menu boasts fresh-made dishes like pine nut crusted chicken breast with herb rice, carrot ginger soup, and sushi. The Pecos chicken is a popular salad. Yes, you can get a hamburger here, and pizza, too. This is college after all.

O's is open for breakfast and lunch. Off-campus visitors are welcome. Lines are usually long, so many people grab a meal at the two "O's-to Go" trailers around campus. One is located at the base of the administration building. We're told it was put there at the request of a frequent diner, the school's president, whose office is inside.

Texas

The Pacific

California, Oregon, Washington, Alaska, Hawaii

IF IT'S A food trend, more than likely it started in California. But there's no way to properly define California cuisine. Does it have an Asian influence, or more of a south-of-the-border flavor? Maybe it's just easier to refer to everything as *fusion*. But what comes to mind first is "fresh," whether it's the ingredients or the ideas.

From our standpoint, the answer is simple. You don't have to put California cuisine into a box. Take a train ride through Napa Valley's famed wine country, or head to San Francisco for the best dim sum you'll ever taste. The Bay Area is also the home of a great vegetarian find, one of the most celebrated French restaurants in the country, and a nifty place where you can still celebrate a high-rolling, high-tech deal.

In Los Angeles, we'll tell you about the best places for star sightings, right down to the exact tables reserved for celebrities.

Those innovative ideas are not restricted to California. Oregon is home to a bistro where all cultures and cuisines seem to collide, producing the best mac and cheese in the land. And you'll discover why you want to relax with the *second*-best martini in Seattle, and how to get a free limo ride to the most scenic restaurant in town.

But the Pacific region also includes Alaska and Hawaii, which share an ocean with the other west coast states but still make their own unique contributions to the culinary landscape.

And speaking of landscapes, it's not hard to imagine that Alaska, by far the biggest state in the Union, has lots to offer the intrepid traveler. It's the perfect place for those with an appetite—both figuratively and literally—for adventure. But you're in for a few surprises if you think Alaska is confined to elk and King Crab, because not only will you discover a sumptuous glacial picnic but also one of the best taco stands in the country.

Finally, what better way to conclude this whirlwind tour of America than on the balmy shores of the Hawaiian islands. You'll find both the exotic and familiar everywhere—from onaga and ono to indigenous pineapple and homegrown coffee. The hospitality, the breathtaking beauty—not to mention every modern convenience and luxury—welcome all visitors to this paradise on earth.

California

Napa Valley Wine Train

1275 McKinstry Street
Napa, CA 94559
(707) 253-2111 or (800) 427-4124
www.winetrain.com

Drink in the scenery of America's most famous wine country while you leave the driving to them. The 3-hour, 36-mile trip from Napa to St. Helena aboard a refurbished-to-the-hilt train offers everything from sandwiches to gourmet wine-and-dine meal packages. All the food is made onboard.

Vincent DeDomenico, who created Rice-a-Roni and once owned the Ghirardelli Chocolate Company, bought the train to keep him busy during his "retirement." Consider it the Napa Valley Treat.

Jarvis

2970 Monticello Road
Napa, CA 94559
(800) 255-5280
www.jarviswines.com

From the outside, it's hard to imagine the jewel that lies within. An oversize door built into a rock is the only clue that this ultra premium boutique winery even exists. Call it "spelunking" for wine enthusiasts. The entire winery is burrowed into the side of a mountain in a cave that spreads 45,000 square feet underground. It took 5 years to build this massive, intricate structure, which opened in summer 1995.

The man behind this seeming madness is William Jarvis. But when talking to him, we realized he's anything but mad. His reasons for going down under make sense.

Jarvis wanted to preserve the 37 acres above for growing his grapes, and he didn't want to take up precious space above ground with fermentation rooms and tasting tables.

But his more practical reason is that the winery doesn't have to use air conditioning or heat to control the temperature. Instead, they rely on Mother Nature. Built-in waterfalls help control the humidity, the temperature in the cave remains constantly cool year 'round at 61 degrees, and the dark surroundings preserve the quality of the wine. Makes sense to us, especially when you take a sip.

Jarvis specializes in chardonnay and cabernet sauvignon, and believe us: These wines will knock your socks off. Just don't let them knock you off your feet!

Tours are by appointment only, with a maximum of 10 people at a time. If you are lucky enough to tour this wine cave, one of the highlights is the "light" at the end of the tunnel—the Crystal Chamber. Entering this spectacular room through the big brass doors is like walking into the Emerald City. Think Oz, as in *Wizard of* . . . Except here, the yellow brick road is dark and dimly lit, and the Emerald City is in a cave.

Domaine Chandon

One California Drive
Yountville, CA 94599
(800) 736-2892
www.chandon.com

The pop of a cork; the fizz of tiny bubbles. It usually means a celebration is under way. But at Domaine Chandon, simply sitting down for a meal is reason to celebrate. That's because every culinary creation here is prepared with a specific sparkling wine in mind. Taking in the whole experience will literally elevate your palate. You'll begin to think you belong to a "bourgeois bubbly" family. As you are transported to this other place, be forewarned: You might actually begin to sparkle (or at least think you are!).

From the wine tours to the tasting, to their ultra-fine dining room, you'll want to take your time. Think of it in terms of wine making, where from grapevine to glass can take 2 to 6 years. We don't recommend staying there *that* long, but it's not an experience you want to rush.

California

California

Lobster Salad on Brioche with Vanilla-Orange Vinaigrette

ADAPTED FROM DOMAINE CHANDON, YOUNTVILLE, CALIFORNIA

MAKES 4 SERVINGS

2 cups orange juice
1 ounce fresh ginger, peeled and sliced
¼ vanilla bean, split and scraped
2 star anise
Juice of 1 lime
1 tablespoon Dijon mustard
1½ teaspoons Thai fish sauce
½ cup pure olive oil
½ cup extra-virgin olive oil
10 haricots verts (small green beans), cooked until crisp-tender
2 (1¼-pound) lobsters
4 slices brioche, cut crosswise
1 avocado, diced
1 fennel bulb, cut into paper-thin slices
¼ cup pumpkin seeds, toasted
Salt and freshly ground black pepper to taste
10 leaves baby lola rosa or red oak leaf lettuce

In a small pan, combine orange juice, ginger, vanilla, and star anise. Boil over medium heat until reduced to ¾ cup. Strain into a bowl, and cool dressing to room temperature. Add lime juice, mustard, and fish sauce. Slowly whisk in pure and extra-virgin olive oils; set aside.

Bring a small pot of salted water to a boil. Remove tips from beans. Cook the beans in boiling water until tender, then cool in ice water. Cut beans into thirds.

Bring a very large pot of salted water to a boil. Add lobsters. When they float (after about 5 minutes), remove them from water. Remove tail and claw meat. Dice claw meat. Slice tails in half lengthwise.

Toast brioche.

Mix beans, avocado, fennel, pumpkin seeds, and claw meat in a large bowl. Season salad with salt and pepper, and toss with enough dressing to coat well.

Divide salad among 4 plates. Place brioche on top.

Toss tail meat and lettuce separately with enough dressing to coat; season with salt and pepper. Place tail meat on brioche. Top with a small bouquet of lettuce. Drizzle some dressing around the plate, and serve.

Gaige House Inn

13540 Arnold Drive
Glen Ellen, CA 95442
(707) 935-0237 or (800) 935-0237
www.gaige.com

If you think of a bed and breakfast and cringe at the idea of paisley comforters with stuffed animals on your bed and proprietors who want to "chat" with you all morning, then this is the place for you. It is the antithesis of all that, and more. We'll call it one of Sonoma County's best-kept secrets. At this amazing bed and breakfast/inn, no expense is spared in making your stay private, relaxed, and romantic (should you wish). For that, you do pay a price, with rooms up to $600 a night. But if your budget allows, you'll luxuriate in deep tubs, cozy fireplaces, a babbling brook outside, and amazing food.

Once you've checked in, you'll feel your breathing start to slow down and the muscles in your jaw relax. After an incredible night's sleep, with the breeze gently blowing across your bed, you'll awaken to find yourself revitalized and also ravenous, which is why breakfast is key here. It is served and, therefore, enjoyed the way it was meant to be: at a leisurely pace and full of indulgence. When we were here, Chef Charles Holmes prepared smoked salmon—which he smokes himself—perched atop a poached egg and drizzled with hollandaise sauce. Zucchini pancakes with an asparagus purée are served on the side. Between the bed and the breakfast here, you'll never think of a B&B the same way again.

Zucchini Pancakes with Cresenza and Roasted Red Peppers

ADAPTED FROM THE GAIGE HOUSE INN, GLEN ELLEN, CALIFORNIA

MAKES 4 SERVINGS; 8 DOLLAR-SIZE PANCAKES

2 cups shredded zucchini
¾ cup all-purpose flour
½ teaspoon kosher salt
½ teaspoon freshly ground black pepper
Pinch ground nutmeg
4 eggs
3 tablespoons butter, melted and cooled
½ cup water
⅓ cup grated Parmesan cheese
Olive oil for sautéing
½ pound Cresenza cheese, crumbled, or 2 ounces
    Brie
4 sprigs thyme
Roasted red bell peppers to serve

Place zucchini in a clean dish towel, and squeeze out water. Mix flour, salt, pepper, and nutmeg in a medium bowl. Whisk eggs in a small bowl until lightly beaten; whisk in butter and water. Stir liquid ingredients into dry ingredients. Stir zucchini and Parmesan cheese into batter; add more water if batter is too thick.

In a large sauté pan over medium heat, heat a thin layer of olive oil. When a drop of water will dance on the pan, spoon 1 heaping tablespoon batter into the pan. When bubbles appear and pancake is lightly browned on the bottom, turn and brown the other side. Continue until all batter is used. Drain pancakes on paper towels.

Preheat the oven to 375°F. Place pancakes in a single layer on a baking sheet. Top pancakes with equal amount of Cresenza cheese. Bake for about 1 minute or until cheese softens. Garnish with thyme, and serve with bell peppers.

Yank Sing

One Rincon Center
101 Spear Street
San Francisco, CA 94105
(415) 957-9300

49 Stevenson Street
San Francisco, CA 94105
(415) 541-4949
www.yanksing.com

The dim sum here will "touch the heart," which is what the words mean in Chinese. Dim sum (or deem sum as they prefer here) are those wonderful bite-size delicacies often thought of as Chinese dumplings. At Yank Sing, they're much more than that.

The restaurant offers 60 different types of "deem sum" daily, and more than 100 overall. Servers roll small carts loaded with choices through the aisles, while diners pick and choose. At Yank Sing, deem sum can be roasted, grilled, stir-fried, or steamed. It can be a dumpling, a spring roll, a barbeque pork bun, or a slice of Peking duck. There are no limits.

The restaurant is only open for lunch, but in just a few hours sells more than 10,000 pieces.

Originally, owners Henry and Judy Chan

California

Preparing Dim Sum at Yank Sing, San Francisco.

were planning careers in medicine. But fate and family obligations led to the couple taking over a relative's restaurant. Now, consider them the doctors of deem sum. Who better to "touch the heart"?

Emmy's Spaghetti Shack

18 Virginia Street
San Francisco, CA 94110
(415) 206-2086

Upon approaching this Mission District diner, you'll know immediately why it's called "shack"—the tin roof is only the beginning. Inside, where old aprons hang from clotheslines above the diners' heads, the word that comes to mind is *cozy*—there's not much elbow room.

Don't get the idea owners Jay Foster and Emmy Kaplan were going for "dive chic." The look and feel of Emmy's just came together naturally—and successfully.

Open only for dinner, locals love this place, even though there's usually a wait. About the only reservations you'll find here are about the neighborhood, which probably isn't on the Chamber of Commerce tour.

The menu, under Chef Sarah Kirnon, changes monthly. She calls her cuisine "Italian and then some," which means you'll always find Emmy's signature spaghetti and meatballs, but the "and then some" is left to Sarah. Sometimes that means Californian; other times Mediterranean. Bills here tend to remain in the single-digit-per-person territory. Oh yeah, one more thing: Bring cash. The "Shack" doesn't take plastic.

Meatballs

ADAPTED FROM EMMY'S SPAGHETTI SHACK, SAN FRANCISCO, CALIFORNIA

MAKES 6 TO 8 SERVINGS; 30 TO 32 MEATBALLS

2 pounds ground beef
1 medium white onion, finely chopped
1 medium red onion, finely chopped
2½ to 3 tablespoons capers, rinsed and chopped
1½ cups dried breadcrumbs
2 tablespoons chopped garlic
1 large egg, lightly beaten
2 teaspoons salt
1 teaspoon freshly ground black pepper
2 tablespoons chopped fresh parsley leaves
2 tablespoons olive oil, for frying
3½ cups marinara sauce
⅔ cup red wine
¾ cup grated Parmesan cheese
Chopped fresh parsley leaves for garnish
About 6 cups cooked spaghetti to serve

Preheat the oven to 400°F.

Combine beef, white and red onions, capers, breadcrumbs, garlic, egg, salt, pepper, and parsley in a large bowl, and mix well, using both hands. Shape meat mixture into golf ball–size pieces. Heat oil in a large, heavy skillet over medium heat. Brown meatballs, in batches, 5 to 8 minutes, turning to brown all sides.

Transfer meatballs to a 13x9-inch baking pan.

California

Cover meatballs with marinara sauce and pour red wine over the top. Sprinkle with Parmesan cheese. Cover with aluminum foil, and bake for 15 minutes. Remove the foil and bake for about 10 minutes, until meatballs are cooked through and sauce is bubbly. Garnish with parsley. Serve over spaghetti.

Scala's

432 Powell Street
San Francisco, CA 94102
(415) 395-8555
www.scalasbistro.com

Who would expect great Italian classics cooked up by a Swede? But Scala's Executive Chef Staffan Terje, a proud Swede, will exceed your expectations when he makes his homemade pasta. He does it any way you like it: thick, thin, rolled, or wrapped. Try the Naked Ravioli (who knew the Swedes were so risqué?) made with fresh spinach-Parmesan gnudis (they're gnocchis, but he calls them "nude-ies"). After he boils them, he dresses them up and covers them in classic tomato sauce. *Ooh-la-la,* or should we say, "Magnifico!"

———

Flea Street Café

3607 Alameda de las Pulgas
Menlo Park, CA 94025
(650) 854-1226
fleastreet@cooleatz.com
www.cooleatz.com

It's a chilly morning in the San Francisco Bay area town of Menlo Park, and Marc and his camera crew are in a backyard in a residential neighborhood, chasing chickens.

It's probably not how most people would spend their time in high-tech Silicon Valley, but then not everyone gets to hang out with Jesse Cool. Yes, that's her last name, and yes, she is.

Jesse is leading this field trip to a neighbor's "Chicken Hilton" to help illustrate her philosophy about dining. In short, she's passionate that people connect with their food. Jesse believes people can better enjoy what they eat by buying locally: knowing where food comes from and how it's raised.

Although not 100 percent organic, Jesse says she's "organic minded." That means she prefers to avoid foods covered with chemicals and pesticides. Nurture the earth, and you take care of yourself.

Jesse knows her theories might sound like "'60s hippy-dippy stuff," especially coming from someone who long ago spent 3 years on welfare. But she insists it's also good business. And she seems to know what she's talking about. She now owns three successful organic restaurants and a catering company. She's also the author of several popular cookbooks. So much for the hippy-dippy stuff.

Since she first opened the casual gourmet Flea Street Café in 1982, she has made it a point to know her vendors, which brings us back to the henhouse. The eggs the birds here produce might not all be the same shape, size, or color, but they're real and natural. Buying from a local grower helps the area's economy—and they even seem to taste better when Jesse cooks them back at Flea Street. Suddenly, it all makes perfect sense, even if it did have Marc running around the yard—like a chicken with its head cut off.

California

California

Bloody Mary Shrimp Cocktail

ADAPTED FROM FLEA STREET CAFÉ, MENLO PARK, CALIFORNIA

MAKES 4 SERVINGS

4 cups organic tomato juice
Juice of 2 limes
1 teaspoon Worcestershire sauce
2 tablespoons sugar
1 heaping tablespoon grated horseradish
2 tablespoons grated red onion
½ teaspoon freshly ground black pepper
Salt to taste
½ teaspoon hot pepper sauce, or to taste
1 cup chopped, seeded cucumber
1 medium avocado, coarsely chopped
2 green onions, sliced
1 pound cooked shrimp (prawns, bay shrimp, langostino, or rock shrimp will work)

In a pitcher or large bowl, combine tomato juice, juice of 1½ limes, Worcestershire sauce, sugar, horseradish, red onion, and pepper. Mix thoroughly, and season with salt and hot sauce. Refrigerate until chilled.

In a medium bowl, combine cucumber, avocado, and green onions, and toss with remaining lime juice. Season with salt.

Divide shrimp among 4 large glasses or bowls. Pour tomato mixture on top. Serve chilled.

CHEF'S TIPS: Seasoned firm tofu, cut into chunks, would be a great way to make this vegetarian. To serve the soup hot, heat the tomato mixture until it boils and pour it over the shrimp.

THIS NOTE ABOUT THE RECIPE FROM JESSE COOL: "As much as I love to indulge in luscious kinds of foods, my regular day-to-day diet consists of lots of vegetables and protein. This is amongst a handful of dishes that I could easily eat once or twice a week for lunch because it is a flavorful way of getting both."

Rose Pistola

532 Columbus Avenue
San Francisco, CA 94133
(415) 399-0499

This upscale Italian restaurant captures the vitality of the late Rose Pistola, a one-time fixture in San Francisco's North Beach neighborhood. Her name alone may be an indication of her lively personality. According to founder Reed Heron, Rose Pistola was one red-hot pistol. Or as he put it years ago when he was first introduced to Rose, "This is the sexiest 88-year-old I've ever met!"

For years, Rose owned a popular corner bar in North Beach. According to Heron, if she liked you, she would cook for you. If not: There are stories of her chasing people out of the place, sometimes brandishing an empty wine bottle.

She was also known to repaint the bar and put up new pictures, then hold a "Grand Opening" party, which happened several times a year.

When Heron started his own restaurant in 1996 (he has since left the operation), he wanted a name that would reflect the neighborhood's character, or perhaps the neighborhood character.

North Beach was settled in part by Italian immigrants (Joe DiMaggio grew up here), was home to bohemians and beatniks in the 1950s, protestors in the 1960s and 1970s, and remains a lively mix of everything good about a city. Still very Italian, it's packed with cafés, coffee shops, markets, and most of all, excitement.

To Heron, no name said it better than "Rose Pistola," who passed away years ago but remains a key ingredient here today.

Millennium Restaurant

580 Geary Street
San Francisco, CA 94102
(415) 345-3900
www.millenniumrestaurant.com

Fine dining veggie style and truly one of those meals that we still talk about . . . The smoked tofu tasted like smoked gouda cheese. The way Chef

Eric Tucker cooked wheat gluten with a marsala mushroom sauce, you'd think you were eating a Steak Diane. Nearly all the ingredients, which come from small family farms in the area, are organic. No genetically modified foods of any kind on the menu. If vegetarian food was always this good, we might have a meat-free society.

Roasted Corn Abdi

ADAPTED FROM MILLENNIUM RESTAURANT, SAN FRANCISCO, CALIFORNIA

MAKES 2 TO 4 SERVINGS

1 teaspoon dried oregano
⅓ tablespoon ground allspice
¼ bunch fresh cilantro, minced
1 red onion, cut into ¼-inch dice
1 tablespoon ¼-inch dice carrot
1 ear fresh corn, kernels removed and roasted in a skillet until some of the kernels start to brown
4 to 6 kumquats, sliced
1 cucumber, seeded and cut into ¼-inch dice
Juice of 1 lime
½ habanero chile, seeds removed
1 avocado, cubed
Salt to taste

Toast oregano, allspice, and cilantro in a dry skillet over medium heat until aromatic. Mix with onion, carrot, corn, kumquats, and cucumber in a medium bowl. Transfer ¼ cup onion mixture to a food processor; add lime juice and chile. Process until finely chopped. Add back to remaining onion mixture. Add avocado, and season with salt.

The Big Four

Huntington Hotel
1075 California Street
San Francisco, CA 94108
(415) 771-1140-restaurant
(415) 474-5400-hotel
www.big4restaurant.com

The Big Four—nineteenth-century railroad tycoons—inspired the name of this stately, masculine place that feels like an old gentleman's club. The irony is that this place is run by women! It's no wonder that Chef Gloria Ciccarone-Nehls, who grew up with a dad and brother who hunted, would find her calling cooking wild game. She certainly has her ducks in a row, not to mention her rattlesnake, alligator, ostrich, elk, and kangaroo. This is a place worth checking out if you want to take a walk on the wild side.

True Colors

On the same day we were scheduled to shoot *The Best Of Game* at The Big Four, we had an early morning shoot at another restaurant for our *Best Of Women Chefs* show. However, the top-ranked woman chef refused to cook on camera for us. It's kind of hard to showcase someone who doesn't want to perform in front of the camera, so we left without rolling any tape.

As it turned out, Gloria Ciccarone-Nehls fit into both our shows: women chefs and game. She was "game" for a double shoot, so we just showed up at The Big Four early and got to work.

With two segments and a heap of game under our belts, we called it a night, convinced that in the end, things often work out for the Best (Of)!

California

Venison Chili with Black Beans

ADAPTED FROM THE BIG FOUR,
SAN FRANCSICO, CALIFORNIA

**MAKES 6 HUGE SERVINGS, ABOUT 1 QUART
CHILI EACH**

¼ cup vegetable oil
3 pounds coarse ground venison or beef chuck
2 pounds coarse ground pork
6 cloves garlic and 2 whole jalepeño chiles,
    pureed in blender with ¼ cup vegetable oil
3 yellow onions, sliced
3 tablespoons chili powder
2 tablespoons ground cumin
1 tablespoon dried thyme
1 teaspoon each dried oregano, celery seed, sweet
    paprika, and black pepper
½ teaspoon each anise seeds, dried chili flakes,
    and cayenne
2 bay leaves
Pinch ground cloves
2 teaspoons salt
3 (10-ounce) bottles chili sauce, such as Heinz
2 (28-ounce) cans diced tomatoes in juice
1 cup tomato paste
3 cups chicken broth
2 cups cooked black beans, home prepared or
    canned
2 cups shredded sharp white cheddar cheese
Honey-Spiced Onion Crisps (recipe follows) for
    garnish

Heat oil in a 12-quart saucepan over medium heat. Add venison and pork, and cook until browned, stirring to break up meat. Add garlic-chile mixture, onions, chili powder, cumin, thyme, oregano, celery seed, paprika, black pepper, anise seeds, chili flakes, cayenne, bay leaves, cloves, and salt. Cook for 5 minutes.

Stir in chili sauce, tomatoes with juice, tomato paste, and broth. Bring to a boil. Reduce heat and simmer, uncovered, for 2 to 2½ hours.

Remove bay leaves, and serve with black beans and cheddar cheese. Garnish with onion crisps.

Honey-Spiced Onion Crisps
2 quarts canola oil for deep-frying

2 red onions, thinly sliced
½ teaspoon chili powder
½ teaspoon ground cumin
¼ teaspoon cayenne
1 tablespoon honey
½ teaspoon salt
2 cups all-purpose flour
Kosher salt (optional)

Heat oil in a deep, 8-quart heavy saucepan to 325 to 350°F.

While oil heats, toss onions with the chili powder, cumin, cayenne, honey, and salt in a large bowl. Add flour, and toss to coat onions well. Let them stand for 5 to 10 minutes, tossing several times. Shake off excess flour.

Have a pan lined with paper towels and a skimmer ready.

Fry onions, in small batches, until golden. Using a skimmer, transfer onions to the paper towel–lined pan to drain.

Sprinkle lightly with kosher salt, if desired.

Ponzu

401 Taylor Street
San Francisco, CA 94102
(415) 775-7979
www.ponzurestaurant.com

Picture this: It's midnight, and as Jill is about to go to sleep, she says to her husband, "I'm kind of hungry." He says, "We have pretzels and chips in the kitchen." She replies, "No, I'm dying for some orange curry sea bass over sticky rice." At that point, he looks at her and says, "I think you've been at this job too long. Goodnight." Lights click off. She's left to ponder and dream about that sea bass . . . .

It's true. Sometimes you're left with the memory of a meal that you can't stop thinking about. Such was the case at Ponzu, where the menu is truly memorable. Asian fusion and influence are apparent in all their dishes—from the bright and bold to the crunchy, sweet, salty, and savory. All kinds of flavors and textures await the lucky patrons of this San Francisco eatery. Now if only that sea bass could be Fed-Exed when those midnight cravings hit . . . Sweet dreams. (At the time of writing this piece, the Orange Curry Sea Bass over Sticky Rice has given way to other delicacies on the menu. But you won't be disappointed by whatever you find.)

———

Teatro ZinZanni

Pier 29 on the Embarcadero, at Battery
San Francisco, CA 94133
(415) 438-2668
www.teatrozinzanni.org

If you the think the name is unusual, wait until you experience this surreal show. Dinner theater this is not.

The producers of Teatro ZinZanni (pronounced *Tea-ah-troe Zin-zahn-nee)*, who started in Seattle in 1998 and expanded to San Francisco in 2000, use three words to describe their brand of entertainment: love, chaos, dinner. We can do it in one: *mayhem.*

It's a semi-circus that goes on in-the-round under a quasi-big top. There's a wild assortment of acrobats, contortionists, and magicians. Not to mention the jugglers, illusionists, and of course, clowns. And, oh yeah, there's a five-piece band.

The whole thing feels like a Cold War–era East Berlin cabaret act, with attention-deficit disorder. Even Felinni would think it's over the top.

Somehow during the 3½-hour show, a 5-course gourmet meal is served. The performers wait on tables, the waiters perform, and audience members are coerced into participating. And that's the easy part to explain. It's not just zany. It's Teatro ZinZanni.

———

Fleur de Lys

777 Suter Street
San Francisco, CA 94109
(415) 673-7779
www.fleurdelyssf.com

After 45 years in business, Fleur de Lys is still one of the best French restaurants in the country. Or the most romantic. Or just the best, period. Executive Chef/Owner Hubert Keller is renowned for his contemporary French cuisine and has received almost every culinary award invented.

But, on September 8, 2001, an overnight electrical fire reduced Fleur de Lys to ashes.

To create and sustain a renowned restaurant is challenge enough, but to re-create it through

California

L'affaire

Fleur de Lys was the first, but certainly not the last restaurant where *The Best Of* ran into the problem of "married/not married" couples. By that, we mean a dating duo where he's married and she's married—they're just not married to each other.

Usually the couple ducks out when they see our crew or just asks us not to videotape in their direction, which is certainly something we can respect. But sometimes, the guy—it's always the guy—gets up in our face and tries to bully us out of the restaurant. It's at that point we politely remind him that we're the ones with the camera, and we're not afraid to use it. Seems to work.

But at Fleur de Lys, the situation was reversed. Not only did a *woman* confront us, she virtually begged that we interview her . . . *and her date!!!* Then she volunteered their married/not married status . . . *on camera!!!!* She followed it up by insisting her date sign our legal release allowing their images to be shown on TV. Hey, we knew the French have different rules about this stuff, but does that extend to a French restaurant?

Did the pair make it on air? Well, they might not have been too discreet, but we will be.

so many tears, seemed impossible. Customers with long-standing reservations were contacted, but some never got the word and showed up anyway. They left with a signed copy of Keller's cookbook. For nearly a year, architects designed and builders built. Phones rang constantly.

Fortunately, one item that survived the blaze was the chef's extensive dossier on customers. Since Keller started at the restaurant in 1986, he had kept cards with handwritten notes listing regulars' likes and dislikes, their dining partners, and their preferred wines. He estimates the file numbered several thousand cards.

Fleur de Lys reopened in mid-August 2002. Even more opulent than before, it still featured its signature harem-like tent over the dining room reminiscent of the inside of an *I Dream of Jeannie* bottle. Keller's menu returned (slightly updated), as did most of the staff. The glowing reviews quickly followed, along with the customers. The place is packed most nights, and once again it's a restaurant that knows success.

Roasted Maine Lobster, Artichoke Purée, and Citrus Salad

ADAPTED FROM FLEUR DE LYS,
SAN FRANCISCO, CALIFORNIA

MAKES 4 SERVINGS

Artichoke Purée:

4 artichokes
1 lemon, cut in half
2 tablespoons cream
Salt and freshly ground black pepper to taste

Roasted Lobsters:

3 tablespoons white wine vinegar
1 bouquet garni
2 (about 1½-pound) live lobsters
1 tablespoon unsalted butter, melted
Salt and freshly ground black pepper to taste

Citrus Salad:

1 orange, peeled and segmented
1 lime, peeled and segmented

1 green onion, white only, minced
¼ teaspoon olive oil
Salt and freshly ground pepper to taste

Citrus Sauce:

1 cup freshly squeezed orange juice
3 tablespoons unsalted butter
Salt and freshly ground pepper to taste
Chervil for garnish

To prepare Artichoke Purée: Bring a large saucepan of water to a boil. To prepare artichokes, cut off stems and thorny tips of leaves. Trim bottom so none of the hard green skin remains. As you work, rub the cut portions of artichokes with lemon to prevent discoloration. Place trimmed artichokes in the boiling water, and cook until tender when pierced with a knife, about 20 to 30 minutes. Remove from the boiling water, drain, and let cool. When artichokes have cooled, scoop out chokes with a teaspoon and slice hearts.

Bring cream to a boil in a small saucepan. Add sliced artichoke hearts, season with salt and pepper, and boil for 3 minutes, stirring gently. Transfer the mix to a blender and purée until very smooth. Transfer into a small saucepot.

To prepare lobsters: Bring 1½ gallons salted water to a boil in a large stockpot. Add vinegar, bouquet garni, and lobsters, head first. Cover tightly with a lid, and cook for 9 minutes. Remove lobsters and let cool. Break lobsters in two where the tail meets the body. Using scissors, cut the underside of the tails and remove meat in one piece. Split each lobster tail lengthwise. Break off claws, crack shells, and remove meat. Lightly butter a small sauté pan, and lay lobster meat in the pan. Brush lobster meat with butter, and season lightly with salt and pepper.

To prepare salad: Cut orange and lime segments into 4 or 5 pieces. Transfer to a small mixing bowl or cup; add green onion, olive oil, salt, and pepper. Mix gently.

To prepare sauce: In a small saucepot, boil orange juice until reduced by half. Lower the heat and whisk in butter a few pieces at a time. Season with salt and pepper and keep warm.

To assemble the dish: Preheat the oven to 375°F.

Place lobster and the plates in the oven for 3 minutes, to warm. Heat artichoke purée, and spoon a mound of purée in the center of each serving plate. Spoon sauce around the mounds. Place half a tail and a claw on the top of each purée mound. Lightly spoon citrus salad, over each serving and garnish with chervil. Serve immediately.

Pelican Inn
10 Pacific Way
Muir Beach, CA 94965
(415) 383-6000
www.pelicaninn.com

Jill might be biased on this one because it was just steps away from the Inn on Muir Beach where she got engaged. How could the moonlight cascading on the rough and rocky Pacific Ocean coast not make for the perfect setting for a breathtaking proposal?

Whether you come here to pop the question or just to rest and relax, this area of Northern California will bring out the romantic in you. The Pelican Inn is steeped in old world elegance, yet it's only 20 minutes from the Golden Gate Bridge. Each room in this bed and breakfast is unique and offers its own charm. Guests who stay the night are treated to a traditional English breakfast: eggs, bangers (British slang for sausages), bacon, and broiled tomatoes.

However, anyone can come dine for lunch or dinner in the restaurant. It's no surprise that they feature English specialties like prime rib and Yorkshire pudding, cottage pies, and lots of good draught beers and European wines.

The Pelican Inn is a good place to relax, unwind, and possibly pop a *certain* question. In case you're wondering: Jill said yes.

The Palo Alto Creamery Downtown
(formerly the Peninsula Fountain and Grill)
566 Emerson Street
Palo Alto, CA 94301
(650) 323-3131

The Palo Alto Creamery at Stanford
Stanford Shopping Center
180 El Camino
Palo Alto, CA 94304
(650) 327-3141

During the boom of the 1990s, Silicon Valley dot-commers sat in the booths of this landmark restaurant and shook hands over deals written on napkins. These days customers pretty much just use the napkins to wipe the egg off their faces.

The Creamery has seen a lot of changes since it opened in 1923—except when it comes to their renowned milkshakes: shakes so rich and creamy they're better enjoyed with a spoon than a straw. One customer, Ormand McGill, was here on the first day the restaurant opened and *still* comes in for his favorite, mocha chip. The place sells up to 500 shakes a day.

The Creamery's décor got stuck some time in the 1950s. There's even an old jukebox that we're sure still plays Elvis and Perry Como. The menu fits right: chilidogs, burgers, and tuna melts. But it also offers more stylish dishes like Caribbean French Toast (breakfast is very popular here) or New England Lobster Rolls.

If nothing, the Creamery is a study of contrasts with such nostalgic offers as "The Bubbly Burger." It costs $150.75. Why so expensive? Because it comes with a bottle of Dom Perignon champagne, a throwback to the glorious old dot-com deal-making days in the 1990s.

California

New England Lobster Roll

ADAPTED FROM THE PENINSULA FOUNTAIN AND
GRILL, PALO ALTO, CALIFORNIA

MAKES 4 SERVINGS

1 pound cooked lobster claw and knuckle meat,
    drained and shredded
½ cup finely diced celery
Juice of ½ lemon
¾ cup mayonnaise
½ teaspoon white pepper
4 hot dog buns, toasted

Lightly toss together lobster, celery, lemon juice,
mayonnaise, and white pepper in a medium bowl until
mixed. Place one-quarter of mixture into each bun.

Naughty Dawg Saloon and Grill

255 North Lake Boulevard
Tahoe City, CA 96143
(530) 581-3294
www.thenaughtydawg.com

Every dog gets to have its day here at this dog
lover's den. Cat owners, beware: Leave your
feline friends behind. At the Naughty Dawg,
canine companions drink free (as is evidenced
by the many dog dishes full of water on the
patio), while owners (or in politically correct
terms "pet guardians") rack up a tab drinking
dog-a-ritas. Yep, here you drink your margaritas
out of a giant dog bowl. There's also the "lush
puppy"—a mix of amaretto, Southern Comfort,
orange and pineapple juices, and dark rum.

The food is basic pub grub: burgers, salads,
fish tacos, and wings. And although there is no
"dog food" on the menu, most people just order
regular food for their pooch (remember, this is
Lake Tahoe, where the fat cats . . . err, should we
say, top dogs . . . hang out).

A word of warning: Look out for the shotski.
It's an actual ski with shot glasses attached. You
and your friends line up, each in front of a glass
(while Waldo and Lassie look on shaking their
heads in dismay), and on the count of three, you
lift the ski toward you and down the drinks. A
word to the wise: Too many of these and your
dog will be leading you home and putting *you* in
the doghouse for a night.

Swiss Lakewood Restaurant and Lodge

5055 West Lake Boulevard (Highway 89 South)
Homewood, CA 96141
(530) 525-5211
www.swisslakewood.com

Think Hansel and Gretel meet Heidi's Alpine
cottage, with Goldilocks in the distance looking for a good meal and place to rest. No matter which fairy tale you like best, a visit to the
Swiss Lakewood Lodge will transport you to a
fantasyland, where you may feel you can stay
young forever.

Working Like a Dog

I have to confess that I'm a huge
cat fan. I carry pictures of my two
cats, Katie and Draino, with me on the
road. So I naturally felt like I was betraying
their confidence by going to an "all-dog" place
in Tahoe. I felt so guilty that I decided to work
Katie and Draino into the piece for *The Best
Of*. We began the setup with cameraman Chris
Peterson focusing on me at home talking to
the cats, explaining to them that I was going to
a place that only allows dogs. Our attempts to
get the cats to "react" on camera was an exercise in futility and a confirmation of how difficult it is to train these feline friends.

Six hours later, I looked like something the
cat dragged in. Completely exhausted, with
cat treats, catnip, and an array of cat toys
spread out all over my apartment, Chris had
gotten only six shots that would work. Suffice
it to say, Katie and Draino got their 15 *seconds*
of fame, and I learned to never let the cat out
of the bag again.

California

It's a hidden treasure, nestled in the woods on Lake Tahoe's magical west shore. They serve up French Continental cuisine with a bit of Swiss influence, like their famous Spaetzle (German dumplings). Try the grilled leg of venison with glazed chestnuts and balsamic vinegar, topped with a lingonberry sauce. Those spaetzle dumplings come with it.

One tip: If you go wandering around in the woods surrounding the restaurant, it's a good idea to drop breadcrumbs behind.

———

Plumpjack Squaw Valley Inn

1920 Squaw Valley Road
Olympic Valley, CA 96146
(530) 583-1576 or (800) 323-7666
www.plumpjack.com

The staff here joke that on day one, the frazzled business person pulls up with luggage, cell phone, laptop, spouse, and maybe a kid or two, ready to have a "working" family vacation. The first couple days, he/she continuously calls the front desk, asking for faxes and messages, as the annoyed spouse and impatient children carry on in the background. But by about day three, the illusory presence of Jack Falstaff takes hold . . .

He's the merry and rather plump Shakespearean character from *Henry IV* whom Queen Elizabeth nicknamed Plumpjack. She so loved this roguish character that she asked the Bard to write another play in which Jack would fall in love. Shakespeare answered her with *The Merry Wives of Windsor*.

At any rate, the influence of Plumpjack (a.k.a. Jack Falstaff) on the guests at this Squaw Valley establishment is not to be underestimated. Once they disconnect from their frenetic world and enter his, they begin to breathe, their muscles relax, and they open their eyes to a 4,000-acre playground that surrounds them. It forces even the most stressed person to "chill out."

This great escape is where the 1960 Olympics were held, and guests can still take advantage of the world-class skiing in the winter. In the summer, biking and hiking trails await, along with a refreshing outdoor pool and a nearby river you can float down. One of the best things about it: Although it *is* expensive, the place is *not* pretentious. Rooms are lovely, done in slightly whimsical medieval décor, but not overdone. The dining room certainly serves up some of the finest food around: seared Alaskan halibut, bourbon-brined pork chop, and Dungeness crabcakes, but the après-ski attitude keeps the atmosphere light.

Their motto: Eat, drink, and be merry. Jack would most definitely approve.

———

Heavenly Mountain Resort Catering

Heavenly Ski Lodge
Wildwood and Saddle Streets
South Lake Tahoe, CA 96150
(530) 542-5153-catering
(800) 692-2246-lodge
www.skiheavenly.com

You've heard of the stairway to heaven? Well, this is the chairlift version—to the same place. At Heavenly Ski Lodge, you truly are closer to the heavens at 9,000 feet up. But you can take your divine experience a step further.

Heavenly Mountain's caterers will do a "picnic in the pines" for you. This isn't your average picnic. With at least a 3-day notice and several hundred dollars, you can find yourself feasting on filet mignon and stuffed salmon, as you feast your eyes on the incredible view looking down onto Lake Tahoe.

No Wrong Turn Here

Right off one of the chairlifts at Heavenly Mountain, at more than 10,000 feet up, you're faced with a choice: You can ski down the mountain on the California side or on the Nevada side. Whichever route you choose, there are surprises around every corner.

When our crew was taping, we went down the California side and came across a couple who had just gotten married on the mountain. The newlyweds were about to take their first plunge as husband and wife down the slopes of paradise. However, they didn't get very far. Just after taking off, the groom took a dive and wiped out. He was fine, but we were glad we refrained from telling the couple to "break a leg."

Caterers carve out the chairs and table in the snow (think open-air igloo) in a secluded spot for you and your sweetie. Fresh cut flowers, silverware, and a personal waiter are all at your beck and call. No need to refrigerate the wine up here. It just chills out in the snow. Good thing is, you can do the same. Sit back, snuggle up, and soak it all in.

We think it's fair to call this a picnic in paradise.

Wilderness Lodge

Royal Gorge Cross Country Ski Resort
9411 Hillside Drive
Soda Springs, CA 95728
(800) 500-3871
www.royalgorge.com
(Open December through March)

In spite of its civilized-sounding address, the *only* way to get to Wilderness Lodge is by sleigh, a 3-mile journey from the trailhead on Hillside Drive. However, once you arrive, the first thing you need to do is listen, and listen closely. What you'll hear is the sound of getting away from everything. The sound of serenity coupled with the sound of fresh snow crunching under your skis is your cue that you've changed from stress-buster to trail-buster.

Covering 9,000 acres, the Royal Gorge Cross Country Ski Resort is the largest cross-country ski resort in North America. The great thing is, even though it's a popular destination, you can still enjoy the solitude that surrounds this vast

area. At times, you'll think you're the only one on the trail.

After a full day of exploring, Wilderness Lodge is a perfect cozy retreat. Breakfast and lunch are served buffet style, and dinner is a sit-down, full-service meal. Keep in mind the menu is limited to two to three choices, but they're good choices like fresh fish, filet mignon, and prime rib. In others words: hearty foods to fill you up because you gotta be ready to hit the trails for their guided night ski.

Rainbow Lodge

50080 Hampshire Rocks Road
Soda Springs, CA 95728
(530) 426-3661 or (800) 500-3871
www.royalgorge.com

While shooting at Wilderness Lodge, we also did a segment at their sister place, Rainbow Lodge. Although you can drive* to this one, avid skiers often take the challenge and cross-country ski the 22 kilometers (13 miles) from Wilderness Lodge. Talk about working up an appetite! But you'll want one here. French and California cuisine are the specialties and are bound to fill you up.

Be sure to check out the pictures that adorn the walls. Many of them date back to the 1860s and tell the compelling—almost unbelievable—story of how the railroad was built over the treacherous Donner Pass. Equally hard to digest is the Donner Party story.

No Gold at the End of This Rainbow

Starvation aside, the Donner Pass was also a favorite stop for gold miners. Legend has it that back in the 1800s a card game here turned ugly. The winnings were buried somewhere on the property. I decided to seek out the treasure while taping here but came up empty handed. My advice: Instead of going home with full pockets, go home with a full stomach. There might be a pot of gold to be found at the end of this rainbow, but for now, your treasure will have to come in the form of a full plate.

During the winter of 1846–1847, a group of more than 80 people was attempting to make it over the dangerous mountain pass. They were trapped in a heavy snowstorm, and more than half the party froze to death. Many of those who were still alive resorted to cannibalism to survive. Nice thought as you're eating, huh?

The irony is, Rainbow Lodge serves some of the best fare around. The mushroom streudel is especially yummy. So dig in and let someone else worry about how to "dig out" of those snow-covered mountains.

*To get to Rainbow Lodge, this is all you need to know: Drive on I-80 to Rainbow Road. Then, exit to Rainbow Lodge. The mailing address will do you no good. The phone number is the same as Wilderness Lodge.

Le Petit Pier

7238 North Lake Boulevard
Tahoe Vista, CA 96148
(530) 546-4464
www.lepetitpier.com

Le Petit Pier, which has helped to toast countless milestones in its quarter century in business, is *the* place in the region to go for a special occasion, celebration or simply an elegant evening. From the fine French food to the stunning view of Lake Tahoe on one side and Mount Tallac rising up 11,000 feet on the other, you won't be disappointed. However, keep this in mind: While the name means *small* pier in French, if you're looking to celebrate in a *big* way, then you better have a *big* budget to go along with it.

Ciudad

445 South Figueroa Street
Los Angeles, CA 90071
(213) 486-5171
www.millikenandfeniger.com

Mary Sue Milliken said it best. "We gave the restaurant a name no one can pronounce, and put it in downtown L.A., where nobody goes."

Tahoe Trivia

If you want to be the Cliff Claven (the know-it-all of television's *Cheers*) of your party, here are some stats we learned while shooting at Le Petit Pier:

- Lake Tahoe is one of the clearest lakes in the world! You can see 70 feet down.
- From the edge of the lake, right below the restaurant, the peaks in the distance look a few miles away. But because the view is so crisp and clear, you'll be surprised to know there's actually 22 miles of water separating you. That's the same distance as the English Channel.
- The sun shines at Lake Tahoe 75 percent of the year, or 274 days. Even more reason to visit!

Here's a toast to French dining and "cheers" to Cliff.

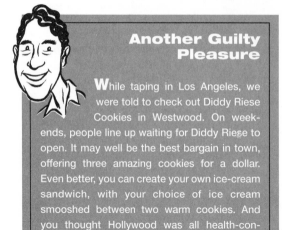

Another Guilty Pleasure

While taping in Los Angeles, we were told to check out Diddy Riese Cookies in Westwood. On weekends, people line up waiting for Diddy Riese to open. It may well be the best bargain in town, offering three amazing cookies for a dollar. Even better, you can create your own ice-cream sandwich, with your choice of ice cream smooshed between two warm cookies. And you thought Hollywood was all health-conscious. You can find Diddy Riese at 926 Broxton Avenue, 310-208-0448. Enjoy!

Don't worry about Milliken and her business partner, Susan Feniger. They're doing just fine. They're better know as the feisty "Too Hot Tamales," famous chefs, restaurant owners, authors, and media personalities. Ciudad, one of their many endeavors, is a festive restaurant that features authentic dishes from all over Latin America.

The restaurant, which is often packed (lunch: Monday–Friday, dinner: Nightly), is doing its part to revitalize downtown L.A. Appropriately, Ciudad (pronounced: *see-oo-DAHD*) means "city" in Spanish.

California

If you can't find Pink's as you whiz by in your car, just look for the lines of customers.

photo courtesy of Pink's

Pink's

709 North La Brea Boulevard
Los Angeles, CA 90038
(323) 931-4223 (sorry, no telephone orders)
www.pinkshollywood.com

Pink's is, quite simply, one of the best places to eat in Los Angeles. Naturally, everyone who hears that statement has the same reaction. Their noses scrunch up, and the rest of their facial features contort into a big question mark as they think to themselves, *A hot dog stand? You have to be kidding!*

Then they try it. Debate over.

Pink's has been at the corner of Melrose Avenue and La Brea Boulevard since 1939. Founder Paul Pink started by selling hot dogs out of a pushcart, and despite the depression, his business grew . . . into a shack. The old place hasn't changed much, even though Pink's has become the most famous hot dog stand in the country.

If you can't see the shack as you whiz by in your car, just look for the line. If Pink's is open (until 2 A.M. weeknights/3 A.M. on weekends), people will be waiting. It's all very democratic, with tourists standing next to corporate suits who are next to celebrities. The owners say Bruce Willis proposed to Demi Moore while they were in line. A small seating area inside is filled with pictures of other famous Pink's devotees.

The chili dog is the most popular item on the menu, but Pink's offers more than 30 different types of hot dogs.

Pink's doesn't take credit cards, so bring cash. Tums wouldn't hurt, either.

Arturo's Puffy Taco

15693 Leffingwell Road
Whittier, CA 90604
(562) 947-2250

If you want to forget the chic Hollywood dining experience, head out of La-La Land and into this hole-in-the-wall taco stand. Look for the truckers who make this a regular stop on their route. Why *Puffy* Taco? Watch what happens when they take your flat flour tortilla and toss it into a vat of hot oil. Then watch what happens when you take a bite. Uh-huh. There's a reason you should eat them outside, on the sidewalk, while standing up and leaning over. The ground beef and cheese, mixed up with the tomatoes, lettuce, and salsa might decorate your shirt in a way you didn't expect.

Chef Franco's at the William L. Morris Dealership

1024 Ventura Street
Fillmore, CA 93015
(805) 524-2619

Even in car-crazy California, Chef Franco's goes the extra mile. By day, the location is the William L. Morris Chevrolet dealership. But at night, Chef Franco Onorato sets up tables and serves Italian food right on the showroom floor.

Unique doesn't quite capture it. Imagine diners sitting among the Camaros feasting on Chicken Parmesan. Or order your Lasagna

In the Pink

Pink's hot dogs have been made by the same company, Hoffy, since the beginning. They're all-beef and have a natural casing that makes the dogs pop when you first bite into them.

Pink's claims that the late actor/director Orson Welles, who ate 18 at one sitting, holds their hot dog-eating record. Otherwise, Welles was the picture of health.

My personal favorites include the bacon burrito dog (two hot dogs, cheese, bacon, chili, and onions wrapped up in a giant soft tortilla) and the 12-inch jalapeño dog, which has the hot peppers cooked *inside* the dog itself.

California

California

loaded with options. Try to conjure up the scent of garlic blending with the "new car" smell. In short, this is one-stop shopping for wheeling and *mealing*.

During our taping, one customer actually bought his third truck while dining.

Onorato has been in the driver's seat since 2000, when he first approached the dealership about letting him prepare dinners in their in-house snack shop. When it comes to portion size, there's no economy or mid-size. Everything the chef prepares is a big as an Impala.

So buckle up and put the pedal to the metal for the 60-mile trip outside Los Angeles to Chef Franco's. We wouldn't steer you wrong.

Chicken alla Padulese

ADAPTED FROM CHEF FRANCO'S AT THE WILLIAM L. MORRIS DEALERSHIP, FILLMORE, CALIFORNIA

MAKES 4 SERVINGS

4 boneless, skinless chicken breasts
1 cup all-purpose flour
2 tablespoons olive oil
1 clove garlic, chopped
1 cup tomato sauce
½ cup heavy cream
1 tablespoon chopped fresh oregano leaves
20 fresh basil leaves
Salt and freshly ground black pepper to taste
Cooked pasta to serve
Grated Parmesan cheese for garnish

Preheat the oven to 350°F.

Coat chicken in flour, shaking off any excess. Heat oil in a large skillet over medium heat. Add chicken, and sauté until golden brown, turning once. Set aside to drain on paper towels.

Add garlic to the skillet, and sauté until golden. Add tomato sauce, cream, oregano, and basil. Season with salt and pepper. Bring sauce to a boil, and remove from the heat.

Place chicken breasts in a baking dish, and cover with sauce. Bake for about 10 minutes, until cooked through. Serve with your favorite pasta, and garnish with Parmesan cheese.

The Gumbo Pot

Los Angeles Farmers Market
6333 West Third Street #312, at Fairfax
Los Angeles, CA 90036
(323) 933-0358
www.thegumbola.com

The original Los Angeles Farmers Market is one of the most popular destinations in the city, and with more than 110 merchants and stalls, you can spend hours here shopping and eating.

The market is located across from CBS Television City, where *The Price Is Right* is taped. On any given morning, you can see dozens of contestant-wannabes in their "Pick Me Bob!" T-shirts scarfing down an early bite and loading up on coffee in hopes that the java jolt will give them just the advantage to be called to "Come on down!"

The market opened in 1934 as in informal meeting place for area farmers. It grew to the point where its slogan, "Meet me at 3rd and Fairfax," became L.A. shorthand for a Farmers Market rendezvous. Legend has it that Walt Disney sat at the market's outdoor tables designing Disneyland and James Dean ate his last breakfast there before climbing into his Porsche and driving off into oblivion.

One of the most popular stands at the market is The Gumbo Pot. Opened in 1986, it was one of the first places in the city to feature New Orleans delicacies at reasonable prices. The gumbo, jambalaya, and fresh catfish are standouts on a menu that features more than 40 items. The Gumbo Pot is so authentic, a jazz band performs every Thursday night, and thousands of people show up for its annual Mardi Gras street party.

Just in case you want to spice up your dish (not that it's necessary), there's a small shop next door that sells more than 300 types of hot sauce.

Sweet Lady Jane

8360 North Melrose Avenue
Los Angeles, CA 90069
(323) 653-7145

She might be a baker, but Jane Lockhart doesn't sugarcoat her response when customers ask about prices. She says she's expensive. In fact, her exact words are "I'm very straight up. When people ask 'how come you're so expensive?' we say, we're probably *the most expensive* bakery in Los Angeles. But we're proud of it because we know we're giving quality."

Open since 1988, Lockhart is famous for hand-painting designs on cakes. Another popular cake features real roses inserted in and around the entire creation. Everything in her small West Hollywood shop is done by hand, right down to cutting the fruit for tarts.

Lockhart is a former hospital worker who used to bake for her co-workers. Their raves helped her build a clientele (Halle Berry and John Lithgow are celebrity regulars)—and gave her enough confidence to open her own business.

Sweet Lady Jane doesn't cut corners, and she proudly won't cut prices.

Pacific Dining Car

1310 West Sixth Street
Los Angeles, CA 90017
(213) 483-6000

2700 Wilshire Boulevard
Santa Monica, CA 90403
(310) 453-4000
www.pacificdiningcar.com

The Pacific Dining Car isn't your father's type of steak house. No, this place has been around so long, it's more like your grandfather's.

Opened in 1921, the landmark restaurant resembles an antique railroad car, right down to the wingback chairs and plush booths. With its maze of dining rooms and subtle lighting, the place just *seems* dark, even in the afternoon.

"And the Winner Is . . ."

Plenty of celebrities eat at the Pacific Dining Car, but the place also had its own taste of fame in the movie *Training Day*. In a scene shot in the downtown restaurant, shady police officials discuss the likely demise of the character played by Denzel Washington. The actor won an Oscar for the role. And the Pacific Dining Car? Not even a Cable Ace nomination for its later appearance in an episode of *The Best Of*.

This is one destination in image-conscious L.A. where people go *not* to be seen.

When it comes to steak houses, "old school" works. The Dining Car invests considerable time and money to employ its own in-house butcher. Its steaks are dry aged on-site, in a temperature-controlled locker, for about a month and a half. The process creates a thick protective shell that seals in flavor, but it also means the butcher has to chop off and throw out a lot of meat. Good steaks don't come cheap.

There's an urban legend in L.A. that the Pacific Dining Car can close unexpectedly. The story stems from the early days before air conditioning when founder Fred Cook would shut down in the summer. He was famous for putting out a rather provocative sign for the times that read, "Too D. hot for L.A. Gone fishing. Why the H. don't you go, too?"

These days: The downtown restaurant never closes. In fact, no one could find the keys during our visit. A second location in Santa Monica is open from 6 A.M. to 2 A.M. daily.

California

Koi

730 North La Cienega Boulevard
Los Angeles, CA 90069
(310) 659-9449
www.koirestaurant.com

If you read the gossip pages, then you've read about Koi. On most nights, a Hollywood A-lister can probably be found doing *something* at this chic New Asian restaurant, often to have it reported on days later. The most notable occurrence might have been when reality-TV mom and talk show host Sharon Osbourne got into a brawl with a Tinseltown talent agent. The police had to be called. But whether it's the *National Enquirer* reporting on George Clooney meeting a gorgeous TV anchorwoman, or the *Star* disclosing a date between Leonardo DiCaprio and supermodel Gisele Bundchen, the location is the same: Koi.

On the night our crew taped there, a pre-rehab Jack Osbourne partied with a date, movie megastar Sidney Poitier dined with his family in a back dining room, and fading TV actress Nicolette Sheridan kept looking over at Marc's table, probably wondering why the executive chef was spending so much time with this nobody.

A little behind-the-scenes: There are two booths in the main dining room set aside for stars. Officially, they're called tables #20 and #21. Look for them against the wall, not far behind the hostess stand. Then, there are five more celebri-tables (#100 through #105) in another dining area called the Back Patio. Of those, the bigger names get to sit in the middle, more desirable booths, #102 and #103.

The real ink should deal with the menu: Delicacies like uni risotto with seared Japanese scallops and truffle vinaigrette taste like Asian comfort food. There's also a large sushi bar.

If you visit Koi, ask for a good seat—and stay out of the tabloids.

Warm Baby Spinach and Mushroom Salad with Ponzu Dressing

ADAPTED FROM KOI, LOS ANGELES, CALIFORNIA

MAKES 4 SERVINGS

1/4 cup ponzu sauce
1 tablespoon grated, peeled daikon radish
1/2 teaspoon sesame oil
1 tablespoon soybean oil
4 ounces button or crimini musrooms, trimmed and cut into 1/8-inch-thick slices
4 ounces shiitake mushrooms, stems discarded and caps cut into 1/8-inch-thick slices
1 (about 3-ounce) package enoki mushrooms, ends trimmed and mushrooms separated
1/2 teaspoon grated, peeled fresh ginger
1/2 teaspoon minced fresh garlic
8 ounces fresh baby spinach leaves
Pinch sesame seeds, toasted
1/4 cup Crispy Shallots (recipe follows)

Not Tabloid Ready

Headline this: NYPD Blue Star Doesn't Nab the Right Man.

Actor Esai Morales plays a cop on TV, but one late night at Koi he was more Clouseau than Kojak. The gregarious *NYPD Blue* star, who also happens to be an investor in the restaurant, was ambling by our table when suddenly he stopped, smiled broadly, and gave a warm welcoming hug—to our photographer, Larry Deal. Larry, who's never seen the actor *or* the ABC drama, politely played along. It wasn't until mid-embrace that Morales realized he had his arms around a complete stranger. After a few awkward moments, he slinked away, leaving us with our minor scoop over the tabloids.

California

Stir together ponzu sauce, daikon, and sesame oil in a large bowl. Set aside.

Heat soybean oil in a large heavy sauté pan over medium-high heat. Add button and shiitake mushrooms, and sauté until they are tender and golden, about 5 minutes (add 1 tablespoon water or dashi if necessary to keep the mixture slightly moist). Add enoki mushrooms, and sauté until just wilted, about 30 seconds. Remove the pan from the heat. Stir in ginger and garlic. Immediately transfer warm mushroom mixture to ponzu sauce mixture. Add spinach, and toss to coat.

Mound salad in the center of 4 plates, dividing equally and surrounding salad with any extra mushroom slices. Sprinkle sesame seeds over salad, sprinkle with shallots, and serve immediately.

Crispy Shallots

MAKES ABOUT 1 CUP

3 to 4 shallots, very thinly sliced (almost shaved)
Soybean oil for deep-frying

Rinse shallots in a fine mesh strainer under running cold water. Drain well. Using a clean kitchen towel (not terry cloth), wring shallots until very dry.

Heat oil in a large, heavy saucepan to 350°F. Add shallots to oil, in small batches, and fry until golden but still limp, about 1 minute. Shallots will continue to brown and will become crisp as they cool.

Using a slotted spoon, transfer shallots to paper towels to drain.

Katana

8439 West Sunset Boulevard
West Hollywood, CA 90069
(323) 650-8585
www.katanarobata.com

One thought comes to mind as you make your way through Katana: *Did a convention of beautiful people just let out someplace?* Opened in 2002, the restaurant was officially put on the map when Hollywood royal couple Brad Pitt and Jennifer Aniston booked it for a party. Located

Only in Hollywood

So many people showed up when Katana first held job interviews that the line stretched out onto the Strip. Given the restaurant's location in the Miramax office building, many thought it was a casting call for a movie. Some hopeful actors actually showed up with their glossy headshots.

on sexy Sunset Strip in the heart of West Hollywood, there's never a shortage of stars nearby. *American Idol*'s Ryan Seacrest is among the celebrity investors. There's so much name-dropping at Katana, you could injure your foot.

Katana features sushi and a full Asian-style menu, but the spotlight is on its Robata-yaki cuisine. The word means "open flame cooking" in Japanese. Chefs use a specially imported wood that burns red hot to prepare small dishes, kind of like Japanese tapas. The cooking is out in the open, right off a main dining room. The process is so fascinating to watch, it's enough to make you take your eyes off all the beautiful people—well, almost.

Real Food Daily

414 North La Cienega Boulevard
Los Angeles, CA 90048
(310) 289-9910

514 Santa Monica Boulevard
Santa Monica, CA 90401
(310) 451-7544

242 South Beverly Drive
Beverly Hills, CA 90212
(310) 858-0880
www.realfood.com

It's not hard to find health food in Los Angeles, but it is hard to find a place that is 100 percent vegan with 90 percent of their produce certified

California

organic. That means no animal-derived dishes, meat, fish, eggs, or dairy of any kind—sounds like a fad that's no fun, right? Wrong.

The place came about by chance. Owner Ann Gentry, a vegetarian for more than 20 years, moved to L.A. to jump-start her acting career. To earn money on the side, a friend of hers talked her into doing a catering job for actor Danny DeVito. He was looking for someone to cook healthy, vegetarian dishes. When she went to meet him, she says she "fibbed her way into establishing herself as a caterer." He bought her act, and she spent the next few months cooking for him on the set of *Throw Momma from the Train*. It was during that time she realized cooking was something she was really good at and loved to do. She gave up on her pursuit of acting and started a home-delivery service called Real Food Daily. A few years later, in 1993, she opened the first permanent location in Santa Monica. The second location in West Hollywood followed in 1998, and a third one opened in Beverly Hills in 2003.

Try their "wheat meat." It's like a Salisbury steak made with Saitan, which is a mix of gluten flour, wheat flour, and spices. It's blended with filtered water, organic soy sauce, and canola oil, then shaped into a loaf and steamed. They marinate it in a mustard sauce and bake it in the oven.

Check out their beverage bar at the West Hollywood location. All the drinks are 100 percent organic. There are no pesticides or chemical residues on any of their fruits or vegetables. They even carry organic wine, beer, and sake.

And get this: They don't have a microwave in any of their stores.

Interested in going macrobiotic? You can do that here, too, by ordering their "Real Food Meals." To splurge, try their desserts. Hard to believe there is no processed sugar in them. A lot of the sweetness comes from things like coconut and fresh or dried fruit, maple syrup, and maple sugar.

No matter what you're into—organic, vegetarian, vegan, or macrobiotic—this place has great-tasting food. 100 percent real. 100 percent good.

Ḱ Chocolatier

9606 Little Santa Monica Boulevard
Beverly Hills, CA 90210
(310) 248-2626
www.dkron.com

Some women can't live without it. Others insist on taking it on their honeymoon. Movie stars are pouring in by the droves to buy it. What is it? Ksensual. It's a little morsel of chocolate that owner Diane Krön says does more than just melt in your mouth. Intrigued? Read on.

Temptress Diane opened this little shop in the heart of Beverly Hills after she and her husband sold their chocolate business in New York City. They moved to California to retire, but past customers kept begging them to go back in business. Diane eventually decided to make a go of it herself, although her husband is now a regular customer.

What some of her chocolates do is too risqué to print. As for the others . . .

Try the whipped milk chocolate with powdered hazelnut inside. It evaporates on your tongue. Her truffles made with her exquisite cocoa beans will send you into orbit. Wanna fire your shrink? Just have the vodka chocolates. They're actually filled with a shot of Ketel One Vodka. All your worries will melt away. (It's true—some psychiatrists in the area send their patients here . . . and probably drive themselves out of business!)

But back to the "one," the Ksensual, said to have orgasmic qualities. Three different cocoa beans are roasted three different ways. They're mixed with 15 different herbs like matrimony vine fruit, horny goat weed, and hare's ear root. What happens from the synergy of the herb combined with the chocolate is what Diane terms, "a wake-up call of bliss in your body," one that will boost your libido.

It might also be a wake-up call for your wallet. They're pretty pricey. A box of 14 tasty morsels costs about $50, but it does come complete with instructions. You're supposed to have one after lunch and one after dinner, with either a warm drink or a glass of wine. An entire box produces seven "happy endings."

California

Talk about a prescription for pleasure and a true sinful sweet!

———

The Cheese Store of Beverly Hills

419 North Beverly Drive
Beverly Hills, CA 90210
(310) 278-2855 or (800) 547-1515
www.cheesestorebh.com

Music is Norbert Wabnig's passion. So much so, he dreamed of hitting the big time and seeing his name in lights. But fate had something else in mind. As he puts it, "I came to California to become a hit songwriter, and I did so well that I slice cheese for a living." Doesn't sound too glamorous, huh? But wait until you walk into his store in the heart of Beverly Hills. As soon as you breathe in, you'll know he's not selling just any old cheese. Well, actually some of it is quite old. This is special cheese from all over the world. So are his clients. Although he won't kiss and tell, he admits that many of Hollywood's A-list are frequent visitors. (Norbert will also mail order just about anything, whether you're an A-list celeb or not.)

This store has been around since 1967, but it's been in Norbert's hands since 1978. He sells more than 600 types of cheeses, along with all kinds of gourmet goodies like jams, jellies, truffles, wines, balsamic vinegars, olives, and unique oils that he gets from all over the world. It's fair to say that Norbert has found celebrity in a way he never imagined—as a cheese man to the stars, cheese connoisseur, and owner of this great shop.

The best thing? When he gets sick of selling cheese, he runs upstairs and pounds out a few notes on his piano. Cheers to cheese and to the man who marches to the beat of his own drum.

———

Pedals Café

Shutters on the Beach
One Pico Boulevard
Santa Monica, CA 90405
(310) 458-0030-hotel
(310) 587-1707-restaurant
www.shuttersonthebeach.com

When you hang out near this happenin' hotel in Santa Monica, be on the lookout. No, not for purse snatchers, but for celebrities! Star sightings abound in this area. (When we were there shooting, we saw David Hyde Pierce from *Frasier* taking a brisk walk on the beach.)

Shutters on the Beach is a glorious hotel that is just fancy enough to make you feel special, yet casual enough to make you feel like "Yeah, I'm a regular just hanging out here in hip L.A. talking about the projects I want to do."

At any rate, dining at Pedals Café, the more casual of the hotel's two restaurants, is the perfect place to have those "meetings" or just hang out with friends. They're known mostly for their pasta plates, but the menu is varied. If you can't snag a seat alfresco under the stars (guess your "project" wasn't big enough), don't worry. Nearly every seat inside has a view of the ocean. Just think, you can watch the sun set over the Pacific and let it inspire you for your next Hollywood "project."

———

Geoffrey's/Malibu

27400 Pacific Coast Highway
Malibu, CA 90265
(310) 457-1519
www.geoffreysmalibu.com

Owner Jeff Peterson's life story sounds like the premise for an Aaron Spelling TV series on FOX. A kid from Modesto, California, moves south to Hollywood to model/act/wait tables. He has limited success in the "biz," but his restaurant career takes off. He quickly moves up the ranks from busboy to waiter to general manager, and then incredibly, he puts together a business deal to become owner of one of the most scenic restaurants in star-studded Malibu.

California

California

Now, celebrities and the area's beautiful people flock to Geoffrey's (pronounced *Jah-freeze*) to sit on the terrace overlooking the Pacific and dine on California cuisine. On second thought, forget Aaron Spelling. This could make a great reality show.

Signature dishes include the Fresh Ahi Tuna Tartar appetizer and Sautéed Day Boat Sea Scallops with a Hudson Valley Foie Gras Risotto.

Ahi Tuna Tartar with Caviar and Spicy Ginger Vinaigrette

ADAPTED FROM GEOFFREY'S, MALIBU, CALIFORNIA

MAKES 4 SERVINGS; ABOUT 1½ CUPS VINAIGRETTE

Spicy Ginger Vinaigrette:
¼ cup sesame oil
½ teaspoon chopped garlic
½ teaspoon chopped shallot
½ teaspoon chopped fresh ginger
1 cup sake
½ cup unseasoned rice vinegar
¼ cup soy sauce
⅓ cup brown sugar, or to taste
3 tablespoons cornstarch mixed with 1 tablespoon water

Ahi Tuna Tartar:
1 pound sashimi-grade ahi tuna, finely diced
¼ cup Spicy Ginger Vinaigrette
¼ teaspoon sesame seeds, toasted lightly
¼ teaspoon black sesame seeds
1 avocado, diced
½ cup diced pineapple
Caviar to garnish

To make vinaigrette: In a medium saucepan, heat sesame oil until smoking. Add garlic, shallot, and ginger. Sauté until garlic begins to change color. Add sake, and stir to loosen any bits from the bottom of the pan. Bring to a simmer, and cook until reduced by half. Add vinegar, soy sauce, and brown sugar. Bring to a boil, stirring. Strain into a clean saucepan. Whisk in cornstarch mixture, and cook, stirring, until thickened. Remove from the heat. Chill before using.

Combine tuna, ¼ cup vinaigrette, and toasted and black sesame seeds in a medium bowl. Stir well, and let marinate for 5 minutes. (The remaining vinaigrette can be covered and refrigerated for up to 1 week.)

To serve as they do at the restaurant: Pack the bottoms of 4 open-ended tubes with avocado and pineapple. Top with marinated tuna, and pack tightly. To serve, turn out onto individual plates. It can also be served by layering avocado, pineapple, and tuna on small plates. Garnish with caviar.

Saddle Peak Lodge
419 Cold Canyon Road
Calabasas, CA 91302
(818) 222-3888
www.saddlepeaklodge.com

Just about every restaurant calls itself an oasis, but Saddle Peak Lodge can legitimately make the claim. It's *so* nestled in the rugged Santa Monica Mountains you can literally drive by without seeing it. Spend time inside the hunting lodge–like restaurant, and you'll forget that you're barely a half an hour from hectic Los Angeles.

The secluded location has been a destination for most of a century. It started out as a one-room cabin for cowboys and fishermen, and through the years it has been a Pony Express stop, a snack shop, and even a bordello. The restaurant isn't far from what was once the outdoor set of the television series *M*A*S*H*. Peer over the mountains, and you can almost visualize the helicopters from the show's opening.

Saddle Peak specializes in game—buffalo, venison, and elk. As a not-so-subtle reminder of its culinary specialties, the place is decked out in trophy heads. The décor looks like it could be an elegant version of Teddy Roosevelt's living room but filled with lots of people talking about the kinds of trophies show-biz types go after.

———

Orfila Vineyards

13455 San Pasqual Road
Escondido, CA 92025
(760) 738-6500 or (760) 765-0102 for tastings
www.orfila.com

Nestled in what's known as the "not so famous wine country" of California is a boutique winery run by Leon Santoro, a native Italian who was recruited to this vineyard from the Napa Valley in 1991.

Santoro is passionate about the grapes he grows and the wine he pours. You can tell that by just one sip. He studied chemistry in college and now applies all those bewildering components to his harvest. What comes out of those bottles can truly be called "nectar of the gods," as opposed to a "periodic table," which sounds too scientific.

Although still considered small by many standards—they only put out about 150,000 bottles a year—Orfilia Vineyards is making a big splash on the wine market, having gathered up enough awards to fill many cases of wine. They specialize in Syrah, Sangiovese, and Viognier.

From the 104-foot-long grapevine-covered arbor, you'll have a panoramic view of the San Pasqual Valley. Orfilia doesn't have a regular restaurant, but you can book private functions here, from corporate lunches to weddings.

Keep in mind while you sip that you are tasting history. San Diego is where Spanish explorers planted California's first grape vines more than 200 years ago. And if you have a mind to bring more than a few bottles home with you, you can join Orifilia's wine club and have it shipped pretty much everywhere in the country.

———

Café Sevilla

555 4th Avenue
San Diego, CA 92101
(619) 233-5979

3252 Mission Inn Avenue
Riverside, CA 92507
(909) 778-0611

3050 Pio Pico Road
Carlsbad, CA 92008
(760) 730-7558
www.cafesevilla.com

It's no surprise that Latinos lead the way in one of the hottest restaurant trends: tapas. You'll find the best smack-dab in San Diego's trendy

Practice Makes Perfect . . .

Don't be surprised if the staff at Café Sevilla come around to your table offering wine out of a porron (*pawr-RAWN*)—a glass wine container with a narrow spout that shoots the wine right into your mouth, similar in concept to the leather bota bag from Spain. Whether you can keep up with this steady stream or not is another story. But your best bet to keep spillage at a minimum is to tip your head back slightly. And if at first you don't succeed . . .

Gaslamp district at Café Sevilla, where they get a leg up on these tasty appetizers.

Tapas originated in Spain more than a century ago when innkeepers served travelers their wine along with a piece of bread to cover their glass to keep out the flies. (*Tapas* means "lid" or "cover.") Over time, various toppings such as olives, chorizo, and cheese were added and, *olé*, the modern-day tapas.

Café Sevilla is the perfect place to go with a group of friends and order a range of those delectable tidbits. Share your finger food until you're all full, then go work it off downstairs when the salsa dancing heats up. They give free lessons on many nights, so even if you have two left feet, after some of their famous Sangria, you'll feel as if you have, well, four!

Azzura Point Restaurant

Loews Coronado Bay Resort
4000 Coronado Bay Road
Coronado, CA 92118
(619) 424-4000-hotel
www.loewshotels.com

Maybe it's the Mediterranean ambience or the magnificent view of San Diego and the Coronado Bay Bridge. Or maybe it's the fresh, flavorful California-French cuisine. Whatever the reason, Lowes Coronado Bay Resort, located on a 14-acre peninsula, is one of the top places to visit in the area. If an overnight stay or even dinner aren't in your plans—or budget—at least come for a drink and watch the sun set over the bay. (Although we wouldn't recommend wearing shorts in the restaurant, the attire is "resort-casual.")

Food fresh from the garden to the table is one of the keys to the superb fare. Not only does the staff keep an incredible herb garden where you can stroll, but the chefs are also dedicated to buying local produce from the farmer's market. You can even sign up to go shopping with the chef and get an inside glimpse of what goes into planning a menu. Of course it also encourages

Farm Fresh

We actually shot the segment at Azzura Point for our *Best Of Farmer's Markets* following the Azzura chef around the Coronado Bay Market (1st and B Streets, Coranado, CA 92118, 760-741-3763). It gave us, and viewers, a real glimpse into the way a chef works outside the kitchen. It's like watching an artist with a new palate.

This farmer's market is held year 'round on Tuesdays, rain or shine, from 2:30-6 P.M. If it works for your schedule, we urge you to check it out. Although not a huge market, it is beautiful, right on the water at Ferry's Landing Marketplace. There are also a lot of good restaurants where you can eat lunch.

The other option, of course, is to sit down right on the curb with all your fresh veggies and eat like the farmers do. Now that's what we call "getting in touch with your roots."

people to dine at Azzura Point that night to see and taste the fruits of the chefs' labor.

Oregon

McMenamin's Kennedy School

5736 NE 33rd Avenue
Portland, OR 97211
(503) 249-3983
www.mcmenamins.com

Drinking. Smoking. General debauchery. Each of these vices is punishable by detention at most schools. Get sent to detention at McMenamin's Kennedy School in Portland, however, and you'll actually be rewarded for such nasty behavior.

From 1915 until 1975, Kennedy was just your standard elementary school. But in 1997, pint glasses replaced the pencils, the headmaster was overtaken by a brew master, and suddenly everyone wanted to stay after school. That's when Portland's McMenamin brothers took the dilapidated Kennedy School and transformed it into one of the weirdest trips down memory lane you're likely to take.

Nowadays, inside the old schoolhouse you'll find 35 guestrooms, a restaurant, a movie theater, and several bars. We weren't kidding about detention, either. When Jill visited, she was sent to the detention bar (in the actual detention room) and punished with a flaming Spanish Coffee drink, made with Triple Sec, Kahlua, and coffee. A shot of rum was poured on top, then lit on fire. And you thought you weren't allowed to play with matches in school! Incidentally, the detention bar is one of only two spots at the Kennedy School where smoking *is* allowed.

For all the goody-two-shoes, they have the Honor Bar, a cozy, smoke-free lounge with classical and opera music playing while you sip your wine and pontificate on the meaning of life.

And although there's no smoking in the boys' room, there *is* brewing in the girls' room. Literally. The Kennedy School is also a microbrewery, and the authentically pink-tiled former girls' bathroom is now where you'll find the brew masters creating everything from their Hammerhead Amber to the Terminator Stout to the Ruby (raspberry-flavored) beer. They cover this subject well by having about 10 types of beer on the menu at any time, making this curriculum accessible to everyone.

In the restaurant, nothing goes better with that beer than their famous burgers, including the Communication Breakdown Burger that's topped with sautéed mushrooms, red and green bell peppers, and cheddar cheese. Note, however, this is a school with lots of electives. You can have your choice of sirloin, seafood, and salads in the restaurant, or pizza, pub grub, and beer in the movie theater while watching your favorite flicks on the big screen.

If you decide to spend the night in one of the guest rooms, be prepared for something of a surreal slumber. The rooms are actually old classrooms, complete with original chalkboards and those massive wall clocks that used to tease you as you waited for the final bell. Not to worry, though, because at McMenamin's Kennedy School, you'll be rewarded for sleeping in class, and we guarantee you'll be true to this school. Hangover notwithstanding.

———

Esparza's Tex Mex Cafe
2725 SE Ankeny Street
Portland, OR 97214
(503) 234-7909

What happens when a Texan gets lost up north? When that place is Portland and the Texan is Joe Esparza, you can count on a lot! It all began when Joe and his wife, Martha, vacationed in Oregon. This Texan couple had already been talking about opening a restaurant when they took a wrong turn while visiting Portland and stumbled upon the place that was to become Esparza's.

Joe had been raised by his widowed mother, who taught him how to cook her famous Tex-Mex concoctions. And when he saw the year of his mother's birth, 1916, inscribed in the sidewalk in front of an abandoned building, he felt her spirit speak to him, urging him to follow his dream.

Among the distinctly Texan ingredients that have made their way to the northwest is the prickly pear cactus, which the Esaparzas used to forage for in the desert when they didn't have much else to eat. It is now used in one of their "gourmet" omelets and also as an appetizer, sautéed and served up salty. We think it's the perfect way to start off your meal, along with a margarita, of course.

Expect long lines of loyal customers, all of whom are grateful for Joe's wrong turn. Sometimes you have to get lost to find your way back home.

———

Oregon

At Montage, if there are any leftovers, you'll get them wrapped in the most artistic way imaginable.

photo courtesy of Jeffrey Dey

Oregon

Le Bistro Montage

301 SE Morrison Street
Portland, OR 97214
(503) 234-1324
www.montage.citysearch.com

If you're not one who likes to share a table with a stranger, then this is not the place for you. At Le Bistro Montage, you might end up sitting with the mayor on one side and a lad with green hair—political origin unknown—on the other side.

As the name suggests, this place is one big montage. From the art, to the menu, to the staff and the customers, it's an eclectic mix. From Cajun to comfort food, the crisp white table linens are about the only formal things in the place. Case in point, their mac and cheese which many say is the best in the city.

If you have food left over, you *must* ask for a doggy bag. Most of the waiters are tortured artists, so wrapping up your leftovers becomes a way for them to express themselves.

Wildwood Restaurant

1221 NW 21st Avenue
Portland, OR 97209
(503) 248-9663
www.wildwoodrestaurant.com

"**C**ooking from the source" is how Chef Owner Cory Schrieber describes what he does with the

food he gathers locally for his Wildwood Restaurant. Set in Portland's historic district, he definitely has a natural advantage. Not only is freshness at his fingertips, with the lush valleys and the coast nearby, but he also has family history on his side.

Schrieber's great-great-grandfather got into the oyster trade in 1864 and, ever since, cooking has been in this family's blood. As a fifth-generation Oregonian, Shrieber has inherited a sixth sense when it comes to finding the best ingredients for his seafood and shellfish delicacies. His contemporary, classy restaurant is the perfect place to enjoy those delicious dishes, especially on a rainy Portland night. His food will warm you up from the inside out.

Apple Cider–Cured Smoked Salmon

ADAPTED FROM THE WILDWOOD RESTAURANT, PORTLAND, OREGON

MAKES 4 SERVINGS

Apple Cider Brine:
1 cup packed brown sugar
¾ cup salt
4 cups apple cider or juice
2 cinnamon sticks
1 teaspoon fennel seeds
1 teaspoon whole allspice
1 teaspoon black peppercorns
1 bay leaf
1 teaspoon red pepper flakes
6 sprigs fresh thyme or ½ teaspoon dried thyme
2 (about 1-pound) large salmon fillets, skin and
    pin bones removed

To make brine: In a saucepan, combine brown sugar, salt, and apple cider, and bring to a boil over medium heat. Add cinnamon sticks, fennel seeds, allspice, peppercorns, bay leaf, red pepper flakes, and thyme; remove from the heat; and cool to room temperature. Brine can be made 2 to 3 days in advance and kept in the refrigerator.

To brine salmon: Add salmon to brine, and refrigerate for at least 6 hours or overnight. Remove salmon from brine and place, uncovered, on a wire rack set in a sheet pan. Refrigerate fillets for at least 6 hours or overnight to dry them out. (A dry fillet will take on smoke quicker than a moist fillet.)

To smoke salmon: Soak a small bundle of wood chips in water while the grill heats. In an outdoor grill, make a small fire using mesquite charcoal or briquettes. Once the fire has burned down to a hot bed of coals, about 1 hour, place the soaked wood on the coals. Position the grill rack 8 to 12 inches above the smoking wood, and place salmon on the rack. Cover the grill, and shut any open air vents. After 5 minutes, check the heat of the grill; large fillets will be cooked and smoked through in about 30 minutes if the heat is low, 300 to 350°F; a hotter fire will cook the fillets in 15 to 20 minutes. Serve salmon hot off the grill.

Washington

Tini Bigs

100 Denny Way
Seattle, WA 98109
(206) 284-0931
www.tinibigs.com

There's a reason this retro-style martini bar boasts of having the second-best martini in town. Owner Keith Robins says that because everyone claims to have the best, he thinks listing theirs as *second* best really makes them *second to none*. Whether or not you follow that particular cocktail culture logic, one thing is certain: At Tini Bigs, they make big 'tini's—10 ounces to be exact.

Although they claim to have the second-best martini, their range of flavors is unrivaled. The Flir-Tini, made with Stoli Vanilla, cocoa, and Bailey's Irish Cream, should be garnished with someone's phone number. The Las Vegas Martini, a fierce blend of vodka and Goldschlager, is decorated with a playing card. The Feng-Shui Martini is a perfectly balanced blend of vodka, gin, and sweet-and-sour mix. The Dot-Com Martini is

described on the menu as "Out of Stock." But our favorite, the "Jill-Tini" (named after a certain co-host of a show), is a bubbly blend of 7-Up, orange liqueur, and vodka—and a cute bartender to shake it all up!

They also serve excellent bar food: Coconut prawns in a hot chili sauce, a blue cheese cheeseburger, Parmesan garlic fries—in other words, salty foods to make you thirsty.

Jill-Tini

ADAPTED FROM TINI BIGS, SEATTLE, WASHINGTON

MAKES 1 DRINK

2½ ounces vodka, preferably Finlandia
1 ounce Parfait Amour (orange liqueur)
½ ounce sweet-and-sour mix
½ ounce 7-Up
Maraschino cherry

Combine vodka, Parfait Amour, sweet-and-sour mix, and 7-Up in a glass with ice, and stir vigorously. Strain into a martini glass, and garnish with the cherry.

Palisade

Elliott Bay Marina
2601 West Marina Place
Seattle, WA 98199
(206) 285-1000
www.r-u-i.com

Palisade offers *at least* four perks other restaurants can't match:

1. An incredible view of downtown Seattle, the Puget Sound, and, in the distance, the Olympic Mountain Range and Mt. Rainier.
2. An eye-catching décor to match the scenery outside: Palisade is all glass and Hawaiian Koa wood. There is a large saltwater pond filled with lobsters and Dungeness crabs for meals. But don't worry; the fish in the pond *are* just for show.

Audio Guys

Audio guys are *different*. Not bad different, or good different, just different.

Audio guys—and it's usually a guy—make sure all the spoken words and natural sounds are captured on tape.

Why are they *different?* We don't know. Maybe it's because they wear headphones and hear things the rest of us don't, so they're more in-tune with their surroundings. So what if many of those sounds aren't actually there?

We usually have our set crew, but every once in a while we'll hire an audio guy on the road.

Hiring on the road reduces travel and lodging costs, but often leaves us with audio guys who are *really* different. There was the one guy who shouted at a woman two blocks away because she was pushing her baby in a stroller that had a squeaky wheel. He doesn't work with us anymore.

Neither does the guy who would break into dance moves during our shoots, whether there was music playing or not. He also bummed extra food at every restaurant we visited.

One time an audio guy got us lost in the Hollywood Hills for 2 hours, even though he lived nearby.

And then there was the very nice but still *different* audio guy who took us to his apartment, against our will. We had been working together all week when he decided we should celebrate a job well done. The next thing we know, he's driving our van into the parking lot of his building and insisting the crew come up for a drink. Not long after we sat down in his apartment, the audio guy got into a loud fight with his girlfriend. You didn't have to wear headphones or be an audio guy to hear them. As evenings go, it sure was *different*.

---

3. Great Hawaiian/Polynesian cuisine: The plank salmon has been a best-seller for years. It's cooked on a cedar plank, so the fish takes on a wonderful scent of the wood.

4. Complementary limo service from any of nearly 20 downtown hotels. All visitors to Seattle have to do is contact the concierge at their hotel, and a short time later, they're enjoying the 20-minute ride to Palisade inside a stylish limousine. (Tip not included.)

FareStart Restaurant

1902 Second Avenue
Seattle, WA 98101
(206) 443-1233
www.farestart.org

Life wasn't easy for Veronica (not her real name). After two of her children died, her life fell apart, and she found herself living on the streets of Seattle. She felt she had nowhere to turn . . .

Similarly, Todd (not his real name), a nervous young man with fear in his eyes, was trying to turn his life around. A former drug user, he ended up in a mental hospital "being a sloth" as he puts it.

How these two turned their lives around is nothing short of miraculous . . .

It all began at the FareStart Restaurant, one of those special places you'll wish was in your town. What started out as a central kitchen to feed nutritious meals to low-income families in homeless shelters has grown into one of Seattle's greatest nonprofit success stories, not only providing good food but also giving restaurant job training and placement for homeless men and women.

Since its inception in 1992, more than 1,000 homeless and disadvantaged people have walked in the door: jobless, destitute, and hopeless. They've walked out *with* hope, confidence, and most important, employment. During the 16-week program, they train under FareStart instructors, then get set up in restaurant jobs around the city. When we were there, Veronica and Todd were learning how to wait tables, while some of their counterparts in the kitchen were learning how to cook. And here's the bonus for the rest of us: The food is good and cheap!

FareStart is open for lunch, but on Thursday nights, some of Seattle's finest chefs come in to help the students put on a world-class meal. FareStart also caters everything from business breakfasts to weddings.

Their success rate is impressive: 80 percent of the students who graduate from the program are employed. One year later, 80 percent of those students are still in the same jobs—far surpassing the standards in an industry known for its high turnover.

So where are Veronica and Todd today? Well, Todd volunteers at FareStart on a regular basis and is getting ready to move out of transitional housing. He's still going through therapy, taking some classes, and getting by with food service jobs here and there while pursuing a profession as a music writer. Veronica decided to head off to join her family in the Southwest, where she planned to put her newly acquired skills to work.

———

Café Flora

2901 East Madison Street
Seattle, WA 98112
(206) 325-9100
www.cafeflora.com

Devoid of macramé, incense, and political jargon, this vegetarian mecca snags even the most committed carnivores. Perhaps it's the airy, light décor, but it's more likely the great vegetarian and vegan food they serve in this friendly, community-based restaurant—one that introduces nonmeat dishes to the masses and does it well.

Some favorites: Indonesian-Style Rice with Banana Curry; Eggplant and Pine Nut Pizza; Smoked Mushroom and Spinach Salad; Coconut Tofu with Sweet Chili Sauce. For dessert, even the vegans can have their cake and eat it, too. Pastry chef Edna Tapawan masterfully prepares sweets without using animal products of any kind. Some of her most popular creations include a soy cheesecake, a vegan coconut cake, and carrot cake with soy cream-cheese icing.

Vegan Coconut Cake

ADAPTED FROM CAFÉ FLORA, SEATTLE, WASHINGTON

MAKES 1 (9-INCH) CAKE; 10 TO 12 SERVINGS

Cake:

2 cups all-purpose unbleached flour
¾ teaspoon baking powder
¾ teaspoon baking soda
4 ounces (½ cup) silken tofu
1⅓ cups sugar
¼ teaspoon salt
1 cup coconut milk
¾ cup sweetened or unsweetened coconut flakes
½ cup canola oil
1 cup sweetened or unsweetened coconut flakes

Icing:

¾ cup (1½ sticks) soy margarine, at room temperature
2 cups powdered sugar, sifted
⅛ cup coconut milk

Preheat the oven to 350°F. Line a 9-inch-round cake pan with parchment paper, and spray with cooking spray.

To make cake: Sift flour, baking powder, and baking soda into a medium bowl; set aside. Add tofu, sugar, salt, coconut milk, coconut flakes, and canola oil to the bowl of a food processor, and pulse until uniform in texture, about 8 to 10 seconds, scraping down the bowl as needed. Add dry ingredients, and process until just combined, 6 to 8 seconds. Pour batter into the prepared pan. Bake for about 1 hour, or until cake starts to pull away from the side of the pan and a toothpick inserted in the center comes out clean.

Cool cake in the pan for 10 minutes. Turn out on a wire rack to cool completely. Cake is best if made one day prior to icing and serving; store loosely wrapped in the refrigerator.

To toast coconut: Preheat the oven to 350°F. Toast coconut on a baking sheet about 10 minutes or until golden brown. Cool completely and set aside.

To make icing: In a bowl, beat margarine with an electric mixer until creamy. Slowly add powdered sugar, and continue mixing until smooth, scraping down the sides of the bowl as needed. On slow speed, drizzle in coconut milk, and beat until icing is smooth and fluffy, about 5 minutes.

To assemble cake: Place cake rounded side down on a flat cake plate. Cut cake in half crosswise with a serrated knife; using a sawing motion, cut toward the center, then turn cake and continue cutting until all the way through. (Keep the knife horizontal with the counter to ensure an even cut.) Flip over the top layer. Evenly spread the bottom layer with about ½ cup icing. Top with the remaining layer. Frost the top of cake and spread remaining icing on the sides. Sprinkle toasted coconut on the top and side of cake. Cake is best served at room temperature. It may be refrigerated for up to 3 days.

Dahlia Lounge

2001 4th Avenue
Seattle, WA 98121
(206) 682-4142
www.tomdouglas.com

Owner Tom Douglas is probably one of Seattle's most famous chefs, but he doesn't take himself too seriously. When we asked why he was so popular in his adopted hometown, the big and burly Douglas claims it's because he looks like a logger. "They look up to loggers around here," he says.

The Delaware native started cooking after high school, working at the prestigious Hotel du Pont in Wilmington. He saved enough money to buy a 1967 Bel Air station wagon from his father for $150, tossed in all his belongings, and set out on his cross-country dream trip. He ended up in Seattle in 1978 because he had run out of money.

For a while, he tried working construction, selling wine, and laboring on the railroad. That could be where he started perfecting his "logger" physique. Having limited success in those endeavors, he realized it might be time to call on training from back East, so he got a job cooking in a restaurant. Even though Douglas didn't have a formal culinary background, his experience in Wilmington taught him how to make crab cakes. But around here, he had to use Dungeness crabs. No one was doing that at the time, and the dish was a hit.

His growing success with ingredients from the Pacific Northwest led to the opening of Dahlia Lounge in 1989. It's a modern but surprisingly intimate restaurant that's as much a part of a visit to Seattle as the Space Needle. (It's since moved, but the original Dahlia Lounge was used in a scene in *Sleepless in Seattle*.) Along with the now-famous crab cakes, the Alaskan halibut and crispy five-spice duck are to be taken seriously.

Douglas has since opened several other restaurants and written two successful cookbooks. The logging industry's loss is Seattle diners' gain.

Earth and Ocean

1112 Fourth Avenue
Seattle, WA 98101
(206) 264-6060
www.earthocean.net

French fries and fine dining don't always go hand in hand, unless you're at the posh W hotel in their signature restaurant Earth and Ocean. Here, the chefs take something as simple as the french fry and put a potato-pleasing spin on it.

Try the Sexy Fries, tossed with Oregon truffle, garlic, parsley, and Reggiano Parmigiano, or the Skinny Fries—thinly sliced potatoes, deep-fried and served in a cocktail shaker with dipping sauces offered in martini glasses. And here's a notch above your everyday spud: thick-cut fries mixed with melted Reblochon cheese from the Savoy region of France.

If you're looking for a more "refined" meal, they have that, too. The lobster basil soup and the grilled king salmon are top sellers. Be sure you save room for dessert—they are edible works of art.

Wild Ginger

1401 Third Avenue
Seattle, WA 98101
(206) 623-4450

There's a lot of confusion about fusion, but Wild Ginger is attempting to set the record straight. Just because this sleek, contemporary restaurant in downtown Seattle has a co-mingling of Asian cultures (the chefs are from all over Asia: Thailand, Japan, Vietnam, China, Indonesia, Malaysia—to name a few) doesn't mean the cuisine co-mingles. Rather, each dish stands alone and is specific to a different corner of the continent. Some of our favorites include the Bangkok Boar, the Niman Ranch Pork served with a sweet-hot sauce, the Thai Green Bean Salad, and the Vietnamese Crab Salad. For the adventurous palate, there are Cambodian Turmeric Mussels or Angkor Wat Clams. Other offerings include curries of crab, beef, and lamb, as well as signature entrées: Fragrant Duck, Pow Wok Lamb, and Emerald Prawns.

If you can, save room for dessert. The ginger ice cream can't be beat. Eat it while sipping on a pot of imported Asian tea, and you've got the perfect ending to any evening. Not to mention the fact that you'll leave with a clear mind—devoid of any confusion over fusion.

washington

Washington

Seven-Flavor Beef

ADAPTED FROM WILD GINGER,
SEATTLE, WASHINGTON

MAKES 2 TO 4 SERVINGS

Marinade:

2 stalks lemongrass, pounded (only use lower 6
   inches)
2 tablespoons minced fresh ginger
1 tablespoon minced garlic
1½ teaspoons salt
¼ teaspoon five-spice powder
2 tablespoons chili flakes
2 tablespoons sesame oil
1½ teaspoons fish sauce
2 tablespoons vegetable oil
1 tablespoon honey

1 pound flank steak, sliced against the grain into
   2¼-inch pieces
2 tablespoons vegetable oil
2 tablespoons hoisin sauce
3 tablespoons finely chopped fresh roasted
   peanuts
½ cup small Thai basil leaves

To make the marinade: Combine lemon grass,
ginger, garlic, salt, five-spice powder, chili flakes,
sesame oil, fish sauce, vegetable oil, and honey in a
medium bowl. Add beef, and marinate for at least 2
hours or up to 8 hours in the refrigerator.

To cook: Drain beef. Heat oil in a wok over high
heat. Add beef, and stir-fry until half-cooked, about
1 minute. Add hoisin sauce, and stir-fry until beef is
about 80 percent cooked. Add peanuts and basil,
and stir-fry for 30 seconds. Serve hot.

The Herbfarm

14590 NE 145th Street
Woodinville, WA 98072
(425) 485-5300
www.theherbfarm.com

It burned down once, was in a temporary location for a year, and yet The Herbfarm finds that

Oink Oink!

If it's any indication of how good
the food at The Herbfarm can be,
look for the pot-bellied pig named
Hamlet, also known as the "recycling
pig" because he eats so many of the leftovers.
Hamlet, who was originally called Rudy until
he moved to his new quarters after the original
restaurant burned down, shares a little house
on the grounds with ducks. Apparently,
between courses guests are known to visit him
with their leftovers, giving this pig one sophisticated palate and one increasing waistline!

true aficionados come back time and again . . .
that is, if they can get a reservation. Even though
their new home now has room for 80, be prepared to wait months to book a table. But if you
love a long, leisurely meal—and are prepared to
pay the price—then it is definitely worth the
wait and the expense.

Executive Chef Jerry Traunfeld puts on a
nine-course, herb-infused dinner each night. As
the restaurant's name suggests, there's a magnificent herb garden out back, where guests can
stroll between courses. It's magical. Servers
hand you champagne along with your choice of
herbs to enhance it. The night we were there,
lemon balm made an incredible pairing with the
bubbly! Not to mention the sorbet made with
fresh rose petals. It was like tasting heaven . . . if
only for a night.

This place is simply one of the best . . .

Lavender Shortbread

ADAPTED FROM THE HERBFARM, WOODINVILLE, WASHINGTON

MAKES 24 COOKIES

4 teaspoons fresh or dried lavender buds
½ cup sugar
8 ounces (2 sticks) unsalted butter, chilled and cut
    into 1-inch cubes
2 cups all-purpose flour

Grind lavender buds with ¼ cup sugar in a spice grinder or blender until very fine.

Mix together lavender sugar, remaining ¼ cup sugar, and butter using the paddle attachment of a heavy-duty electric mixer until smooth but not fluffy. Add flour all at once, and mix until flour is just incorporated and a dough forms, but no longer.

Pat dough into a disc on a large sheet of plastic wrap, wrap it up, and chill it for about 15 minutes.

Unwrap dough, and roll it out on a floured surface into a rectangle ¼-inch thick. Cut dough into bars about 3x1½ inches, or cut out shapes with a cookie cutter. Transfer them to a baking sheet lined with parchment paper, allowing at least ½ inch between them, and chill for at least 30 minutes.

Preheat the oven to 300°F. Bake cookies for 22 to 25 minutes, or until they just begin to turn a sandy tan color. Do not brown them. Cool on the pan. Store in an airtight container.

CHEF'S TIP: If you don't have a heavy-duty mixer, you can mix the dough by hand or with a handheld mixer if you soften the butter a little first and chill the dough longer.

5 Spot

1502 Queen Anne Avenue North
Seattle, WA 28109
(206) 285-7768
www.chowfoods.com

The 5 Spot is the home of "The Bulge," a dessert so decadent customers have to sign a waiver before they eat it. The tongue-in-cheek

photo courtesy of Peter Levy, 5 Spot

The Bulge—the dessert that requires a release form from customers who tackle this sinfully fattening treat.

document releases the restaurant from legal action in case diners end up with junk-in-the-trunk or love handles. Obviously, the whole thing is a shot at the recent wave of obesity lawsuits and fat-cat attorneys.

But it gives you an idea of the attitude at 5 Spot, which can be summarized as "We take our food seriously, but not much else."

Opened in 1990 in Seattle's fashionable Queen Anne neighborhood, 5 Spot is open for every meal of the day, plus late-night drinks. The menu is constantly changing, and every three months, the food and décor highlight a new theme.

For instance, 5 Spot once offered a menu as an ode to Springfield, USA, hometown of FOX televsion's *The Simpsons*. Among the dishes: the "three-eye" fish fry and donut bread pudding. Homer's favorite Duf beer was also available, the second "f" kept off the label to, once again, keep the attorneys at bay—this time from the FOX network.

Over the next few months, 5 Spot featured items from various nationwide food festivals, including shrimp fritters from the Louisiana Shrimp and Petroleum Festival, and a brat from the Sheboygan, Wisconsin Bratwurst Days celebration.

You get the idea.

As for "The Bulge," co-owner Peter Levy says it's made with a good banana gone bad. First it's quartered, then rolled in sugar, and deep-fried.

Washington

It's topped with an oversize scoop of vanilla ice cream, sprinkled with powdered sugar and cinnamon, drizzled with chocolate and caramel sauce, and then finished with a handful of Macadamia nuts. They (legally) serve about 18 a night.

How many calories? As Levy says, "I don't know, and I don't care."

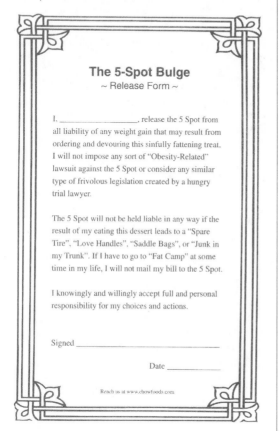

The 5-Spot Bulge
~ Release Form ~

I, _____, release the 5 Spot from all liability of any weight gain that may result from ordering and devouring this sinfully fattening treat. I will not impose any sort of "Obesity-Related" lawsuit against the 5 Spot or consider any similar type of frivolous legislation created by a hungry trial lawyer.

The 5 Spot will not be held liable in any way if the result of my eating this dessert leads to a "Spare Tire", "Love Handles", "Saddle Bags", or "Junk in my Trunk". If I have to go to "Fat Camp" at some time in my life, I will not mail my bill to the 5 Spot.

I knowingly and willingly accept full and personal responsibility for my choices and actions.

Signed _____

Date _____

Reach us at www.chowfoods.com

Milford's Fish House
719 North Monroe Street
Spokane, WA 99201
(509) 326-7251

You don't think of eastern Washington state as a place to find fresh fish, but at Milford's, think again. Owner Jerry Young is very picky about his fish and only has the best brought in. Sink your teeth into pan-fried Puget Sound oysters;

wok-fired Penn Cove mussels served with ginger, sake and lime butter; grilled Oregon salmon and baked almond-crusted Alaskan halibut. After eating here, you might think twice about making the trek to Seattle for seafood.

Pan-Fried Oysters
ADAPTED FROM MILFORD'S FISH HOUSE, SPOKANE, WASHINGTON

MAKES 2 SERVINGS

Breading Mix:
1 (15-ounce) box cornflakes
4 cups all-purpose flour
2 tablespoons ground black pepper
¼ cup celery salt
¼ cup onion powder
⅓ cup granulated garlic
16 extra-small oysters, shucked
2 eggs, lightly beaten
½ cup vegetable oil

To make breading mix: Process cornflakes in a food processor until just ground. In a bowl, combine flour, pepper, celery salt, onion powder, and granulated garlic, and stir in cornflakes.

Place about 2 cups breading mix in a shallow bowl. (Refrigerate remaining mix for another use.) Dredge oysters in eggs, then place oysters in breading mix, one at a time. Cover oysters with mix by pressing lightly. Heat oil in a medium sauté pan over high heat. Add oysters, and sauté until golden, turning once. Do not overcook.

Alaska

Café Michele
Mile 13.75 Talkeetna Spur Road
Talkeetna, AK 99676
(907) 733-5300
www.cafemichele.com

We have yet to find a restaurant that offers dining on the moon, but we've found one that

Alaskan Favorites

One of the questions we often get asked is "What is your favorite place to go?" For me, Alaska is one of them, which is why *The Best Of* has traveled there so many times. Although all our favorites can't be included in this book, we do want to mention some other choices in case you make it to this special state.

If a bed and breakfast is your thing, take in the view from the **Denali Overlook Inn** (Mile 8.5 Talkeetna Spur Road, 907-733-3555, www.denalioverlook.com). This charming B&B, run by the Gilroy family, is clean and comfortable. Steve Gilroy is a wilderness photographer, so when you get tired of looking at the view from their backyard, you can enjoy some of his wildlife photos that grace the walls.

The Talkeetna Alaskan Lodge (Mile 12.5 Talkeetna Spur Road, 877-258-6877, www.talkeetnaalaskan-lodge.com) also serves up a million-dollar view of Denali and some equally impressive food. Alaskan ingredients featured on the menu include oysters from Prince William Sound and salmon and halibut caught fresh in nearby waters. You'll find the rooms rustic and cozy, although not cheap.

For a family adventure, check out **Talkeetna River Guides** in the heart of town (800-353-2677 or 907-733-2677, www.talkeetnariverguides.com). Raft down the rivers that converge on the town, and keep your eyes open for incredible wildlife. Some of their excursions include a gourmet lunch cooked up on the beach. *Talkeetna* means "river of plenty," and you'll find plentiful amounts of stuff to eat and look at on this excursion.

comes pretty close and is a much shorter flight. Plus, in the summer, you get 24 hours of daylight. What you do need is a wad of cash and a good pair of sunglasses.

Michele Faurot, a native New Yorker, got into the restaurant business in the 1970s when she was a young woman living in Manhattan. But when the love of her life decided to head west, she followed, eventually ending up in Talkeetna. She opened a small catering business but always dreamed of owning a restaurant.

Talkeetna might seem like a tough place to make a living. After all, this tiny town caters primarily to alpinists who come to climb in the magnificent Alaska Range, home to North America's highest and most prominent peak, Denali. It means "The Great One" to the Athabascan people, although the more familiar name is Mt. McKinley. At more than 20,300 feet, Denali is a sight to behold. Thing is, for those of you who know climbers, they are a group who spend what disposable income they have on climbing, not eating in restaurants.

But Michele is able to make a living because this incredible wilderness also attracts a lot of tourists who want to marvel at The Great One from afar. Come summer, Talkeetna teems with visitors on their way to Denali National Park. Michele has seized upon this opportunity, and instead of just offering her customers a great meal *inside* her restaurant, she has found a way to take those who can afford it *outside* and up close and personal to this majestic wonder.

For a few hundred bucks or more, you get a scenic flight tour in and around Denali, courtesy of Talkeetna Air Taxi (800-533-2219 or www.tal-keetnaair.com). You land on a glacier, where Michele cooks up a gourmet, four-course meal. Trust us, there's not a bad seat in the house. However, this is when you'll want sunglasses. With the sun reflecting off the glacier, all that snow can be blinding.

Jill shot this piece with her dad and brother as part of their *Best Of Places to Take Dad* show. Her father, Sam Cordes, had already visited 49 states, and Alaska was the last one to make his list complete. He says it was worth the wait. As the wine and champagne flowed, Michele cooked up some marvelous Alaskan fare on her portable stove, including fresh Alaskan halibut.

Alaska

Four courses later, after sipping wine and feasting on fine food in a setting that was nothing short of spectacular, it was time to head back to earth. Like we said, we can't give you the moon, but this comes pretty close.

———

Double Musky Inn

Mile .3 Crow Creek Road
Girdwood, AK 99587
(907) 783-2822
www.doublemuskyinn.com

If you ever ask Jill what her favorite recipe is, she'll go on for hours about her Aunt Nancy's Louisiana Crawfish Pie. So you can imagine her surprise when she came across an equally delectable New Orleans crawfish pie in the wilds of Alaska at the Double Musky, about 30 miles from Anchorage. Described as the "last great American roadhouse," it truly belongs among our top spots.

Bob and Deanna Persons are born Southerners who found themselves in this northernmost climate in 1979. Alaskans have been grateful ever since. The Musky first opened in 1962 as a place where customers cooked their own steaks over an open fire. But when Bob and Deanna bought the place, they took it to new heights.

With an atmosphere that walks a line between fine dining and your grandmother's attic—the Musky is something you simply must experience. The Persons hesitate to call this a Cajun restaurant, even though most dishes have a New Orleans accent. You'll find decidedly Alaskan fare on the menu, including Alaskan king crab, Alaskan salmon, and Alaskan halibut. All are truly outstanding. But if you're a meat-eater, Jill suggests trying their steaks. Her favorite: the French Pepper Steak.

Even though the Double Musky isn't far from the middle of nowhere, you might have trouble getting a table. Lines are known to snake out the door—even in an Alaskan winter. It says something about a place that can provide true Southern comfort in the heart of Alaska. It also

photo courtesy of Jill Cordes

Jill's audio guy Tom Forliti and her photographer Dan Dwyer gear up for a shoot near Girdwood, Alaska.

says something about a place that can rival Jill's Aunt Nancy's cooking. During the shoot when Bob asked Jill which crawfish pie was better, his or her aunt's, Jill took the diplomatic road and told him his was "just as good." Fair enough.

Crawfish Pie
ADAPTED FROM THE DOUBLE MUSKY INN, GIRDWOOD, ALASKA

MAKES 6 MAIN-DISH SERVINGS

½ cup butter
¼ cup all-purpose flour
⅓ cup minced yellow onion
½ cup minced green bell pepper
¼ cup minced celery
¾ cup chopped green onions
1 teaspoon minced garlic
1 pound crawfish tails, taken out of the shells
Spice Mixture (recipe below)
1 cup heavy cream
Purchased 9-inch pie crust, baked

Melt ¼ cup butter in a heavy, preferably cast-iron, dutch oven over medium heat. Add flour all at once; stir or whisk quickly to blend together. Lower the heat to medium-low. Cook, stirring constantly, until medium brown in color. Do not burn. Remove roux from the heat. Stir in minced onion, bell pepper, and celery.

Alaska

Melt remaining ¼ cup butter in a skillet over medium heat. Add green onions and garlic, and sauté until softened. Add crawfish, and heat well. Sprinkle with Spice Mixture. Add this to roux mixture, and add enough cream to create the desired consistency (not soupy or too thick).

Pour hot crawfish mixture into pie crust, and serve hot.

Spice Mixture

MAKES ABOUT 1½ TABLESPOONS

1½ teaspoons salt
1 teaspoon sweet paprika
½ teaspoon white pepper
¼ teaspoon onion powder
¼ teaspoon garlic powder
¼ teaspoon dry mustard
¼ teaspoon cayenne
¼ teaspoon black pepper
⅛ teaspoon dried thyme leaves
⅛ teaspoon dried basil leaves

Mix together salt, paprika, white pepper, onion powder, garlic powder, dry mustard, cayenne, black pepper, thyme, and basil in a bowl, and store in an airtight container.

Marx Bros. Cafe

627 West 3rd Avenue
Anchorage, AK 99501
(907) 278-2133
www.marxcafe.com

What Chef Jack Amon cooks up will knock your socks off, which is why we recommend reservations. Some of his signatures include Macadamia Nut Crusted Halibut and King Salmon served over King Crab. So what did Jack and Jill make in the kitchen when she shot here? Turkey. Yep. Sounds pretty elegant, right? Especially when you consider she had to put on rubber gloves and help Jack inject the raw birds with Cajun flavoring. Yum.

We shot Marx Bros. for one of our Thanksgiving shows because come Turkey Day, Jack makes Cajun deep-fried turkeys and ships them all over the state. They put together about 300 Thanksgiving meal packages each season, which means they make about 1,400 pounds of stuffing (the best kind is with andouille sausage), more than 600 pounds of their garlic roasted mashed potatoes, and nearly 700 pounds of yams for the Bourbon Yam Casserole. Oh yeah, and all those turkeys, too.

The restaurant was originally the brainchild of Jack and three other guys. Initially they found themselves in all sorts of madcap blunderings as they tried to get the hang of running a restaurant. That's what led to them calling themselves the Marx Bros. Nowadays it's just three partners, including Jack, but nevertheless, the things they cook up—like the Thanksgiving dinners—make for quite a production.

And although Jack has created a unique niche here, injecting his birds with all things Cajun, we suggest you come for a regular dinner. You'll have a lovely meal no matter what you order, and there will be no wishbone to fight over.

Baja Taco

Red bus off Nicholoff Way
Cordova, AK 99574
(907) 424-5599

For a town with no roads leading in or out (the only way to get here is by boat or plane), it's pretty remarkable to find a restaurant inside a school bus. Then again, it's not like it's going anywhere, unlike the owners, Liz and Bob Pudwill, who make a 5,000-mile pilgrimage to Baja, Mexico, each winter. Come spring, they head back north to Cordova. But instead of leaving all of Baja behind, Liz has made it her mission to bring part of it with her by way of her fish tacos.

Ironically, in this tiny town of Cordova, locals are probably feasting on better fish tacos than they could get south of the Rio Grande. That's because Cordova is home to the famous Copper River Red Salmon and King Salmon, both of

Alaska

which are considered the finest wild salmon in the world due to their high oil content, rich flavor, and delicate texture. If you're not a fish lover, especially of salmon, don't blab it around, because this town makes and breaks itself on the fishing industry. However, we'll let you in on a little secret: You can get other Mexican specialties at the bus—you just might want to whisper your order through the window.

When she opened in 1989, Liz didn't want a permanent place to maintain because she's only there half the year. What you'll find is a small cabin where you can dine inside, picnic tables if you want to dine out, and the red school bus complete with a walk-up window where you place your order. It's also where Liz does all her cooking. Guess this take-out joint gives new meaning to the term "meals on wheels," even if it's the cook, not the wheels, who is going somewhere.

Fish Tacos

ADAPTED FROM BAJA TACO, CORDOVA, ALASKA

MAKES 4 TO 6 TACOS

Beer Batter:
¾ cup all-purpose flour
Dash of yellow mustard
Enough beer to make batter consistency of
    pancake batter

Vegetable oil for frying
1 red salmon fillet, skinned, boned, and cut into
    2-inch strips
Salt to taste
4 to 6 flour tortillas
1 cup shredded cabbage
Chipotle Mayonnaise (recipe follows)
Tomatillo Salsa (recipe follows)

To make batter: Stir together flour, yellow mustard, and beer in a small bowl until smooth.

Heat ½ inch vegetable oil in a heavy skillet over medium-high heat. Dip fish strips in batter to coat. Arrange fish strips in hot oil, without touching. Fry until golden, 2 to 3 minutes. Turn and fry until golden

on the other sides. Drain on paper towels, and season with salt.

Heat a dry cast-iron or heavy skillet over medium heat. Heat tortillas, one at a time, until warmed. Assemble tacos by layering fish, cabbage, mayonnaise, and salsa on tortillas.

Chipotle Mayonnaise

MAKES ABOUT 1½ CUPS

½ cup mayonnaise
2 tablespoons milk
1 or 2 canned chipotle chiles in adobo sauce
1 cup finely shredded onion

Mix together mayonnaise, milk, chiles, and onion in a bowl. If making ahead, cover and refrigerate until needed.

Tomatillo Salsa

MAKES ABOUT 2 CUPS

1 cup canned or chopped fresh tomatillos
¼ cup canned or chopped fresh jalapeño chiles
¼ cup diced onion
¼ cup chopped fresh cilantro
¼ cup canned diced mild green chiles

Add tomatillos, jalapeños, onion, cilantro, and green chiles to a food processor or blender. Process until combined. Transfer to a nonreactive saucepan, and heat over medium-high heat until just boiling. Serve warm. (If using fresh ingredients, simmer until vegetables are tender.)

Cordova Lighthouse Inn

212 Nicholoff Way
Cordova, AK 99574
(907) 424-7080
www.cordovalighthouseinn.com

There's a secret you can smell when hanging out in the fishing village of Cordova. Close your eyes and let the scent guide you away from the boat docks and into the Lighthouse Inn. That's where you'll find Lisa Marie Van Dyck and her husband Glenn, toiling over a wood-fired brick oven. And therein lies the secret to those good smells. The Van Dycks believe it's the brick oven that makes their baked goods turn out so good.

Neither of them have a formal baking background. In fact, Glenn entered the business by accident. He was a commercial fisherman by trade, but after surviving a major storm in which the boat he was on went down, he decided to rethink his career. Life on land seemed like a welcome change of pace, and hanging around a hot oven was the icing on his cake.

He and Lisa Marie bake all their bread, cakes, cookies, and pizza in the now-famous oven. And because it gives off conduction, convection, and radiant heat, everything bakes in about one-third the time of a regular oven. That way customers don't have to wait so long to bite into these delights.

So walk down the streets of Cordova, and inhale the smell of sweet success. After all, the couple who built this business brick by brick is taking comfort in that smell and in the fact that neither of them is going to drown baking bread.

Chocolate Macaroons

ADAPTED FROM THE LIGHTHOUSE INN, CORDOVA, ALASKA

MAKES 18 LARGE MACAROONS

1 pound 2 ounces semisweet chocolate, broken into chunks
9 ounces unsweetened chocolate, broken into chunks
9 egg whites
2¼ cups superfine sugar
1½ tablespoons vanilla extract
12 cups sweetened flaked coconut

Preheat the oven to 325°F. Line 2 large baking sheets with parchment paper. Melt chocolates in a double boiler over simmering—not boiling—water, stirring occasionally. Beat egg whites in a heavy-duty stand mixer to soft peaks. Gradually beat in sugar; beat on high speed until stiff peaks form. Mix

in vanilla. Reduce the mixer speed to low, and slowly incorporate melted chocolate.

Pour chocolate mixture into a large bowl. Fold in coconut. Use a 4-ounce ice-cream scoop or ½ cup measure to portion the cookies onto the prepared baking sheets.

Bake for about 25 minutes. When ready, cookies will look like melted chocolate; they will not be firm or look done. Do not overbake them. Cool slightly on the baking sheet and transfer to a wire rack to cool completely.

Orca Adventure Lodge

2500 Orca Road
Cordova, AK 99574
(907) 424-7249
www.orcaadventurelodge.com

It's not every day that one gets to make up their own address, but after UPS and FedEx insisted upon it, Steve Ranney decided that his lodge was at 2500 Orca Road. Mind you he is the only business on Orca Road and his lodge sits at the end of the road to nowhere. (Literally the only way in and out of Cordova is by boat or plane, and Orca Road is just a gravel strip off the main highway.) He says he thought the high number made his place sound more "official." Guess one of the benefits of living in this final frontier is you get to make up your own rules!

One rule he likes to live by is that life should be full of adventure. And in this land of the midnight sun, you can really count on an adventure or two. With all the sunshine in the summer there are ample hours to fish, hike, kayak, and sightsee. If you're coming to Cordova to do all that, we think this is a good place to base yourself and soak up some history while you're at it.

The lodge is actually an old cannery that dates back to 1886. In its heyday, there were seven canning lines that produced 2 million pounds of fish a day. But in 1991, when it closed down, all that business went to the birds. Enter Steve, who saw the potential in the place. After replacing the old canning lines with linens, the 34-room lodge

Alaska

opened up to adventure seekers. And although they don't catch and can any fish on the property, they serve plenty of it in the main dining room (open only to guests of the lodge).

So when you fly or sail into Cordova and realize you forgot your hiking boots or fishing poles, rest assured. You can have them delivered right to your door at 2500 Orca Road.

Walnut-Crusted Salmon

ADAPTED FROM THE ORCA ADVENTURE LODGE, CORDOVA, ALASKA

MAKES 4 SERVINGS

Marinade:

½ cup white wine
¼ cup fresh lemon juice
2 tablespoons olive oil
1 teaspoon chopped garlic
½ teaspoon crushed dried rosemary
½ teaspoon crushed dried thyme
¼ teaspoon salt
¼ teaspoon freshly ground black pepper
2 pounds salmon fillets

Crust Mixture:

1 cup finely chopped walnuts
1 cup finely chopped croutons
1 tablespoon chopped fresh oregano
1 tablespoon chopped fresh chives
2 tablespoons olive oil
2 tablespoons fresh lemon juice

To make marinade: Mix together wine, lemon juice, olive oil, garlic, rosemary, thyme, salt, and pepper in a glass baking pan.

Add salmon, and marinate for 10 minutes.

Preheat a grill until very hot. Line a baking sheet with foil. Preheat the oven to 400°F.

To make crust mixture: Combine walnuts, croutons, oregano, chives, olive oil, and lemon juice in a small bowl.

Remove salmon from marinade, reserving marinade. Place salmon on the grill rack, meat side down. Grill for 4 minutes or until seared. Remove and place salmon on the foil-lined baking sheet, skin side down. Lightly brush with marinade. Sprinkle crust mixture on top, pressing it in slightly. Bake for 4 to 8 minutes or until desired doneness.

Prince William Sound Lodge

No official address
(907) 248-0909
www.alaska.net/~pwslodge/

A mere six people call Ellemar, Alaska, home, at least on a year-round basis, thus the reason there's no "official" address for this place. Technically, the "town" (although it's a stretch to call it that) sits on the serene shores of Virgin Bay, which you probably won't find on a map, either. We fell in love with it because it is still largely undiscovered—not even by Exxon Valdez! It's also home to a lush rain forest, towering mountains, glacial waters, and an unparalleled beauty.

Don't expect your cell phones to work. In fact, shame on you for even bringing them. This is a place to leave the e-mail and high-tech world behind, except for the helicopter, plane, or boat you take to get here.

When we shot, we took a helicopter from Valdez to Ellemar, which took about 20 minutes and was full of breathtaking sights. When you land on the shore of Prince William Sound (PWS) Lodge, owners Chris Saal and Megan McDiarmid are there to greet you with some of the finest food you'll ever taste. Megan is a chef, and most of what they make here is foraged by them. She has her own garden where she grows nearly all the vegetables and herbs she cooks with. And you can even feast on fresh oysters and clams caught right outside the lodge, not to mention all the fish that is caught in the cool waters of the Sound. They even ice fish—for their ice. They're not too far from Columbia Glacier, so when the ice breaks off, they go fishing for it, gathering it up in their boat and hauling it back with them. Who needs a fancy ice-making machine anyway?

Rooms are rustic yet have modern amenities such as indoor plumbing and heating. However, don't expect a television or phone. They have one satellite phone in the lodge in case of emergencies.

You can tailor your own trip and your own adventure, whether it's fishing, kayaking, flightseeing (Chris is a pilot and owns a plane), or just taking in your surroundings.

Alaska

Be sure to ask Megan to make her famous sourdough pancakes with spruce tip syrup. She actually boils down the tips of spruce trees, which incredibly, turn pink. After she sweetens it and you try it, you might never go back to the bottled stuff again.

After spending a couple days gazing from meadows to mountains, and from the sea to the sea life, you'll find it refreshing that places like this exist. Who knows, after being without your cell phone and e-mail, you may decide to take up residence here and boost the town's population to seven.

Rhubarb Peach Pie with a Crunchy Macaroon Topping

ADAPTED FROM THE PRINCE WILLIAM SOUND LODGE, ELLEMAR, ALASKA

MAKES 1 (9-INCH) PIE

Filling:
5 tablespoons all-purpose flour
¾ cup granulated sugar
¼ cup packed light brown sugar
¼ teaspoon ground nutmeg
½ teaspoon salt
1 egg
Zest and juice of 1 orange
14 ounces (1¾ cups) chopped rhubarb
12 ounces (1½ cups) sliced, peeled peaches

Topping:
2½ cups crumbled coconut macaroons
¾ cup whole pecans
¼ cup packed light brown sugar
6 tablespoons unsalted butter, chilled, cut into ¼-inch cubes
1 (9-inch) pie crust, preferably made with butter, baked

To make filling: Mix together flour, sugar, brown sugar, nutmeg, and salt in a medium bowl. In a large bowl, beat together egg and orange juice. Add rhubarb, peaches, and zest. Sprinkle dry ingredients over the top, and toss gently to combine.

To make topping: Put macaroons, pecans, brown sugar, and butter into a food processor, and pulse until mixture resembles a coarse meal.

Preheat the oven to 375°F.

Pour filling into pie crust. Sprinkle topping over filling. Bake pie in the bottom third of the oven for about 1 hour or until filling bubbles.

CHEF'S TIPS: If making the crust yourself, make the rim of the crust thicker so it won't get too dark during its second baking. If you make your own macaroons, bake them about 25 degrees lower than the recipe calls for, so they will dry out with no browning.

Potato and Sweet Potato au Gratin

ADAPTED FROM THE PRINCE WILLIAM SOUND LODGE, ELLEMAR, ALASKA

MAKES 4 SERVINGS

2 teaspoons salt, plus more to season the pan
½ teaspoon freshly ground pepper, plus more to season the pan
20 ounces yellow or white potatoes, peeled and sliced into ⅛-inch thickness
5 ounces orange sweet potatoes, peeled and sliced into ⅛-inch thickness
1½ cups milk
½ cup shredded sharp cheddar cheese
¼ cup sliced fresh chives

Preheat the oven to 350°F. Butter a 13x9-inch baking pan, and sprinkle with salt and pepper. Simmer potatoes, sweet potatoes, milk, salt, and pepper in a large saucepan over medium heat until potatoes are partially cooked, about 10 minutes. Pour potato mixture into the prepared baking pan. Arrange potatoes so they are evenly layered. Sprinkle top with cheese and chives.

Cover the pan with foil. Bake 35 to 45 minutes or until potatoes are tender. Remove the foil, and increase the oven temperature to 400°F. Bake for another 15 minutes. Place under the broiler until the top is golden brown.

Alaska

Jill getting ready for a traditional Hawaiian luau.

Hawaii

Sushi Sasabune

1417 South King Street
Honolulu, HI 96814
(808) 947-3800

First rule: If you can't take instructions, don't come here. Second rule: You must trust the chef. Third rule: You better *love* sushi.

At Sushi Sasabune, Chef Seiji Kumagawa will tell you straight out that not everyone is welcome here. Huh? What's this guy doing in the hospitality business then? Well, he's feeding people the right way, the only way: *his* way.

Chef Kumagawa is the equivalent of the Soup Nazi, made famous in *Seinfeld*, only this guy is selling raw fish. No rice on the side, no California rolls. In fact, he'll tell *you* if and when you're allowed to dip your fish into soy sauce or wasabi. But hey, when you're this good, you get to make the rules.

A true perfectionist, he has his buyer hand-select each fish every morning in Los Angeles, then has it flown to Hawaii in time for lunch. That's how fresh it is. No wonder this stuff liter-ally melts in your mouth. Before you know it, you'll find yourself begging him to let you stay longer and let you try more. You'll begin to realize he is the master of the sushi universe, and you might even kneel down on the floor and take a bow to his majesty . . . okay, so maybe not that extreme, but you get the picture.

The good news about a place like this is that you never have to worry about what to order. What you *do* have to worry about is how big your final bill will be, because you really have no say in that, either. The only choice you have is deciding if you should walk in the door in the first place. It's his way or no way. Is it worth it? You decide.

Halekulani Hotel and La Mer Restaurant

2199 Kalia Road
Honolulu, HI 96815
(808) 923-2311 or (800) 367-2343
www.halekulani.com

This is one of those places the critics rave about. The AAA Four-Diamond Halekulani Hotel sits in the shadow of Diamond Head, a famous inactive volcanic crater. It's a place that boasts of being "an oasis of tranquility in the heart of Waikiki" and has a laundry list of famous celebrities who like to stay here. It's definitely a place to see and be seen. Although this area on Oahu is not exactly Jill's cup of tea, we feel it's worth a mention. To us, Waikiki—the hustle and bustle beach area in Oahu—is like an upscale and more scenic version of the Jersey Shore: frenetic, throngs of tourists, lots of traffic. She prefers the more subdued feel on other parts of the island.

Their five-star dining room, La Mer, has a beautiful view of the ocean and fine French food to go along with it. Be sure to bring your suit and we don't mean your bathing suit. This is one of the few places in all of Hawaii with a jacket requirement for dinner.

Rooms start at just over $300 a night and can go up to more than $500. If it sounds like your kind of place, check in and check it out. As for Jill, you'll find her in a sundress and flip flops eating dinner in a less-formal place and lounging on a beach that's not packed with hordes of people. To each their own.

———

Kahala Mandarin Oriental

5000 Kahala Ave
Honolulu, HI 96816
(808) 739-8888
(800) 367-2525 for reservations
www.mandarinoriental.com

We think the Kahala Mandarin Oriental is one of the nicest hotels on Oahu and, arguably, in the world. Far from the hectic beach scene of Waikiki, the Kahala gives you what you come to Hawaii for—luxurious peace and quiet.

The island of Oahu is known as the "gathering place," and this is one place we think you'd like to gather—or hide out, if you have a mind to do so. The hotel has a reputation for protecting the privacy of its guests and has long been a haven for celebrities and royalty who prefer a secluded setting.

You'll find this gem in one of the more prestigious neighborhoods on the island. With its beautiful beach and its own family of dolphins that swim in the hotel's lagoon, you'll feel like you've walked into a different world. You'll begin to unwind the moment you step onto the sandy beach and feel the water swirl around your toes.

There are several restaurants to choose from, and we think they're all top-notch. The service here is equally impeccable both in the eateries and in the hotel. So lacking any "story" to tell, the best we can do is to tell you to enjoy this lovely place and go make your own stories and create your own memories.

———

Beach House Grill

5022 Lawai Road
Koloa, HI 96756
(808) 742-1424
www.the-beach-house.com

Dusk is falling on the island of Kauai, and at the Beach House Grill, diners are relishing their meals. Music plays softly in the background, and the murmur of voices can be heard throughout. Our cameras roll on this picture-perfect scene for our *Best Of Date Destinations* show. Suddenly, the talking lowers to a whisper, people stop eating, some even put down their forks. Within a few seconds, the crowd begins to applaud. Cameraman Dave Dennison looks around to see what's going on . . .

You know you're at a special place when first-rate food takes a backseat to the sunset. Nearly every night at this beachfront restaurant, the sunset gets an ovation.

Here in the Hawaiian Islands, locals talk about the aloha spirit. You'll find both that and the spirit of romance here. How could you not? Soak it up and savor it—especially when the curtain falls and all eyes look to the west. Now *that's* paradise.

———

Gaylord's at Kilohana

Highway 50, one mile west of Lihue
Lihue, HI 96766
(808) 245-9593
www.gaylordskauai.com

In Hawaiian, *Kilohana* means "the greatest, not to be surpassed." This place could very well live up to its name. Originally a sugar estate built in 1935 by Gaylord Parke Wilcox, it was the largest private estate home constructed on the island at the time.

Now you can dine in this fine home, courtesy of Russ Talvi and his wife, Paige, who offer a delicious menu of Hawaiian specialties like Grilled Ahi and Macadamia Nut Crusted Sea Bass in the setting of their 35-acre plantation.

Hawaii

But if you're here with the kids, we suggest experiencing one of Hawaii's oldest traditions: a luau, which they offer on Tuesdays and Thursdays, just across the yard from the restaurant. Their buffet is tasty, and it's always a treat to see the cooked kalua pig coming out of the pit.

The Polynesian Review, complete with fire-eaters, hula dancers, and drum players, takes you through Hawaiian history—from ancient times to present—and is a decent, albeit touristy, way to spend a night.

Be sure to try the poi (a dipping sauce made from the taro root). This is a Hawaiian staple used as a condiment on just about anything.

In short, a night at the luau is a good way to pig out, and a night at their regular restaurant is a charming way to spend an evening. No matter which setting you choose, at Gaylord's, they'll leave a lasting impression in your mouth and in your memory.

Tidepools

Hyatt Regency Kauai
1571 Poipu Road
Koloa, HI 96756
(808) 742-1234
www.kauai-hyatt.com

Okay, so it's another chain resort. But hey, we're tourists, too, so we feel like we need to point out some of these places.

When it rains on these islands, the locals call it a blessing. Let's take it a step further and say anyone who comes here should *feel* blessed. Kauai is probably Jill's favorite island mainly because of its lush and mountainous terrain. It's an astounding place to hike and there are some especially challenging trails if you're up for it. If you remember some of those scenes from *Jurassic Park*, you'll know what we're talking about. The cliffs you saw in the movie were part of the Na Pali Coast. They will literally take your breath away, especially if you hike to some of the overlooks. However, getting this island green

comes with a caveat. This is the rainiest of the islands, so don't be surprised if you get a good soaking.

The day we shot at Tidepools, the skies opened up and gave us a *huge* blessing. Crazy thing is, 4 hours later, with Jill mostly drenched and a rain bag over our camera, we were all still smiling. In fact, we didn't feel cursed at all by the elements. That's because the setting and the food make you forget about the rain. Plus, in the restaurant, while open-air and floating on a lagoon, you sit under thatched-roof huts so you can stay pretty dry.

Local-Style Ahi Poke

ADAPTED FROM TIDEPOOLS, KOLOA, HAWAII

MAKES 2 SERVINGS

8 ounces tuna sashimi block, cut into small dice
⅛ teaspoon Hawaiian sea salt or other sea salt
⅛ teaspoon ground kukui nut or macadamia nut (optional)
½ teaspoon light brown sugar
Pinch chili flakes
1 teaspoon soy sauce
1 teaspoon oyster sauce
1 teaspoon finely chopped green onion
1 tablespoon finely chopped onion
1 teaspoon chopped garlic
1 tablespoon furukake spice
1 tablespoon Asian sesame oil

Combine tuna, sea salt, nut (if using), brown sugar, chili flakes, soy sauce, oyster sauce, green onion, onion, garlic, furukake spice, and sesame oil in a stainless-steel bowl, and gently mix. Make this on the day of use. Serve with chips, crackers, or toasted bread.

CHEF'S NOTES: Kukui nuts are from the candlenut tree, the state tree of Hawaii. They are slightly toxic unless roasted. Furukake spice is a Japanese spice mixture used to flavor plain rice.

Kauai Coffee Plantation

On Highway 540 just off Highway 50
Kauai, HI 96705
(808) 335-0813
www.kauaicoffee.com

It's a sound that millions of us wake up to every morning: Drip, drip, drip. We're talking coffee!

If you're curious about the famous Hawaiian coffee and how they harvest it, take a trip to the south side of Kauai. Watch for a sea of coffee trees that look as if they fall off into the sea. This may very well be the coolest (and most caffineated) outdoor office we've seen.

But don't be fooled by the picturesque beauty of this place. Making coffee isn't easy. To begin, there are 3,400 acres with 4 million trees to be harvested. What's unique about Kauai Coffee is they produce their own fruit, which means everything from the seedling to the final cup happens here.

Quality control at Hawaii's largest coffee estate consists of a bunch of people sitting around sniffing, then slurping, and finally spitting out coffee. The official name sounds a little more refined. It's called "cupping," and there is a logical reason for such behavior. Think of it like wine tasting, but instead of grapes you have beans. What the testers look for are any bum beans in the batch.

There is no formal tour, so you'll have to be content with a visit to the gift shop and watching videos on how it's all done. But a visit to this estate gets you a free coffee sampling. If you like what you taste, there are lots of beans to buy and take back home. Now that should get you all jazzed up.

―

Hali'imaile General Store

900 Hali'imaile Road
Hali'imaile, HI 96768
(808) 572-2666
www.haliimailegeneralstore.com

When you visit Maui, you don't always have to dine at the beach. There are a handful of eateries away from the ocean that prepare superb food, like this one 1,200-feet up on the slopes of the world's largest dormant volcano, Haleakala. This massive crater sits 10,000 feet above sea level at the highest point on Maui. We're told the entire island of Manhattan could fit inside it. At the restaurant there's a lot to fit inside your tummy. Hali'imaile General Store is known for its stylish menus featuring island-fresh ingredients and flavors that define owner and executive chef Beverly Gannon's particular style—eclectic American with Asian overtones. Gannon started in the food business by catering to the stars. She traveled as a road manager with entertainers like Liza Minnelli and Joey Heatherton and discovered she loved cooking so much, she should study it. After completing cooking school at Le Cordon Bleu in London and after several stints in Europe and the United States, she ended up in Maui with her husband, Joe, an entertainment producer. They own two other restaurants together on the island, plus a catering company.

Now she's making her star-pleasing food for anyone who makes the trek "up" to the Upcountry. This is sort of the Hawaiian version of the Wild West. You'll find lots of ranches and farm fields. In fact, the General Store sits in the midst of 1,000 acres of pineapple fields and was once the main shop for the plantation workers. Beverly takes advantage of her surroundings and pulls her produce from the area. You'll find dishes such as Szechuan Barbequed Salmon, Blackened Ahi, and Chocolate Macadamia Nut Pie.

Hawaii

No wonder stars such as Helen Hunt and Bill Murray make pilgrimages here. It's not exactly the Hollywood Hills, but we'll take the hills of Maui over those any day. We think you'll agree. Maui No Ka Oi—Maui is the best.

Pork Loin with Dried Fruit

ADAPTED FROM THE HALI'IMAILE GENERAL STORE, HALI'IMAILE, HAWAII

MAKES 4 SERVINGS

2½ pounds pork loin, cut into 4 fillets
Salt and freshly ground black pepper, to taste
6 dried pears
12 dried prunes
12 dried apricots
½ cup apple juice
½ cup water
2 tablespoons unsalted butter
1 tablespoon olive oil
3 shallots, chopped
½ cup rich chicken stock
1½ tablespoons Calvados (dry apple brandy)
1 cup heavy whipping cream
1 tablespoon fresh lemon juice

Preheat the oven to 325°F. Season pork with salt and pepper; set aside. Place dried fruit in a saucepan; add apple juice and water. Bring to a boil. Simmer fruit until tender. Strain off and discard any liquid.

Heat butter and oil in heavy sauté pan over medium-high heat. Add pork, and sauté until golden brown, turning as needed. Add shallots and chicken stock. Cover and cook until the center of pork is 160°F for medium done or 170°F for well done. Remove pork to a platter, and keep warm.

Remove excess fat from the pan. Place the pan over high heat, and add Calvados. Stir with a wooden spoon to scrape the browned bits from the pan. Reduce the heat and add cream; simmer until reduced to a sauce consistency. Add lemon juice. Taste for seasonings, and adjust as needed. Strain sauce through a sieve, and pour over pork. Garnish each plate with some dried fruit.

Wailea Four Seasons

3900 Wailea Alanui
Wailea, HI 96753
(808) 874-8000 or (800) 332-3442
www.fourseasons.com

There's a Hawaiian legend that says if you wish to nurture your body, mind, and soul, then head for the water. We did just that when we shot on the southwest coast of Maui for our *Best Of Waterfront Places.* We're not ashamed to point out another chain resort in this chapter—not if it's a good one like the Four Seasons. It's expensive and certainly there are lots of people here, but the service is supreme, the views are glorious, and the staff is always smiling.

There are definite advantages to staying at a place like this. Namely, you don't have to lift a finger if you don't want to. And if that Hawaiian legend holds true, then this resort does its job well in nurturing you in every way, shape, and form. After staying here, you'll have a relaxed mind and a rejuvenated spirit, and it's hard to put a price tag on that.

Hawaii

Index

Page numbers in *italic* indicate illustrations.

A

Acme Oyster House, 115
Ahi Poke, Local-Style, 274
Ahi Tuna Tartar with Caviar and Spicy Ginger
    Vinaigrette, 254
Ajax Diner, 109
Alabama, 105–8
Alaska, 264–71, *266*
Aldo's Ristorante Italiano, 58, 59
Al Forno, 16
American Coney Island, 143, *143*
Amy Ruth's Restaurant, *27*, 27–28
Anchor Bar, 38
Angelo Brocato Ice Cream and Confectionary,
    Inc., 119
Annie Gunn's/The Smoke House Market, *158,*
    158–59
Apple Cider-Cured Smoked Salmon, 258–59
Apple Upside-Down Cake, 86
Arctic Char, 75
Arizona, 209–15, *211, 213–14*
Arkansas, 122–25, *123–25*
Arthur Bryant's, 153–54
Artichoke and Tuna Salad on Kalamata Olive
    Bread, 179, *179*
Arturo's Puffy Taco, 247
Azzura Point Restaurant, 256

B

B. F. Clyde's Cider Mill, 21, *21*
B. T. McElrath Chocolatier, 172–73
Babani's Kurdish Restaurant, 168–70, *169*
Babe's Chicken Dinner House, 221
Bacchanalia, 92
Baja Taco, 269–70

Bananas Foster, 116
Bar Abilene, 171
Barbary Fig, *167*, 167–68
BB's Jazz, Blues and Soups, 157–58
Beach House Grill, 275
Beaumont Inn, 80
Beef Odessa, 37
Bellagio, 215–16
Bern's Steak House, 101–2, *102*
Bertha's, 56–57, *57*
Beverly's at the Coeur D'Alene Resort, 182–83,
    183
Big Fella's, 133
Big Four, The, 237–38
Billy Goat Tavern, 135, *135*
Biltmore Estate, 85, *85*
Bistro Maison deVille, 114–15
Black Bean and Florida Citrus Salsa, 51
Black-Eyed Pea Fritters, 95, *95*
Black Olive Crust, 15
Black Pearl and Hot Dog Annex, The, 19, *19*
Blacksmith Inn, The, 164–65, *165*
Bloody Mary Shrimp Cocktail, 236
Bomboa, 12–13
Bootlegger Bistro, The, 217–18
Bottega, 105
Bottletree Bakery, 109
Brennan's Restaurant, 115–16
Brie Stuffed French Toast, 52
Brownie Enormous, Wuollet's, 172
Bryant Lake Bowl, 174
Bubbalou's Bodacious BBQ, 70, 97
Buckhorn Exchange, 201
Buckhorn Exchange Bean Soup, 201
Buddakan, 50
Buddy Guy's Legends, 135–36
Buddy's Pizza, 144

Buffalo Pot Stickers with Asian Napa Cabbage Slaw, 198–99
Butter Onion Steak Sauce, 186

C

Café Annie, *224*, 224–25
Café Du Monde, 116
Café Flora, 255–56
Café Glechik, 37
Café Latte, 170–71
Café Latte's Turtle Cake, 170–71
Café Michele, 266–68
Café Milano, 62–63
Café 1217, 124, *124*
Café Sevilla, 255–56
Cafeteria, 32
Café 210 West, 54
Cakelove, 64–65
California, 229–54, *232–33, 239, 241, 244, 251*
Camellia Grill, 113, *113*
Canoe Bay, 165–66
Cantler's Riverside Inn, 59, *59*
Caramel Rum Sauce, 14
Caro-Mi Dining Room, 89
Casino Clams, Flo's, 17
Castle Hill Inn and Resort, 18
Celebration Restaurant, 219
Chanler at Cliff Walk, The, 18–19
Charlie Gitto's, *156*, 156–57
Charlie Gitto's Toasted Ravioli, 157
Charlie Trotter's, xiii, 133–35
Cheeky Monkey, 20, *20*
Cheese Store of Beverly Hills, The, 253, *253*
Chef Franco's At The William L. Morris Dealership, 247–48
Chef Joe Randall's Cooking School, 95–96
Chef Rene's Shrimp, Mussel, and Scallop Orecchiette Pasta, 98–99
Chef's Special Omelet, 113
Chick and Ruth's Delly, 60
Chicken alla Padulese, 248
Chicken Piccata, 133
Chicken Tagine with Tomato Chutney, 168
Chile Pasilla Broth, 225
Chiles Rellenos Topped with Ranchero Sauce and Garnished with White Cheese and Cilantro, 223
Chipotle Mayonnaise, 270
Chocolate Macaroons, 271
Church Brew Works, *54*, 54–55
Ciudad, 245–46
Coconut Vegan Cake, 260
Coffee Pot, The, 212–13, *213*
Colorado, 199–205, *202–3, 205*
Commander's Palace, 116–17

Conch Flyer Conch Chowder, 105, *105*
Conch Flyer Restaurant and Lounge, 70, 104–5, *105*
Connecticut, 20–22, *21*
Cordova Lighthouse Inn, 270–71
Corky's Ribs and Bar-B-Q, 84–85
Corner Room, The, 54
Cowgirl Hall of Fame, The, 33
Cranberry-Pumpkin Bread Pudding, 87
Crawfish Pie, 268–69
Cream de Brie Sauce, 224
Creamy Shrimp and Grits, 106–7
Creamy White Grits with Bitter Greens and Wild Mushrooms, 225
Creole Sauce, 173
Crunchy Macaroon Topping, 271

D

Daddy D'z, 69, 93
Dahlia Lounge, 262–63
Daily Pie, The, 218–19
Daniel's on Broadway, 41
Dante's Down the Hatch, 93
David Family Kitchen, 125, *125*
d'Bronx Deli, 154
Delaware, 56
DeLeo's Park Theatre Café and Deli, 201–2
District of Columbia, *62–63*, 62–68, *67*
Dizzy's, 35, *35*
Domaine Chandon, 231–232
Dorsett 221 Truck Stop, 226
Double Musky Inn, xiii, 268–69
Dried Cherry Scones, 165
Dried Fruit, Pork Loin with, 276
Driskill Grill, 225–26
Duck-In, 73

E

Earth and Ocean, 263
Ed Debevic's, 136, *137*
Eggs à la Crème, 120–21
Eiffel Tower, 218
Elias Corner, 37–38
Elizabeth on 37th, 94, *94*
El Tovar, 214–15
Emmy's Spaghetti Shack, 234–35
Esparza's Tex Mex Cafe, 257

F

FareStart Restaurant, 260–61, *260–61*
Fat Mo's Burgers, 82
Filet of Beef Roasted with Coffee Beans with Pasilla Chile Broth and Creamy White Grits with Greens and Wild Mushrooms, 224–25
Finale Cheesecake, 12
Finale Harvard Square, 11

Finale Park Plaza, 11
Fish Camp Bar, The, *90*, 90–91
Fish Tacos, 270
5 Spot, 263–64, *263–64*
Flea Street Cafe, *235*, 235–36
Fleur de Lys, 239–41
Florida, 97–105, *98, 100, 102–3, 105*
Florida Citrus and Black Bean Salsa, 51
Flo's Clams Casino, 17
Flo's Clam Shack, 17
Focaccia Bread, 153
Fogo de Chao, 221–22
Food Network *best of* The Best Of, xi–xiii
Fort, The, 200
French Dip with Peach Mustard, The, 19
French Toast, Brie Stuffed, 52
Fresh Herb and Garlic Aioli, 179, *179*
Fried Chicken, Strawn's, 121, *121*
Fried Chicken, Traditional Southern, 84
Fried Green Tomatoes, 107
Fried Shrimp, O'Steen's, 99
Frittata, Hot Brown, 78
Frittata Pasta, 142–43
Fritters, Black-Eyed Pea, 95, *95*
Fritz's Railroad Restaurant, 154
Fudge (Hot) Cake, 182

Gaige House Inn, 232–33
Garlic Aïoli Shrimp, Spicy Toasted, 124, *124*
Gateway Café, 203–4
Gaylord's at Kilohana, 275–76
General Joe's Chicken, 46
General Lewis Inn, The, 76
Gennie's Bishop Grill, 219–20
Geoffrey's/Malibu, 253–54
Georges' of Tybee, 96
Georgia, 92–96, *94–95*
Georgia's and the Owl, 183–84
German Potatoes, 132
Gina's Cappuccino Café, 37
Gino, xiii, *30*, 30–31
Globe and Laurel, The, 71–72
Glorioso Brothers Grocery, 161
Grand Central Oyster Bar and Restaurant, 29–30
Great Plains and the Mountains, 177–205
Greenbrier, The, 74–75
Green Room, The, 56
Greens and Wild Mushrooms, Creamy White Grits
    with, 225
Grill, The, 148
Grilled Peppered Beef Tenderloin, *158*, 159
Grimaldi's Pizzeria, 34, *34*
Grounds for Sculpture, 43
Ground Zero Blues Club, 108–9, *109*

Grove Park Inn Resort and Spa, The, 86–88, *87*
Gumbo Pot, The, 248
Guy's Steakhouse at Lolo, 180

Halekulani Hotel & La Mer Restaurant, 274–75
Hali'imaile General Store, 277–78
Harbor Sweets, 8
Hawaii, *272*, 272–76, *275*
Heavenly Mountain Resort Catering, *243*, 243–44
Hennessy Tavern, 41–43, *42*
Herbfarm, The, xiii, 264
Hereford House, 155
Highlands Bar and Grill, 106
High Plains Homestead, 196–97
Hog Heaven, *80*, 80–81
Hoover's Cooking, 226–27
Horseradish Crust, 29
Hot and Hot Fish Club, 106–7
Hot Brown Frittata, 78
Hotel Pattee, 151–52
Hot Fudge Cake, 182
Hunter's Table and Tavern, 185

Iaria's Italian Restaurant, 132–33, *133*
Idaho, *181*, 181–83, *183*
Illinois, 133–43, *135, 138–41*
Ina's, 142–43
Indiana, 131–33, *132*
Inn at Little Washington, The, 71
Inniskillin Wines, 39
Iowa, 150–53
Irma's, *222*, 222–23
Irondale Café, 107–8

Jacob's Table, 150–51
Jakes, 187–89, *188*
Jarvis, 231
Jean-Georges, 25
Jestine's Kitchen, 89–90
Jewish Mother, The, 73
Jill-Tini, 259
Jimmy's Restaurant, 57
Joe Huber Family Farm and Restaurant, 131
John Bull's Trading Company, 88
John Volpi Company, 156
Joseph Poon Asian Fusion Restaurant, 45–46
Jumbo Lump Crab Cakes, 66
Just Truffles, 166–67

Kahala Mandarin Oriental, 275
Kansas, 179, *179*

Katana, 251
Katz's Delicatessen, 25–26
Kauai Coffee Plantation, 277, *277*
K̆Chocolatier, 252–53
Kentucky, 77, *77*–80
Kinkead's, 62
"Kitchen Sink" Chocolate Chunk Cookies, 32
Koi, 250–51
Kopperman's Delicatessen, 158
Kristi's Cinnamon Rolls, 88

L

Lafayette Coney Island, 143–44
Lafitte's Landing at Bittersweet Plantation, 119–21
Lake Lure Tours, 88–89
Lamb (Rosemary) Skewered with Black Olive Crust, 15
L'Auberge de Sedona, 214, *214*
Laura's House, 88
Lavender Shortbread, 265
L & B Spumoni Gardens, 36
Le Bec-Fin, 48
Le Bistro Montage, 258, *258*
Legendary Jambalaya, 136
Leon's Frozen Custard, 162
Le Petite Chateau, 40
Le Petit Pier, 245
Lindy's Diner, 6
Littel Nell, The, 204–5
Little Dooey, The, 111
Little Sister Resort, 163–64
Lizzie Border Bed and Breakfast-Museum, 15–16, *16*
Lobster Roll, 4
Lobster Salad on Brioche with Vanilla-Orange Vinaigrette, 232
Lobster House, The, 41
Lobster Shack, The, 3–4, *4*
Local-Style Ahi Poke, 276
Log Inn, The, 131–32
Los Dos Molinos, 209
Louisiana, *112*–*13*, 112–21, *118, 121*
Louis's at Pawleys, 90, *90*–91
Lou Malnati's Pizzeria, 141–42
Lou Mitchell's, 141, *141*
Loveless Motel and Café, 81–82
Lover's Leap Vineyards, 196
Lumière, 13–14
Lyceum Bar and Grill, 9
Lynn's Paradise Café, 69, *77, 77*–78

M

Macaroon Crunchy Topping, 273
Madidi, 108–9, *109*
Maggie's Pickle Café, 123–124
Maine, *1*, 1–5, *3*–*4*
Maisonette, 130

Mama Mexico, 28
Mamma Maria, 10–11
Mandarin Oriental Miami, *103*, 103–4
Mangy Moose Buffalo Meatloaf, 193
Mangy Moose Restaurant and Saloon, 192–93
Maple Chicken with Cream de Brie Sauce, 224
Market Place, The, 85–86
Marx Bros. Cafe, 269
Maryland, 56–61, *57*–*59*
Massachusetts, 8–16, *16*
Matzo Ball Chicken Soup, 151
Mayfair Diner, The, 53
McClard's Bar-B-Q, 122
McClellanville Lump Crab Cakes with Whole-Grain Mustard Sauce, 91
McMenamin's Kennedy School, 256–57
Meatballs, 234–35
Merridee's Breadbasket, 82–83
Merriland Farm Café and Golf, 4–5
Metrazur, 28
Michael's at the Citadel, 210–11
Michigan, *143*, 143–50, *149*
Mid-Atlantic, 23–68
Midwest, The, 127–75
M & I International, 36–37
Milford's Fish House, 266
Millennium Restaurant, 236–37
Million Dollar Cowboy Bar, 192
Miniature Pumpkins Filled with Maine Lobster Ragout, 68
Minnesota, 166–75, *167, 169*
Mirror, xiii, 69, 81
Mississippi, 108–11, *109, 111*
Mississippi Catfish and Hushpuppies, 111
Miss Mary Bobo's Boarding House, 83–84
Missouri, 153–59, *155*–*56, 158*
Missouri Baking Company, 156
Molasses Sugar Cookies, 83
Molten Chocolate Cakes with Rum Caramel and Vanilla Ice Cream, 14
Montana, 180–81
Mother's Restaurant, 112, *112*
Mountains and The Great Plains, 177–205
Moxie, The, 76
Mr. Bartley's Burger Cottage, 14
Mr. Beef, 139, *139*
Mrs. Miller's, 123, *123*
Mulate's, 118, *118*
Murray Bros. Caddyshack, *100*, 100–101
My Brother's Bar, 199

N

Nacho Mama's, 57–58, *58*
Nancy's Home Cooking, 130
Napa Valley Wine Train, 231
Napoleon House, 114

Napoleon Pheasant, 189
Naughty Dawg Saloon and Grill, 242
Nebraska, *194*, 194–97
NECI Commons, 5
Nevada, 215–18
New England, 1–22
New England Lobster Roll, 242
New Hampshire, 6–7, *7*
New Jersey, 40–44, *42*, *44*
New Mexico, 218–19
New York, 25–39, *27–28*, *30–31*, *34–35*, *39*
95 Cordova, 97–99, *98*
No. 9 Park, 12
Noodles (Curried), Singapore, 104
North Beach Grill, 96
North Carolina, *85*, 85–89, *87*
North Dakota, 183–87
North End Market Tours, 10

O

'Ohana, 97
O & H Danish Bakery, 162–63
Ohio, 129–31
Old Ebbitt Grill, 66
Olde Tymes Restaurant, 20
Old Talbott Tavern, 79
Old Town Tortilla Factory, *211*, 211–12
Onion Butter Steak Sauce, 186
Opera, 138, *138*
Orca Adventure Lodge, 271–72
Oregon, 256–58, *258*
Orfila Vineyards, 255
Osso Buco alla Gino, 30–31
O's Campus Café, 227
O'Steen's, 69, 99–100
O'Steen's Fried Shrimp, 99
Osteria Del Circo, 216
Outback Crabshack, 100

P

Pacific, The, 229–78
Pacific Dining Car, 249
Palisade, 259–60
Palo Alto Creamery at Stanford, 241, *241*
Palo Alto Creamery Downtown, The, 241, *241*
Pan-Fried Oysters, 266
Pasilla Chile Broth, 225
¡Pasion!, 48
Pasta Frittata, 142–43
Pastime Club and Steakhouse, 185–86
Pat O'Brien's, 113–14
Pat's King of Steaks, xiii, 49, *49*
Pedals Café, 253
Pelican Inn, 241
Pennsylvania, 44–56, *47*, *49*, *54*
Peppermint Twist, 174–75

Pheasant Napoleon, 189
Philadelphia Cheese Steak, The Original Pat's King of Steaks, 49
Pine Creek Cookhouse, 205, *205*
Pink's, xiii, 247
Pitchfork Fondue, 186–87
Plaza III, 155
Plumpjack Squaw Valley Inn, 243
Pocahontas Pancake and Waffle Shoppe, 73
Point Restaurant, The, 198–99
Poke (Ahi), Local-Style, 274
Ponzu, 238–39
Pork Loin with Dried Fruit, 278
Potato and Sweet Potato au Grautin, 273
Potato Cakes, 82
Potato-Crusted Red Snapper, 94, *94*
Primanti Brothers, 55
Prince William Sound Lodge, 272–73

R

R. Thomas Deluxe Grill, 93–94
Radius, 13
Rainbow Lodge, 244–45
Ralph's Italian Restaurant, 47
Ranchero Cubano, 173
Ranchero Sauce, 223
Ranch House, The, 195–96
Ranchman's Café, 221, *221*
Rat's, 43
Reading Terminal Market, 44
Real Chili, 160
Real Food Daily, 251–52
Red Fish Grill, 102–3
Red's, Eats, 3, *3*
Red Snapper, Potato-Crusted, 94, *94*
Rhode Island, 16–20, *19–20*
Rhubarb Peach Pie with a Crunchy Macaroon Topping, 273
Rhubarb Walnut Muffins, 165, *165*
Richardson's Ice Cream, 9–10
Rico Mexican Market, *197*, 197–98
Rider Ranch, *181*, 181–82
Ristorante Antipasti, 60, *61*
Ristorante Café Cortina, 147–48
Ristorante Fausto's Antipasti, 60
Ristorante Sandolo, 212
River Café, The, 34–35
Roasted Corn Abdi, 237
Roasted Maine Lobster, Artichoke Purée, and Citrus Salad, 240–41
Robert's, 90
Roma Café, 145–46
Rosa Mexicano, 33
Rosemarie's Peanut Butter Pie, 220
Rosemary Skewered Lamb with Black Olive Crust, 15
Rose Pistola, 236

Ruby et Violette, *31*, 31–32
Rum Caramel Sauce, 14
Russian Dressing, Zingerman's, 150
Ryland Inn, The, 40–41

S

Sabatino's Italian Restaurant, 58
Saddle Peak Lodge, 254–55
Safe House, The, 159–60
Sai Café, 134
Salts, 15
Sambuca Jazz Cafe, 223–24
Sandwich (Reuben), Zingerman's, *149*, 149–50
Santa Fe Chicken, 58
Sarah's Secret Flat Chocolate Torte, 65
Sautéed Shrimp, 96
Sautéed Squash, 219
Scala's, 235
Schmidt's Restaurant und Sausage Haus, 130
Sciortino's Bakery, 161
Scones, Dried Cherry, 165
Seared Olive-Rubbed Chilean Sea Bass "in the Style of Niçoise," 210–11
Seared Salmon with Braised and Raw Endive and Beet Reduction, 29
Seared Scallop Ceviche, 81
Seeger's, 92
Seven-Flavor Beef, 264
Shack Up Inn, xiii, 109
Sheikh Babani, *169*, 170
Shepherd's Pie, 42–43
Shrimp Ceviche Tostadas, 198
Singapore Curried Noodles, 104
Sioux Sundries, 194, *194*
Skewered Rosemary Lamb with Black Olive Crust, 15
Smoked Fish Pate, 164
Smokey's on the Gorge/Class VI River Runners, xiii, 75
South, The, 69–125
South Carolina, 89–91, *90*
South Dakota, 187–92, *188, 191*
South Union Bread Café, 152–53
Southwest, The, 207–25
Speed Queen Bar-B-Que, 161–62, *162*
Spicy Toasted Garlic Aïoli Shrimp, 124–125, *124*
Splash, 21
Stanley Hotel, The, 202–3, *202–3*
State Game Lodge and Resort, 189–90
Steinhilber's Thalia Acres Inn, 72
Stone-Ground Grits and Shrimps, 88
Strawn's Eat Shop, 121, *121*
Strawn's Fried Chicken, 121, *121*
Sugar-A Dessert Bar, 137–38
Sugar Molasses Cookies, 83
Susanna Foo, 45

Sushi Sasbune, 274
Suzabelle's, 95, *95*
Sweet Lady Jane, 249
Sweet Potato and Potato au Grautin, 271
Swiss Lakewood Lodge, 242–43

T

Tacconelli's Pizza, 51–52
Tavern on the Green, 26–27
Taylor Grocery, 110–11, *111*
Teatro ZinZanni, 239
Ted Drewes Frozen Custard Stand, *155*, 155–56
Temple Bar and Grill, 44, *44*
Tennessee, *80*, 80–85
Termini Brothers, *47*, 47–48
Tessaro's, 55–56
Texas, 219–25, *221–22, 224*
Thomas Henkelmann-Homestead Inn, 22
Three-Cheese Mornay Sauce, 78
3950, 217
Thurman Café, 129
Thurman's Salsa Burger, 129
Tidepools, 276
Timballo, 61
Tini Bigs, 259
Tombs, The, *63*, 63–64
Tombs Gumbo, The, 64
Top of the Falls, 38–39, *39*
Top of the World, 216
Topolobampo and Frontera Grill, 139
Top Ten, Food Network *best of* The Best Of, xiii
Tortilla-Crusted Salmon with Fire-Roasted Corn Salsa, 215
Traditional Southern Fried Chicken, 84
Trellis, The, 72
Tribute Restaurant, xiii, 146–47
Tuna and Artichoke Salad on Kalamata Olive Bread, 179, *179*
Turtle Cake, Café Latte's, 170–71
Twisted Spoke, 140, *140*
Twisted Spoke Pot Roast, 140
Twist O' the Mist/The Misty Dog Grill, 38–39, *39*
Two Sisters, 180–81

U

Uglesich's Restaurant and Bar, 69, 117
Under the Eagle, 146
Union Oyster House, 11
University Creamery, The, 54
Utah, *197*, 197–99

V

Valley Green Inn, 52
Vegan Coconut Cake, 262
Venison Chili with Black Beans, 236
Vermont, 5–6

Versailles Restaurant and Bakery, 103
Victor Café, 46–47
Victor's 1959 Café, 173
Vincenzo's, 78–79
Virginia, 71–73

W
Wailea Four Seasons, 278
Wall Drug, 190–91, *191*
Walnut-Crusted Salmon, 272
Warm Baby Spinach and Mushroom Salad with
    Ponzu Dressing, 250–51
Washington, 257–64, *258–59, 261–64*
Waybury Inn, 5–6
Waybury Inn Vermont Cheese and Ale Soup, 6
Web site for Food Network *best of* The Best Of, xii
West Virginia, 74–76
WheatFields Bakery and Cafe, 179, *179*
White Chocolate Bread Pudding, 120
White Dog Cafe, 50–51
Whitney, The, 144–45
Whole-Grain Mustard Sauce, 91
Wilderness Lodge, 244
Wild Ginger, *261,* 261–62
Wildwood Restaurant, 258–59

Willard InterContinental Hotel, *67,* 67–68
Windsor Court Hotel, 117–18
Wisconsin, 159–66, *162, 165*
Wooden Knife, 192
Wort Hotel, The, *193,* 193–94
Wuollet Bakery, 171–72
Wuollet's Brownie Enormous, 172
Wyoming, 192–94, *193*

Y
Ya Mamma's, 6–7, *7*
Yank Sing, 233–34
Yavapai Restaurant, 213–14
Ye Olde College Diner, 53–54
Ye Olde Pepper Companie, 8–9

Z
Zen Palate, 33
Zingerman's Delicatessen, 148–50, *149*
Zingerman's Reuben Sandwich, *149,* 149–50
Zingerman's Russian Dressing, 150
Zip's Cafe, 130–31
Zola, 66–67
Zucchini Pancakes with Cresenza and Roasted Red
    Peppers, 233

About the Authors

IN JANUARY 1995, **Jill Cordes**, newly graduated from Penn State, left the mailroom at the NBC affiliate in Washington, DC, where she had been working and headed to Rapid City, SD, for her first reporting job at KEVN-TV.

For ten months she covered the local news, anchored the weekend news, and—in a market where everyone is a Jack (or Jill)-of-all-trades—learned how to shoot, write, edit, and produce. In November 1995, she landed her second on-air gig in Sioux Falls, SD at KSFY. By 1997 she was the morning anchor at KETV in Omaha, NE, and two years later moved to Minneapolis where her husband, Phil Johnston, had taken a job as a reporter at KARE-11. Shortly after, Jill was offered what she calls her "dream job" with Food Network, cohosting *The Best Of* with Marc Silverstein.

Her adventures with *The Best Of* have led her to play golf with actor and restaurateur Bill Murray, dine atop a glacier in Alaska, and dance with leading man Morgan Freeman.

Jill has been featured in newspapers and magazines all over the country for her work on Food Network, as well as appearing on local and national television talk shows, including *The Oprah Winfrey Show*.

Jill, Phil, and their two cats, Katie and Draino, now live in Brooklyn, NY.

You can visit Jill's website at: www.jillcordes.com.

Marc Silverstein has been described as "fresh," "lively," "irreverent," and even "ornery." He came to Food Network's *The Best Of* as an Emmy Award–winning news reporter who worked in Washington, DC, Baltimore, MD, Columbus, OH, Tulsa, OK, and Corpus Christi, TX.

Marc started in broadcasting while still in college, covering Capitol Hill and official Washington for national radio and television outlets. For almost a decade he had been a consumer/investigative reporter at WMAR-TV in Baltimore, and, before that, at WSYX-TV in Columbus, exposing scams, cutting red tape, and leaving more than a few bureaucrats and politicians seething. As a political reporter earlier in his career,

Marc uncovered a scandal that led to a politician's expulsion from the Corpus Christi City Council.

Along with the Emmy and other honors, Marc's long-running crusade for child safety seats earned him the Public Service Award from the U.S. Department of Transportation.

Marc has a B.A. in broadcast journalism from The American University in Washington, DC. He also attended Tulane University. He lives with his wife, Kathy, and their two children, Spencer and Lexy, in Maryland. Marc can be contacted through our website, www.bestofbook.com, or via e-mail at BestofBook@aol.com.